WHAT WE LEAVE BEHIND

Barb Solberg

BookLocker
Trenton, Georgia

Published by BookLocker.com, Inc., Trenton, Georgia.

Printed on acid-free paper.

Booklocker.com, Inc.
2022

Library of Congress Cataloguing in Publication Data
Solberg, Barb
What We Leave Behind by Barb Solberg
Library of Congress Control Number: 2021923140

"I was enjoying a beautiful early fall morning in my room at the Vettakollen Hotel with a few hours to myself before I had to report to work with the children. Light, cool breezes floated in through the open window moving the curtains back and forth. The musty smell of fall and the crunching of dried leaves underfoot occupied my attention as I watched the children play outside. Then the sounds quickly changed. I heard rhythmic stomping of boots in the short hallway outside my room. My heart skipped several beats as my eyes surveyed my room to be sure no underground newspapers were visible. I had been careful to keep those papers and anything American hidden. The sounds of boots stopped in front of my door. Bang! Bang! Trying to remain calm, I peeked out the door. Eight German soldiers pushed open the door and charged into my room. The one in front shouted, "*Sie arden verhaftet.*" I was being arrested.

"Why? I'm a student here. I work with the children. They need me here."

"Gather a few things including your American passport. You are coming with us."

I did as I was told and put a pair of pants, underwear, a sweater, my hairbrush, my US passport, what was left of the kroner Bibben had given me, a package of Venus napkins, and my toothbrush and toothpaste into a bag. One soldier held tightly onto my arm as they marched me down the hallway to the stairwell, down the stairs, and out the front door to a German war truck. I was pushed up and into the

backend of the truck. Four German soldiers jumped in
behind me…"

Dedication

To my mother, Margaret,
who kept the story alive for me.
&
To this family, who, in spite of all obstacles, has
stayed connected for over one hundred years.
&
To lovers of history, relentless researchers and savers
of family stories and history, puzzle solvers, and
keepers of archival materials who preserve the past
and present for the future.

Table of Contents

Preface

What We Leave Behind began in 1975 when my grandmother's youngest sister Else, who lived in Norway, showed me the picture on the cover of this book. For the past several decades curiosity about my mother's family has nagged at me. How could I find more pieces to the family puzzle? My mother, Margaret, kept a number of family documents. They were not organized, but they were kept. When she passed away, I took that box home with me. It sat in the closet for a few years until I thought to clear things out. My obsessive organizational genes kicked in! I also had spent the last fifty years in the same county where my grandparents had homesteaded. I had ready access to the county's courthouse files.

Puzzle pieces began to fall into place. Then technology! Computers! Internet! Search Engines! My husband and I were empty nesters with time on our hands. I decided to tackle putting my family history in order. My organizational work began. Each decade was labeled on a file folder, and into those folders went the appropriate information. I kept chronological records on the file covers and in pencil noted what I was missing and as well as questions that remained for that decade.

I knew my grandparents had immigrated from Norway. I never knew them, but I knew they had sent three of their daughters back to Norway. How would the family ever know what had gone on in Norway?

In 2015 on my third trip to Norway, I learned that one of the girls, Borghild, had written her story. Her story! The story of Norway from her vantage point! In Norwegian – 35 pages of family history! What a thrill! More puzzle pieces were falling into place. Borghild's daughter and granddaughter translated the Norwegian narrative for me --- and technically for the family history.

And then COVID 19. Lock down. Everyone suffered loss, but it also presented an opportunity. I decided to apply to the Little Mo' Writing Incubator, a program provided by Humanities ND. "I'm going to apply," I told my husband, "and if I get one of the eight spots, I'm going to write the narrative!" And that's how this book came to be.

I pledged to myself to write from 1:00 – 4:00 every day. Sometimes that meant research, sometimes writing, sometimes crying as I imagined the lives of my grandparents and their children. I was reconstructing my family's story as best I could. I have not changed any names. I have not altered the basic story line. I have, however, had to imagine relationships, conversations, feelings, motivations. So, I present the skeleton with my interpretation of how life may have unfolded for the Martin and Asta Aadnes family in its intimate layers.

To members of the Aadnes family who might read this, may I suggest that you read it as a historical novel with considerable family connections. These characters are your relatives and the facts in this novel parallel those in the family history book. Sit back on a quiet afternoon and think about how conversations may have occurred, how relationships may have or may not have been built, how emotions probably were held tight to the chest. Consider the inner strength of these women: Asta, Clara, Borghild, and Eleanor.

For readers not part of the family, I hope this family's story may invoke in you a desire to learn more about your family. I hope that the information about immigration, Ellis Island, homesteading, and WWII in Norway reveal to you some history that you may not have known or perhaps had forgotten.

What We Leave Behind is historical fiction. The story takes place between 1911 and 1951 – a forty year span that encompasses immigration, homesteading, The Great Dust Bowl, and WWII and the Nazi invasion and occupation of Norway. The major characters are strong women who confronted obstacles they must work through. It is compelling and emotional to consider these women as part of my heritage. Their story is both heartbreaking and joyful.

I hope you appreciate the read.

Family Trees:

Martin and Asta

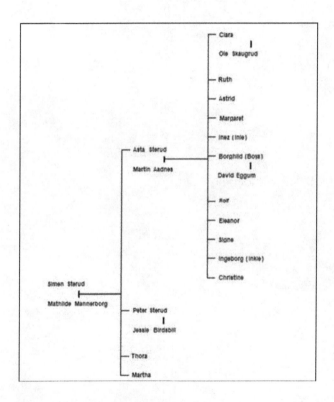

Martin Aadnes

Ancestor Chart

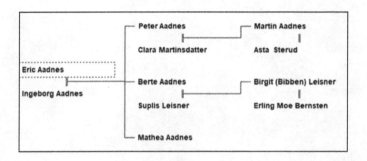

Peter Aadnes — Martin Aadnes

Clara Martinsdatter — Asta Sterud

Eric Aadnes

Ingeborg Aadnes

Berte Aadnes — Birgit (Bibben) Leisner

Suplis Leisner — Erling Moe Bernsten

Mathea Aadnes

Prologue

Spring 1932
Van Hook, North Dakota

Asta whispered softly trying to wake her husband. "Martin... Martin." After a long day plowing and then picking the rock by hand in the wind, Martin often collapsed into bed, exhausted. Just as always, sleep came quickly for him.

Asta found it difficult to sleep these days. She had been awake most of the night, listening to her husband's breathing. The crops were poor due to the drought, and she worried about how they were going to take care of the family.

"Martin, "she whispered again. Her lips quivered, and her eyes welled up with tears. "Please." She wished they could talk before the day carried them away to their various chores. She cried quietly as she struggled with thoughts of her children. Clara, the oldest, wasn't at home anymore. Ruth left school last year at sixteen to work at the Lumo Ranch, but she came home often to help on the farm. And there were the others. Her mind raced through her other seven children – Astrid, Margaret, Inez, Borghild, Rolf, Eleanor, and Signe. How she loved them all. She had been in the United States just nineteen years and had borne nine children. Only one son. And she was only 38 years old

1

In the dark of the night, Asta thought about her homeland—her parents back in Norway. They ask often in their letters if she and Martin couldn't bring the family home for a visit. But raising children during poor farming years certainly meant they couldn't possibly afford that trip.

They had important family matters to discuss, and time was running out. Martin's aunt, Tante Mathea, had sent a letter suggesting they send a couple of kids to Norway for two years. This idea weighed on her mind. She knew it would be a better existence now for the girls and easier for those left on the prairie, but how could they send any of their girls away for even a year? Which ones should go?

The six girls at home shared a large bedroom upstairs in the second house Martin had built since they immigrated in 1913. The first house, oh so small, at just 12' x 24' worked almost perfectly until Margaret was born in 1920 and she was the fourth. Martin had worked hard those first few years proving up the land, building a house, two barns and a granary, and digging a well. Planting and harvesting. Trips to town to get supplies. Then four children and a too small house meant he had to build another. He worked hard to establish their settlement on the land and take care of his family. But Asta had worked hard too. Baby after baby, small children, raising chickens, selling eggs, cooking, cleaning, gardening, and sewing clothes for the kids. Small children up at night. Once one child was sick the others were sure to get sick as well. Never a full night's sleep. Adjusting to the prairie, the wind, and the harsh winters. How much could she take.

"Martin... Martin... Vær så snill å våkne." Asta urged quietly in Norwegian to not wake the kids. Martin stirred and opened his eyes just in time to see his wife wipe her tears on the pillow.

"Martin... we need to talk about the letter from Tante Mathea. Should we send a couple of the girls? Which ones? What do you think about this Martin?"

Martin turned in the bed and rubbed his eyes. "I don't know, Asta, what the future holds here. The weather has been so hot the past couple of years. No rain. No snow. The ground is very dry." Asta understood the situation, too. There was little grain to sell, and farming may not improve next year. Asta felt certain that Martin's 40-year-old single cousin in Norway, Birgit, would be so happy to have some girls. She has money. Afterall, her dad started the huge department store, Glass Magazinette, in Oslo. She goes to Switzerland. The girls could travel, take dance lessons, and eat good food. They'd brush up on their Norwegian and meet their Norwegian families.

"Maybe we should send... maybe three," Martin suggested. "Isn't that what Tante Mathea suggested. She'd pay for the round-trip tickets good for two years."

Asta started to cry again. "But, which three—who shall we send?"

"Let's send Ruth and two of the younger girls," Martin offered. "Ruth would probably be happy to go to Norway."

"We can't send Ruth, Martin, I need her." Asta peered out from the top of her eyes. "Remember that I'm pregnant again, Martin," she whispered, "and I need Ruth to come home to help me."

Martin sighed. "Oh Asta. I've been so busy with my own worries about the drought and the lack of money to make payments to the bank. I haven't paid attention to you. I'm sorry." Martin's eyes dropped and his arms comforted her. "We won't send Ruth. I think Clara is a good choice. How about Margaret? She's eleven and can manage herself."

"Yes, Clara is a good choice, Martin," Asta wiped her tears. "But Martin, I don't think Margaret should go. She and Astrid are doing so well in school and at such tender ages. They are so close in age and both play basketball. Not Margaret and not Astrid."

"Let's think about this tomorrow, Asta," Martin said. "It's too hard to think at night. Then we can't get to sleep. I need to get to sleep."

Asta said, "But we do need to decide, Martin. Time is running out."

#

It had been almost twenty years since Martin and Asta had left their homeland, and when they left, it wasn't under such good terms. Asta's family wasn't happy that one of their daughters was hanging around with Martin. He was the second son with no chance for the farmland. What kind of a future would Asta have? They had hoped for better for her. They wanted their daughters to marry a first-born son who would inherit the farm. But Martin was tall and handsome and strong, and Asta delighted when he threw her over his shoulder and laughed and teased that he was going to toss her into the fjord. Asta felt protected and safe with Martin. Besides, Asta had left home when she was sixteen. How could her parents tell her what to do when she had already been out of the house for two years?

#

With thoughts of family on both sides of the Atlantic, Martin fell asleep. Asta contemplated her choices. Clara for sure, she was the oldest and could take care of the younger ones. She could send a telegram to Clara in Minneapolis and offer her the trip to Norway. Eleanor was four and could easily adjust. She is so cute and would win the hearts and attention of the Norwegian family. Who would be the third? Borghild at eight? How could she send these two young daughters?

Beside her in the bed, Martin snored. Asta fell asleep with her face in the pillow.

The next morning, breakfast was served in silence. Martin's look was distant. Asta knew from the last letter from Tante Mathea that she had little time left to write about which girls would be arriving. Little time for them to get ready. Little time for Norway to prepare the way and arrange for the tickets. Yes, Asta thought, she must get to Clara to arrange for her to come home and get ready.

Asta watched her daughters as they cleared the breakfast table, heated the water on the stove and did the dishes before they readied for school. Once she turned away and touched her apron to her cheeks. She stepped outside to talk to Martin before he left for the fields.

"So we agree that Clara should go. Is that right?"

"I think that's best, Asta. *A svelge noen kamier.* It will all be fine. They'll be back in no time." He held her in his arms; they looked at each other.

Supper brought the family back together. Even Ruth came home to spend the evening with them. Martin spoke first.

"Do you kids remember hearing about my cousin, Birgit, in Norway? You remember, the one who lives in the big house with a huge garden? We've told you about her before."

The kids eyed the chicken and potatoes as they were passed around the table. Asta had hated to butcher that chicken today, but it wasn't producing eggs as it had earlier, and she needed something for dinner. The potato bin was about empty, and the sprouted potatoes were going to be her seed potatoes for the garden. Just enough to go around. She waited until everyone was served before she served herself.

No one spoke; then Martin broke the silence.

"Well, we got a letter from Tante Mathea and Birgit a while back." Martin put potatoes on his plate and handed the bowl to six-year-old Rolf. "They'd like to meet a few of you girls, show you Norway and where your mom and I grew up." Martin noticed there weren't enough potatoes for Asta. He put some of his on her plate. "Birgit goes to Switzerland each year. It's a beautiful country in the mountains in Europe. She loves dancing. Clara is going to go. She wants to see Norway. Would any of you like to go?"

Ruth's eyes lit up. She wasn't particularly happy working at the Lumo Ranch, but she knew if she quit, she would be working at home. She was strong enough to help with the farm work, and Asta had taught her well around the kitchen and with the younger children. Ruth thought it might be a good idea to get away.

"I'd like to go with Clara," she said. Asta looked at Martin. Martin looked at Asta. They both looked at Ruth.

"We probably need you here, Ruth," they said at the same time.

"We just can't let you go, Ruth, we need you," Martin continued. "You are such a great help to Mama. We can't send Signe --- she's only two. We can't send anyone too small for Clara to handle on the trip and for Birgit to care for." There was a long silence. Nine-year-old Inez, who was eating the wings and the neck, was looking around the table for more food. It seemed she was always hungry, growing so fast.

"That leaves Astrid, Margaret, Inez, Borghild, and Eleanor," Martin looked at each of these daughters. He never mentioned six-year-old Rolf nor two-year-old Signe.

Astrid excused herself saying she had homework. Margaret looked down and said nothing. Inez continued to pick at the food scraps. Ruth began to clear the dishes as she usually had done. Uninvolved in the conversation, Borghild and Eleanor got up from the table and played dolls together on the floor. Their dolls were simple, but their play was real.

Martin looked at Asta and nodded to the two younger girls on the floor. Asta watched them with smiles and with pain. She knew in her heart that these were the two to go to Norway with Clara. Borghild was old enough at eight to be of some help to Clara yet young enough to play with and be company to Eleanor, both on the trip and in Norway. Eleanor would be with her sisters and probably wouldn't feel the absence of her parents quite so much. Asta looked at Martin. Tears rolled down her cheeks. Margaret looked up and saw her dad put his arms around her mom.

Not much was said.

Margaret watched her two little sisters closely for the next few weeks. She played with them, laughed with them, and tried to imprint their faces in her mind. Nothing further had been mentioned about the Norway trip, but Clara did arrive home the next week. A couple of days later a neighbor came over and took a family picture for Martin and Asta. They laughed and spoke in Norwegian while the kids played hide and seek in the tree rows Martin had planted eighteen years earlier.

About a week later the neighbor returned with the family picture. Asta took the picture, looked at it closely, and showed the girls. Later that day she held the photo to her heart and cried as she placed an X over the heads of Clara, Borghild, and Eleanor. She wrote a quick letter to Birgit, kissed the photo and put it with the letter. She addressed the envelope, stamped it, and put it in the mail.

For the next few weeks, Asta watched the mail closely for a letter from Norway. Finally it arrived. Asta stepped quietly outside, sat on the step, opened the letter, and cried.

May 10, 1932

Dear Asta and Martin, please excuse me for making all this mess but I have to admit that by the time I heard from Tante Mathea that you would be sending Borghild, age 8 years old, instead of Signe who is 3, I was very disappointed for getting such an old girl. Most of all, I was afraid she would get homesick. After thinking it over, I have now decided to go for it, if you also think it will work. When I got Asta's letter with the pictures the other day, I really like the looks of Borghild – she looks so sweet – they both do – and now I hope I can start to look forward to their coming to Norway.

I am sure I will get to love them, and I promise you that I will do all I can to make them feel like home and enjoy it here. I understand it must be hard for you to send them so far away, but I will write you often and tell you about them and I will see that they won't forget their parents. It will give me more to live for and I hope everything will turn out good.

It is still time to get them on board the Bergensfjord the 11th of June. I sent a telegram to Tante Mathea yesterday telling her to send one back if there was any trouble – if not, I will buy the tickets so they can pick them up in New York. Tante Mathea will order the railroad tickets.

Love, Birgit

It was the middle of May, and the three girls would leave home in a couple of weeks to get to New York in time to get on the boat. They would catch a ride to Shakopee, Minnesota, with a family friend who had a car, and from there they would take the train to Chicago, change trains for New York and meet Tante

Mathea who would have their tickets. They would stay with her for a couple of days before she took them to the pier. Then they would board the Bergensfjord for Oslo. The trip would take ten days. Eighteen-year-old Clara would be in charge. Birgit and Tanta Signe would be at the Oslo pier to meet the boat.

The day to leave came too quickly. Their bags had been carefully packed with just essentials, a new dress, and Borghild's and Eleanor's dolls. Their early breakfast was at times quiet and at times full of chatter. When the neighbor drove into the yard, all the sisters gathered around while their only brother slept in. There was hugging. There was crying. Martin loaded the bags into the neighbor's car as Asta clung to the little ones as long as she could and then sobbed as she walked with her three daughters and helped them climb into the car. The girls clung to their mother as the neighbor started the car. Martin closed the car doors. Clara, Borghild, and Eleanor cried and waved goodbye as the car began to pull away. Martin held Asta. They all waved as the car disappeared down the road.

**PART ONE:
ASTA**

Twenty-one years earlier

Chapter One:

Store Odnes, Norway 1911

At twenty-one years, Martin was as handsome as he was tall. His 6'5" sturdy, muscular frame was enough to attract the attention of many ladies. And Martin also loved life! Dancing, joking, laughing, playing pranks. That was Martin. He had all he needed—except the first son birthright. Martin's older brother, Erik, had that, and that meant Store Odnes, that had been in the family for generations, would be Erik's. Martin's great, great grandfather had sold Store Odnes to his first-born son, as had Martin's great grandfather, and his grandfather. It was simple tradition. Martin's older brother Erik would get the farm.

Even though Martin was studying animal husbandry, gardening, farming, and construction at the Lillehammer agricultural college, he knew he was not in line to inherit or purchase the farm. There was the Odnes Hotel, also part of the family estate. Both the farm and the hotel served as a hub for all traffic on Randsfjorden from Gjovik to Valdres and as a post farm for over 500 years. The more current two and a half story hotel built in 1885 provided Martin a place to work and a good social environment. He could work there for certain, but he couldn't own what belonged to the family and namely to Erik.

Store Odnes

But all that didn't matter because Martin saw the world at his feet. Friends everywhere talked about opportunities in the United States, and many of Martin's college friends schemed for ways that they too could take advantage of these opportunities.

"I've heard that there are plenty of immigrant ships heading for Canada and the US," one of Martin's school buddies offered. "I'm not in line for any land here. I need to figure out a way to go."

"Are you thinking of going to Canada? I hear they need strong men with skills and stamina. I guess the work is in the mines and the lumber industry," Martin offered.

"Ja, but I'm not so sure about working in the mines. I'm more of the farming type,"

"Have you heard about that bill signed by President Lincoln?" Martin asked. "Something about 160 acres free if you just improve the land and build a residence."

"160 acres? How many hectares is that?" his buddy asked. "Can we figure that out?"

"Let's see," Martin recalled his classwork. "I think one acre is a little less than half a hectare. That means about 45 hectares, I think."

"That's a hellova lot of land. Think of what we could do with that," Martin's buddy shook his head and lifted one eyebrow. "*Drittbra*! How can a government give away so much land to people who aren't even citizens?"

"I've heard all you need to do is declare your intention to become a citizen and improve the land," Martin offered.

"Ja? Sounds like a good deal. I'm nervous here anyway," the friend shared. "Our government is going to require any unmarried mother to declare the father of her child. Then that father needs to provide for the mother and kid. This isn't good. I might be getting caught in the middle of something I don't want."

Martin thought about Johanne, the chambermaid who worked in the family's hotel in Odnes. Her gentle manner was attractive to Martin. She was much older and knew more about the ways of life. Martin had secretly visited her chambers several times. They never spoke much in public, but Martin now began to worry about any predicament he might be getting himself into.

"How can we not go," the friend questioned. "We both need to improve our lot in life. No opportunity here for us. What do you say, Martin?"

Martin felt confident that he should look at this opportunity. Yet, the hotel provided entertainment and work for Martin in the meantime. So he continued to study at the Lillehammer college and to work as a hotel host at Odnes Hotel when he wasn't in school. And to say the least, Martin liked the work. Saving money was now a priority so working as much as he could was important.

#

When the hotel filled with guests, Martin became one of them. Their celebrations were his celebrations, and he easily became one of the crowd. There were the regulars and most weekends a few newcomers. But everyone, guests and staff, knew when Martin was around. Hotel guests and staff responded to his warm personality. Things ran more smoothly and were more fun with Martin there. And the work got done amidst the fine-tuned flirting and coquetry. Afterall, the hotel was located at the foothills of some Norwegian mountains as well as on the shores of the beautiful Randsfjorden. Ski guests were regulars at the hotel and that meant young people. What could be better than a ski crowd gathering at the hotel? After a day in the snow and cold, these folks were ready for the evening activities that appropriately concluded such a day!

"I haven't seen you dancing, Johanne," Martin nodded toward the dance floor. Johanne dusted off her apron, then on second thought she took the apron off and followed Martin to the dance floor. It was late, work was done, skiers were tired and wanted to be ready to strap on their skis again in the morning. Soon the stars and the moon signaled the end of the day and all supposedly went to their respective rooms. Martin and Johanne lingered a while and then slipped away to her room as they had in the past.

#

Martin headed back to school the next day. He couldn't stop thinking about Johanne. But he also couldn't stop thinking about the 160 acres of free land in America. Times were tough in Norway, and Martin didn't think he'd ever have enough to just travel to America to check things out. He had to think logically. Sometimes he'd lie awake at night weighing the advantages and disadvantages of going and of staying. One advantage of staying was Johanne. She was nice looking, loved to dance and laugh and had a young spirit. She was teaching Martin a great deal about life... and love. Martin liked that. But she was more than twice his age. How would she fare on a long oceanic trip, working the new land, being away from home? Martin would be so busy he wouldn't have time to entertain her. And besides, he needed a helpmate and sons to help with the work. At twice

Martin's age, Johanne didn't have much time left to bear children. And Martin did want children and a family.

Wanderlust. Adventure. The urge to get away and go abroad churned in his head.

Several of Martin's friends were packing up and leaving. They told Martin they'd get to America, get some land, and work hard. Others had done it. They weren't worried about the money. The land of opportunity. "Life for us is not here," they'd tell Martin.

Martin couldn't talk to Johanne about his restlessness, but she sensed it. Sure, he'd come to her chamber at night, mess up the covers, giggle, and kiss her gently as much as he could. But he never mentioned restlessness. He could go back to school and immerse himself in that world.

When Martin was back at college, he often ventured into Lillehammer for something to do. It was there that he met a handsome young lady. Asta Sterud, the fifth child of Simen Peterson Sterud and Mathilde Mathiasdatter Sterud, was staying at Schee farm not far from Lillehammer. Asta had left home before she was sixteen and found work as a typist in a Lillehammer office. One of Martin's school friends introduced the two of them, and they visited and laughed and began to see each other as often as Martin went to town. It wasn't long before the relationship became more than just friendly, and conversation turned to emigration and how many friends were leaving for America. Asta shared that her oldest brother, Peter, had gone to America five years ago.

Martin was anxious to hear what Asta knew about her brother's trip. How did he do it? Which vessel did he travel on? How much did it cost? Peter and his trip to America dominated their conversations. Asta was only nine when Peter left in 1903 so she didn't really have all the details, but she remembered hearing some of them in her parents' conversations.

"He went alone," Asta said. "He was supposed to leave on the Montebello, but since it was just a transport vessel to get him to a larger port, we don't really know how he got there. He used to say to the folks—*a koka bort i kålen*—a plan comes to nothing with waffling. But we don't hear from him very often. He went to Wisconsin, I think, and worked as a farm hand for a while. I think he left there. I could check when I see my folks next time."

Asta decided to write to Peter on her own. She had several questions she wanted to ask him privately. Questions like *if I came to America, could I come to you? Could you help me get settled? Where would I find you?*

The farm and the hotel just weren't going to be enough for Martin. Erik would eventually inherit it all -- the farm, the hotel, and probably the sawmill on the fjord. What would Martin have? He wanted a larger society, he wanted to try his luck in this new land, and he wanted to tempt fortune. And if it didn't work? He could always come home. It wasn't forever. He was young and strong in body and mind. But he was intrigued by this Asta, and he decided to visit with her more. He read up on the opportunity in the United States to prepare for a conversation when he would meet Asta at the market in two weeks.

"Is he still there? What is he doing? Did he homestead?"

"Mom and Dad don't hear from him much. He was a tanner, you know, like Dad. I think he probably continued to make leather belts and purses, but the last letter came from the Dakotas. I think it said Rugby, ND. He writes home only every so often." Asta was careful not to indicate that she had written to Peter about going to America.

Martin liked Asta. She was easy to talk to. She liked to have fun. Asta liked Martin. He was easy to talk to. He liked to have fun.

As the time passed, Martin and Asta saw more and more of each other. Martin had to be careful because he still saw Johanne as well. Martin knew he was putting one foot in two shoes at the same time, and he felt the pressure but was uncertain about what to do. He knew he wanted to leave Norway, go to America, and get some of that homestead land. One weekend at the hotel he did notice Johanne was getting thicker around the middle. Then one evening Johanne told him.

Now what? And now the upcoming Norwegian law regarding illegitimate children would make him responsible for the child and the mother. Now what?

The conversations that ensued were private. Private between Martin and Johanne. Private between

Martin and Asta. *Should Asta know about this? How could he tell her? Should Johanne know about Asta? How could he tell her?* It was time for Martin to come to terms with his predicament. Maybe Johanne was seeing someone else too? How could he know?

He and Asta had talked about the opportunity in America so many times. *Should he bring up marriage?*

During this time, Asta also heard from Peter who wrote that he was working as a farm hand for Charles A. Nute who homesteaded just south of Rugby, North Dakota. Asta was anxious to share this information with Martin. Peter said that Asta could come to him and he could help her.

Lillehammer had several freelance ticket agents hanging around selling passage on many different shipping lines. Passports for immigrants were not necessary. All that was needed was a ticket and a smallpox vaccination certificate. Once these items were in hand, the adventure could begin. Martin decided to have a deeper conversation with Asta to talk more about the two of them and going to America.

Martin met Asta in the town square the following day. It was just the two of them meeting late in the afternoon. They were alone and Martin decided to broach the subject.

"Asta. I've been thinking about this opportunity. The opportunity to go to America... and... and about us," Martin hemmed and hawed. "I'm wondering... I guess I don't know what you've been thinking...I mean, Asta, about us. We've been seeing each other for quite a while now. We get on well. I hope you feel the same. We haven't talked about it much, but Asta, I've fallen in love with you. I mean, I love you. I'm thinking we should marry and go to America." Martin was silent but kept his eyes on Asta. He leaned in closer to her and whispered, "Asta, will you marry me and go to America with me?"

Asta had thought about America as well. Her brother had gone, and now she entertained thoughts of going to where he was. Asta was independent of her parents. After all, she was the fifth child, and after she was born, seven more kids were born. She had nine siblings, well, that didn't count her sister who died as a baby. Oh, and it also didn't count her half-sister, Erna, whom her dad had fathered when he was just seventeen. Her dad's parents had raised Erna. She never lived as Asta's sister, so she didn't really count.

Asta wouldn't really be missed. Perhaps she would miss home more than they would miss her. The decision was painful. How could she leave her homeland and her family? The newspaper ads she saw promised security and comfort. Others were leaving. She had both friends and relatives who had left on different ships. Martin would probably be good support for her; his mother had died when he was only five years old, and his dad had remarried three years later. Martin wasn't attached to his stepmother, and they had had a daughter, Ingeborg -- Martin's half-sister, who needed their attention. Martin has been independent for many years. He is strong and he always watches out for Asta.

Asta didn't really want to be a typist the rest of her life. She wanted a life away from the typewriter. She wanted a change. She wanted more excitement, and she was falling in love with Martin. Plus, Peter was in America.

"Yes, Martin. Yes. I will marry you," Asta blushed and looked down as Martin took her hands in his. She paused. He waited. She looked up and into his deep blue eyes. "And yes, Martin, I love you and I will go to America with you!"

"I love you Asta, and I want to make a life with you. We can work together; it will be hard work." Martin held her, kissed her, and whisked her up in his arms and danced around with her. "We can have a family. Life can be good." They were a couple. They were happy, but they had much to think about and plan for.

"Oh Martin. I've been writing to Peter and he says we can surely go to him in North Dakota!"

"We can get married, book our tickets, and pack our trunk! Think of it Asta!" Martin smiled. He was planning their future. Time to figure out all the pieces of his puzzle. He needed money. He needed to end his relationship with Johanne. He needed to figure out the logistics of the trip. He needed to finish school.

"Will you quit your job at the hotel? What about school, Martin?" Asta needed the details. "Have you thought about all of this? Where will we leave from?"

"Asta, my dear. The plans will unfold. Let's take one thing at a time. Let me finish school this term and let's both save some money." Martin was being direct. Asta could see she had lots to ponder.

She needed to share her plans with her family – her parents and her siblings at home. They hadn't been too happy earlier when she told them she was seeing Martin.

"He has no future," her mother had said. "No chance for farmland, no chance for hotel. How will he care for you? We had hoped you'd find someone with a future."

Asta knew her mother was right, but she had fallen in love. Certainly now, they will be excited for her to see Peter; Asta's being in America would give Peter some family connections. *Should she take Martin with her when she tells her parents? Should she even tell her parents? Will she go with Martin to tell his parents? How could they afford a wedding?* Her older siblings hadn't had any weddings. A wedding would take too much time to prepare and cost too much. She and Martin should marry without anything public because time was running out.

August 12, 1912, Johanne bore a child—a son, Helge.

Just six months later, in February 1913, the Justice of the Peace in Hov, the administrative centre of Sondre Land, declared Martin Aadnes and Asta Sterud husband and wife. The municipality officers served as witness.

Martin at twenty-two

Asta at sixteen

May 3 – 12, 1913

Chapter Two:

Caledonia of the Anchor Line

Martin knew he could not afford first- or second-class passage to the United States. He knew, and Asta knew, they needed money when they got to Ellis Island to continue to Peter in North Dakota. Martin decided they needed the lowest priced tickets. He had heard that steerage meant the lower deck of the ship where the cargo was stored and that it was the lowest class of travel. He purchased steerage tickets on the Caledonia of the Anchor Line.

Their steerage tickets included an immigrant guidebook and a steamship brochure. The guidebook explained how to navigate Ellis Island and addressed the fear of rejection that loomed foremost for prospective immigrants. Rejection, it said, was usually due to physical or medical issues. The information eased Martin's worries. Neither had any physical nor mental issues. The guidebook also explained that each ship carried a manifest, a list of all the people on the ship and their answers to twenty-six questions that would be asked before the ship left the port for America. The guidebook explained the questions to help the passengers understand them before they were asked.

"Asta, they will want to know our names, ages, occupations, and birthplace as well as where we are going, who paid for the tickets, how much money we have with us, can we read and write. These are easy questions. They will also ask if we are a polygamist or an anarchist. The answers to those two questions are NO. All our answers will be written in the manifest that will go with the ship. This will be easy."

Martin continued. "We are young and strong, and when we get to Ellis Island, we will pass the medical examination. *Frisk som en fisk*! But officials will be watching us walk to determine our physical condition. We will be fine."

So with excitement and anxiety, Martin and Asta packed necessities in a trunk. Asta wanted to take some things to Peter, but Martin reminded her "Just necessities, Asta. Just necessities. Some things need to be left behind. Seeing you will be enough for Peter." He held tight to their tickets, their trunk, and her hand. They took the train to Oslo where they rented a room at the Amerikalinjen Hotel close to the port of departure. Asta hoped to take some things to Peter, but Martin convinced her that somethings needed to be left behind. "Just necessities, Asta, just necessities. We need to leave some things behind."

Arriving two days before departure gave them adequate time to rest, get their bearings, and secure their trunk's brackets and straps. Several ships were docked in the port --- so many people, so many trunks, so much hustling and bustling around the area.

Martin and Asta mingled in the group boarding the Caledonia. Family and friends of passengers were waving and crying. Martin and Asta stood with the others on the deck to take part in the excitement of the ship's departure. Once out to high seas, the decks began to clear as porters directed passengers to various areas.

Some passengers were directed to a specific area where necessary vaccinating and disinfecting of each passenger occurred. They were prepared for this, so Asta followed the women and Martin the men. After the vaccination and disinfecting, they were led with the other steerage passengers to their accommodations. They squeezed through the tiny deck space and around the Caledonia's machinery and made their way down steep stairways into the enclosed lower decks, their home for approximately ten days of ocean voyage.

What Martin didn't know was that first and second-class passengers would be courteously "inspected" at departure and also quickly disembarked for New York City when they arrived in America. When Martin learned of this on the journey, his spirits fell. Only the steerage passengers were processed at Ellis Island; he had read about that in the guidebook. He hadn't wanted the trip to be overwhelming for his bride, so he had kept that information secret.

"Oh Martin, this will be okay," Asta assured him even though she felt like a prisoner in the bowels of the ship. "Our tickets promised us a berth, food, and the journey. And that will be fine."

Asta did the math often in her head: *our tickets were $30.00 each and we have now $50.00 left. That can get us to Peter. If we had bought first or second-class passage, we wouldn't have much money to get started.* Asta was mostly concerned that they stay together. "We can just stay close to each other, Martin, when we process in America. Let's not lose each other."

"I'm not going to let go of you, my dear!" Martin reassured her.

Steerage passengers quickly learned that steerage was not going to be comfortable. Money could buy comfort, but they had not come from wealthy families. Had they, they would have purchased first class passage. Now they knew for certain that first class comforts were not going to be theirs. The bowels of the ship were dark, dank, with limited ventilation. With more steerage tickets sold than first- and second-class tickets, the area was crowded.

"This place stinks," Asta offered. "I think it's going to get worse. Look at the toilet facilities. Unsanitary. Do you think it will be cleaned during the trip?"

"Hard telling. It's only ten days, Asta. I think we can handle it. But I agree it isn't the best."

It didn't take long for the air in the bowels to smell of urine and feces. Many passengers got seasick which added the smell of vomit to that of body odor due to lack of adequate bathing facilities. Some passengers suffered colds, sore throats, lice, and other germs that traveled faster through the ship than fresh air.

"Let's go up on the deck," Martin often said to Asta. "The air is fresh, and we don't need to observe others getting sick. Let's go up there early each day before it gets too crowded. It's the best we have for this journey. *Glad I deg*, my dear."

The steerage deck for fresh air was in the worst part of the ship and was subject to the most violent motion as well as the dirt and stench from the ship's hold and the galleys. When passengers weren't on the deck, they stayed in their berths which meant they spent many hours smelling the foul air. Yes, money bought comfort.

Martin and Asta spent long hours with each other in their berth, but Martin's 6'5" frame certainly crowded the space. At 5'6", Asta wasn't short, but she could wriggle her way up to Martin's neck, snuggle her face in close to his, and then tuck her feet between his knees. This little love cocoon provided protection and comfort. When the ship rocked in the waves, spooning worked the best; whatever the conditions, they tucked themselves in together.

When they left the berth, they spent time visiting with other Norwegian passengers both on the deck and at mealtime. If they were lucky, they could get into a dining room and find a seat by someone familiar. If no seats were available, they leaned against the walls of the cafeteria to eat. Yes, money bought comfort. They had neither.

"I'm scared," Asta finally confessed about halfway across the Atlantic. She spoke quickly pouring her heart out. "It's not the weather, Martin, and it's not the fear of sea storms. It's not even the smell. These days Martin... they just seem so long, and I feel miserable. Yet I know we must hold out for our future. A future that is so unknown. I hope it's easy to find Peter. All we really have is the address on his letter, Box 75, Rugby, ND. We don't know if he got our letter telling him we are coming. How can we find a box number? What if we get turned back at Ellis Island, Martin? We don't even speak English. How will we know what they are saying to us?"

"*Å svelge noen kameler*," they said at the same time and laughed. They agreed that they had to do some things that they didn't like.

"My dear Asta. Some people on board speak English. Let's find them and see if we can learn more words and phrases. We studied some English in school and that may come in handy. That will make us more confident. We have lots of time each day to talk and learn. I've seen some playing cards and singing. Let's try to be part of those groups."

Sure, this was easy for Martin. His work as a hotel host proved invaluable. He could talk to anyone. Asta was a bit more shy, but she'd stay by Martin as they began to befriend some passengers. She sensed the sweetness of being a newlywed was ending.

They began to listen to the conversations, join in, ask questions. Most days the conversations revolved around questions the officials would ask when docking in Ellis Island. The Eriksen brothers were quite helpful. They were Swedes but hung around with the Norwegian passengers. The older brother, Erik, had already spent several years in Wisconsin and had gone home to Sweden to get his younger brother Lars. Erik spoke Swedish, English, and some Norwegian and had passed through Ellis Island years before. He knew how to get through Ellis Island, what the inspection was like, how to understand money exchange, how the trains worked. He was popular with the other passengers, and everyone wanted to sit by him. Many of the Norwegians practiced English with Erik, rehearsed answers to the Ellis Island questions, studied money, and got to know each other.

"Say this after me," Erik would say. "Farmer. Yes. No." And the group would respond. Sometimes Erik asked a question, "Are you a polygamist?" Then he'd wait for an answer to see if they understood the word. Polygamist. Anarchist. Sometimes he'd ask, "Where are you going?" and they'd take turns answering. Sometimes they just shook their heads. "*Herregud.*" Sometimes they laughed out loud with each other. Sometimes they wanted to cry.

The ship continued west over the North Atlantic waters. Sunlight and fresh air barely reached the bowels of the ship. When sunlight began to appear below, passengers scurried to get up the stairs to see the sunrise and breathe some fresh air. Luckily, the seas were not as rough in May as in other months. When the ship did roll on the waves, the passengers held onto each other or leaned against a wall for safety. Someone always seemed to get seasick at those times. Finally, the last of the days on water was near and the shores of their new world began to appear.

"Look!" one of the passengers shouted below. "Come on the deck and see. Land ahead!"

People rushed up the narrow stairs to the deck. "We are almost there!" Pushing and shoving, but generally an atmosphere of excitement! Shouts of joy! Shouts of survival!

"We made it!"

"I can't believe it. This trip is almost over!"

"My husband will be waiting at the dock."

"I'm exhausted but I'm so happy," Tears of relief streamed down Asta's cheeks. She knew the journey wasn't over. America was a big country and Peter was still half of that new world away. She couldn't wait to see him!

Their Atlantic journey was almost over, and many passengers raced to their berths to repack their trunks to stand ready to see land and begin a new chapter. Tears of joy accompanied tears of uncertainty as they faced the reality of seeking a new life. Some passengers eagerly searched for others in their party so they could all stay together.

"Stay close, Anna!" "Don't go walking so fast Marcus." "Grab Elsie and keep her close to you." Family members shouted at other family members. The air was thick with excitement and chaos. But all that excitement soon gave way to lots of waiting.

Just because they were in the Lower Bay of the New York Harbor didn't mean they could leave the ship. They reached the harbor after 5 pm which meant that ship had to anchor, and they had to stay aboard for another night. Asta and Martin were happy about this as they wouldn't have to pay for accommodations for that night. Even the realization of spending another night in the foul-smelling bowels of the ship seemed okay knowing that tomorrow they would put their feet on American soil. Their hours aboard were now numbered. Asta spent the evening sorting and repacking their trunk. She took out her bunad, her precious traditional dress, and held it up to see the wrinkles, folded it, and put it into the bottom of the trunk. She refolded their heavy Norwegian sweaters knitted of wool, hers a cardigan and his a pullover. She placed them in the bottom of the trunk with the other warm clothes, and between them she placed the few bowls and spoons and tools they had packed. She tucked her Bible, a couple of family pictures, the

 leather gloves her father had made for her, her hairbrush and combs closer to the top and carefully placed Martin's gardening seeds under her hairbrush. Then she held the necklace her mother had given her, looked closely at it, and placed it by her Bible. She knew

that they had packed the most important things into the trunk together with their hopes and dreams. Martin closed the trunk's rounded lid, fastened the wrought iron brackets and straps, and took hold of Asta's hand.

"We have fit our old lives into this trunk to begin our new lives," Martin held her tight to his chest and kissed her gently. "I love you and am so happy to have you with me."

Early the next morning medical examiners boarded the ship to examine the first- and second-class passengers. The examinations of these higher-class tickets were cursory, and those passengers quickly disappeared. Any US citizens aboard simply passed through. Once this layer of examination was complete, the ship began to move again. The crew shouted something to the remaining passengers, but with little English under their belts, they didn't understand what was happening. *Where, oh where, was Erik to translate for them.* They looked around trying to find him. Soon Erik spotted Martin's head above the rest and hurried over to them.

"We are sailing through the Narrows to get to the upper bay and into the harbor," Erik told them. "This is where we will depart the ship and go through the examinations."

"Martin, Martin, look. Can you see it... way up there!!" Asta said.

"I heard someone say that is the tip of Manhattan," Martin told her. "Look over here. I think that is the Statue of Liberty."

No one spoke. The bigness of Lady Liberty was overwhelming.

"She is like a goddess, and we know she represents the big, powerful country which is to become our future home," one man shouted to the others.

One half a mile northwest of the Statue appeared Ellis Island. Once the Caledonia docked, the first- and second-class passengers were released into the freedom of New York. Steerage passengers were then moved across the pier to a waiting room. The ground below them swayed like waves beneath their feet. Ten days on the seas certainly had affected their balance. Shrill shouts in several Northern European languages gave instructions to the various cultures. Baggage was piled on the lower decks while each passenger was given a name tag with his/her name and a number written in large figures.

"There are 30 in a group," the inspector shouted. "These 30 names are on the same manifest page, and you thirty will move together through the inspection. When I call your name, you come forward."

"Hjalmer Jacobsen.... Sverre Olsen... Erik Eriksen.... Lars Eriksen... Anna Hanson... Martin Aadnes... Asta Aadnes... "and all thirty names were called and all thirty stepped forward one at a time. It looked to be a crowd of mostly under thirty-year-olds. Several were just teenagers. Asta had counted. Only four women and 26 men.

"Look Asta. Anna Hanson. We met her on board and told us she was going to North Dakota. She's in our group. Let's get her to stay close to us."

"You're going to North Dakota, too," Martin asked.

"Yes," Anna responded. "I'm going to my uncle in Kulm."

"Where is Kulm? Is it near Rugby?" Martin inquired. No one was quite sure exactly where Kulm was located, but they knew all three had to get to North Dakota. Such luck. Lots of Norwegians in this group of thirty. Some Swedes. Many were just going to stay in New York with family, but some Swedes were going to Wisconsin. This group of thirty quickly got to know each other. Several had met on board. There was Karl Karleson, a Norwegian going to Wisconsin. Hjalmer Jacobsen, the oldest it appeared, from Vormsund in Norway was going to his wife in Brooklyn.

Anna and Asta felt better. Now these two women – just 21 and 19 – were with four strong young men all going west: Martin, 23; Karl, 21; Erik Eriksen, 21 and his brother, Lars, 18. Karl, Erik and Lars were going to Wisconsin. Erik would be a great help to Martin, and he, Asta, and Anna wondered about their train ticket to North Dakota.

"I can help us all get to Chicago," Erik told the small group. "Karl, Lars, and I will get off in Chicago to go north to Wisconsin. Martin you will need to take care of Asta and Anna and get the three of you to North Dakota."

Soon an interpreter approached them and explained the in-processing protocols.

"Listen up. Make two straight rows and walk forward to the doctors at the end of the line."

Martin and Asta knew they were already being inspected. The two doctors for each row first surveyed the passengers as they walked forward. They watched the feet, the legs, the body and then the hands, arms face, eyes and head. A doctor at the top of the stairs watched for lameness or for heavy breathing that may indicate a heart condition. A "bewildered gaze" could be symbolic of a mental condition. In any case, if anything suspicious was noted, a large white letter indicating the issue would be put on the passenger's lapel.

Martin stayed close to Asta checking to be sure she had no markings.

"Continue up the stairwell over here to the disinfecting baths. They won't hurt you. Women on the right and men on the left," the clerk pointed to the correct direction as he shouted. "You'll meet on the other end of the baths. Move along now and hurry." Asta and Anna went right. Martin, Karl, Erik, and Lars went left.

Martin worried. This was the first time he and Asta had been separated since they left Norway. He watched Asta disappear into a room. Anna was close behind. He followed Karl, Erik and Lars into a room.

"Ah," Karl sighed. "This is great. I haven't had a bath since we left Norway. That was about ten days ago according to my calendar."

"Too bad we have to put our stinky clothes back on," Lars chimed in.

"We are entering America with clean bodies!" Martin offered. "That's a damned good deal in my mind."

"Martin. Over here. Anna and I are here," Asta shouted as they left the bath. Martin inched his way to her side. "It felt good to get a bath... but these clothes!!"

"Keep moving! We have many to process today. Stay with the group. Hurry along." The clerks moved the passengers along as fast as they could. The group of six new friends had reconvened and were moving together.

The last of the inspections was the dreaded eye exam. Asta watched as those ahead of her were inspected.

"They are using something on our eyes," she said. "What are they doing?"

"Next." And Martin stepped forward. He liked to go first to be sure of what would be happening. The doctor flipped up his eyelids looking for signs of trachoma. Martin moved to the next doctor as Asta stepped forward for her eye exam. He looked back to check on her as the doctor inspected Martin's scalp before he sent him on.

Asta passed through the eye and scalp inspection but was told to proceed to a nearby room. Only the women were in that room. *What is this? Why do I need to lie down on that table? Why do I need to remove my panties?* Female inspectors moved from table to table saying nothing as they inspected the women for venereal diseases. When the inspection was completed and okayed, the woman was released.

"I'm scared," Anna nervously shared with Asta. "I had no idea what they were doing to my eyes. It hurt. I don't like this. I didn't like that last inspection. Do you think anything else is going to be done to us? Asta, this is awful. Are you okay, Asta?"

"Yes, Anna, I'm okay. I think you are too. This was unpleasant. We weren't told that these things would happen to us. It seems wrong, but we have no control. Just stay close to me, Anna." And the two moved together to locate the men.

"That eye inspection hurt, didn't it," Martin said to Asta and the group. "What was it about? And what was the scalp scraping for?"

Erik had been through this before. "They are looking for contagious diseases in both eyes and scalps. If you have one of them, they don't let you into the country. And I'm not sure why they take the women into a separate room."

"I can't talk about it," Asta shared with tears in her eyes. "I just want to forget about it."

"Oh," said Erik. "Looking for signs of prostitution. Usually those women have diseases, and they don't want those women entering either."

Martin and Asta, bewildered and exasperated and confused, had passed their inspection.

"I felt violated," Asta shared. "I just wish I had known exactly what was going to happen and why. I was nervous the whole time." Anna agreed as did the rest of the group. The experience itself was intense and traumatic.

"Sometimes I wonder if this immigrating is worthwhile, but then I think about how the United States needs to protect itself," Martin offered. "At least the inspection is over, I think, and we can move forward. We can't turn back now."

Standing before a large staircase, the registry clerk shouted, "Step forward to the front of this Grand Hall. This is the Stairs of Separation. You will see three aisles. I'll ask you a question and then tell you which aisle to go down. Then you go down the staircase to the next level." Individual names were called one at a time, questions were asked, and then the person was directed to one of the three aisles. "Stay in the aisle I tell you to."

"Martin Aadnes and Asta Aadnes." They were called to the front. "Where are you going?"

Martin had been listening closely to the questions others were being asked. Erik and Lars had gone before Martin and Asta and he had heard them say Wisconsin. Martin decided the clerk wanted their destination.

"North Dakota."

"Go to the right side of the staircase and keep moving." Martin repositioned their trunk on his shoulder as they moved quickly to the right and down the stairs. Erik, Lars, Karl, and Anna were waiting for them.

"What happened if you had to go left?" Anna asked. "And what about those in the middle. I noticed they all had chalk marks on their collars."

"Those going north or staying in New York went left, Anna," Erik answered. "The ones with chalk marks were going to be detained and probably sent to the hospital here or home. Some deficiency showed up in their inspection. No marks on any of us. We are all good here!"

Martin held Asta's hand while he balanced their trunk on his shoulders and looked around. Almost everyone was headed to what appeared to be money exchange booths. He followed. He wished they had more money. He secretly wanted to save a few of the coins he had. He looked at the ore and kroner in his hand. He had counted it on the ship with Erik and knew he had about $50 US dollars. He walked to the money exchange window and handed the clerk his Norwegian money. They didn't have much money to exchange, but Martin exchanged it all. They were not going to need any kroner here. The exchange clerk handed him several bills and some change. He looked at it, recognized the numbers 1, 5 and 10. Three 10s, four 5s, three 1s and a little change. *Tre tiere, fire femmere, og tre. Det er femtitre.*

The inspection wasn't over. They were shuffled into a long line where people were opening their trunks and men in official uniforms were digging inside. A quick inspection of luggage, Martin supposed. What were they looking for? Martin and Asta followed and noticed Karl, Erik, Lars, and Anna in the same line. Once their trunk was checked, nothing was said. They were cleared and told to head to a cafeteria where workers helped them buy a box lunch for the next part of their journey. Sandwiches and fruit were exhibited in glass cases, so all they needed to do was point and hope that someone would help them determine which coins to pay with. Erik chuckled and stepped in to offer his services.

"I've heard some days 6,000 people process through here," Erik commented. "Be careful with your money and tickets. Sometimes swindlers and pickpockets are around. They are quick, so don't take any chances." Martin felt for his money pouch to be sure he hadn't been taken advantage of.

Once all five had exchanged money and purchased a box lunch, they headed toward the ferry boat to New York City. A ferry boat left every 20 – 25 minutes and the guards counted passengers to keep in compliance with safety regulations. All six boarded the same ferry, sighed a sigh of relief and laughed aloud. The hard wooden seats held only so many passengers. Asta and Anna took seats. The other passengers huddled together guarding their baggage between their feet.

Martin kissed Asta on the forehead. They were in America. They were almost to New York. They were tired and hungry.

"Just think, Asta," he smiled broadly as he looked into her eyes. "We have traveled the Atlantic, made new friends, learned some English, passed our inspection, exchanged our kroner for dollars, and now we need a train ticket. Not so bad."

Asta returned his smile, sighed, and nodded agreement. They would make it. Comfort in a group, comfort in sharing excitement, comfort for Asta and Anna to have four strong men to help them through the chaos.

No one met them at the docks – no family, no friends. The severing of old ties and the lack of familiar places and language was real. All they had was their trunk and each other. Some things had to be left behind, and now newness appeared on the horizon and reality was settling in.

Chapter Three:

Westward Ho!

Passengers grabbed their bags and trunks. Men, women, children. Pushing and shoving. So many languages. So much shouting. Hurry, hurry. So many trains. So much noise. So many people. Everyone was excited to buy a train ticket. All six of us needed to get on the same train. Stay close to each other. Tend to what Erik says and does.

"Look for Great Northern Railway," Erik advised as he pointed to the logo's three big words with the mountain goat in the middle. "This train goes all the way to the West Coast with stops on the way. Lars, Karl and I will buy tickets to Wisconsin. Martin, you and the girls need to continue west to North Dakota. Anna to Kulm. You and Asta to Rugby. Shout at me if you need help."

Everyone was heading west. Everyone carried big trunks with their worldly goods pressed into them. Heavy trunks, some painted with the fancy rosemaling from the area of their homeland. Some looking new. Some old, tattered, and obviously weathering part of the family's history. Regardless, the train cars were going to be full! Asta hoped they'd get seats together.

"Great Northern ticket office this way," was shouted repeatedly into the crowd. Erik commandeered the group to get in line to buy their tickets. "Trains leave every 45 minutes. Get your tickets and then check the chalkboard to see the train schedule. You'll need to be on the ramp fifteen minutes before boarding. Have your tickets ready when you board."

Martin kept his ears and eyes open trying to catch some words that he might know. He didn't want to lose Asta nor the trunk, so he knew his height was a blessing. He reached down to Asta, put his arm around her shoulder, and squeezed her. "We are going to make it to Peter," he assured her. "Just hang on to me."

"Two please. Rugby, North Dakota," Martin told the ticket agent. "Anna. You buy to Kulm."

'Three legs to your trip. New York to Chicago. Chicago to Minneapolis. Minneapolis to Rugby. That will be $11 for each or $22." Martin was confused by what the agent said, but he didn't let on. He reached into his money pouch and gave the ticket agent three tens. Martin waited to see if he got any change. The agent reached for change. Ah, good, Martin thought. He didn't want to spend all their money on the train tickets. He knew they needed to practice the new money system while they were on the train. He tucked the change back into his money pouch and secured the pouch in his pocket.

"Money and language," he told Asta. "We need to understand English and money. We'll have time on the train to practice." All six were off to the Great Northern #6 headed west. The end of each train car had room for baggage, and soon Martin was putting the trunk on the shelf. Anna came in behind them with a smaller trunk. Martin helped her with her trunk. Anna took the seat across from Martin and Asta.

"I need to change trains in Minneapolis," she shared as she looked at her ticket. "Do you?"

"Yes, and we take the leg to Rugby. And you go on to Kulm?"

"Yes, to Kulm," Anna said. They spotted a railway map on the train wall and using their fingers drew out the route and noticed that in Minneapolis they would be splitting. "Oh well," Anna shared, "My uncle will meet me in Kulm. We've had several good times, some scary times, some nervous times. We can do this. Let's try to enjoy the train ride while we can."

Soon the whistle blew, the train wheels slowly began to turn, and they were on their way to Box 75, Rugby, ND, and Peter Sterud!

Barb Solberg

1910 Map of Central North Dakota
Showing Rugby, Barton, Minot, Drake, Plaza, and Van Hook
Fort Berthold Indian Reservation

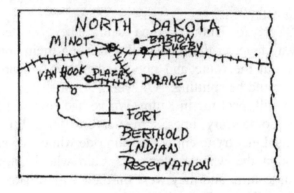

Chapter Four:

Rugby, North Dakota

Asta peered out of the window of the rail car, "Oh Martin, Look over there. I think I see Peter," she exclaimed. "He must have gotten my letter. That looks like him, but I haven't seen him for several years now and maybe he's changed."

Peter looked over the passengers getting off the train. Many passengers carried trunks containing all their possessions. Many were dressed in heavy clothes and most of the conversations Peter could hear were in Norwegian, so he listened for his sister's name. Nothing. Soon he was certain it was Asta stepping out of the railcar. Oh, how grown up she looked. She had been just a little girl when he had last seen her. A tall young man was carrying a trunk on his shoulders and helping her down the stepping block. The young couple looked tired but happy. They looked right at Peter. Peter saw the name *Martin Aadnes* on the side of the trunk, and he knew.

Asta recognized her brother and ran to him. Home. She was touching a part of home and family. Home, Peter was touching a part of home and family. Tears streamed down both of their cheeks as they hugged each other, backed away and looked, and hugged again. Somehow homesickness diminished for a while.

"Oh Peter. It's so good to see you. It's been a long, hard trip. Oh, here's Martin, my husband. Martin, this is Peter." Martin put the trunk down and extended his hand to Peter.

The men shook hands and looked each other over and then grabbed each other in a family-friendly hug. Martin felt quite certain that he and Peter would be friends.

"Come," Peter said. "I have a buggy over here. You are coming with me to the Nute homestead. I have a little place of my own there. It will work for a while as you both rest up and decide what to do next." He reached over to help with the trunk, but Martin, strong man that he was, picked it up and put it over his shoulder. Peter noted Martin's strength and let him handle the trunk himself while he led his little sister to the buggy.

"It is beautiful. North Dakota is beautiful," Martin and Asta commented almost at the same time. Of course, it was spring. The grass was green, the trees were in full bloom, and the air was fresh. After several days in a crowded train with only a berth and filthy bathrooms, the open spaces and fresh air were welcome. "No mountains," Martin pointed out.

"No mountains,' Peter said. "Oh, we have some higher hills north of here. The Turtle Mountains. They are nothing like home. But you get used to this."

"How long have you been here," Asta asked.

"Just a few years in this spot. I came to the United States from Canada and made my way west. I have been working as a farm hand for Charles Nute just south of here. His wife is Lettie. They are a nice family—in their forties with three kids: James, Cary, and little Edith. They came from Wisconsin. But I'm hoping to get my own homestead place. I've learned the government opened some land about 100 miles from here. We can talk about that soon enough. How was your trip?"

Martin looked at Asta and she looked at him. They looked at Peter, raised their eyebrows, and shook their heads.

"Yes, I know," Peter said. "It wasn't easy, was it. It's all so new. First the language then the money then knowing what to do next. I guess we talk with others and decide what's best for us."

Asta sighed a sigh of relief. Martin shook his head in agreement and thanksgiving. *If only we can get organized and decide on something,* he thought. *The sooner the better. Our money won't hold out forever. Maybe I can get some work like Peter.* Peter had hitched a couple of horses up to the buckboard and lifted the trunk into the backend, helped Asta onto the seat, and motioned to Martin, who was staring into the west, to climb up beside him. The buckboard seat wasn't really meant for three riders let alone two tall Norwegian men, but Martin squeezed onto the seat and hung on tightly to Asta. Soon the horses pulled the cart forward and they were on their two-mile ride to Peter's place.

"You are an old hand at this," Martin declared. "We hope you can give us some direction and some help. How long have you been here in Rugby?"

"Just a few years. It's a stopping place for me, and I was lucky to meet the Nutes who needed help. I've been here since. They lived in Wisconsin, but Nute wanted some homestead land and had read about the land available in North Dakota. They got the land here in 1904. They've had already almost ten years on the place, so he has proved it up and life is pretty good. They are anxious to meet you two. I've met a lot of people. I think we can get you settled."

Peter had prepared for their arrival. His residence close to the Nute residence was small. They could work with it for a while. Lettie Nute had invited them all to dinner and given Peter extra blankets for his family. Supper was better tasting than anything Martin and Asta had had for several weeks. Potatoes, roast beef, flat bread and homemade wheat bread with strawberry jam, and custard pie and a good cup of coffee. The Nutes didn't speak Norwegian, but they could tell from the looks on Martin's and Asta's faces and their voracious eating that the dinner had hit the spot. Peter translated as much as he could, but his broken English gave way to Norwegian.

The Nute kids were intrigued by their guests even though meeting immigrants wasn't new to them. Their parents had taken in other newcomers to the area looking to get settled. Several kids had entered their school the past few years speaking only Norwegian or German. Helping them out with language was a familiar experience for them. The kids felt important to help the newcomers learn new words so teaching them the names of the food came first. "Potato." "Flatbread." "Pie." "Coffee." Martin and Asta repeated each word and everyone clapped!

Soon the sun was setting in the West, and chores had to be done before dark. Peter excused all three of them, thanked Nettie for the delicious dinner, and said he would be back to help with chores as soon as he got Martin and Asta settled.

Peter had given up his bed for his sister and her husband. He took the old sofa that sat in the corner. Fresh water was pumped, a fire in the woodstove heated it, and Asta began to clean up. Martin left with Peter to help with the chores. The warm water felt good on Asta's face. She was glad Peter had put enough hot water into the makeshift bathtub in his kitchen. She took a quick bath but didn't have a clean nightgown. Tomorrow she would ask Peter how to wash some clothes. Life was good today. She eyed a real bed that would be hers and Martin's tonight. A real bed, not a wooden train seat, not a crowded berth on a ship. A real bed with a mattress and blankets.

Asta was asleep by the time Peter and Martin returned. Martin added a little hot water to the same tub water, cleaned up, and put his dirty clothes in the corner with Asta's. He too wore his week-old pajamas and fell quickly asleep beside his bride. Peter was happy to wash up and go to sleep on the sofa. How nice, he thought, to have some family with him.

Morning came quickly, and Asta took a few moments to step outside. Blue skies, birds singing, sun coming up in the east. She was happy to be outside in the fresh air. She took a deep breath as she surveyed her new land before she walked inside and helped make breakfast. Toast, jam, and fried eggs. She was happy to be with her brother. She was happy to be around others whom she trusted. She was happy not to be in a ship nor a railroad car. She was mostly happy to be able to wash her hair as well as their clothes and to hang the clothes outside to dry. The sun was warm this late May morning, and the breeze helped dry her hair and the clothes. She smelled her hair and her clean clothes. Yes, this was a good day.

Martin wasted no time pitching in to help Peter and Charles. He was intrigued by the 1912 Bull Tractor that Charles used. Martin felt more comfortable on the horse drawn farm machinery, but he liked the looks of that Bull Tractor. Martin noted that Charles had quite a collection of tools as well. A harrow. A plow. A cultivator. Lots of hammers, sickles, axes. A guy could do just about anything with this equipment. All the observation, however, didn't stop Martin from taking advantage of any opportunity to talk about getting a homestead. Charles was happy to be the authority on that subject, and since he had been in Rugby for a decade and spoke English, he had garnered lots of information over the years.

"Minot," he said, and Peter did the translation. "You need to go to the US Land Office in Minot to make application for a homestead. The train goes

there from Rugby, and you can go on that. The Land
Office is a short walk from the depot. Anyone can
direct you." Charles looked at Peter, "why don't you
and Asta and Martin take the horse and buggy into
Rugby tomorrow and talk with some folk to see what
you can learn. I'm not sure when the train goes west
nor the cost, but we need some supplies from Rugby
and perhaps you do as well. You could combine the
trips." Charles was proud that he could provide some
early assistance to the newlyweds.

Peter informed Martin that it appeared to be a
good time to farm. The May 22 issue of the Pierce
County *Tribune* reported that the 1913 farm prices
were even better than the crop in 1912. Wheat was
$1.00 a bushel, durum was $.81, oats $.25.

"If you had a bushel of wheat, a bushel of durum,
and a bushel of oats, you have about nineteen kroner,
Martin. With all the rain in May and the warm
weather now, you'd be off to a good start." Peter
intimated that he might like to go farming on his own,
make that money for himself.

And so it was. The three went early to Rugby and
returned shortly before sundown loaded down with
sugar, salt, lard, bacon, matches, kerosene, lumber, the
mail and recent newspapers, and a whole lot of tips
about homestead application. It was decided that Asta
would help Lettie with work around the farm and
Martin would take the train to Minot to see about a
homestead.

After some conversation about transportation to
Minot and advice about the homesteading process,

Martin went to bed. Sleep wasn't easy that night as he thought about what he needed to do and how he was going to do it. He rehearsed English words in his brain, he mentally counted his money, and he thought of alternate ways to secure some work to generate income he would probably need. The next morning Peter took him to Rugby and put him on the 12:05 pm Great Northern train for Minot.

Martin's trip to the Land Office resulted in Section 19 in Township 152 Range 91 assigned to him. Martin accepted the land and signed the Declaration of Intention to become a citizen of the United States of America and renounce "all allegiance and fidelity to Haakon VII, King of Norway." The Martin Aadnes Homestead Application #09809 was completed on June 5, 1913 and filed later at the US Land Office in the Ward County Court House, Minot, on July 7, 1913.

Martin's work was about to begin. He had until January 7, 1914, to build a residence on the land and to be prepared to break land and plant crops. He needed to get back to Asta to make plans. The train left for Rugby late afternoon and Martin was on it. He took out his money pouch and counted what he had left of the fifty plus dollars he had when he got to New York. Fourteen dollars. Martin was running out of money.

Martin needed to discuss these things with Peter and Asta. His train ride back to Rugby gave Martin time to contemplate what was next. *Lumber, I need lumber, tools, nails. Plaza, they said Plaza is where to buy them. I'll need transportation to Plaza and on to the land. Where will Asta and I live while I am building a place. Perhaps she should stay with Peter until I have something in place. Maybe she should come with me. Maybe there's a neighbor nearby that we can stay with for a short time while I build a little home.*

The walk to Peter's place wasn't far. It was early June and the sun set late in the evening. He could walk. He knew the way.

Chapter Five:

Building A New Life

Martin shouted as he neared Peter's place. "Asta! Asta!" He saw her in the yard. "Asta! We have applied for homestead land!" He ran to her, picked her up, and sang as he danced her around. Asta laughed as Martin sang her a Norwegian folk song about a suitor and his money!

Det nak ein friar uti gar'e, mor lilla, hau, hau!
Kor mange pengar haver han, du mi dotter Dalia?
To hundre riksdaler seier han at han har.
Sei han nei, vis han vei, du mi dotter Dalia!
No 60nak ein friar uti gar'e, mor lilla, hau, hau!
Kor mange pengar haver han, du mi dotter Dalia?
Femhundrede riksdaler seier han at han har.
Lat opp døra, slepp 'n inn, du min dotter Dalia!

"Oh Martin! *Ach Mej*! Don't ever put me down!" Asta giggled; Martin kissed her cheek.

"We are going to do this, Sweetheart! It will be some work, but we can do this. It's only June 5th, Asta, and we arrived at Ellis Island on May 12th. In three weeks we have traveled halfway across America, found Peter, and claimed a homestead. And I really like Peter!"

"I'm so proud of you, Martin. You have done so much. And I'm so glad you like Peter! I know he likes you!"

"Now, off to tell Peter of our good fortune," Martin suggested. "We can have dinner and then rest!"

Peter watched as Martin and Asta met each other on the path. He knew Martin would be successful, but he mostly liked the idea of Martin swinging Asta around and having some fun. Asta hadn't had much fun for the past month, and Peter saw the twinkle in her eye tonight. Martin will be good to her, he thought.

Peter took a bottle of Akvavit out of the cupboard and the three of them toasted Martin's accomplishments and discussed what to do next.

"I've been thinking, Martin," Peter looked straight at him. "I've been thinking that you may be running out of money. You don't need to explain. But I'd like to help you and my sister with a loan. I've been able to put some money away, and you probably need it. What do you say?"

"*Å snake rett fra leveren*! You are correct," Martin stood in amazement. "We would be pleased to accept your help."

"We can talk details later. My offer is good. Now let's talk about going into Rugby tomorrow," and Peter outlined his plan to take his horse and buggy into Rugby the next day for the Sons of Norway Odin Lodge festival. The seventeen member Norden Chorus from Devils Lake would be performing, orations would be given, and baseball would be played.

"It's time to have a little fun with some other Norwegians," Peter laughed. "We can meet some others in the area, make some new friends, and have a celebration. Come with me!"

June 7, 1913 was a mild with only a slight breeze. The horses knew the way, the town square and market were busy with chatter and gaiety, and people were happy to meet newcomers to the area. After the Norden Chorus program, Martin and Asta visited with the young couple sitting next to them who lived in Barton about sixteen miles northwest of Rugby. The gentleman was a farmer and did handyman construction in the winter months. The couples got along well and were pleased to know that they came from the same area in Norway. They, too, had immigrated not long ago. The couples shared their Atlantic voyage experiences. A quick friendship was formed, and the Barton couple invited their new friends to visit anytime.

As the day drew to a close, Martin and Asta met up with Peter and made their way back to Peter's house. Lots of conversation about their day, the great Norwegian music, food, and the new friends they had made.

Martin and Peter sat up late that evening discussing the money and the next steps.

"I can lend you $150, Martin. You won't need to make payments until you have harvested at least two years. I have that money here and can give it all to you now or you can take it in installments."

Martin let out a deep breath. One of his first hurdles had been crossed. "How can I thank you, Peter, for your generosity. You are sharing more than what we came to America with. I'm humbled, but in thankfulness I accept. Shall we shake on it?"

"No need, my brother! We trust each other, I think. We can work together. Now what will you do next?"

They decided Martin needed to locate the homestead land and meet the neighbors. Make some contacts. Determine what would be best for him to do first—build a residence, break the land, plant some potatoes, put up a granary? What should he do first? They needed to ask Asta if she'd like to join Martin for the first visit or stay with Peter.

Asta decided to stay on with Peter while Martin located the homestead. The Great Northern would take Martin to Minot where he would switch to the Soo Line and go to Drake where he would change trains again and head west to Plaza. From there he could find transportation to the homestead. Perhaps the post office would be a place to start looking. Seems everyone gathers at the post office on occasion and information passes quickly there. The postmaster may have some suggestions. Somehow the mail had to go west, and that may be a way for Martin to catch a ride in that direction.

Into his pocket Martin put the seeds he had brought from Norway; he put $50 into his money pouch, kissed his bride, and left the next day for Rugby. He reviewed his route over and over to be sure he didn't miss any train changes. By the time he got to Plaza, he knew his itinerary. First the post office to secure a ride; second, buy a shovel and some potato and onion seedlings to plant along with the seeds in his pocket. It was mid-June, but he still might be able to at least get a vegetable crop for winter eating.

#

The Amanda Post Office, opened in 1906, held the mail for many of the homesteaders in the area. It was eight miles from Martin's homestead, but it would probably be Martin's post office and he needed to talk to the postmaster about a post office box. The Plaza Post Office could tell him who the postmaster was and how to find him. Martin learned that Gus Sather was the postmaster and was collecting the Amanda mail in the Plaza Post Office when the train arrived. Gus usually timed his trips to the train schedule to see if anyone needed a ride going west. He liked the few extra coins he'd collect for the ride as well as the company he'd have on the long twenty-mile ride, and it was a good way to get to know new neighbors and make contacts for his country store.

Sather was picking up the mail and loading his buggy with merchandise for his country store when Martin got to Plaza. He would gladly take Martin with him. They soon learned that Sather's homestead place was just a few miles from Martin's. Sather, a thirty-two-year-old widower with a four-year-old son, was recently remarried, but Martin could stay with them, and Gus would help him make plans. No need for Martin to buy supplies in Plaza since Sather had the store closer to Martin's land and was hauling merchandise for the store anyway.

Sather was born in Wisconsin and spoke English, but he had spent many years as a kid with Norwegian and German friends, so he and Martin could communicate a little. Martin was glad to learn some English from Gus, and Gus was glad to brush up on his Norwegian since many of the homesteaders in his area came from Norway. He needed more Norwegian to communicate with them in the post office and his store.

"I'm quite certain your land is next to the Frangs," Gus said. "Simon and Hage are grand old couple originally from Norway. Simon's in his sixties, I believe, but in good health. Hage is his second wife. No children. I think you'll like them. I'll drop you by their place as I'm delivering their mail."

Martin stayed with the Sathers for one day meeting the neighbors, checking out supplies in Gus's store, and sharing a little hootch and a laugh. The next morning he put his bag in Gus's wagon and traveled with Gus on his mail route. It was a good way for Martin to see where his new friends lived and get familiar with their names.

"Simon! I've brought you a new neighbor," Gus shouted. "Get Hage out here, get your mail, and meet Martin. He's going to be farming next to you."

'Welcome, Martin," Simon shook his hand. "Hage and I are happy to have neighbors. Come inside and we can visit. Gus, you come inside too."

"Thanks, Simon, but I've got mail to deliver and need to get home to Mabel. We're newlyweds, you know, and I had to leave her to go to Plaza. Guess I better hurry home."

As was the custom, neighbors invited a new neighbor to stay with them while they built a residence. Most homesteaders in the area were getting settled and indulged in this unwritten good neighbor program. In addition to inviting Martin to stay with them, Simon offered to lend him some farm implements so Martin could get a start.

"We are neighbors now, Martin, and in my way of living, we share. You can use my tools, Martin. Be sure to take a good look at the creek that runs through that area. I think you might find good water there. We dug a well and the water's good. You could do the same."

Martin accepted the offer of a place to stay and the use of his tools. The next day he took one of Simon's shovels with him and walked the perimeter of his land looking for the best location for a residence, where he might get water, and the best place for a garden. It didn't take long for him to push the shovel into the dirt to begin cultivating land for a garden. He decided to take a chance that something would grow, so he planted the vegetable seeds and prayed for rain! In the meantime, water could be hauled from the creek. He was lonesome for his bride even though he'd been quite busy. He felt he'd started his homesteading and it would be okay to go back for Asta.

"Bring your bride back and stay with us," Hage suggested. "We don't have a big place, but we have enough room for the four of us. And we'd sure like the company!"

"Too kind, Hage, but I appreciate it. I'll bring Asta back, and we can stay here while we get a residence. *Mange takk.* We should be back within the week."

Martin was anxious to tell Asta about their Norwegian neighbors. His trip back to Peter's included a ride to Plaza with Sather, a Soo Line ride to Minot followed by the Great Northern ride to Rugby. Martin was consumed with details—what he had learned, what he had accomplished, and what was in the near future. And he felt confident now that he knew the way!

The walk from Rugby to Peter was easy. Martin's step picked up, and he talked to himself. "I've married; we've traveled over the water and half of the United States; I've secured a homestead claim; I've planted a garden; I've met some neighbors. I made a good choice to come to America." Martin ran the last quarter mile to Peter's and to Asta.

"Asta! I'm back! So much to tell you and Peter. Best of all, we have kind neighbors, the Frangs. They've invited us to stay with them while we get settled. Will you do that with me?"

"Of course. Slow down, Martin," Asta assured Martin. "I am happy to meet our neighbors and to stay with them," Asta knew she didn't have any household supplies. No pots. No pans. Few dishes and utensils they'd tucked into their trunk. No bedding. How could she do this? She and Martin didn't even have a house. Perhaps, she could get a few chickens. She could tend the chickens and the vegetables, meet the neighbors and decide what else to do later.

"Peter," Martin began, "it was a successful trip. I've learned the way to our place, I've met the neighbors, I've planted a little garden. Peter, we are on our way. I think we'll pack up and go there tomorrow. What do you think?"

Peter shook Martin's hand. "Good work. I'll be anxious to visit you. And leaving soon is a good decision. Let's have dinner tonight, get a good night's sleep, and I'll get you to Rugby tomorrow."

Asta and Martin packed their trunk, thanked Peter for lending them the last $100, and rode with Peter to Rugby to catch the train to Minot. Hopefully, Martin thought, Sather would be back in Plaza getting merchandise and the mail. He wanted Asta to meet the Sathers; perhaps she and Sather's wife Mabel could be friends.

Asta hadn't been further west than Rugby, so she spent lots of time looking out the window, taking in the countryside, and thinking. Not many trees. No fjords. Wild prairie grasses. Birds singing. Small shacks every so often, not many towns. She hoped to adjust and learn to love her new home. Her thoughts shifted to what she could be doing to help with their settlement. The need for household supplies. Could she help Martin in the field? What would she be doing? She shifted in her seat and looked over at Martin. They held hands but each was consumed with thoughts.

"What are you thinking about, Martin?" she shyly asked.

"Oh, I'm making plans for the next few months before snow flies. I'm thinking about how I can prove up the land and build a residence," he shook his head and raised his eyebrows. "Lots of work to do, Asta. I need to break some land so I can plant a crop next spring. I need to think about paying Peter back too." They both took a deep breath and squeezed each other's hand. "What are you thinking about, my dear?"

"Oh, some of the same things, but more about how to create a home here where it is so different," she shared. "I'm thinking about my family back in Norway. I've even relived that trip across the Atlantic. That was something! We made it, Martin. We left some things behind, and now we need to move forward."

The train rolled west across rolling hills that gave a pleasant relief from the flat land in the eastern part of North Dakota. The rolling hills looked a little like home, but there were no mountains and no fjords. They stopped in Minot to change trains. That meant a short walk from the Great Northern depot to the Soo Line depot. Asta's eyes widened as she stepped into the brown pressed brick Soo Line depot. It's cream-colored dome ceiling gave the waiting room a grand feeling and shoes clicked on the handsomely tiled floor. She took time to visit the small resting room for women and peeked into the gentlemen's smoking room. Asta had never been in such an inviting depot on her journey across half of America. She stood as tall and dignified as she could when they boarded the train to head east out of Minot to Drake. The conductor held her hand as he helped her unto the stepping stool and into the passenger car. She nodded a thank you and smiled at Martin. They took their seats.

The conductor called out the names of the little towns: "Logan." "Sawyer." "Velva." "Balfour." "Drake. Everyone heading west will need to change trains." Martin took her hand, grabbed their trunk, and they waited for the train heading west.

"All aboard for Makoti, Ryder, Douglas, and Plaza." The new conductor placed a small stepping stool in front of the passenger car and helped Asta into the car. They took seats and waited for the train whistle to blow, the wheels to begin to roll, and the train to head west. The conductor walked through the car and took their tickets. Sometimes the train stopped to let passengers on and other passengers off. Usually the mail bag was tossed out or another one picked up. This was a new world for both Asta and Martin. They were helping settle the American West.

"Plaza station. The end of the line. Detrain here for Plaza. Ten minute stop." Martin hoisted the trunk on his shoulder. They detrained and headed for the post office. Lucky for them Sather was in Plaza picking up mail and merchandise.

"Ah, Martin. The gods must be with you! I was going to skip coming to Plaza today and come tomorrow instead, and here you are. This must be your bride! Welcome young lady!" and Gus reached out to give her a hug. Asta nervously looked over at Martin, and he assured her with a nod of his head that it was fine.

They understood only a little of what Gus had said, but they did recognize what he meant when he pointed to his wagon, took their trunk and put it in the wagon with the merchandise, and nodded to them to hop in.

"It's a dusty ride, Asta," Martin explained to Asta, "and it will take a few hours, but Gus knows where he's going. And Asta, isn't it a great day to be outside."

She smiled and settled into the seat behind the horses and headed west. The splendor of the rolling hills and the charm of the depot had given way to bumpy, potholed dirt paths. Hot breezes and the smell of horses permeated the air. No mountains. No fjords. Just a barren stretch of prairie that now seemed stern, inhospitable, and windy. It was all earth and sky.

The tall grasses blew in the wind. Asta looked around for civilization. Not much. Oh, a few homestead shacks, some clothes blowing around on the clotheslines, a few horses here and there, some small children playing in the dirt. No towns. Where were Martin and Asta to live? How could they ever make this a home? Asta wasn't spoiled; her family in Norway worked hard, didn't have much but made do with what they had. She had no right to expect anything else. It's just that here it was her turn to create a life. She had nothing to move into. Nothing had been prepared for her.

But she did have Martin, and he loved her. Strong. Smart. Industrious. Gentle. Fun-loving. He would make it a pleasant home. She looked lovingly at him as he attempted to visit as much as he could with Gus. The language barrier was there, but the two men were working through it.

"New residence there," Gus pointed at a homestead shack for Martin to see. "Digging a well now."

"Ja, I see," Martin responded. "They found water?"

Asta could see that Martin liked people and people liked Martin. She and Martin would make friends, but how far from others would they be living? Asta hadn't seen a town since Gus' horse and buggy headed west out of Plaza.

Oh how the thoughts rolled in her head...thoughts of home, of her parents, of loneliness, of worry, of excitement, of newness, of challenge. She had Martin and she had a trunk.

Gus suggested they come to his house first.

"We will stay with Gus and Mabel tonight, Asta. We can see what he has in his store and you can meet Mabel and others that come to the store. I planted some garden seeds, and we will need some gardening supplies you can look for."

Martin beamed with pride as he introduced Asta to the others. So many spoke Norwegian, and both Martin and Asta were happy to be part of the conversations. He smiled when Asta joined in the conversations. She was part of the group. These neighbors were happy to share work and equipment. They too had been homesteaders on the land and knew how much was needed to get things going. And how they loved to hear the stories of home. Martin and Asta were happy to share those stories and to be able to use their help. But the Sathers were a good eight miles from Martin's land, and Martin was anxious to get to his place and get to work.

"Tomorrow, Martin, tomorrow," Gus spoke slowly, his gestures helping communicate his message. "You and Asta... with me... to your place. Tonight, we sleep here." Gus gave them a tour around his general store while Mabel set out meat and potatoes and pie. A separate guest room was ready with an open window letting in the warm summer breezes and the light of a waxing crescent moon.

"Asta," Martin whispered to her as they lay in bed. "We are here. We are about to make our homestead. I am so happy, and I hope you are too." She snuggled in closer to him. The sound of crickets chirping filled the night skies until the light of dawn seeped into their room. The roosters crowed; the birds began to sing. A new day had dawned.

"*Takk. Takk. Takk*," Martin and Asta said at the same time. "Thank you for all, Gus and Mabel." A healthy hug and a firm handshake helped to move the goodbye along. Bags and a few gardening supplies were put in Gus's wagon and the group of three began the few miles to Martin's land. Asta would soon be making her first steps on their homestead land. She took a deep breath!

"Simon. Hage," Gus shouted as the horses brought the wagon, the mail, and Martin and Asta up to the Frang house. "I've brought your neighbors back to you!"

"Velkommen! Hage, kom utenfor for å møte Martin's kone. Vi har naboer!" Simon slipped into Norwegian so Asta could understand. *"Velkommen Asta!"*

"I'm going to leave them with you. I know they are in good hands with you two next door," Gus offered as he turned and climbed back up into the wagon. "Here's your mail, and I'll be off. See you next time."

Hage served up a three o'clock coffee with a nice tray of krumkake. She understood Norwegian but did not speak it. "Simon, tell them we've been here since 1908 and we've helped many settle in. Tell them we are happy to help them."

"We've been happy to help others who have come here to homestead," Simon nodded to Hage and spoke Norwegian. "We'd like to do the same for you. You stay with us and we can help you and you can help us with some things. Hage and I aren't as young as you two!" Simon chuckled as he stood up and walked around like he was an old man! Everyone laughed, but Martin could see that Simon had several more years under his belt, and Martin would gladly help Simon with his work.

Simon treated Martin like he was a son, and Martin was happy to have a father-like friend next door. Martin and Asta decided to stay with Simon and Hage into the fall. The Frangs were happy to have house guests.

"Let's put together a neighborhood gathering for this weekend, Hage," Simon said. "I know that Carl and Della like to celebrate, and they'd be good for Martin and Asta to meet," Simon turned to Martin and Asta and continued, "the Elgins homestead right across the way. You passed their place with Gus. Did he point their place out to you?"

"Simon, tell Asta that Della will be happy to have a young woman as a neighbor," Hage said. "Della's new to the area as well, and those two might form a good friendship. They don't have any children either. So, we'll have a party!"

"And I think Della speaks some Norwegian, too," Simon said.

Hage showed Asta the room Martin and Asta would share. Asta put their things down, thanked Hage, and stepped back outside to Martin.

"Martin, show me where we will live!" Martin took Asta by the hand, and they began to walk to their land.

Martin had stepped off the location for the residence earlier, but he engaged Asta in a conversation about where to put the residence. "I put the garden here, Asta, because it was easy to break up some of the dirt. Look, the garden has even begun to sprout. Carrot tops," and he pulled up a little carrot, wiped it on his pants, and handed it to her. "Your first homegrown American carrot, my dear! Enjoy," he looked around for other signs that rain had helped the seeds. "Look here, Asta, potato and onion tops well into their season. We will have vegetables for the winter!"

"I can see that we will need a vegetable bin, Martin. And where do you think we should put the residence?" Martin had already planned where to put the residence. "How about right here by the garden!" He and Asta picked a few rocks to mark where the corners of the residence might be.

"I have big feet," Martin laughed. "I'll step it off. How about 12' x 24'?" and he began to walk a straight line and count. "*En... to... tre... fire... fem... ti... elleve... tolv*," and he put down a stone to mark the corner. He turned a military style 90-degree turn, grinned at Asta, and began again to count this time to twenty- four. "*... tjuetre... og tjuefire*." He put down a stone. The residence was marked. Martin walked over to Asta, picked her up, and pretended to carry her over a threshold. "Where should we put our bed? Where should we put our table? Mark those spots, my dear. Let's make a home!" He put Asta down and she walked around in their house placing rocks and carrot tops where their household goods would go. Martin watched with a twinkle in his eye, walked over to her, and held her in his arms.

#

Summer 1913

Using Simon's equipment, Martin began to break land for next year's seeding. Asta walked the short half mile every day from Frangs to their land to tend the garden. Crane Creek ran through their land, so she hauled water from it to keep the garden growing. A creek on their land certainly made it easier to not only haul water but to consider where to dig a well. It also provided a nice place to have a picnic and a little alone time. Living with Frangs was good, but the newlyweds took advantage of as much private time they dared steal.

Hage engaged Asta with cooking and tending the chickens and taught her the English words for each little thing. Martin helped Simon with some of his chores, dug as much rock off his own land, and talked about a well. Martin wanted to be ready for the spring. He needed land ready to seed and a residence to be able to show he had made improvements on the land. All this was necessary to meet his obligation on the homestead contract.

Long summer days with late sunsets gave Martin the opportunity to work hard for long hours. He put what he had learned in agriculture school in Lillehammer to work. And yet he was learning a lot from Simon and was happy to be an extra hand for Simon.

"Simon," Martin said one evening, "I think I can get a residence up in about two weeks. What do you think? Is that too fast?'

"Ja, Martin, I think we can do it in that amount of time. We've got some supplies and a lumber yard close."

"I'm thinking about 12' x 24'. Smaller than yours, but doable, I think, and can show we've proved it up."

"You think maybe next week we should begin?"

"Let's plan on it, Simon. Sounds like you're thinking to help me?" Martin winked at Simon who chuckled and shook Martin's hand.

#

Martin noticed in the fall that Asta wasn't as helpful as she had been. She didn't complain, but he could tell she was not feeling well and was often sick in the morning. One evening at dinner Hage said, "Asta. *Tror ikke du tror du kan være gravid?*" Soon it was confirmed. Asta was going to have a baby.

Her sickness didn't improve with time. She felt weak and queasy. Each morning it became more difficult for her to carry water to the garden and bring back any vegetables that were ready. So, Martin took on this responsibility which took time away from his digging rocks, breaking land, and getting a spot ready to put up a residence. Martin felt lucky to have Simon and his other neighbor, Carl Elgin, close by for advice and friendship. They assured Martin things would be okay and they were there to help. He listened to what they said and hoped he could return the favors to them. Asta, on the other hand, didn't find much help regarding pregnancy. Hage had no children of her own and was not personally familiar with the process. Although Della was young, she and Carl had no children yet; she had nothing to offer.

"Asta. We won't be able to stay here for the winter. Simon and Carl both say the winters can be pretty rough, and we won't have a decent place to live," Martin chatted with Asta after dinner one evening. "And you are going to need care. We are too far from any medical help. Let's think about going back to Peter's place, maybe try to find something in Rugby or Barton. We could get a doctor there. What do you think?"

"That may be good, Martin, but what will we do for money? Do you think you might find some work there? It seems that Barton is growing. We saw lots of signs around Rugby, but they were in English. Oh, Martin. I'm sorry. We just didn't need this quite yet."

Martin bent down, kissed her forehead, took her in his arms and said, "It's great, Mamma. We want a family, and this is the way it goes. Cheer up. We're doing just fine."

#

The trees had shed their leaves. The days were getting shorter. Days and nights cooled down. Autumn signs were in the air. No residence had been built yet, and now Martin needed to consider that come early next spring, he would have a family. He'd heard that coal could be found in the dirt on the banks of the river, and others were mining their own. Martin hadn't had time to mine any coal for winter heat plus he didn't have any of the needed equipment. Martin and Asta needed to make plans to head east to Peter. Train tracks hadn't yet come to their area, so Martin needed to talk to Gus Sather soon to see if he and Asta could catch a ride to Plaza to catch the train. No need to write a letter to Peter; they would get to Peter before the letter. Peter will just be surprised to see them. Asta, however, took the time to write a letter to her parents to let them know about Peter, about their new land and new friends, and with the news that they were going to be grandparents.

Martin helped Asta into Gus' wagon early one morning for the ride to Plaza. An extra blanket was placed around her legs to keep her warm in the cool October day. Another neighbor and his wife were also going to Plaza for supplies and were riding along. The ride was long... twenty miles in a horse drawn buggy, but language was not a barrier since the others also spoke Norwegian. Martin and Gus enjoyed catching up with what was happening with Martin's homestead as much as they could considering the language barrier.

"Well, Martin. Congratulations. It's not surprising that Asta is pregnant. This happens to most of the homesteaders when they finally get assigned their land. Most who come into my store or the post office lament the situation, but when the year passes, they are pretty proud to show off the little one," Gus assured Martin. "Shucks, maybe you'll get a boy,

Martin, and have an extra hand in a few years. Kids grow up pretty fast, you know."

Martin chuckled. He knew he had left a son in Norway, and that little guy would be just a little over a year by now. He didn't mention this to Gus nor to Asta, but he wondered how the little guy and his mom were doing. He and Asta left Norway just five months ago and so much had happened to them in this short time. Martin knew he had a lot of work in front of him. He had to stay strong and positive for the two of them. Best to put Norway behind him.

"I think you had better apply for an extension on your homestead agreement, Martin. Your agreement says you will have a residence on the land within six months of signing the agreement, and I don't think you will make that. Didn't you sign that agreement back in July? Well, that means come January you will need to show proof."

"How do I do that, Gus, get an extension, that is?"

"Someone in Rugby should be able to help you. Maybe Asta's brother or the fellow he works for can give you some direction."

Martin had a lot to think about. Asta had a lot to think about. Their thoughts were not about the same things. Martin needed advice about getting an extension, he needed advice about a job, money, and a place for them to live. Asta needed a doctor and a good female friend to encourage her and share what she knew about delivery and babies. And could they afford all this? Babies cost money. They needed clothes. She figured that she was probably about three months pregnant and would be having her baby in the spring. *I'm going to need other clothes to wear as well. I should have paid more attention to Mama. Seems she had a baby every year. I hope that's not me.*

Martin talked to everyone he could gleaning information and advice. Asta stayed quietly beside him. New things were happening to her. Her body was changing, she could tell. At the same time, she wasn't feeling well. *Was everything going to be okay? Would she be able to get some help? Where will she end up? Where will Martin be? Can she do this alone?*

#

Peter was surprised to see the two of them walk up to his place. "Come in you two. Let's celebrate and hear about what's new in your lives. Did you get a place set up? What kind of neighbors do you have? Meet any Norwegians there?" The questions came one after another without time for Martin nor Asta to answer. Soon the three of them looked at each other and laughed. It had indeed been a while since they had seen each other, and so much had happened.

"I'll be quiet now, Martin. You two tell me what's new with you."

"Well, first, Peter, you are going to be an uncle! What do you think about that?"

"It will be great. Congratulations my sister! And you too Martin. Mom and Dad will be so proud. When is this going to happen?"

"Oh, in the spring sometime. We aren't sure yet, Peter. I haven't felt very good, so we need to get to a doctor hopefully in Rugby and get some help."

"Let's walk up to the Nutes' house to ask some questions," Peter said. "Nettie can give more advice than I can. I don't know anything about this sort of thing." And to the Nutes they went.

"All three of our children were born in Rugby," Nettie said. "She should see my doctor there. Dr. Alfred R. Sorenson. I'm certain that he can help you and perhaps even give an indication if the sickness would soon end."

"Tell her thank you so much," Asta said. "I don't have a mom or sister nearby to help me with this." She hugged Nettie and said, "*Takk. Takk. Takk.*"

#

It was early November and Martin was feeling the pressure of winter coming on. Those who had been in the area for a few years told him about the harsh winters, and Martin was anxious to get them settled. No snow had fallen yet, and the temperatures were still comfortable. Martin took his twenty-year-old bride by the hand and asked if she was able to take the three mile walk into Rugby. The late autumn day was beautiful, and the walk felt good to them both. Asta's tummy was beginning to round. The walk gave them time to talk. So happy to have Peter and the Nutes to give some advice.

Rugby on the horizon, and it was only 9:00 AM. They had plenty of time to search for the doctor's office. They headed for Dr. Sorenson's office at the local Lutheran Good Samaritan Hospital. He examined Asta and advised them to find a place close to a home hospital until the child was delivered. The delivery was estimated to take place sometime in April.

Martin and Asta needed a place to stay, and Martin needed work for the winter months. He also needed to apply for an extension on establishing a residence on the homestead. The original date had been set as January 7, 1914. Martin now knew that would be impossible. How was he going to handle all of this? Proving up a homestead many miles away. Finding winter work to generate an income. Helping his young, pregnant wife in a strange town. Martin had a great deal on his mind.

Chapter Six:

Barton, North Dakota 1913-1914

Tacked to the bulletin board in the Rugby drug store was an announcement about work and housing in Barton. "Look here, Asta," Martin said. "Housing and work in Barton. Remember that nice couple we met last June at that celebration? They live in Barton."

"Yes, I remember them," Asta said. "She told me that Barton is a growing community with homesteaders." It was most likely that the work in Barton included both farm work and construction. Martin could do both.

"Let's go to the depot and to see if a train goes to Barton," Martin suggested. "Maybe we could go up and back in one day to learn about the place. "

A Great Northern line out of Rugby ran north through Bottineau and stopped in Barton. Martin and Asta could easily train from Barton to Rugby and Rugby to Barton. A seventeen-mile ride that cost fifteen cents one way per person. That would be sixty cents total. Martin had the money. They could afford the trip. The schedule showed the train went to Barton in forty-five minutes and another train would go from Barton to Rugby late afternoon.

"Do you feel good enough to go today, Asta?" Martin asked.

"Yes, Martin. I think we should go. I can do this." Martin bought the tickets, they took a seat, and Martin put his arm around Asta. "My little mama," he said winking at her. "I need to take good care of you."

#

Small town, but a growing town. Barton had five elevators, four lumber yards, two livery stables, mercantile stores, five grocery stores, two meat markets, two hotels, two barbershops, a post office with a telephone exchange, gas stations, Baillie's Drug Store, a feed mill and a portable grinding mill, two implement shops, harness and shoe repair shops, hardware and furniture stores, cream station and ice cream parlor, confectionary store, photo gallery, 'Optimist' newspaper, two dance halls, pool hall and bowling lanes, blacksmith shop, garage, fire hall, jail, two churches and the Barton Hall. It also had a home hospital, two doctors, a drayman, a mortician, two real estate agents, and a rural route mail carrier.

Martin was sure to find work here, and most businesses posted jobs on a bulletin board or with the shop owner. It wasn't going to take long for Martin to find work. Barton had everything they needed including places to live. A couple of shop owners gave them tips on that topic as well.

#

Soon they rented a room from a Norwegian family; Barton became their home. Asta would help the family to help offset the room and board charge. It would be tight, but they could do this. So, they settled in for the winter, and Martin had no trouble finding work.

Martin knew that he also needed to get back to the homestead plot so that he could build a residence. *First things first, Martin, apply for an extension.* Certainly someone could give advice about how and where to do this filing, and the Norwegian Lutheran Church of Barton was a good place to ask.

Martin was told to enlist legal aid from James Johnson, Attorney at Law, from Minot, regarding his extension application. Martin visited Johnson's office in Rugby where Johnson drew up the legal request including a medical affirmation on Asta's condition. Johnson contacted Dr. Sorenson, and on December 20, 1913, Dr. A.R. Sorenson wrote a note to add to Martin's letter to the U. S. Land Office in Minot.

> *This is to certify that Mrs. Martin Aadness [sic]is now under my care and will need medical attention for some time yet. AR Sorenson, MD, Rugby, ND.*

Johnson wrote "owing to [his wife's] delicate condition it would not be safe to take her out on the land... as it would be remote to obtain medical aid taking into consideration the clemency of the weather and the distance of twenty-five miles to the nearest place where medical aid can be obtained.... and that it is necessary for [Martin] to remain with his family and to care for them..." The application requested that Martin's residency requirement on homestead entry serial NO. 09809 be changed from January 7, 1914, to July 7, 1914.

Martin and Asta waited. Martin worked construction jobs; Asta helped with domestic duties and with the children. Their first Christmas away from home was celebrated with their new family, but Asta thought about family celebrations in Norway. She was happy to have Peter nearby. Martin checked at the Post Office every day for a letter from the General Land Office in Minot. Finally on New Year's Eve, a letter was there. Martin anxiously opened it only to be disappointed. How would he tell Asta?

"Asta, I'm so sorry," Martin explained. "We are granted an extension but only until April 30 not July 5. How will I build a residence on that land before April 30? How can I leave you here? You and the baby? We aren't even exactly sure when the baby is due."

"Oh dear Martin. What if I don't have this baby by then? How long will it take you to put up a residence? What will this weather be like? How will we do this? Martin, what do you think?" Martin wasn't sure what to think. He needed to talk with Peter. Maybe he should make a quick trip to Rugby and then get down to Peter to visit about this. Maybe Peter could go with him to their land for a few days and help him get started on a residence. It was early January and not a blizzard had yet happened. Could it be they'd have a clear winter? Martin had heard about prairie blizzards from the guys he worked with. They can be dangerous and deadly. It was risky to go back in January.

What Martin didn't know was that Peter had decided to apply for a homestead plot himself hoping he could get one in the same area as Martin's. He had visited the Land Office in Minot mid December 1913 and was told about available land that looked to be about six miles south of Martin. Peter accepted the plot sight unseen. He was ready to make some important decisions himself. When should he tell the Nutes? When should he plan to go to his land? What would he take with him? Thoughts of the next step in his life occupied his time. He wondered what had happened to Martin and Asta. Where were they?

Peter was quite surprised when Martin showed up on his doorstep in early January.

"Martin!!! So good to see you! We have lots to catch up on. Where is Asta? How is she?" The questions kept coming. Martin tried to answer as quicky as he could. But he too wanted to ask Peter for help.

"Martin. I now have a homestead quarter just a few miles from yours. I'm going to establish a residence to prove my intent. Won't this be great. We can help each other."

Martin breathed a sigh of relief. "Oh Peter, thank goodness. We will be so happy to have family close, and we will be able to help each other. Now let me tell you about my situation." Martin told Peter of his filing for an extension due to Asta's health and getting one just til the end of April. He told of where he and Asta were living and what they were doing... Martin doing odd jobs, renting a room with a family that Asta was helping. Making friends at the local church.

"Maybe I could help you get your residence built and then you could help me," Peter offered. "Our dates for proving our residence are a few weeks apart and that gives us time to get them built. I'm sure you are an *arbeidshest*!"

Martin laughed and returned the compliment. "We are workhorses, Peter. But that's what we need to be. Now let's talk details. Would we go now in the winter?"

"No, I don't think so," Peter replied. "I need to inform the Nutes. You need to work and take care of Asta. And the weather... it's unpredictable, but it will be cold and windy. Maybe lots of snow. We just don't know."

Martin and Peter developed a plan that involved each of them getting things in order— Peter gathering his earthly goods, talking with the Nutes, and figuring out what they needed to buy. Martin—getting back to Barton, telling Asta, working to get some money together, determining when he needed to get back to the homestead land. Peter would go to Barton in mid-March so they could complete their plans.

It was a relatively warm January day, so Martin could walk to Rugby. He needed some time to think. The two looked at each other, grinned, thumbs up, and bid each other goodbye.

The walk to Rugby went quickly. Train ticket in hand, Martin was on his way to Barton. It had been a good day—no - a great day. He was pleased to have

Peter as a brother-in-law. They worked well together, and both were well-built, strong, sturdy Norwegians with hard working ethics. Now to just keep Asta healthy and to welcome the new member of the family. It would be several weeks, he thought. *Work hard, Martin, save some money, help the family you live with, and learn all you can.* The lady in the seat beside him nudged him and told him he was thinking out loud!

#

Asta was excited to welcome him back. It was a long day for her when he was gone. She wasn't happy tending children but knew that it was good experience. She had lots of younger siblings back in Norway and had done her share of caring for them, but she had left home at sixteen and was happy to have a life of her own. Oh well, she thought, it's good for me, and Martin is working hard putting our lives in place. I need to help.

The family spoke both Norwegian and broken English, so Asta was learning more words and phrases. The people in town were always good to her. She didn't have many clothes that fit her now, and a couple of the church women offered to lend her some of their maternity clothes. She was grateful for that and took good care of them. But she also worried.

Would life have been different had she said NO to Martin? Not married him. Not come to America. How will she make friends on a homestead plot that is a ways from the next homestead? What if her baby isn't healthy? How does a delivery work? She walked by the home hospital and tried to sneak a peek into the windows, but she couldn't see anything. Further down the street she happened to meet the young lady she and Martin had met at the Rugby festival.

"Good morning," Asta said. "Do you remember me? I met you and your husband at the festival in Rugby last summer."

"Why yes, I do," the woman replied. "How are you? Have you moved to Barton? I'm so happy to see you again."

"Thank you," Asta replied, "and I am happy to see you again too. I am here in Barton... well, as you may be able to tell, I am expecting a baby in the spring. Martin got a homestead about 150 kilometers from here, but I needed medical care that wasn't available there. So, we came to Barton where he found some construction jobs."

"Wonderful! I thought I saw you in church last Sunday, but I wasn't sure. We can meet there. I don't have any children, but I've heard it is important to eat well, get fresh air, exercise, and don't wear corsets! See you Sunday."

#

The first snowfall happened January 22. Snow fell, the temps dropped. The wind blew. The winter went on and on. And as those months passed, the baby grew and Asta found it increasingly more dangerous to get around on the snow and ice. She didn't see the lady from Rugby that Sunday.

Last year's crops and prices had been good, and people were looking to improve their living quarters. Martin was available and good at construction. He made acquaintances in town and his workload was heavy. Martin had lawyer fees and occasional medical fees. They were going to need more money soon. He hoped Asta would have the baby before he had to leave.

"How are you doing today, *Kjære?* I'd like to pick you up and throw you over my shoulder, but perhaps not today," he'd joke. Asta would smile and reply, "Maybe tomorrow? Maybe not for a few more months." Martin could tell that Asta's spirits were low somedays, so he joked with her to get her to laugh and relax.

The calendar rolled over to March and Martin was going to have to go back to the homestead to build a residence before the end of April. He and Peter agreed to meet in March. Martin wondered about the timing of the baby. He knew it would be best for Asta to stay in Barton for a while after the baby was born, and he thought it best they discuss that with the family they were living with.

Martin opened the conversation one morning. "We don't know if Asta will have the baby before I need to leave," he began." Babies cry and need attention, and perhaps Asta won't be as much help around the house or with the children. Do you think we should find another place?"

"Nonsense,' the lady of the house replied. "She and the baby will stay here with us. You are family now. We love babies and having another one in the house won't make a difference. Don't you worry about her, Martin. You have work to do."

So much to do, so much to think about, so much unknown, so much to be excited about.

Mid-March came quickly, and Peter arrived. Taking an overnight room in a small boarding house, he asked for help to locate Martin, and soon Peter, Martin, and Asta were together.

"My how you've grown, sister," Peter said to Asta as he reached over to pat her stomach. "I'd say you are about to have a boy. It looks like it might be sooner than later. How are you feeling?"

Asta blushed and held her tummy. "I'm pretty good, Peter. It's good to see you and to share this with you. Martin tells me we are going to be close neighbors! This makes me happy. I do write home and tell them what we are doing. They are happy to learn about our being together. Maybe some will join us!"

"Tell me, sister, when do you think you'll have this little one?"

"I think probably mid to late April. I hope Martin is here when the baby comes. Barton has a home hospital, so I'll be staying there for a couple of days. I just don't know."

'You seem to be in good company here. I'm sure they will be helpful. I'll take care of Martin if he must leave before the baby comes. We both have lots of work to do to make a residence in time."

Asta nodded agreement but hoped in her heart that she would be able to go with them. She had mood swings and was often tearful. Tears about homesickness. Tears about Martin leaving. Tears about caring for a baby. Martin was careful about what he said, and he tried often to reassure her things would be fine.

Peter left early April to find his homestead land. He would check things out for Martin and himself and purchase some implements for farming and for constructing a wooden residence. Martin would take the train to Plaza on April 23. He would return to Barton for Asta and the baby when the residence was completed. He had until April 30th to complete the residence. Martin counted on Peter to begin the work. He and Peter would have to work fast.

And so it went. Peter left. Martin completed a construction job and helped with a farmer's spring's work. Martin and Asta celebrated her 20th birthday on April 20th. Martin purchased a handmade baby blanket from one of the ladies at church and gave it to Asta for her birthday. However, no baby yet. Martin and Asta both knew that she would have the baby when Martin left.

"Asta, my dear. I leave on Thursday. I must finish a residence for our little family," he said holding her as close as he could. "I hate to leave you now and so wanted to take you and our baby with me. But I cannot wait any longer." They both cried.

Tears were shed the morning Martin boarded the train to Rugby. He hated to leave her behind. Asta waved to him as the train pulled out of the station.

Martin threw a kiss and waved to Asta. Asta was now on her own.

But not for long. Shortly after Martin boarded the train, Asta felt the pangs of childbirth. She was going to need help, so she packed a light bag and walked to the home hospital. Dr. G. O. Bundy attended to her and at 3:00 pm on Friday, April 24, 1914, a daughter was born in Barton. Martin was on the train.

April 1914

Chapter Seven:

Motherhood

Asta. Just barely twenty. A new mom. No mother to help. No sisters to help. No husband to help. She was alone. She held her little girl as tears ran down her face. *What was she to do now? What happens next?* She was tired from the labor. She needed comfort. She needed someone to talk to. *When does this bleeding stop? How do I know if my little girl is getting enough breast milk?* Oh how she wished she had some family close by to talk with, to share her joy and her worry. What if her baby got sick? She needed some baby clothes but how could she shop? What will her little girl sleep in? How long would she be at the home hospital? Did Martin leave her enough money to pay for all of this? If only she could go home to Norway… no, she had said YES to Martin and this is where she must be. *Stay strong Asta. Martin will return and get you and the baby. But how long will he be gone? How will she know when he will be returning to get them?*

A name. She must declare a name for the birth certificate. They had not talked about names. Asta pondered. Clara was Martin's mother's name. Mathilde was Asta's mother's name.

"Her name is Clara Mathilde," Asta told the nurse. She knew Martin would be happy about the connection to their Norwegian mothers. She looked down at her little Clara wrapped in the baby blanket Martin had given her. She was so little and beautiful. Asta cried. She was a mother now. What did she know about motherhood? For the past few months she had been worried about Martin leaving, about the delivery, about so many things but how to be a mother hadn't crossed her mind. Now here she was a mother. A new chapter. No experience. She will need to watch other mothers.

But for now, she needed to be sure she ate well and got the rest she needed. If she could eat well and drink lots of water, then little Clara would have enough milk. Asta held her little girl to her breast and watched as Clara snuggled in and sucked. Tears ran down Asta's cheeks. Yes, she was a mother. No turning back now. She would take care of her baby and wait for Martin. It wouldn't be too long. Martin had to have a residence by April 30. Then he could return for them.

Asta. A mother. She hummed a Norwegian lullaby as little Clara fell asleep in her arms.

Chapter Eight:

Proving Up The Homestead

Martin told Peter go to the Plaza post office and ask for Gus.

"When you get to Van Hook, Gus will introduce you to others. Be sure to meet Simon Frang. He's got the homestead quarter next to mine. Simon and his wife, Hage, will be helpful. Explain to them why I'm not there yet. They may even take you in."

#

Peter climbed into Gus Sather's wagon outside the Plaza Post Office and the two headed west. Gus took plenty of time to give information and instructions to Peter and he took Peter home with him.

"Leave your things here with us," Gus suggested to Peter. "Martin's land is about eight miles from here. I'll take you there tomorrow since I need to deliver some goods to Simon anyway. Help me lift these things into the wagon box." Peter did as he was told.

Simon was in his field when Gus and Peter pulled into the yard. They unloaded the goods.

"There's Simon over there," Gus pointed Peter toward Simon. "Greet him for me." Peter walked across the field to Simon and Gus left.

"Du må være Simon," Peter held out his hand. Simon shook his hand and replied, "Yes." Simon was speaking English! Peter quickly changed to English as well.

"I'm Peter Sterud, Martin's wife's brother. I have a homestead quarter a few miles south of here, but I'm going to help Martin get a residence established. You may remember that Asta is pregnant and needs care, so they are living in Barton a few miles north of Rugby. Martin filed for an extension into July but was granted only to April 30. He is staying with Asta hoping she has the baby before he has to leave. I'm going to get things started."

"Well, welcome Peter. It's nice to meet you. Perhaps I could give you a hand. It's late into April and Martin doesn't have much time to get a little house built. You stay here with us in the meantime. Perhaps we could trade. I help you build a residence and then you help me get some planting done, but we will need to watch the weather because if a storm comes up or the wind blows too hard, we may need to work faster or take a break."

It was agreed that Peter would stay with Simon and Hage. Simon would help Peter get a start on Martin's residence.

"Let's walk over there and see if Martin left a mark for where he'd build the house," Simon suggested. The two of them walked the land and found a small rise that had stones laid out on it. "This must be the spot," Simon said. "Why don't you take my wagon in the morning and see if Gus has the materials you might need. Check the lumber yard as well. You may not even need to go to Plaza. Of course, Van Hook is a busy place right now with all the settlers moving in and the train crews working, but you should find most of what you might need. Carl over there --- another neighbor – and I work together really well, so he should be of some help as well."

Peter knew the wooden residence was going to be 12' x 24'. That evening he penciled out what it would look like and what materials he would need. Soon he had a list and was ready to leave in the morning. A house that size wouldn't take them too long to put up once they got the materials. It would be a wooden structure with asbestos for insultation. Peter hoped that Martin would arrive during the construction so that he could not only be part of the process but also oversee how he would like it completed.

Martin left Rugby on April 23 and was on his way. Late the next day he appeared at Simon's house and became part of the process. It wasn't long before a couple of other neighbors stopped by to help. Carl Elgin brought John Kasa over with him. Both had homestead plots kitty corner from Martin. Kasa, a single man in his early thirties, was born in Minnesota and had visited with the Frangs many times. Elgin, a Norwegian born man in his mid-twenties, and his wife, Della, lived next to Kasa. It was easy to see a neighborhood of young families was developing. Sixty-year-old Simon had a few young men close by whom he could shepherd as they grew their families and their livelihoods. The young men in turn helped Simon with work that he needed done.

Hage had extra seed potatoes that she gave Martin. "Put these in your garden, Martin. Come fall you will have potatoes for most of the winter. That will make plenty of lefse and klub!"

It was an exciting few days for all. Soon Martin's house was completed, and minimal furnishing were donated by the Frangs and the Elgins to provide a home for Asta and the baby when they arrived. Martin needed to get back to Asta since he hadn't heard any news of her. However, he knew he needed to break at least an acre and plant a crop. He was hoping to have ten acres cultivated and seeded this first year, so getting started was important.

Simon provided his horses and cultivation equipment for Martin. The horses needed a rest in the middle of the day, so work began early morning with a midday break. Then they would be back at work in the late afternoon. The horses needed water and food, so Martin had that responsibility as well. It was hard work, and Martin was finding out that he was a lot stronger and tougher than he had thought. He worked sunup to sundown for three days just to break an acre.

"Flax" Simon said. "Plant flax. They make linseed oil from it and that's used in paint. You'll make more money and flax can be planted later in the season. You don't need to learn much about it. It's a good crop to begin with."

Martin planted flax and stayed in his new residence. At the very end of a long hard day, he stood in the doorway to see what he had accomplished. A sense of satisfaction poured over him, and yet he knew the next day he had to get up and do the same work again. He was so busy that some days he hardly noticed the wind that swept across the prairie almost daily.

In Barton, Asta planned for little Clara to be baptized on Sunday, May 24, at the local First Lutheran Church. She sent a telegram to Martin in care of the Frangs letting him know. A few days before the event, Martin appeared in Barton and surprised Asta. Asta cried while Martin held her and his new little daughter and cried. They were a family. A family ready to baptize their baby, gather their goods, thank their Barton friends, and begin the journey to their new home. Barton to Rugby. Rugby to Minot. Minot to Drake. Drake to Plaza. And the last family journey in Gus Sather's wagon! It was a long trip, but it was good to be together and hold their little Clara.

"She's so precious," Martin said. "I'm so proud of you, Asta. You are a good mother already. Clara's a month old and look at her look at you with such love. Precious little girl. Thank you, Asta. I hope our home will be okay for us."

"It will be perfect, Martin," Asta assured him. "We just need to be together. *Er hun ikke søt.* I can't believe how much I already love her. Our little girl!"

#

Gus took them right to their homestead. Simon and Hage saw Gus coming down the path and ran to meet the horse and wagon. Old friends already in the neighborhood, hugging, congratulating, looking at the baby, and helping them get settled. How lucky they were. Soon John Kasa and Carl Elgin and his wife Della appeared. Asta felt loved yet at the same time anxious. Language moved between Norwegian and English. Overwhelming. How would she ever learn this?

It was late May, and the weather was still cool but not cold. Hage called it "spring pretty" – leaves on the trees, birds singing, and Crane Creek which ran through their land was running strong with spring runoff. This water couldn't be used for cooking and drinking, but it could be used for washing clothes and dishes as well as bathing. Asta knew she was going to have to do some washing real soon as both she and Clara smelled of sour milk. How would she handle that? Hopefully, a little stove with a side container of warm water would be available. She could soak those clothes and then put them outside to dry. Maybe Martin would put up a clothesline.

The chores that accompany homesteading and farming began. Drinking and cooking water needed to be hauled from local wells and then heated on the coal burning stove. When wells were dug, veins of lignite coal were exposed, so Martin, like many of the area homesteaders, mined coal for heating purposes until the easily obtainable coal was gone.

Martin had dug a well, broken some land, and planted a garden. Now it was time for him to plant more flax and help Asta learn about the land and the work she could be part of. Summertime made living easier. The sun was out longer, and lanterns were not needed as much. Many of the cooking facilities were outdoors, and the use of the outdoor privy was acceptable.

Most pressing was to report to the land office that he had established a settlement on Lot 1 of 152 91 Section 19 in Crane Creek Township. He needed to ask Simon and Carl to witness his work. Every time he filed a document, there was a charge. A little income on the side would help. He thought he should get some chickens, maybe buy a cow – they needed milk, cream, and eggs not just now but also through the winter. But what about refrigeration? How would they keep the supplies cold during the summer? Martin hadn't had time to dig a deep hole, cut ice to put into the hole to keep food cold. Spring had been too busy for him. And he'd spent money on flax seed and supplies and knew that he wouldn't have any money from harvesting and selling until into the fall and winter.

Carl said banks were anxious to lend money to hard-working homesteaders and with three banks in town – First State Bank of Van Hook, Farmers State Bank of Van Hook, and Northwestern Bank – surely Martin would get a loan. Martin thought his progress on the homestead land certainly proved that he was a hard worker, and he had neighbors to attest to his character. Finding a bank would be a necessary part of this trip to town. He decided to go to the bank and hope his Norwegian and broken English would see him through. Afterall, many of the homesteaders here were from Norway, so things would probably work out. Maybe the banker spoke Norwegian.

Martin left the Farmers State Bank with a $1500 loan at 10% interest and with a checking account. He needed the money to get his operation going. Writing checks was new to him and to Asta as well. They were accustomed to dealing in cash and learning the American money system was something new as well. He was more nervous about writing the checks than he was about paying back the loan. Feeling happy, anxious, and a bit nervous, he went to the general store for basic supplies. Because he was walking, he needed to be careful how much he bought. He was thankful that Ed Egedahl delivered meat on a regular basis, so he didn't have to worry about meat and refrigeration.

"Asta," Martin shouted. "I'm back with goods!" Asta was sitting outside on a small bench holding Clara and enjoying a warm breeze. She smiled when his tall strong silhouette could be seen coming up the road. She wondered what he had bought. Probably staples: Coffee. Bread. Milk. Bacon. Eggs. They could have bacon and eggs for dinner then boil the left-over eggs. She was certain the hot water in the stove reservoir would heat to boiling as she managed to fry the bacon and eggs. Maybe she should mention to

Martin that they should have some chickens. She could gather eggs and maybe even sell some.

Life felt rather good in the evening even though she felt quite homesick during the day. She'd heard about prairie fever that some homesteading women suffer, but she felt mentally strong with some women neighbors. Carl's wife, Della, had walked over to see her this morning. Della had no children of her own yet and was happy to hold Clara and visit with Asta about motherhood. Carl had finished building the barn and thought a neighborhood social would be a good idea. Della invited her and Martin to a neighborhood dance Saturday night. Frangs and John Kasa would join them as well as some of the others in the area. It would be a good time for Asta to meet the others. "Bring Clara too! And if you see Peter, invite him as well."

#

"Asta, I took out a loan and got a checking account. We need a milk cow, some chickens, and a barn as well as things for the house. We'll use some of the loan for them."

"Slow down, Martin," Asta grinned. "I'm anxious to see what you brought and what happened at the bank, but I too was thinking about chickens."

"Let's talk tonight. I need to stockpile some firewood and mine some coal by the river. Our stove will need to heat water for washing and to heat the house this winter. We'll need hay for the cow for winter feeding as well. Lots to be done before harvest."

Martin kissed Asta and Clara, put the supplies in the house, and went to chop firewood. Asta smiled as he walked away. She, too, wanted to help their lives. She thought about tending the garden, hauling water, raising chickens and gathering eggs, milking a cow. She might be able to sell eggs and milk and maybe even buy a butter churn. The cash she could earn would help. She thought about a sewing machine; she could make clothes for little Clara. Maybe she could take milk, butter, and eggs to the general store and get credit on a sewing machine. She would talk to Martin about these things tonight.

"I heard in town today that things aren't looking good in Europe and war seems likely. I hope Norway stays neutral in this. Norway doesn't need to go to war." Martin shook his head. "I hope our brothers aren't called to war."

Asta thought about her older brothers, Sverre and Marcus, both military age. She didn't want them to go to war and hoped for a letter from home. She'd written home but any mail she received would come through the Amanda Post Office and Gus Sather, but Martin hadn't been to Amanda for some time. Maybe no word from home was okay.

Their little house was beginning to feel like home. Clara was a good baby, and Asta was a good mother. A good night's sleep was rare but always welcome. Martin worked hard each day and even though Clara sometimes cried in the night, he slept.

The rains fell at the right time that summer. A couple of inches in June and then again in August. Of course, the wind blew and at times the garden felt dry, but still the potatoes and other root vegetables were growing. When a summer storm would roll across the plains, Asta and Clara would stay in the house. The small homestead shack was confining and Asta was always happy to get outside. She'd put Clara on a blanket in the yard so she could gather the eggs and milk the cow. Hauling it all back to the house often took a couple of trips, but she was part of a team. Martin wasn't alone in providing for the family.

#

As the weeks passed, charming light blue blossoms on Martin's flax began to appear. To Martin they looked like a reflection of the sky. Martin liked taking a few moments to look at that field. It gave him a sense of satisfaction that he was living the dream promised to those who took on the adventure of settling America. Just knowing he could break more land for seeding next season energized him. He hoped the price of that flax would give him a chance to improve their living situation. He had a family. He had a bank loan. He needed his own equipment. He needed a granary to store flax. Perhaps he would not sell this fall but hold out until spring. They had money to live on, and the talk in the town was that once the Soo Line got to Van Hook in October, getting grain to market would be easier, and the price was going up. Martin built a granary and was prepared to wait.

Martin continued to break land, build a barn, put up a clothesline, string fence, and be a husband and father. Homesteading families had a silent bond to work together and to build a community. They were committed to their neighbors to share workload and tools. The little towns springing up needed schools and community halls. Roads needed maintenance. Van Hook was no different.

The days grew shorter, the crop was harvested, and twenty-five acres had been cultivated for seeding in the spring. The mild fall temperatures and the fall colors pointed to the certainty of winter. As the leaves dried up and fell to the bare ground, Martin prepared for winter by cutting wood and mining coal. Their little neighborhood seemed to squeak out few extra hours every so often to share a meal and prepare root vegetables for winter eating. Even Peter took the time to venture the few miles north to see Martin, Asta, and Clara before winter came. He stayed a couple of days, played with his niece, built a potato bin for the kitchen, and helped Martin stack his wood.

Asta finally heard from home and was anxious to share the letter with Peter. They talked about their family in Norway relieved to learn that Norway was neutral in the war and their brothers were safe. The post office had moved to Van Hook; Asta knew she could send and receive letters more often.

As the daylight hours grew shorter, Martin continued working long hours outside. Asta felt pangs of loneliness. Longer hours of darkness, the lack of warm breezes and the smell of flowers, and a chill in the air and often in the house didn't help. What could she do to lighten her spirits? She talked to Martin about going to town to buy some fabric so she could use her new sewing machine. "This will be a good project for me while Clara sleeps," she told Martin. "The daylight streams in the window and makes it easier to see when I sew. I think this would be good for me." Martin agreed and they went to town.

The mild winter weather made it possible for all three of them to travel to Peter's one Sunday to share news from home. Peter and Asta's younger sister, Thora, was planning to come to America! Just seventeen and single, she was planning to travel alone. Asta worried about that. She was so young and so small, only 5'4" tall, but she had saved what equaled $25 US working as a telephone operator. She had already purchased passage on the Kristianiasfjord. She, just like Peter and Asta, was intent on pursuing a new opportunity. Certainly, her telephone experience in Norway would be useful here in the US.

"Oh Peter, I hope she makes it. I wrote that we are not in Rugby anymore. The train comes right to Van Hook from Fargo, but I don't know if she knows that. It's too late to get a letter to her as she's leaving early February."

"We will have to trust that she can do this. Lots of people along the way can give advice, and she certainly is independent!" Peter assured Asta. "I don't know Thora as a young woman, but if she's like you, she'll be fine."

Asta thought about her younger sister heading out across the waters alone. *Does Thora really know what it is like here? Few trees. No mountains. Dry, hot summer days. Oh some nice days, too. But the wind. The relentless wind that seems to blow all the time. Few nice things. It's not easy, Thora,* Asta thought, *but yes, do come because I need a touch of home here. Martin and Peter aren't enough. I need a sister.*

#

February 29, 1915

When Thora got off the train in Van Hook, it didn't take long for her to find her brother. Tears. Hugging. News from home. Talk of her new little niece, Clara. *Where should Thora stay? Who has room? Who needs help? What were her plans?* Peter took his little sister home with him just as he had Asta and Martin. Time to reconnect. Family. He needed to look after her, help her adjust and find her way. Peter had come to America alone so many years ago now had two sisters close by.

Martin, too, was happy to see Thora. She would be good company for Asta. The sisters could chat while Martin and Peter talked about marketing flax and buying more seed for spring planting. Thora held Clara and told her sister about home and her trip. They had much to share about what had happened the last couple of years. Asta set the table with as much flatbread as she could and lefse – always enough potatoes to roll a little lefse. Peter brought a good bottle of homemade brew; he would always bring something special from Gus Sather's store. Often it was pickled herring. The feast was prepared, a toast was made, and a day of togetherness ended too soon. Thora stayed with Peter. A couple of weeks later she left for Minneapolis. Asta felt alone when she heard the train whistle blow as it pulled out of the station heading east.

The mild winter began to wane early in 1915. Not much snow had fallen, and the ground was quite dry. Families prayed for rain, soft rains to moisten the soil and fill the wells. It wasn't until into April that the rains came, and then just in time. The Van Hook newspaper reported how much rain had fallen, and the spring reports were good. Martin bought a couple of horses from Peter and a plow to break more soil. He was hoping to break about 15 more acres in the spring. That would give him 25 acres of cropland with the ability to plant not only flax but also some oats. He planned to cut prairie grasses to feed the cow and the horses. Simon was always ready to help, and he had the tools and experience. Martin liked helping Simon in return.

Van Hook was a buzz of activity. The presence of the Soo Line Railroad boosted the population which led to the establishment of new businesses and a main street. The village leaders prepared incorporation paperwork. This was all the talk on May 17th when the Norwegians gathered in the town park to celebrate Syttende Mai. Accordion music invited many to step up and dance. Others sang Norwegian folk songs and the Norwegian national anthem. Everyone brought a

Norwegian dish to the picnic. Most of the Norwegian women took their traditional costume out of the trunk and hoped it still fit so they could wear it to town.

Asta wasn't so lucky. She hadn't lost the weight from carrying her first child and her bunad wouldn't fasten. She was tiny as a teenager when she received the bunad, but now just a few years later, it didn't fit, and Asta was pregnant again. She hadn't told Martin. He was much too busy to have to worry about another baby right now. Asta, experienced with pregnancy and childcare, needed to figure out if Van Hook had a midwife. They did not need another child right now, but then maybe it would be a boy who would be a helping hand for Martin. These worries kept her awake at night as well as Clara who was only thirteen months old.

Carl and Della joined in the Syttende Mai celebration that day as well. So many stories to share and so many women to help with Clara who loved to toddle around. All the young women liked mothering her. Asta was happy to have the help.

The men discussed the rains, an answer to prayer. They shared market prices of various grains, what to plant, putting up hay for the livestock, and the town of Van Hook and which boards they might serve on. It was an afternoon full of conversation, food, and fun. The women talked of cooking, cleaning, washing clothes, and children. Della shared that she was pregnant with her first child. Cheers went up and Della blushed when some of the women raised their eyebrows to suggest they knew what Della and Carl had been doing during those dark winter nights! Asta didn't mention her pregnancy but listened closely to suggestions for Della. Mrs. DeTienne, some of the women said, was a midwife and Della should talk with her.

Van Hook's newspaper contained local gossip and farming news. But Carl and Della read the Ward County Independent when available. Della had read in the Ward County Independent that Mrs. DeTienne, a trained nurse, is talking about remodeling her home in Van Hook for a home hospital. "It isn't ready yet, so I've heard she will come to your house and help. But we have time to figure this out!"

Soon the sun began to set, and the men knew they had busy days ahead of them and needed to get their families home. Many walked home but those who came from further away climbed into their wagons. The dust on the dirt road swirled in the air as horses and wagons made their way out of town. Martin and Asta and Clara walked home. A perfect day.

Planting and putting up hay were most important. Neighbors shared implements – mowers, rakes, hayracks and pitchforks. Working together they knew they could get the work done. Being the tallest, Martin was in high demand when stacking hay began. He was able to pitch the hay to the top of the stack! Manpower was necessary but women also helped. The days were long. Breaking up more land was next. And of course, always rock picking. Some of the rocks

Martin and his neighbor hauling hay.
Looks like winter!

were so embedded that it was necessary to pry the
rocks out of the ground with a pick or shovel or
crowbar. Not a job for just one man, so the men
teamed up. Carl had a stone boat to toss the rocks
onto. Horses pulled the stone boat to haul the rocks to
a central pile. It was difficult work for the men and for
the horses, so it couldn't be an all-day project. Both
man and horse needed water, food, and rest. Jelly
sandwiches on homemade bread with apple butter
made a great afternoon lunch.

Van Hook incorporated as a village in 1915.
Schools were established, churches were formed, city
government offices were set up, and city officials
were elected. Asta and Martin's neighbors were not so

concerned about the schools as none of them had school age children, but they were interested in the formation of a church where they could share culture, foods, language and festivities. While the basement of the church was being built, Norwegian services were held in members' homes. Some members felt church should be in English since the children were learning English in the school. Asta wanted to learn more English so she could teach Clara words for things in nature, foods, and daily activities. She hoped when Clara started school she wouldn't be too far behind in English. Ladies Aid was a good place for Asta to both learn some English and to participate in activities with other women plus it gave Clara some friends to play with.

Martin, Asta, and Clara in front of their homestead shack. Asta is six months pregnant.

As the summer turned into fall, the walk to church became more difficult. The wind blew almost every day and walking with little Clara was slow and difficult as Asta got closer to the time of her baby's birth. She stayed home more often. Days could be long, lonely, and full of hard work. Once late fall arrived and the wind had blown the dry leaves from the trees, the garden had been harvested, and a potato bin had been filled, Asta began to need more information about the midwife. And then the great neighborhood news: Della had delivered a baby boy! Asta and Clara walked the mile to Della's to learn more about the midwife.

"Mrs. DeTienne will come to your house. Martin will need to get to her. I think he could saddle up the horse and buggy and bring her to you. What about Clara? He can drop Clara here with us," Della was full of information and happiness. Asta rocked the little boy and wondered if she would have a boy. Clara played on the floor.

The weeks went by, the wind blew, the snow fell, and Martin continued with winter work until one day Asta told him he needed to fetch Mrs. DeTienne. Tuesday, November 30, 1915, Ruth, the second daughter, was born. Clara was nineteen months. Busy and tired, Asta washed diapers, tended babies, cooked, and baked. She thought about her own mother and how lonesome she must be. Clara and Ruth may never know their grandparents, she thought sadly. And then the reality that she may never see her parents again made her cry.

How she longed for word from home. She wrote home regularly, but the post office was quite a ways from her home and she couldn't venture out alone with two small children in the cold and wind, so she waited for Martin to go. She knew the mail came west on the train in the evening and she often sat by the window listening for the whistle. Sometimes in the winter the train was snowbound, and it would take days for the mail to get through. At times she felt sad, often depressed, and wondered how she could keep her spirits up. Just having Martin walk through the door brought a smile to her face, but he was busy feeding the cow, the chickens, and the horses, as well as gathering eggs and going to town for supplies. He had a family now, and his work was never done. Asta rarely got out.

With two little ones in diapers, Asta was always washing clothes. Martin hauled water from the well or the rain barrel every day, and she heated it on the stove. Laundry was always hanging on a line Martin had strung close to the wood stove. Asta had made a large batch of lye soap in the early fall so she would be ready for winter laundry. She knew the recipe for lye soap by heart: five pounds of melted grease, one pound of lye, cold water, Borax, salt and sugar, and ammonia. She dissolved the lye in the cool water and then slowly she added the grease and other ingredients stirring constantly until the mixture became thick and light colored. Then she poured it into pans lined with cloth, cooled it, and cut it into individual bars and stored them in the cellar. First the clothes were soaked in the hot water and lye soap. Exceptionally dirty clothes were rubbed on the washboard before being put in the rinse water. When the sun shone, she hung the clothes outside allowing the heat from the sun to do the work.

#

Winter gave way to spring, and Clara's second birthday was just four days after Asta's twenty-second birthday. Martin took part of the day to take his three girls into town to Malloy's Drug Store for ice cream. They stopped at Bye Clothing Store to find some new clothes for Asta. She used her old clothes to sew clothes for Clara. In addition to sewing, she tended the garden, picked the eggs, baked the bread, and did the laundry. This year she planned to pick some berries to make jam or pick apples to make apple butter, The work never stopped. She'd pause and look out in the distance and see Martin seeding, breaking ground, haying, feeding the animals, picking rock. They did the same things every day. She hoped all their work would pay off.

There were days she hated the prairie. Those were the days when the wind blew, the skies grew dark with threats of tornados, hailstorms forced them inside, and mosquitos swarmed around them. There were days she loved the prairie. Those were the days when the birds sang, the sea of tall prairie grasses swayed in the breezes, and wildflowers colored the open skies as she looked out at the vast horizon. "I can't walk to it," she'd tell Martin about the horizon, "and I can't touch it. But I do feel it and I like to listen to the whisper of the wind as the sun sets." Martin liked to hear that; he wanted his bride to be happy in their new home. Sometimes he worried that she wasn't.

#

News about the war in Europe began to take up more space in the local paper. In spring, 1917, most of the local talk revolved around the Scandinavian countries and the United States maintaining neutrality even though Britain, Russia, Italy, and France were struggling to hold the line against the powerful Germany. U. S. President Woodrow Wilson worked hard to bring about an agreed-upon solution – a peace treaty - but to little avail. On April 6, 1917, the United States declared war on Germany knowing it did not have a large army to deploy to Europe. On May 18, 1917, US Congress passed the Selective Service Act requiring all men between the ages of twenty-one and thirty to register for the military. On the first day of the registration, millions of American men registered for service. On June 5, 1917, Martin walked to the local draft board and J. A. Bartell of Van Hook signed his Selective Service registration.

"Martin, I'm so afraid," Asta said. She started to cry.

"Why?"

"I'm afraid you may be called to war," Asta held her apron to her eyes. "I know you are twenty-seven and you need to register... "

"Asta, my dear," Martin interrupted, "my Selective Service card states that I am not yet a naturalized citizen but a declarant. Do you see that?"

"Yes, Martin, but you could still be called up."

"I have asked for an exemption because I have a wife and two children to support. The Selective Service will call others before they call me but registering is my duty now that we are in America."

"Ja, Martin. I hope you are right. Two little ones and me alone on this prairie in the winter would not be good for any of us. We need you, Martin. I hope you are right. Peter is thirty-one. Carl is thirty-five. They didn't have to register, and I'm sure if you must go, they will help me. But please don't go, Martin, please."

Martin wiped her tears, took her in his arms, and swung her around. "We will all be fine, my dear. We need to trust and have faith and hope. We've come this far. We will be fine."

Worries about the US involvement in the war was a nagging concern, but farmers also realized the war's positive effects on the farming economy. German blockades had cut off Europe's access to Russian wheat. To meet the demands for food for the fighting troops, American farmers broke more land and increased production. The federal government set the price of wheat at slightly over $2 a bushel. This was more than double what Martin received the past couple of years. Led by the slogan "Wheat will win the war," farmers, Martin included, planted more wheat. Finally the hard-working homesteaders felt the prosperity they came seeking. The extra money allowed them to buy better machinery and build better homes for their growing families.

#

Each homesteader had to live on the land, build a home, make improvements and farm for five years before being eligible to "prove up." Martin had applied for his homestead quarter in June 1913. It was now June 1918; Martin's time was up. Martin applied for final proof on his homestead reporting that he had established a 12 x 24 residence, two barns – one 16 x 32 and the other 16 x 20, a 14 x 24 granary, cultivated and seeded ninety acres to wheat, oats, and millet. Ninety acres at current grain prices would certainly provide Martin with more fluid cash to improve his operation. On August 13, he received notice stating that he was not yet a naturalized citizen and he had not made final payment of $5.35. He learned he could not get final proof on the land if he was not yet a naturalized US citizen. His bubble burst. He had planned a celebration with Asta and his girls, but now that had to be postponed.

"We don't own the homestead yet, Asta," Martin confided one night at dinner. "But don't worry. We are waiting for my naturalization papers to arrive. Then I can claim the proof."

Asta left those issues up to Martin. She had a garden, chickens, laundry, and two daughters to take care of. Plus she was now pregnant again. Oh how she hoped for a boy. It would be easier if it was a girl since she had clothes for girls, but if it was a boy, she would dress him in the dungarees the girls had worn.

On September 15, 1918, Mrs. DeTienne came to the house and delivered another girl, Astrid.

Asta was so busy she didn't realize that on November 11, 1918, the war had come to an end until Hage fought the cold, November wind to bring a newspaper to their house and to see new baby. Hage traded the paper for the baby, and Asta read the headline. **WORLD WAR IS OVER**. She laid the paper on her lap and started to cry.

"Now I know Martin will not be called to serve. I'm so thankful. I need him. We need him." Hage agreed as she cooed to the baby. Martin came in, took off his winter work coat, hat, gloves, and boots and smiled at all the girls in his house. "Let me count my girls," he said, "one, two, three, four and Hage, you make five! Good to see you."

Asta opened the paper to one full page devoted to the Van Hook celebration for the end of the war and the establishment of an American Legion Club in honor of Charles Beck, a local boy who had been killed in the war. She showed it to Martin.

"Will you go?" Hage asked Martin and Asta. Asta shook her head and wrinkled up her nose.

"Martin, you should go," Asta said. "I don't think I should take the girls. We have heard about the influenza pandemic. Hage said that some entire families have been sick with no one to care for them. I can't get sick, Martin, and I can't have the little girls get sick. What would we do?"

"You are right, Asta. We can't get sick. We need to stay as close to home as we can this winter and hope this influenza goes away."

"But you go to the celebration, Martin."

"We'll see. I can't leave you home alone with the little girls. Wouldn't be right."

"But we need to celebrate with the town. Charles Beck, I've heard, was a nice young man. He came here with his brother who homesteaded. Did you know him?"

"No, I hadn't met him nor his brother."

"I guess they buried him in France. Nice of the town to remember and honor him in such a long-lasting way."

Martin went to the celebration in Legg's Hall. for a couple of hours, visited with the men, and came home with new worries. He'd heard that wheat prices could fall now that the war was over. And Martin had bills to pay. What was he to do? He had repaid Peter half of the earlier loan, and he wanted to be able to pay off the entire debt.

"How was the celebration?" Asta asked holding Astrid on her lap with Ruth cuddled up beside them. "Were there lots of people?" Clara played dolls at her mother's feet.

"It was a nice bunch. People are happy the war is over, and Bert even decorated the Hall with red, white, and blue. And you'll be surprised to hear that Peter was there, and he had a fine young lady with him. He introduced me to her; her name is Jessie Birdsbill. She's a Hidatsa or another name was Gros

Ventre. I think that's how Peter said it. I visited with them. They seemed to have stars in their eyes, but she is still quite young. We'll see. I think she may be a horse woman and he raises horses, you know. Anyway, it was a nice gathering and people asked about you."

"What did you tell them?"

"I said you are a busy mother with three beautiful little girls just scrambling to get on your lap! And they all said to greet you."

"I sure hope Peter brings this girl by sometime. We have a nice neighborhood, don't we, Martin. I'm sorry to have missed the celebration. Taking the little ones out in the winter isn't easy, and I did need some rest. I'm glad you are back. Let's hope you didn't bring that influenza with you!"

Martin reached down and swooped Clara up into his arms, marched her around, and sang "Over there, over there, send the word over there." Clara threw her arms around her dad's neck, giggled, and kissed his cheek. "I love you, Papa."

Asta smiled at both, kissed little Astrid's forehead, and nodded toward Ruth suggesting he march her around, too. Martin marched her around and sang, just as he had done with Clara. "I love all of you!" he said. "And we are going to do plenty of dancing and singing around here! Afterall, you girls are going to need to know how to dance!"

Martin and his neighbors talked among themselves and decided it would be a good idea to cultivate more land so they could seed more wheat. They feared the price might drop after the war, and more land in production would lessen their loss. Martin had plowed and seeded ninety acres to wheat, oats, and millet in 1918. He sold 750 bushels of wheat for $2.07 a bushel or $1,558. Martin felt rich. He knew he could plow more land come spring if he got everything lined up in the winter. He planned to keep his eyes open for a plow - probably a used plow advertised in the local paper. He could break up about twenty-five acres if the weather agreed, but he would need to put up plenty of hay for his horses.

Word spread about the Spanish influenza as fast as the virus spread. Martin needed to keep his family safe until the pandemic was under control. He took on a greater share of the workload as a form of protection but also because Asta was busy with three little girls. They settled in for the winter, and Martin worked on his plan. By late April 1919, Martin had purchased a plow, worked twenty-five new acres, and was ready to plant 115 acres. Surely this would produce a good crop and a good income for the year.

Martin's Certificate of Naturalization arrived on June 21, 1919. Now Martin was a naturalized United States citizen. Derivative citizenship was granted to wives of naturalized men. Asta, too, was now a citizen as were all three little girls. The Martin Aadnes family was Norwegian American.

Martin walked to Bert Legg's Land Office in Van Hook, naturalization papers in hand, and applied for a patent on his homestead land. His good neighbors --- John Kasa, Carl Elgin, and Simon Frang--- served as witnesses to his proving up the land. The final certificate on Martin's homestead was posted on November 2, 1919, and approved April 14, 1920. Martin now owned 146.78 acres of land. A celebration was in order.

Martin ran into Peter in town and gave him the news. "We not only are citizens," he told Peter, "but we also now own this land. Come for a celebration on Saturday. We will organize a neighborhood party. We are Norwegian Americans!"

"Martin," Peter said, "I married Jessie, the girl you met at the celebration in town at the end of the war. I married her, Martin. She's a good partner for me."

"Ah, congratulations, Peter. Bring her to the party on Saturday; we can celebrate your wedding at the same time."

Peter and Jessie rode horse to Martin and Asta's place stopping at Campbell's Variety Store in Van Hook to buy a couple of toys for the girls. The Frangs, Elgins. Reuben Olsons, and John Kasa would join at the Aadnes homestead, raise a glass, and toast Martin's news and Peter and Jessie's marriage. It promised to be a great celebration.

Martin had loved the festivities at the Odnes Hotel, and now in Van Hook he felt the same excitement when his neighbors gathered at his place. While she tended small children, Asta also baked and cleaned for the event. Martin called the neighbors and suggested the ladies bring something for potluck. Potlucks always worked out since everyone's luck for dinner depended on what was in the pot! No one ever complained! Oh the homestead wasn't as fancy as the hotel, but it was a neighborhood party regardless, and everyone enjoyed the camaraderie,

Everyone was excited to celebrate with Peter and Jessie. Peter explained that Jessie was born in Arkansas and moved with her family to Like-a-Fishhook Village when she was two years old. "We met a couple of years ago when I was selling horses. I became good friends with her father, Buffalo Tongue Birdsbill and her mother, Plain House Blackhawk Birdsbill. Jessie and I fell in love almost immediately."

Asta, Clara, Ruth,
and Astrid

Jessie was timid, but she stayed in with the ladies as Peter went out with the men. The ladies kept watch on the children – Asta now had three girls ages 5, 4, and 2; Della had a four-year-old son and was pregnant again; and Olga Olson had a two-year-old girl. Five little ones between 2 and 5! While the kids played, the women wondered about Christmas.

"Do you think Bye's Grocery will have any lutefisk this year?" Della asked. "Carl said he tried to get some last year, but with the war and all, he just couldn't get any. Don't know why I'm worried," she laughed, "I don't know how to make it! But Carl talks about how he misses it!"

"Easy to make but time consuming," Asta said. "It comes dried in bundles. You saw it into chunks that will fit in your kettle. Then you soften the chunks in a crock with soaked up ashes. The fish chunks must be rinsed several times in cold water. Then we boil it and serve it with lots of butter and lefse."

"Simon likes his with loganberries," Hage said. "And he really likes my glorified rice topped with cinnamon! We should invite John for dinner since he's a bachelor. He'd probably like some good home cooking!"

"What about you, Jessie?" Della asked. "Will you make Norwegian dishes for Peter?"

Jessie looked down and thought for a moment. "I'll do the cooking. My mother taught me how to cook venison and wild turkey. We also cook with lots of vegetables and wild berries. Peter has never complained when I've cooked."

"This talk is making me hungry," Della laughed. "What do you say we call in the men?"

"Come to eat," Asta shouted out the front door.

Gathered around Martin's new plow, the men had been discussing what they had planted and how the new machinery seemed to be working for everyone. The threshing ring they formed last summer was working well. They'd pooled their resources to buy threshing equipment and share the work and the machinery. The only consideration was who would get their threshing done first.

John, a bachelor, had purchased a tractor, and he'd joined the threshing ring as well. "I've been farming longer than you whippersnappers, but I kept my horses," he said stroking an imaginary beard. " I don't need to worry about starting an engine in the winter when I still have horses just in case! All they need is hay."

"I'm no whippersnapper, only nine years younger than you! But say, what did you pay for that tractor?" Martin asked. "The harness shop had a Fordson tractor on display last week. Cost about $750. I'd sure like to have one, but I can't count on the tractor producing more tractors whereas my horse can reproduce!" The men chuckled, and John confirmed that $750 was close to what he paid.

Simon, quiet most of the time, pulled the 1919 edition of Farmers Almanac out of his back pocket and opened to the ear-marked page reporting predicted weather patterns.

"Looks like this could be a good year," Simon said. "We may all be buying tractors come spring. Listen to this. Warm breezes in the summer months, scattered showers regularly. Even predicts that harvest months should be good."

"That's normal weather around here," Peter interjected. "But what does it say about wind, tornadoes, and prairie fires?"

"Ja, we get those," Martin said, "but I think we may be in for a good year. Let's hope so." And the men headed to the house.

Gathered around the table, they all held hands. Hage put an American flag on the table recognizing the Norwegian Americans and Simon offered the prayer.

> *I Jesu navn gar vi til bords*
> *a spise, drikke pa ditt ord.*
> *Deg, Gud til aere, oss til gavn,*
> *Sa far vi mat i Jesu navn.*
> *Amen.*

Simon agonized as the food was passed and then quietly interrupted the conversation. "I'd like to share some information with you all." Everyone paused and looked at Simon. "We are so happy to have Jessie joining our group. Thank you, Peter, for bringing her to us. But now I think we should all recognize that land we are homesteading was taken from the Fort Berthold Indians. This was land that belonged to Jessie's people. I knew this was Indian land when I applied for my homestead, but I don't know if the rest of you knew this." Mouths dropped and eyes widened. Some looked at Jessie and then quickly looked away. Jessie sat quiet.

"What?" Martin looked confused. "Explain this, Peter, in Norwegian."

"Ja, Martin, I will," Peter looked at Martin and then continued in English. "I knew this after I got here," Peter shared in English. "Jessie and I have talked about the United States government taking land from her people so that immigrants and American citizens could homestead. We know it isn't right, but you must realize that you and I didn't take this land. The government took it. That doesn't excuse it. And I think it is nice to have Jessie know that we know this." He put his arm around Jessie's shoulders, turned to Martin and Asta and, in Norwegian, explained what they were discussing. Martin and Asta listened intently and when Peter had finished, they both got up from the table and went to Jessie. They too put their hands on her shoulders. Jessie stood and the three of them hugged.

"*Jeg er så lei for det*," Martin said, and then in broken English said, "I'm so sorry, Jessie. I had no idea. It was not my intent to homestead land that was taken from anyone." The others at the table stood and gathered around Jessie. A new sense of camaraderie filled the air; the rest of the dinner was lively with conversation.

"The government had moved the Indians onto reservations about twenty-five years ago so the govt could have the land for homesteads," Simon tried to explain how this had happened." Then a few years ago the government seized a large section of land from Fort Berthold and open the land for white settlement. Probably not right."

"How do you know it is our land?" Martin asked Peter.

"Do you have your homestead papers close by?" Peter asked Martin. Martin went to the bedroom and came back with his homestead entry papers. They were in English, so he handed them to Simon.

"See here, Martin," Simon pointed to some words on the paper. "It says right here. Fort Berthold Lands. Subject to Act of June 1, 1910. That tells you. We all probably have that on our papers."

"Du har faen meg rett!" Martin blurted out as he shook his head. *"Skulle ønske det ikke var slik."*

"We can't fix it, Martin," Simon offered. "But we do need to recognize and respect it."

The group was quiet for a while until Hage suggested they eat before everything got cold. Jessie said nothing but stayed close to Peter. Asta saw Jessie wipe a tear from her cheek, went to her and put her arm around her. Asta set Astrid, the two-year-old, on Jessie's lap and sat down beside her. She gently laid her hand on Jessie's back.

The sun seemed to stand still in the west that late June evening. The meadowlarks sang. The trees had blossomed. The prairie roses bloomed. The kids played tag in the yard. All was well.

#

June 1920

Asta stepped out the front door and sat down on a three-legged stool in front of their house. In the distance she saw the familiar site of her husband picking rock and preparing the soil for planting. She walked over to the garden Martin cultivated yesterday.

134

Clara, now six and ready to start school in the fall, was a little mother to almost 4-year-old Ruth and two-year-old Astrid. Clara was digging little holes in the freshly turned dirt and showing Ruth how to drop the seed potato into the hole.

"You put the eye of the potato facing down, Ruth. See this little spot with the sprout? That's the eye, and it will help make a new potato." She had learned this from her mother. Potatoes, a staple in Norway, were well- suited to the growing climate in North Dakota and provided a staple for the table.

Asta's thoughts turned to her mother in Norway and the myriad of ways she could prepare potatoes. Lefse. Potato klub. Mashed potatoes. Potato pancakes. Scalloped potatoes. Every meal seemed to circle around the potato. She smiled thinking of her mother, and a wave of sadness overcame her as she thought of how quickly she had left home. She would probably never return. She realized she might never see her mother again. She hadn't heard from her family for over a year and hadn't written home either. So busy with kids, gardens, cooking, sewing, cleaning, laundry. She smiled and touched her tummy knowing she had just felt her fourth child moving in her womb. Would it be a boy this time? How would she take care of four children?

The fourth child would require a bigger house for them. The 12 x 24 wouldn't fit six people! Martin planned to build a two-story house when he got the crop in. As for today, let Ruth help Clara plant the potatoes. Asta decided to write home!

She fetched a pen and paper.

May 9th, 1920

Dear Mama and Papa,

I haven't been such a good letter writer, but I'm going to give this a try. Now that the war is over, perhaps the mail will go through. I am very busy with three little girls, and part of our news here is that I am expecting again in late summer. Maybe a boy – who knows. Naturally we take what arrives, but a boy would be nice for Martin. Clara, now six, is so helpful. Right now she has four-year-old Ruth helping her plant seed potatoes in the garden. Astrid just plays in the dirt! Guess I'll have some clothes washing to do tonight. They love to go barefoot even when the ground is wet!

It was so nice to have Thora here with us. She's a lovely young lady and so helpful. I miss her now that she has gone on to Minneapolis. But we do have another lady in the family. Peter got married --- I know he doesn't write home, so I'm telling the news. He married Jessie Birdsbill, a charming and pretty Indian woman. Peter has been doing some great improvements on his farmstead – remodeled his shack into a neat little living house. I think you'd like Jessie; we sure do.

I'm getting better at English. Our church now does services in English and Sunday School is in English. Clara's school is in English, so we are learning bit by bit. My neighbor, Hage, speaks only English, so I learn from her too. Her husband, Simon, speaks Norwegian and English, so Martin is able to switch back and forth. We are many Norwegians here and we help each other.

Asta heard the girls fighting in the garden, put her pen down, and went outside to see what was going on. "Clara! Ruth doesn't like to be bossed around!"

The crop was peeking through the soil. Martin picked the little girls up, called Clara and Asta to follow him to the nearest field. "Look out there," he pointed west. "It's all ours and it's all planted. See those little green shoots, Clara and Ruth? They are going to make wheat that we will sell when Clara starts school this fall. Then we'll all go to town and have ice cream!"

He put the girls down and reached for Asta. "And we are going to take this new little one with us! Time to show off our winter seeding!" Asta blushed and Martin kissed her cheek. "I'm so happy we are doing fine. And maybe, just maybe, we'll have a boy. But I love my girls!"

In late August, Asta called to Martin in the barn. "Better fetch Mrs. DeTienne. We are about to have four children." August 20, 1920, at 5 a.m., Asta delivered their fourth daughter. "We are running out of girl names," she joked with Martin. "Let's just name her after me --- Asta Margareth! Let's name her

Margaret. No middle name. We better save some girl names in case we need them!"

Asta cuddled and nursed her baby to the eternal lullaby the prairie provided. Gentle, swaying, soft whispers of the grasses in the wind. Soon to change to cold and snow. How she hoped the crop would be good and the harvest plentiful.

Ten years later

Chapter Nine:

Van Hook, 1930

Asta sat on her favorite living room chair sipping hot coffee and nursing Signe, now six months old. Eleanor, the two-year-old, played dolls at her mother's feet. Rolf, her only son now four years old, watched out the window as his dad drove the school bus out of the yard taking Rolf's sisters and the neighbor kids to school.

In the ten years since the war, so much had happened. Many families mourned the loss of their loved ones who "gave their all," while others were thrilled to welcome home their sons and daughters. Young people returned eager to work in a robust economy. Post war prosperity led to carefree living, fashion changes, and the passing of the 19th Amendment giving women the right to vote. Congress passed prohibition which led to black market alcohol, organized crime, and social upheaval that goes with underground activity. The Stock Market flourished, wealth for some doubled, and the United States became a superpower. People either had money or bought on credit new, advanced cars and machinery. Society dubbed this the Roaring Twenties.

But the only roar that Asta experienced was the decline in farm prices and the ever-increasing cost of goods. Inflation hit the farmer hard. Sadly, some farmers overbought on credit when grain prices were good at the end of the war. But farm economy spiraled downward as the decade closed with the collapse of the stock market in October 1929.

And here sat Asta recalling all she had read in newspapers and heard on the Philco radio sitting in a prominent spot in the living room. Here sat Asta with her three little ones. The six older girls had made their beds, finished the breakfast dishes and headed off to school with their dad as the bus driver. How blessed she had been that all her pregnancies had been good, and her babies were healthy. Poor Peter and Jessie had lost little Marian Mathilda when she was just two weeks old. Asta found it difficult to comfort Jessie when she herself had been so blessed. Married seventeen years with nine healthy children! A few times every year Asta opened mail from Norway requesting she and Martin and the kids make a trip home just for a while. Afterall, the letters said, "We hear the life is good in the United States right now, and we'd love to have you visit." Both Martin and Asta hoped that things would turn around and perhaps they could make a trip back, but it wasn't going to be this year. Martin had taken on additional work as school bus driver and road grader operator to supplement their income. He had bought an old Ford car, but their family was too large for everyone to go somewhere together, so it was often just a few that would go to an event. Asta needed to write home and give the accurate picture of their life on the prairie.

Making ends meet became more difficult as the decade progressed. What could she say in her letter? Life hadn't been all bad. She had birthed five children during this decade. Two girls, Inez and Borghild, were both born at home with the help of the local midwife. Rolf, their only son, was born in a hospital as were Eleanor and Signe. The hospital stay had certainly given Asta a respite. Thank goodness Clara and Ruth were both helpful with the housework and children while their mother was hospitalized.

It had been wonderful to have Asta's younger sister, Martha, emigrate to America in 1927 and visit them in Van Hook. Now Asta had two sisters, Thora and Martha, and one brother, Peter, within a five-hundred-mile radius, and that made it feel like home. Simon Frang became a father-figure for Martin, and then in 1926, Simon died and Hage moved away. Martin missed him but never said much about it. Asta could tell and often suggested he visit Peter for a day or two. They both would benefit from a visit, and she would be fine with the children.

In early 1930, Bennie Tollefson approached Martin regarding his desire to sell his farm. The additional land would give Martin more land and the family a larger house. Martin pondered the idea, counted his money, and told Asta he thought they should buy the place. That for certain meant no trip to Norway. Clara would be graduating high school in a couple of years and Ruth, Astrid, and Margaret were not far behind. The girls needed more space, more privacy, a larger bedroom, more beds, and always clothes, clothes, clothes. Asta agreed that they should purchase the Bennie Tollefson place and move.

#

Asta laid Signe in her crib and returned to her coffee. She must have been lost in thought as her coffee was stone cold. She giggled about that, poured it into a small kettle to warm it. Eleanor and Rolf were busy playing so she sat down to rest before starting her morning chores. It was Tuesday and she generally ironed the girls school blouses on Tuesdays, but she needed to make bread so they would be able to pack their lunches the rest of the week. Laundry and cooking took up most of her time. Ruth had talked often about quitting school and getting a job so she could help with finances and with work around the house. What would Asta have done without her these past years? She was so good in the kitchen and so helpful with her sisters. Of course, Clara was her dad's helper in the fields and around the farm. They were fifteen and sixteen and it was time for them to be thinking about their own lives. Astrid and Margaret were just eleven and thirteen but were so involved in school activities that they were hardly home. And Margaret with her eczema was not able to help much around the house. Better to let those two excel in school.

#

The year flew by; they prepared for their move to the Tollefson place. It took some time to box things up, move them, and then unpack. The girls had gotten a lovely package last spring from Ingeborg, Martin's half-sister, and Asta had not thanked her yet. She decided to write to Ingeborg.

Van Hook, October 7, 1931

Dear Ingeborg,

Ruth and I have been writing you for a long time ---in fact, Ruth has already done so and is just waiting for me to do my share and now she gave me strict orders to sit down and write. Should have written a long time ago but hope you forgive us and don't think we are so ungrateful as it looks like. Thank you so much for the mittens you sent this spring. They are so beautiful and pretty soon they will be good to use. They have been so admired by everyone who has seen them, and I really would like to send them to this summer's exhibition, but you're supposed to send only things that you have made yourself, of course. I couldn't send them with a clear mind! Ruth saw a picture of Crown Princess Martha in a newspaper, and she was wearing a pair just like them. So Ruth is very proud of hers!

We hope to get a lot of snow this winter – have had so little snow and rain these last years so we really need a lot of it before we can put more seeds in. It has been a quiet fall – no harvesting or hay and we sure hope not to have another year like this. In the letters from home they say they have a lot of rain and the summer was cold.

We bought a different farm not too far from here. It will give the girls more room. Some farmers have been moving up to Alberta in Canada. The climate is almost like in Norway with pine trees and birch trees and have wild berries as at home. Even more would like to move but being raised in this country they are afraid to be ruled by the English king.

We got a bunch of Norwegian papers the other day sent to me from a place in Colorado, but no address so we wondered if you had sent them with someone. It was sure nice to get Norwegian papers again, of course and we get the main news in the papers here but getting them from Norway is like a breath from home.

I see the communists are really up in numbers and there are a lot of them here. Most of them from Finland and Russia. They demonstrated outside the city hall yesterday --- demanding flour, potatoes, plus free doctor and dentist, no taxes for the next four years. Of course, that's asking too much.

Martin took Clara and Ruth to town tonight. The girls were going to a party at the Sunday School and Martin to a farmers meeting, so it's so quiet here now. Clara and Ruth are invited to a dance on Friday night and want me to talk Martin *into letting them go. I think they are old enough to get out and have some fun, but I am not sure Martin will let them go. There are really nothing for the young people to do in their spare time ---- no sports like in Norway and never any private parties for the kids either. This is Clara's last school year, and she will have to find something to do – like work. Hard to get work around here now, but I hope for better times.*

Hope grandpa and grandma are doing fine and tell all hello from us and to Erik and Maja too. It's so nice to get letters from you, Ingeborg, and we hope to hear from you soon again.

Love from all of us here. Asta

"Martin," Asta said as he walked in the back door. "I've written to Ingeborg tonight. Is there anything you'd like to say before we mail it?"

"Thank you but no, Asta, there is little good news from here. We shouldn't bother them with how tough times have been here. I think it will turn around, but let's keep that quiet."

"Ja, I guess you are right," Asta replied. "But they keep wondering why we don't come home or at least send a couple of kids. I don't mention that topic in my letters, Martin. Better left unsaid. But you do remember that Tante Mathea and Birgit asked if we would send some girls, and they offered to buy their tickets and have them live with Birgit. They suggested just a couple of years. Do you think we should consider this?"

PART TWO:
Borghild (Boya)

June 1932

Chapter Ten:

The Bergensfjord Of The Norwegian
American Line

Clara 18, Borghild 8, Eleanor 4

I climbed into the back seat of our neighbor's car. Eleanor climbed in next to me, and Clara got in the front with our neighbor. Mama cried while Dad put our bags in the trunk.

"You will love playing with these," he handed Eleanor her doll. "Have fun with these dolls. Remember that I love you and we'll see you soon." I saw tears in his eyes when he handed me my doll. "Now remember, I sure love you girls." He walked to Mama and put his arm around her.

Why are we doing this? Going to Aunt Thora's and then to New York. I thought I heard Norway, but where are these places? I looked at my family standing in the farmyard. My sisters were hugging Mama and crying. Mama was holding her belly. I knew I was going to have a brother or sister in the next few weeks. I wanted to stay to see the new baby.

Putt... putt... putt... the engine was running. Our neighbor waved to our family and put the car in gear. We were moving. I looked out the back window of the car and watched our house and my family disappear. Eleanor and I hugged our dolls.

"Clara, where are we going? Why isn't the rest of the family going too? What are we going to do?"

"Oh Borghild," Clara said. The three of us have an exciting trip in front of us. Mama and Dad explained this to us last week. Remember the map of Norway where they showed us where we will be.... do you remember that? We are going to Norway for a couple of years to meet our grandparents and aunts and uncles."

A couple of years? What about school? Aren't I going to go to school?

"We are going to Aunt Thora's in Shakopee. Aunt Martha is there with her," Clara continued. "You've met Aunt Martha, but I don't know if you remember her. Thora and Martha are Mama and Uncle Pete's sisters."

I was listening, but I was also watching Eleanor. She was talking to her dolls. "Here we go now for a ride. Hang on." "I'm hanging on." "You can watch out the window." Sometimes one doll cried, and Eleanor held that doll to her chest like she was its mother. "Now, now, little one. Don't cry," she said. And she rocked back and forth.

"'I've been at Aunt Thora's," Clara continued. "She's nice. She has four kids including two girls. We are going to stay there for a couple of days before we get on the train to New York. The train ride to New York will be fun. Then we get on a ship and cross the ocean."

Hm, I thought about what Clara said. Playing with two girls should be fun especially if they have a doll house. I've never ridden on a train before. I've watched it go through Van Hook, and I've seen people get on and off the train, but I've never been inside one. That should be fun. I don't know anything about New York nor the ocean. I'm not sure I want to go that far. I guess I'll have to let Clara be in charge. She's always been like a mom anyway.

All day we rode in the back seat with not much to do. The land was so flat and the ground was black showing just the green sprouts of crops. Dad always liked this time of the spring. He'd say "there's hope out there. We put the seed in the ground and now it's starting to sprout and do its work." I thought about that and wondered if Dad had seen some sprouts in our fields yet this year. Then the flat land turned to rolling hills; we drove through lots of little towns. Kids played ball on the side streets since school was out. Sometimes I played dolls with Eleanor, but she wiggled around a lot. Sometimes she cried. Sometimes she was just quiet and looked out the window. Sometimes I cried. Those times Clara turned around and visited with us and asked Eleanor questions to take her mind off crying. I was homesick and Eleanor said she wanted to go home. Clara said we couldn't go home because Aunt Thora was expecting us. Sometimes Clara tried to play Old Maid with us but leaning into the back seat was uncomfortable, so she visited with the neighbor who was driving.

When a train went by, Eleanor and I counted the cars in English and then in Norwegian. Eleanor could count in Norwegian. She learned that from Mama. I helped her count in English.

When it started to get dark, our neighbor stopped in front of a hotel in a town. I had never been in a hotel. This one had high ceilings, stuffed chairs, heavy red drapes, fancy lamps, a fireplace, and a high desk. Eleanor and I sat in the stuffed chairs while Clara talked to the tall, skinny man behind the desk. The chairs were soft like the velvet dress Mama made for Margaret. She got too big for that dress, so I got to wear that dress a couple of times last year. We touched the drapes and they felt just like the chairs. The man behind the desk put his cigar down and handed Clara a key. We took our bags up a wide staircase to the second floor. Clara and Eleanor and I had our own room, but we shared the bathroom down the hall. Three white, fuzzy towels and three washcloths were on one of the beds.

"I'm not walking down the hall alone," I told Clara. "And I don't think Eleanor should either."

"Oh, I'll go with you girls." The floor creaked and the door to the bathroom squeaked! The bathroom was too small for all three of us. Clara went in with Eleanor. I kept watch in the hall so nobody else would go in. Then it was my turn. Clara and Eleanor waited for me so we could walk back to our room together. I felt important and rich staying in a hotel, but I also was afraid when I saw Clara locked the door. I didn't know if someone would come into our room. I woke up a couple of times in the night and listened for strange noises, but we were okay.

The next morning we ate eggs and toast and juice in a little cafe, and then we got back in the car and rode most of the day.

We finally got to Aunt Thora's, and our neighbor dropped us off. Aunt Martha was there too. Both aunts greeted us at the door with lots of hugs. Aunt Thora's house was much bigger than ours and fancier. She let us look around while she put dinner on a table with a lace tablecloth and fancy dishes. We were really hungry, so Eleanor and I ate two open-faced sandwiches each and a banana. We didn't talk much because Clara visited with the aunts.

Then Aunt Thora's daughter Thelma looked at us and said, "Do you want to play dolls in my room?" We jumped up and followed her. She had lots of dolls and doll clothes and a nice tea set. Her dad had made a two-story doll house with little pieces of furniture, a living room, kitchen, three bedrooms, and a bathroom. The top story was a playroom. We played dolls and had tea parties all evening.

Aunt Thora and Aunt Martha were good to us. We ate cakes and cookies, and Aunt Thora gave Eleanor and me new dolls with clothes and said we could take them with us. I saw Aunt Thora give Clara an envelope and tell her to take good care of it.

The next day the aunts drove us to the Minneapolis train station in Thora's car to catch the train to New York to Aunt Mathea's. I didn't know who Aunt Mathea was, but Clara said she was Dad's aunt. We were dropped off at the entrance to the train station. Clara had taken a train before, so she knew what to do. We took our bags and our dolls and walked into the station. The station was noisy with lots of people and trains and shouting. We were careful not to get lost or to lose our bags or dolls. Clara found the ticket booth and took out the envelope Aunt Thora gave her.

"Where are you headed?" the man in the booth asked Clara.

"New York."

"Round trip?"

"No, just one way."

"You'll need to change trains in Chicago later this evening. I'll get you transfer tickets. Do you want a berth from Chicago to New York?"

"Yes, please."

"Ok. Kids under five ride free and from five to eleven for half price," the man in the booth said. "How old are the little ones?"

"Four and eight."

"You'll need one full ticket and one-half price ticket," he said, and Clara gave him some money from the envelope. He handed her the tickets and some change. "Head down to platform #23. Turn left at the next platform and follow the signs to #23. Your train leaves in about forty-five minutes. Be sure to be on it. Have a good trip." I saw him wink at Eleanor. "Enjoy the ride, Sweetheart. Take care of your doll."

Clara found our train and the correct car. A man in a blue suit stood by the stairs that led into the car. He helped us up the steps and into the train. When everyone was settled, the same guy shouted "All Aboard" and the doors closed. The whistle blew and the wheels turned.

Choo choo. Chuga choo

After the train was moving, the blue suit man came down the aisle and stopped at every seat. Clara handed our tickets to him. He punched a hole in them and handed them back to her. Then he helped Clara arrange our luggage in a special compartment. Eleanor and I watched closely to see that Clara wasn't leaving us. When she came back to her seat, Eleanor asked, "What did you give him?"

"I gave him our tickets for the ride. Borghild and I need a ticket, but you ride free! We bought tickets for this train and for the next train. We will get off this train and get on another train tonight. You'll notice a man will stop for our tickets on that train, too. These men are called conductors."

"Is that the envelope Aunt Thora gave you?" I asked. "Did she pay for the tickets? Who paid for the tickets?"

"Yes, Borghild. Aunt Thora gave me that envelope before we left. I think Aunt Mathea bought the tickets, but I'm not sure."

Later that afternoon a man in a white coat came down the aisle with a tray of sandwiches and fruit and cookies. We got to pick what we wanted to eat. I took a roll and an apple, and Eleanor took a peanut butter sandwich and an orange. Clara took money out of that envelope again. The man handed us our lunch and some crayons and coloring books about trains and people who work on the trains. I think we were supposed to learn more about trains from these coloring books. I read the information on each page to Eleanor as we were coloring the pictures. It was fun to have our own colors and coloring books.

When we got to Chicago, we gathered our bags and dolls to get on a different train. We waited for some time for the next train, but the depot had lots of little shops. Some shops sold magazines and newspapers, and some sold candy and snacks and I saw one with toys. We looked in some of the shops but didn't buy anything. Clara made us hold hands in the depot so we wouldn't get lost. Most of the time we just sat on a bench and held onto our dolls. Eleanor danced around and sometimes she'd talk to the lady next to us. I think that lady really liked Eleanor. I didn't know any of my grandmas, but the lady had a soft voice like a grandma, and she bought us ice cream cones.

When we were to get on our next train, Clara handed the conductor outside the train our tickets.

"You have a reserved berth in car 14. Your berth is Room C. The porter inside will assist you. Up you go girls." I was confused when I heard the word "berth," but Clara explained it to me.

"It's like a bedroom. We will ride all night so we can sleep in this room."

The porter carried our bags and took us right to our berth. It had three beds with pillows, blankets, and sheets. Clara took her own bed, and Eleanor and I took the bunk beds. We put our pajamas on, and Clara pulled the heavy curtain across the front of our little room and hooked it somehow. I climbed a small ladder to the top bunk and found little lights by our beds. I wasn't scared, but Eleanor was, so she grabbed our dolls and curled up beside me in my bed. We tried to see outside, but it was already dark.

The train made the same noise all night. When we woke up in the morning, we were almost to New York. We dressed, packed our things, and pulled the curtain up. The porter came with a breakfast of rolls and fruit juice that we ate as we watched the city go by. The city went on forever. There were lots of trains and tracks. The train whistle blew every time we came to a crossing. Then suddenly we were in a huge train station in New York. The porter came by again to help us get our things together. He stood with us while we waited for the train to stop. Clara held Eleanor's hand and I carried one of her dolls. The porter helped us into the station.

"Enjoy your stay, girls. This is a big city. Don't get lost!"

We looked around to see where we were supposed to go, and then we heard a voice shouting "Clara? Clara?"

Aunt Mathea spotted us, waved, and shouted and came over to help. She was an older woman and looked fancy because her hat had a feather in it that matched her dress, and she had white high heels and a matching purse.

Aunt Mathea took us in a taxi to a big hotel. Our room was on the eighth floor and had lots of windows that gave an amazing view of the whole city. Aunt Mathea had decorated the hotel room with flowers and balloons and a basket of snacks. We had our own bathroom and our own towels. We took baths by ourselves! Aunt Mathea wanted Eleanor or me to sleep with her, but we wanted to be with Clara. So Clara and Eleanor and I all slept in one bed. Aunt Mathea slept in the other bed.

The next morning Aunt Mathea said, "It's June 10th and your ship leaves later today. Let's gather your things and get ready to go." We rode in a taxi past skyscrapers, buses, cars, and people on bikes. Horns were honking all the time. It was so noisy. Eleanor sat on Clara's lap. Soon we saw water.

"Look over there at the all the water," Aunt Mathea said. "That's the Atlantic Ocean. You will be crossing it in a ship." So many ships were there that I didn't know how we would know which one was ours.

"Look for the Bergensfjord," Aunt Mathea told us. "It is a Norwegian-American ship, and it will have two flags flying on the ship. A United States flag and a Norwegian flag." She took out a picture of each flag so we could see what they looked like, but I remembered them from home. The Norwegian flag was always on Mama's dresser. And I knew the United States flag from school. *Do Norwegians pledge to the flag? Do they say it like we did in school? If I go to school in Norway, will I say the*

pledge to the Norwegian flag? I wondered about these things. How will I know what to do?

"There is our ship," Clara shouted. "The Bergensfjord. Do you see the two flags?" She lifted Eleanor up so she could see. "Look straight ahead, Eleanor. The flags are flying in the breeze. Hurry now. We need to say goodbye to Aunt Mathea now and go on our own way."

Aunt Mathea handed Clara some papers, and then Aunt Mathea started to cry. "You girls stay together now. You will love Norway. I was born there. It is so pretty, and our family will be so good to you. Give Birgit a big hug from me. I will see you again because I hope to travel to Norway every two years." She threw her arms around Eleanor and me, and then she hugged Clara real hard. If she came every two years, wouldn't we be gone then?

"Thanks for all you've done for us," Clara told Aunt Mathea. "Girls, you should thank her, too. We've had a nice time in a big city. And now we are ready for the next part of the adventure."

"Thank you," Eleanor and I said at the same time.

Clara took Eleanor's hand and motioned to me to follow her. We walked to a ramp that took us onto the ship. We turned around and waved to Aunt Mathea.

Everybody was waving. The people walking on the ramp were waving. The people on the dock were waving, standing on their tiptoes and shouting to each other. Eleanor handed me her doll and put her hands over her ears to drown the noise. Everyone was taller than I was, but Clara was tall like Dad and could see. She held Eleanor's hand and told me to stay close.

When we got to the deck of the ship, we stopped and put our bags down beside us. Clara lifted Eleanor so she could see. The people in front of us let us move closer to the rail so we could see better. We couldn't see Aunt Mathea right away, and then Clara spotted her.

"Look over there, Borghild," she said. "Aunt Mathea is holding up her umbrella. Can you see her? Can you see her Eleanor?" I stood on my tiptoes and looked all around until I spotted her flowered umbrella. And then Eleanor spotted her. We all waved to each other.

Pretty soon the ramp to the ship was removed and a loud horn blew. The ship began to move slowly. I noticed small boats were pulling the big ship.

"What are they doing? How can a little boat pull a big one?" I asked Clara.

"Oh, they are called tugboats. They help the big ships move so they can get out to the ocean," Clara said. "Look at how many ships are here and how close we are to them. The big ships can't move around without a tugboat to help. The tugboat sort of pulls the ship out to the ocean." Clara lifted Eleanor up again. "Can you see the tugboats, Eleanor? The horn tells the other ships that this ship is leaving the pier. It's a ship language."

I could see over the rail, but Eleanor couldn't, so Clara held her higher onto Clara's shoulders so she could see the tugboats.

"I see them, Clara. They're little boats," Eleanor said. "I'd like to ride in one."

The boats moved away, our ship was on its own, and the city slipped by. People on the shore were still waving as our ship went by. Pretty soon we couldn't see the shore or the people. It was like they disappeared.

"Look at Lady Liberty over there," the lady next to me said as she pointed. "She is the Statue of Liberty and greets everyone when they enter and says goodbye when they leave. She's saying goodbye to us. Look close because we won't be able to see her in a while."

Eleanor held tight to my hand. "I can't see," she said, "everyone is too big. Is it a real lady? Is that liberty lady waving at us?" I tried to lift Eleanor up, but I couldn't get her high enough, so Clara helped .

"No, Eleanor. She's just a statue." Clara seemed to know all about these things. I saw her reading a pamphlet in the hotel lobby, so maybe that's what she was reading.

Lady Liberty disappeared. I looked around and all I saw was water. Water everywhere and nothing else. We were on the ocean.

"This is a huge ship," I told Eleanor as we walked into a large room. "Look up at the tall ceilings and the lights. This is a big room. I wonder what happens in here. Clara, can we come back here sometime? What happens in here?"

"We can. We are going to be on this ship for ten days, so we have lots of time. Let's find where we will be staying." A gentleman in a uniform helped Clara with directions to our room and with the bags just like the porter on the train. He led us down a long hall where there were lots of rooms. Our room was #143. It had 3 beds, one by itself and then bunk beds. A small sink and a three-drawer dresser were between the beds. Clara took the single bed, and I chose the top bunk. Eleanor had the bottom bunk across from Clara.

I've thought about this ship many times over the years. Mama had talked about taking a big ship to America, and now I wondered if the ship Mama and Dad took to America was just like the one we are on. They never talked about what the trip to America was like just that they took a ship. It was strange thinking that Mama and Dad took a ship in one direction and now we are going the other direction.

"This is just like the bed on the train when we left Chicago," I said. "But this is a ship."

"Yes, you are right," Clara said. "I think they call them berths, Borghild, but that's berth with an *e*. Spelled *b e r t h*. Can you see the difference from birth to berth?"

"Yes, Clara. I see that. It's two different words that sound the same. We studied that in school. Words like flower and flour. Eight and ate."

We had dinner in a big dining hall. We sat at one table with a white tablecloth and fancy cloth napkins and silverware, and we were served a fancy dinner by a man who had a white cloth on his arm and sometimes wiped crumbs off the table. Mama would have laughed at that. We always had crumbs on the table when we ate. A piano player played soft music, and then a gentleman stepped up to a microphone.

"Welcome Friends to the Bergensfjord! I am Captain Anzjøn. First mate Velle and I will be guiding the Bergensfjord across the Atlantic Ocean. We want you to be comfortable and enjoy your trip. The staff of the Bergensfjord is here to serve you. Please ask any one of the staff for assistance. Welcome aboard and enjoy your trip over the waters and on to Norway."

We went back to our room and unpacked our bags into a little dresser between the beds. Eleanor and I took our dolls to bed with us, but Eleanor ending up climbing up the little ladder and sleeping with me again. The ship rolled like a rocking chair, and that put me to sleep. The next morning we went back to that same dining hall for breakfast. We had a lot of food --- eggs, toast, sausage, juice. I couldn't eat it all.

"I wish I could give some of this breakfast to Inez," I told Clara. "She'd really like it. I can't eat it all."

"Just eat what you can," Clara said. "We can't send any home!" We all laughed.

After breakfast we went outside to see the ocean. The blue sky was big and the air was gentle like a spring breeze back home. Big white birds flew around the ship and some landed on the deck. One bird had a wiggly fish in its beak. We watched that bird nibble on the fish until it picked it up in its beak and flew away. Some people were walking around on the deck, looking at the ocean and the birds.

"Look at that cute little girl," a lady said nodding toward Eleanor. She bent over to smile at Eleanor. "I'm going to call you the little American doll," she said to Eleanor, and she pinched Eleanor's cheek. Eleanor moved closer to Clara. That's what that lady said the whole time we were on the ship. "Little American Doll." "Little American Doll." "Little American Doll." That got really old. We tried to avoid her but when we saw her, Eleanor always got close to Clara and put her head down.

We did the same thing every day.... walk outside, go to plays in the big auditorium,... listen to music,... play with our dolls,... eat in the dining hall. Day after day. Clara had put numbers 1 – 10 on a piece of paper and put it in our room. We started with ten, and then every day we crossed off one number so we knew how many more days on the ship. Most days the sun shined, and we'd sit outside, but a one day we had a storm. The waves were high, the sky got cloudy, the wind blew, and it rained. The ship rocked back and forth. People ran back to their rooms. Clara took us by our hands and led us to our room so we would be safe. She made us try on our life jackets "just for safety." We had tried them on when we first got on the ship, so we knew what to do. Nothing happened that made us put them on again. Some people got sick and threw up, but we didn't. We just slept through the night.

The longer we were on the ship the worse the smell became. We had to pass by the galley to get to the dining room. The galley stunk of food and smelly garbage. Disgusting. Made me want to throw up. By day nine, I couldn't stand it anymore. I plugged my nose when I walked by. And I never looked into the galley. I just didn't want to know what was stinking.

Then one night over a speaker we heard: "Tomorrow morning we will be arriving in Bergen, Norway. Those passengers with tickets to Bergen will depart the ship. If you are departing, please come to the main deck by 8 am tomorrow. The rest of the passengers should not come up to the main deck but should stay on the ship. Do not get off. We will be in port for two hours."

"Are we getting off here?" Eleanor asked.

"Not here," Clara said. "We will go on to Oslo. We are here for just a couple of hours."

The Bergen port was beautiful. Such colorful buildings beside the docks. We stood on the deck and looked out at the town. I saw some fishermen with nets full of fish.

"What are they doing?" I asked Clara. "Are the fish rotten? It stinks here."

"They fish here in the North Sea and then bring the fish to this port to sell to the market. There are lots of fish in the sea, and this is how the fishermen earn a living. The fish aren't rotten; they just have a smell."

Lots of men were shouting at each other in Norwegian. They were tossing fish into some wagons and then they rolled away the wagons with the fish. It really did stink.

Some people got off the boat and some other people got on. That same horn blew long and loud, and the tugboats helped the ship again. More waving and shouting. We stood on the deck and watched the ship go back into the big ocean. We waved just like everyone else. We had to spend the night on the ship, and the next morning the announcement came: "We will be docking in Oslo in four hours. The passage ends here and everyone departs the ship. Please gather your things and meet on the main deck in three hours."

"Mama wants us to wear the dresses she made for us. She said we should meet our Norway relatives in those dresses," Clara said. Eleanor threw a little tantrum because she didn't want to wear the dress. "We want to look nice when we get off the ship," Clara said as she put her dress on. I didn't think I needed to wear a dress either, but I put it on so Eleanor would put hers on. We had to wear them. Eleanor and I looked alike. Just knowing Mama had made them made me feel homesick for her. I thought about Mama most of that morning. Eleanor hung onto me until the ship docked.

"Here we are!" Clara said. "We are in Norway, and we are going to meet our Norway family. See the Norwegian flag ahead. That's our flag now!" We gathered our things and waited for the official to tell us to walk off the boat.

The "Little American Doll" lady was beside me when we were walking. She bent down to me and grinned. "Are you going to see your grandma," she asked. "I'll bet you are excited. This is a big trip for you and the little American doll. You are lucky little girls!"

"We don't know our grandma," I snapped. And I moved closer to Clara and Eleanor so I wouldn't have to talk to that lady. She disappeared then, and I felt better. We didn't see her again as we walked out into the crowd that was desperately looking around, shouting, and waving. We were directed into a big room with people lining up in front of some booths.

"Notice the sign that says IMMIGRATION," Clara said. "That's where we are going. I'll show them our paperwork and we should be on our way." We inched up in the line until we reached the booth. The man in the booth looked at the papers Clara handed him, read them quickly, and then simply said, "Takk. Move on."

"What was that about?" I asked Clara.

"We had to show our American papers and report what we were doing in Norway," she replied. "They wanted to know how long we will be here, where we will be staying, and what we will be doing. Then they make a record of it and keep track of us. I needed more papers than you and Eleanor because I am over eighteen. You and Eleanor are just with me."

Outside the room, we walked down a ramp lined with lots of people. Some were waving Norwegian flags, some were waving hankies, some were waving their hats. I held onto Clara and Eleanor.

"Over here, Clara," I heard someone shout. We looked that direction and saw eight or ten people holding a picture and pointing. Then they motioned to us. "That sure looks like them," one of them said.

"Little blondies. Over here girls. Clara, we're here." And they all were waving.

We didn't know any of them. Not even Clara knew any of them. We didn't have a picture to go by. How would we know for sure? I stayed close to Clara and kept an eye on Eleanor. Eleanor just hid by Clara's legs most of the time and didn't say anything. I didn't talk either.

"Clara," one lady said. "Welcome to Norway." She was speaking English! "I am Birgit. You will be staying with me. These are two schoolgirls who live with me, too. Help us with the bags, girls.... Just pick them up and carry them to the cars," she told the girls. "And here's Tante Signe and Onkel Hans, and Tante Maia. She's your dad's brother Erik's wife. And this is your Bestemor Aadnes."

I still didn't know who was who. There were so many people with strange names and how would I remember who was who. Everyone wanted to hug. I just wanted to go home. Eleanor stayed by Clara's legs. People tried to coax her out. She started to cry. Clara reached down and picked her up and held her. I stayed close to Clara.

Then the woman I thought was Grandma Aadnes said something to me, but it was in Norwegian. Some people spoke English so that was better. "She likes your dresses," one of the girls told us. The schoolgirls spoke English. Eleanor and I just smiled. I wondered what was next. Where would we go? Would all these people live there? How will I remember who they are?

Clara visited with Birgit. She had to put Eleanor down, but she held her hand while we all walked a long way to two big black cars. I followed Clara not looking at anyone else but hanging onto my doll.

"Clara, you and the girls ride with me and Tante Signe," Birgit said. "The others can follow in their car." The girls put our bags in the car, and we drove away. Eleanor and I didn't say anything. We were in Oslo, a big town with big buildings and lots of cars and people. We had a long drive through the city before we drove up a long driveway lined with pink blossoming trees and many colorful flowers. We crossed a bridge and went around a circle driveway to a big brick house with fancy windows and porches.

Villa Rein was a mansion.

Eleanor (4) and Borghild (8)

Chapter Eleven:

Villa Rein, Slemdal, Oslo, Norway

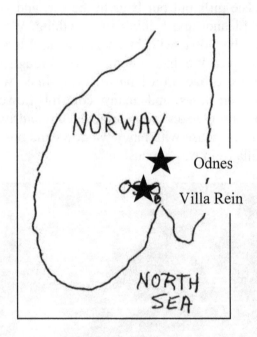

Slemdal, a neighborhood in the borough of Vestre Aker in Oslo, consists of several villas owned or at least inhabited by wealthier citizens of Oslo.

"Here we are in Slemdal," Birgit's hands gave a sweeping motion over the area, "and this is Villa

Rein." We got out of the car, and the girls disappeared with our bags. Eleanor didn't let go of Clara. "Let's walk around the gardens so you can see your new home," Birgit said. "I think you will like it here. See the little bridge over the small stream? We'll cross over that bridge and go to the gazebo."

The air smelled fresh and flowery not like the smell in the ship. I reached down to pick a couple of flowers and smell them. I smelled them again and again. I handed them to Eleanor, and she smelled them. She let go of Clara's hand and picked a couple of flowers of her own and carried them with her smelling them as she walked.

"You can come to the garden anytime you want," Birgit bent down to talk to us. "But you must never walk outside this fence." She pointed to a big white fence. She had a harsh voice. "We have a family who lives here in our basement – the Kristiansens. The parents and their two adult daughters take care of the garden and the house. You will meet them later. They spend lots of time outside here. Just don't go outside the fence."

Why can't we go outside the fence? Are there scary animals? Are there mean people? We were never told why.

"Let's go into the house so you can see your room," Birgit said. We walked back to the house and she opened the door. A wide staircase led us up to the third floor. Our room was huge with two beds and lots of pillows, pink bedspreads, pink curtains. Our bags were standing in the corner of the room by the armoire. Our dolls were sitting on our beds. Eleanor and I looked out the windows while Clara put our things in the armoire and the dresser drawers. I could see the gazebo from the window. Birgit said we were each to sleep in our own beds. *This is nothing like home. We all slept together there.*

Eleanor started to cry. "I want to be with Clara," she said. "Where will Clara be? I want my mama." I felt the same, but I didn't want to cry because they'd think I was just a little girl. I'm not a little girl, I'm eight years old and shouldn't cry in public.

"You will be fine here, Eleanor. We have lots of things we are going to do, and then before you know it, you will be getting back on the ship and going home. I think we will be fine," Birgit touched Eleanor's head to console her. "Clara will be right down the hall in the end room."

"Where are your kids?" Eleanor asked.

"I don't have any kids, Eleanor. I'm not married, and that's why I asked if you could come to Norway and stay with me for a couple of years. I am so happy to have you here. Didn't the housekeeper decorate your room nicely?" She paused and turned toward the door. "And remember, Clara will be in the room at the end of the hall."

We did what we were told. We followed Birgit around the villa looking in each room. Each room was formally decorated with brocade couches, heavy drapes, bookcases, fancy pictures on the walls, area carpets, glass vases, and lots of statues. Then we went down the wide staircase again for dinner. A long table had been set with a tablecloth, napkins, flowers, and fancy dishes. Many of the people who met us at the ship were in the dining room.

"We are having a traditional Norwegian dinner to welcome you," Birgit said. "Fish, boiled potatoes, brown cheese and some berries. Clara, you sit here. Borghild here. Eleanor between the two of you. Grandma, you sit here. The Kristiansens will serve us." We all sat down, and I watched to see what everyone did. They put the napkin in their laps, so I did, too. I nudged Eleanor to do the same. She shrugged her shoulders at me, but she put her napkin in her lap. No one spoke. The dinner was served. During dinner, the adults talked with each other in Norwegian. Sometimes they'd look at us and smile, and sometimes they asked us questions in English.

"How old are you?" "Eight.

"Do you go to school?" "Yes."

"Can you read?" "Yes."

"You look just like the picture we got of you girls." That's great, I thought. Our neighbor took the picture this spring. We should look the same.

After dinner Eleanor and I walked up the big staircase holding onto the heavy wooden rails until we got to the third floor. I held Eleanor's other hand so she would be okay. We could look down the staircase into the big hallway, but we couldn't see into the dining room. We went into our room, grabbed our dolls, and crawled onto one of the beds. Clara visited with the adults for a while but stopped in our room so we could visit and say goodnight. Eleanor and I were both crying.

"Okay girls. Let's settle down and try to understand this. Birgit wants us to be happy, and she has a lovely home she is sharing with us. I know we miss Mama and Dad, but we will have a nice time here before we go back home. This is a beautiful villa and so different from our house on the prairie. Let's try to enjoy our time here. Can we do that?"

I looked at Eleanor and through my tears I said, "But we want to go back now. I want my mama. And I miss the prairie." Eleanor cried louder.

"I know it feels strange right now. Let me hold you, Borghild, and you come closer too, Eleanor," Clara said. "We will stay in your room tonight so we can be close to each other. Ok? We can all three stay in the biggest bed here. We have each other and that's good. Eleanor, let's get our pajamas on and crawl into bed." Then we all cuddled into my bed and fell asleep.

#

That summer we rode in Birgit's swanky, black, open-roofed car to Sondre Land to meet our mother's family. When we were out of the city and driving through narrow, winding roads with lots of turns through mountains and trees and streams, we stood up in her car and looked out the top. I had never seen anything like this. Home is so flat with no trees and no mountains.

Too many aunts and uncles and grandparents met us at Sondre Land. They spoke mostly Norwegian.

Some of them spoke English and that was even hard to understand. The adults had coffee and sweets as they sat around a table in front of the couch. Birgit called it a coffee table. Eleanor and I had juice and just sat and listened. It was boring. Then we drove to Odnes.

"I don't get it," I told Clara. "How can we be going to a place that is really our last name. It's confusing?"

"Yes, it is," Clara laughed as she explained that the little town is the same as our last name because that's where Dad lived with his family. They call it Store Odnes. Store means farm, so it is the Odnes farm."

"In Norwegian it's spelled O-d-n-e-s. Dad changed it to English when they arrived in America. So now we are Aadnes. We are going to the village where Dad was raised," Clara seemed to know a lot more about everything. "Birgit's mom was an Odnes. Her name was Berte and she was Aunt Mathea's sister. Berte and Mathea are dad's aunts just like Thora and Martha are our aunts."

I was confused by all these names and aunts and uncles. I didn't know who was who. Everything was so new and different. I felt empty, alone, and unwanted even though these were supposed to be my relatives. Maybe I'll feel better in Odnes.

Our grandparents in Odnes had a big house that looked out over a fjord. They also had a big hotel, and in front of the hotel was a pond with ducks and lily pads. People staying at the hotel were sitting on benches by the pond. Eleanor and I played outside and ran in the grass down the hill past a sawmill and to the water. We had so much fun just the two of us. Clara checked on us a few times. She also visited with a young man riding his bike by the hotel. He looked to be about the same age as Clara, but he spoke only Norwegian, so they didn't visit long.

"I think you should be careful about who you talk to, Clara."

"Oh, Borghild, I think he's harmless. He said his name was Helge and that he lives here in Odnes. No need for you to worry."

When it came time to go back to Oslo with Birgit, Clara took us to one of the benches in front of the hotel. Eleanor and I sat down. Clara looked closely at us, took a deep breath, and said, "Um... I am going to stay in Odnes and go to school. I am going to improve my Norwegian and learn how to be a housewife."

"What?" I interrupted. "You are going to do what? Stay here? But what about us? What about Eleanor and me? Can't you take us home first?"

"I want to know the family here before we go back home. You two will stay with Birgit in Oslo, and you, Borghild, will go to school. I will see you often." Eleanor and I both sobbed.

"I want to go home," Eleanor pleaded. "I want my mama and dad and sisters. I'm not going with Birgit."

Clara took her luggage out of the car and sat it down by the hotel.

"Come girls, it's time to go," Birgit called. Eleanor refused to move. "Eleanor, my dear, we have lots of fun things to do at Villa Rein. We will come back and see Clara often. Let's say goodbye now and get in the car." Birgit motioned to me to get in the car so that Eleanor would get in.

I didn't see any way out of this. Clara was going to stay there, and we had to go back to Villa Rein with Birgit. It was a long, sad ride as we watched Clara disappear from view.

#

Birgit took us to the Glass Magazinette to shop for clothes and toys. It was a huge store downtown in Oslo with so much stuff. It sold pots and pans, dishes, furniture, clothes, shoes, hats and gloves. We didn't have a store that big in Van Hook. Eleanor held my hand and we both held on to Birgit so we wouldn't get lost. Many people in the store stopped to visit with her. We just stood by. They were speaking Norwegian, so I didn't know what they were saying, but they looked at us and smile several times. Birgit must have been telling them about us.

"This was my father's store," Birgit told us. "He owned it and ran it for a long time before he died. I like to shop here," Birgit held up a dress with lots of lace and a big collar. "Don't you love this dress, Borghild. It would look so nice on you, and you will need some clothes for school, so let's try some on. How about this one? And you Eleanor. You too will need some clothes, but you also need some toys."

At home it was hand-me-downs from our sisters, and we didn't have many toys. Things were different here. We left the store with so much stuff we could barely carry it. All new. When we got back to Villa Rein, the housekeeper took our new clothes to our rooms and hung them up. We played with our new toys in our bedrooms. We had dolls, wooden toys, color books, paper dolls, and puzzles. It seemed like we could have anything we wanted.

We spent the summer playing in the garden. The gazebo was our playhouse, and we lined up all our dolls and played house just like we did at home. "Let's name our dolls after our sisters," I suggested. "Here's Margaret, and here's Astrid, and which ones do think should be Inez and Signe?" Eleanor picked two dolls to be the youngest sisters. She didn't want a doll to be Ruth because she wanted to be Ruth. Then she could take care of the dolls like Ruth took care of us.

"Ok, Eleanor, you be Ruth. I'll be Mama. Let's make this area the kitchen. The garden can be outside." We built our own little pretend home. It was just like home.

We played house in the gazebo the rest of the summer. We never went out of the fence. Birgit didn't come to the garden very often, and we rarely saw the Kristiansens. Then one day Birgit came out to the gazebo.

"I have some news for you girls," she smiled and said, "You got a letter from your mom today and I'd like to read it to you." *Why didn't she let me open it and read it? I can read.* "You have a new little sister!" she told us. "Her name is Ingeborg. She was born when we were in Odnes! Your mom said she would send a picture when she gets one. What do you say we write a letter back to her?"

"Sure," I told her. "What else did she write? Did she say anything else? We'll tell you what to say and you write it."

We followed Birgit into Villa Rein and wrote a letter home.

Dear Mama, Dad and family,

Thank you for the letter. We hope our new sister is good. We wish we could see her. We pretend our dolls are our sisters and now we will need a doll for Ingeborg. We went to Odnes and another town to meet your family. Clara stayed there. We are lonesome and want to come home, but we can't come without Clara. Birgit has a nice house. Norway is pretty.

Love, Borghild and Eleanor

Now we had another sister, but no more dolls. What will we do? Eleanor had a teddy bear, so we went to our room and brought it to our playhouse. We named the teddy bear Ingeborg. Sometimes little Ingeborg cried, and Eleanor held her and fed her. At night we took our dolls to our bedrooms and put them into bed with us. Either Birgit or the housekeeper said good night to us, but most of the time it was the housekeeper. After they left and turned the lights out,

Eleanor crawled into bed with me. She always had little Ingeborg the teddy bear with her.

"Borghild, are you lonesome," Eleanor asked almost every night. "Don't you wish you could see Mama?"

"Yes, Eleanor, I'm lonesome too. But we can't go home without Clara and she is in school now. So, we stay here. Birgit has lots of nice things and I like the garden, don't you?"

"I suppose," Eleanor murmured as she turned to hold onto her teddy bear.

"That's about all we can do, Eleanor. Remember how Mama always said that we have to make the best of any situation. I guess she was right."

#

Birgit took me aside one afternoon. "Tomorrow we will register you in a private, international school, Borghild. You should wear one of your new dresses. Eleanor won't go to school yet, so she will stay here at the Villa with the housekeeper. We will be home at dinner time."

I chose the dress she bought for me at Glass Magazinette and wore it to breakfast. It was not like any dress Mama had made for me, but I liked it. It had a big collar and puffy sleeves with a gathered skirt, and it was yellow. Mama said I looked good in yellow. I wondered how many kids would be at the school. Would I have any friends? Will they speak English? So many things to worry about.

A gentleman brought the open-roofed car up the driveway after breakfast, and Birgit and I climbed inside. He drove us to a big building in Holmenkollen, another area in Vestre Aker. Birgit reached out to take my hand, but I didn't want to hold her hand, so I avoided it. I was eight and a half years old. I didn't need to hold her hand.

The teacher asked Birgit some questions in Norwegian and then I was put into a classroom that had a 3 on the door. I guess it meant third grade. I thought the dress made me look so Norwegian, but I couldn't speak much Norwegian. The teacher smiled at me and showed me to a desk where I would be sitting. Then she showed us the cafeteria, the toilets, and the playground.

#

Learning Norwegian that year was challenging. I counted eleven other kids in the class. The other students spoke many different languages, so we couldn't even talk with each other. The teacher spoke only Norwegian. The best part of school was in the winter when we cross-country skied for recess. When I got home at the end of each day, I showed Eleanor how to cross-country ski. Birgit had bought us skis and poles so we could play outside. Every day when I got home, Eleanor wanted to ski, so we skied around the garden, but we never went outside the fence.

Poor Eleanor didn't have anyone to play with when I was in school, so some days when I got home, I'd play paper dolls with her. We tried to speak

Norwegian with each other, but Eleanor was better at it than I was. We didn't get many letters from home that winter. I guess Mama was busy with the new baby. I wondered if Ruth, our older sister, had come home to help her.

#

The first Christmas in Norway was exciting. In many ways it was like Christmas at home. Mama worked so hard to make it festive. We had lots of good food, Norwegian cookies, a Christmas tree, homemade presents, and lots of company. We went to church on Christmas Day and sang lots of carols in English and in Norwegian. Christmas made me more lonesome for home. But here in Norway it was wonderful, too. Birgit took us shopping. So many shops filled with wooden toys, unpainted and painted animals of all sorts, Norwegian dolls, wreaths, and Christmas tree decorations. People from the countryside had cut down Christmas trees and sold them on the street corners in Oslo. Everyone was busy running here and there, making fancy foods, decorating every room. We had a tall Christmas tree with lots of candles and ornaments. Birgit took us shopping for new Christmas dresses to wear in the Sunday School Christmas play. Eleanor and I got the English speaking parts, and we performed the play one Sunday during church. Lots of people were there. We sang Christmas songs in Norwegian. One song Mama had taught us.

Jeg er så glad hver julekveld,
For da ble Jesus født;
Da lyste stjernen som en sol
Og engler sang så søtt....

Some of the ladies at church patted our backs and told us we were "så bra." I looked at the audience and thought I heard Clara's voice. I couldn't see her though. Suddenly I saw her sitting with Birgit. My heart jumped, and I poked Eleanor and pointed to Clara so she could see her, too. I couldn't wait for the play to be over so we could run over to her.

"Surprise, girls. I'm here for Christmas. You were so good in the play and you look precious." She stayed with us in our room; we really liked that!

The next week was filled with carols and cooking. A couple of days before Christmas we made a gingerbread house with Mrs. Kristiansen whose daughters were in the kitchen busy making risengrynsgrøt. Mama had made the same hot rice pudding many times putting sugar and cinnamon and butter on it. Mrs. Kristiansen put one almond in the pudding.

"What's that for?" I asked Mrs. Kristiansen.

"Oh Borghild. Just you wait. We have this pudding every year on Christmas Eve. You will see a fancy white pig with a red bow on the table. Not a real pig, but a candy pig made of marzipan. Whoever gets the almond in their pudding gets to keep the pig! It's a tradition."

Late in the afternoon we all went to church. The church was beautifully decorated and crowded with people. We sang songs and heard the Christmas story. All of us kids got little bags of Christmas candies. When the city bells rang at 5:00, everyone went home. At Villa Rein we gathered in the parlor and all the adults drank a glass of what they called glogg. We sang Christmas carols, and the adults toasted with the glogg.

"Here's to 1933!" and they clinked their glasses.

"Here's to another Christmas together." They clinked their glasses again.

"Here's to our new American relatives." Clink.

"Here's to their family at home in Van Hook." Clink

Finally we got to eat. We had roasted pork, turkey, ham, boiled potatoes, sweet carrots. We never had that much food at home for Christmas or ever. And there in the middle of the table was the pig! Everyone cheered when a young man I didn't know raised his hand, shouted, and showed the almond he found in his pudding. He got the pig.

After dinner we went to the living room and sat around the Christmas tree. Eleanor and I got more presents than we had ever gotten at home--toys, new dolls, candy, and knitted sweaters and beanies. The sweaters and beanies were light-colored with snowflake-like decorations on them.

Borghild and Eleanor wearing their new sweaters and sitting on their toboggan

"My good friend, Astri Berg, did the knitting," Birgit told us. She was happy to see that they fit us. We didn't know Astri, but we liked our new, warm sweaters and wore them outside.

"Astri is going to knit a sweater for you, too, Clara," Birgit told her. "She needs to measure you. She is going to come to Villa Rein in the next couple of days before you leave." Birgit tried to figure out Clara's size. She had Clara try on one of her sweaters, and it fit. "How's your Norwegian coming along?" she asked Clara.

"*Ganske bra. Jeg husker mye av det da jeg var yngre. Jeg kan faktisk fortsette en samtale. Og jeg lærer om å ta vare på et hus. Jeg tror jeg allerede visste mye om det.*" Eleanor and I looked at Clara and laughed. She sounded like she was a Norwegian. We understood some of it, like Ganske bra. Clara said she remembered some from when she was younger and spoke Norwegian at home. Then she said she was learning how to take care of a house. She laughed because she was good at that because she helped Mama at home. That made us laugh but also felt lonesome. What were our sisters doing for Christmas? What did they get?

A big present addressed to all of us was under the tree. It was a toboggan so big that we could all sit on it and slide together through the snow. The next day Birgit took us to the top of a big hill. All three of us girls sat down on the toboggan. Clara controlled it with a long wooden steering rod. We flew down a long, snowy path passing trees and little shops until we got all the way to Slemdal. Tobogganing was more fun than skiing since I didn't have to do the work. We could go fast. Eleanor laughed and sometimes shouted "Slow down!" We went down the path so many times that day that our cheeks were rosy and our mittens were wet! We couldn't wait to come back to this big hill and ride the toboggan again.

"I have another surprise for you girls," Birgit told us at dinner that night.

We each opened a package to find a beautiful silk dress. "Try them on," Birgit said. "We are going to go to the National Theater to see a performance tomorrow night. Clara is going to come with us. You will wear these dresses, and we will have a wonderful time. Aunt Astri is going to bring children, too, so you will meet new friends."

How will I talk to them? I don't know Norwegian very well, and Eleanor doesn't know it either. Do you suppose they speak English? I guess I'll have to try or just pretend I know what they are saying. We get to sit

*with Clara. I think I'll ask her if she saw that boy
again in Odnes.*

The next night we wore our new blue silk dresses
to see *The Journey to the Christmas Star*. We sat in
the front row! It was the story about a girl looking for
the Christmas star and she got lost in a forest. They
had to look for her, but there was a witch. Finally,
they found her, but I didn't understand all of it
because it was in Norwegian. I did like the way the
star looked and all the white angels that were flying
through the air. It was scary sometimes, and Eleanor
held Clara's hand and cuddled into her. The other kids
were really involved in it, and we didn't talk much.

On the way back to Villa Rein, I looked right at
Clara. "Have you seen that boy again? The one you
were talking to in Odnes?"

"Yes, Borghild. He's in my class in school, but we
don't talk. I've heard his name is Helge. He rides his
bike every day and is very quiet." I wondered why she
wasn't curious about him.

The rest of the winter we skied and tobogganed,
and sometimes we played Christmas Star and used the
gazebo as our little house. Birgit had some strange
ways, but she didn't have any children of her own, so
maybe she didn't know much about kids. One thing
that was strange was that Birgit would not let us take
our shoes off in the house. We had always taken them
off at home, but here we were not allowed to do that.
She was real strict about shoes, and sometimes, when
she was gone, we'd take our shoes off. The
housekeeper would shake her head at us and then

laugh. When the housekeeper put us to bed, she let Eleanor crawl in right beside me. "Ssh. *Ikke fortell Birgit*," she said. We knew what that meant. We promised not to tell Birgit, and we told the housekeeper we liked it best when she tucked us in.

And then on April 20, my ninth birthday, Clara came for the party. Mama and I have the same birthdays, so the kitchen staff made two cakes. One for mama. One for me. Mine had candles but Mama's didn't. Everyone sang "*Gratulerer så mye meddagen*" to me. And they included Mama's name too. I remembered the happy birthday song in Norwegian because Dad always sang it to us.

Clara brought a boy to the party. He didn't look like the boy I had seen Clara talk to when we were in Odnes.

"Girls, I want you to meet Ole," Clara said. "Ole's my boyfriend." Ole reached his hand out to me so I could shake it. I'd never done that before. Eleanor shook his hand, too. Then we all laughed.

This new boyfriend had driven Clara to Villa Rein from Odnes. He had a car with a funny seat in the back. He lifted a big lid and a seat appeared.

"It's called a rumble seat," he told us. "Climb in girls, and we'll go for a drive." We looked at Clara. Then we looked at Birgit. They nodded that we could go for the ride. Eleanor and I fit in the rumble seat just perfectly. We got in first and then Clara got in, and this boy drove us all around Villa Rein just for fun.

"Where did you find him?" I asked Clara. Eleanor stayed close to me and just stared at Ole.

188

"You mean where did I meet him?" Clara and Ole both laughed. "I met him at a dance in Hov. Sometimes students in my school go to dances at Hov. I met Ole at one of the dances. We love to dance, and we have decided to get married next year."

"Married?" I asked. "I thought you were in school."

"Yes, Borghild, I'm still in school. But often in school we go to dances."

"Aren't we going home soon? Aren't you too young to get married? Isn't this too soon? We just got here. What will Mama say? Does that mean you aren't going home?"

"Slow down, Borghild. Mama will understand why I've decided not to go home but to stay here with Ole," Clara explained. "She married Dad when she was just eighteen. I want to stay here Norway plus my Norwegian is improving. How about your Norwegian? *Kan du norsk?*"

"*Ja, men ikke veldig bra ennå,*" I said, and we both laughed. "Do we get to come to the wedding? Eleanor and me? Will Mama and Dad be there too? Will they come?"

"*Nei. Jeg er redd ikke.* Mama and Dad can't be there, but I'd like to have you there," Clara said. She turned to Birgit and said, "It will be May 22nd in Hov at Ole's mom's house. We hope you and the girls come? Do you think you can?"

"Ja. We will be there. Congratulations, Clara and Ole. We will love having you close for years to come," Birgit told them. I'd hoped Mama and Dad would be there, too.

#

"Eleanor seems so much bigger than when we left home," Clara pointed out to Birgit during dinner. "She's growing like a weed. The clothes we brought from home don't seem to fit her very well anymore." Then Clara turned to me. "Let's have a look at how your clothes are fitting, Borghild. You are at the age where you will be growing fast, too." She was right. So Clara and Birgit took us back to the Glass Magazinette to buy new clothes. We had never shopped like this at home. Mama always made our clothes, or we got some hand-me-downs from our sisters. Birgit seemed to have a lot of money for toys and shopping.

#

In May, Birgit took us to Hov for Clara's and Ole's wedding. Hov was a little village about an hour and a half from the villa. It was cozy just like Van Hook. Clara and Ole got married in Ole's mother's house. They were all dressed in Norwegian clothes. Clara called her dress a bunad and said it was a traditional folk dress from the Odnes area of the country. Clara looked so pretty and so happy. Ole wore a men's bunad, too. His trousers were loose fitting, and he had a big hat. Ole's mother had baked a Norwegian wedding cake, and we each had a piece before we ate dinner. Mama made that cake every once in a while, just for fun. She said it had to have an almond taste and eighteen layers and each layer got smaller. That way the cake looked like a pyramid. After dinner, some neighbors came over wearing bunads, and we had a dance. A band played, and Clara and Ole danced. So did the neighbors. They had drinks and laughed, and everyone seemed happy. It was nice to see Clara so happy, but I wondered what was going to happen to Eleanor and me now that Clara was with Ole. We left in Birgit's car and both Eleanor and I fell asleep on the ride back to the villa.

#

That fall, Birgit was often in bed with a bad cough and a fever. She had chest pains when she breathed. We didn't see her very much. We had two housemaids and a nurse, so we were taken care of. I hated to hear Birgit coughing at night, but I couldn't help her, so I just went about my business. I went to school every day to practice my Norwegian, and Eleanor stayed home with the housekeeper. But Birgit didn't seem to be getting better.

"I think some rest and recreation would be good for me," Birgit told me one morning. "The nurse says that I have water in my lungs and fresh air would be good for me. Staying in the mountains for a few months would help me get better. I'd like to take you with me, Borghild, to the Park Hotel in Holmenkollen. It's a fancy hotel close to sledding and to your school. Wouldn't it be nice to go to Holmenkollen?

"What about Eleanor? Can she come with us?"

"I think it's best if she goes with the housekeeper to Tonsberg for those months. You will need to go to school, but Eleanor isn't of school age yet, and I just can't care for her now. She'll get along fine in Tonsberg."

"Where is Tonsberg? What will she do there?"

"Tonsberg is a small town about an hour's drive from where we are now. It's the oldest town in Norway and is right on the water. A big fortress looks out over the water. Eleanor will have fun with the housekeeper's family. She has a couple of grandchildren for Eleanor to play with. We won't be away for too long. The nurse says a few weeks in fresh air will do me good."

"Does Eleanor know about this?" I asked. "Won't she miss me?"

"The housekeeper has invited her to go home with her for a while. She showed Eleanor pictures of her grandkids and of their place in Tonsberg. Eleanor will be fine. She will have lots of fun while you are in school."

What could I say? I wasn't in charge. The housekeeper packed my things one afternoon, and Birgit and I left in her car for the Park Hotel in Holmenkollen. She coughed all the way there. She sounded so sick. When we got there, a man took our bags to our rooms and another man took the car. Birgit told me he was called a valet and would park the car. I had never heard of a valet but was excited to go into the big hotel and look around.

My mouth dropped open and my eyes got so big! I had never seen anything like this.. "Look at the big staircase. I wonder what our rooms will be like," I said out loud to no one in particular. "How will I get to the school from here?"

"I will take you there tomorrow, Borghild. You will have your same teacher and the same class as before," she said. "I think your Norwegian is improving from being in that school. Now, let's walk around and explore this place and then get settled. I will need to rest this afternoon." We had three rooms and a bathroom. Birgit had a room. I had a room. We had a sitting room. It was fancy.

When we arrived at the school, Birgit realized that the students couldn't pronounce my name very well. They were learning Norwegian too, and my name was difficult for them to pronounce. I guess Mama and Dad gave us Norwegian names and the students were trying to learn Norwegian.

"Bogild? Borgy? Boghit? What is the way to say your name?" Birgit decided that we should make our names easier for people to pronounce.

"Why don't I be Bibben and you be Boya," she suggested. "These two names can't be too difficult to say. Maybe our names sound too much alike. This will make it easier."

I had no say in the matter, but from then on, I was Boya, and she was Bibben. I guess I didn't care, but what would my parents think. *What was Clara going to say? And how about Eleanor? Will she call me Boya or Borghild? What should I call myself? What name should I put on my school papers? This is so confusing.*

School was okay. My Norwegian got better and after school the other students and I could go skiing and sledding. Bibben got better in the mountain air, and it wasn't too long before the snow was gone, and we were driving back to Villa Rein. Eleanor was already there and waiting for me at the door! I told her about our new names.

"Boya? What kind of a name is that? Why did you change names? Why is she Bibben?" Eleanor was old enough to need to know.

"It just made it easier for the people there to say my name right," I told her. "I think I like Boya. It's easier to say and to spell. You can call me Borghild. That's ok."

School was almost over, so I didn't go back school when we got to Villa Rein. I practiced my Norwegian with the housekeeper and the Kristiansens. Soon I was learning to speak and read Norwegian. Eleanor seemed to pick it up easily. We didn't see Bibben much that spring. She was feeling better and was gone quite often. We liked playing hide and seek in the gardens especially when we went barefoot. The gardens had so many places to hide. Once we lost our shoes in the flowers and couldn't find them. Panic! We were not allowed to run barefoot, so we scrambled until we found our shoes.

One day a young man picked Bibben up in a fancy car. We watched from behind a curtain in the living room. *Who was that guy? Where were they going?*

"He's been here before," Eleanor told me. "I've seen her leave with him lots of times."

Finally Bibben told us. "I have a friend I want you to meet. His name is Erling and he's coming for dinner tonight to meet you. He's a pharmacist who I met a couple of years ago."

Erling came for dinner that night. He seemed younger than Bibben.

"How old are you?" Eleanor asked him. I told her that asking someone's age wasn't nice. Erling just laughed and told Eleanor that he was thirty-four. Bibben was forty-two. I did the math. She's eight years older. I thought maybe she met him when she picked up her medicines and that he was helping her get better. Or maybe he was just delivering her medicines. Erling smiled at Bibben and she smiled back. It seemed to me like something was going on.

He often came to Villa Rein, and he and Bibben walked in the gardens, went for rides, had coffee in the gazebo. Eleanor and I spied on them all the time. We'd hide behind the trees or the big flowers. Sometimes we'd peek out the curtains in the house. They held hands most of the time, but one afternoon we saw him kiss her. Yuk. Erling even came to my tenth birthday party. Since both of them came to my party, I thought that my birthday present was that they were going to take us home to Mama and Dad and our sisters. But that didn't happen.

A couple of days after my birthday Bibben came to the gazebo. Eleanor and I were playing wedding with our dolls. "How would you girls like to spend the summer with Clara and Ole in Hov?" Bibben asked us. "They would like to have you come and live with them over the summer. What do you say?"

"Yes. We want to go to Clara!" Our bags were quickly packed and away we went to Hov. "I get to tell them about your new name, BOYA!" Eleanor was mostly excited about my new name. As soon as we arrived, she ran to Clara. "Clara. Borghild has a new name. Her name now is Boya. Birgit is Bibben. What do you think of those names?"

Clara and Ole looked at me with inquisitive eyes. "Is this true?" Clara asked. I told them about the kids in school and how they couldn't pronounce Borghild right. "I'll still call you Borghild," Clara said. "That is your real name. Is that all right?"

"Sure," I said. "I can be both Borghild and Boya. It doesn't matter. But I guess Birgit is now Bibben and that's what she wants us to call her."

Clara and Ole had a small house, so Eleanor and I got to share a room and a bed. Clara was a good cook. She had learned how to butcher, can, sew, tat, and do handiwork. She taught us some of that, but other times we went on picnics where we picked flowers and made bouquets and crowns for our heads. We were happy with Clara and Ole. It was almost like being home.

Their house had a basement with a big griddle attached to the furnace. Clara stoked the furnace for heat to make lefse and to heat water for our baths. Their outhouse was nasty, so we waited until nighttime so we could use the bucket in our room. The bucket always smelled in the morning, but Clara emptied it right away.

Clara raised rabbits and pigs. One day she said, "Today we need to butcher a pig and prepare to can the meat." I had seen Mama butcher chickens but never a pig. "This is a messy job, but you both can watch. Ole will kill the pig with a big butcher knife that is very sharp. The pig will squeal, but it will die quickly. Don't worry about the pig."

We went outside. Ole had brought the pig and next to it was a big tub of boiling water. He stabbed the pig and pig blood was squirting all over on their hands and on their clothes. Ole and Clara lifted the dead pig into the tub of boiling water. Ole scraped off the pig's skin and then they hung the pig up on a big hook to let it cool. Later that day after the pig cooled down, they cut it open and pulled its insides out. Clara showed us the heart, the liver, and the guts. Then she handed me the bladder and said it was like a balloon. She blew into one end and then tied it together. It was just like a balloon. Eleanor backed away and hid her head in her hands. Then Clara handed me the pig's feet so I could touch them. They were funny feeling; Clara said she was going to pickle them. She said some of the pig would be boiled and made into headcheese. Yuk. Clara canned most of the meat. It took three or four days to do all of this. It was disgusting but interesting!

We had fun that summer. It was just like being home except the wind didn't blow as much and it wasn't so dry. We had Clara, and that made us not feel too homesick. Clara and Ole took us for rides so we could sit in the rumble seat. We made some visits to our relatives in Odnes. One afternoon when Eleanor and I were playing outside, Clara came running out shouting,

"Boya! Eleanor! Come quick. We have a letter from Mama." Eleanor and I raced into the house. "It's a wedding card for me, but there's a letter in it too. Sit down and I'll read it to us." We sat on the floor in front of Clara, eyes wide open.

"Ok. Are you ready? Let me just read it and tell you what it says. It says she is sorry she hasn't written for some time and sorry that she couldn't send a wedding gift. She said that times are tough at home right now... and... " Clara stopped talking.

"What does tough mean, Clara," Eleanor asked.

"It means that the crops at the farm aren't doing very well. It hasn't rained much, and crops don't grow without water. So they don't have much money, Eleanor. We are lucky to be here with Bibben." Eleanor wrinkled up her nose but didn't say anything.

"Ok. Let's go on now." Clara read ahead, stopped, and told us to sit close. "This is not good to hear." Then she told us the bad news. All the kids had the measles.

"What's measles?" Eleanor asked.

"It's a dangerous disease and you get red spots all over and sometimes those spots itch. It's easy to spread to others in the house"

Then Clara read to us:

March 1934

First Inez got sick. She had a high fever, a cough, a running nose, watery itchy eyes. Then she broke out in a rash just before Christmas. Then Ingeborg got the measles, and she was not yet two. Gradually everyone was sick. Ruth has been working in Stanley, so she wasn't home and didn't get it. Astrid and Margaret had mild cases, but Rolf and Signe were quite sick like Inez. You may not know this, but I was pregnant again, and the baby, a little girl, was born when everyone was sick. She was born January 13, and she got the measles too. She could barely breathe and coughed all the time. It was so hard on her. I had so many kids to take care of, and Dad was helpful, but we couldn't save our little girl, Christine. She died on January 27. She lived just two weeks. She was so little, and the winter was so cold that we couldn't get a doctor to the farm. We couldn't get a preacher to have a funeral either. Dad made a little wooden box, and we wrapped Christine in her baby blanket and put her in the box. Dad put the box on a shelf in the garage. We all cried. And we have been crying ever since. All the other kids got better, but measles is a bad disease. The kids didn't miss much school because we were sick over Christmas vacation. Astrid and Margaret didn't get to practice basketball with the team, but now they are playing again. They are really good at it I think because they are tall like Dad. This is not all good news, but we are healthy now. We will have a little funeral for the baby in the spring.

Eleanor covered her ears with her hands and shut her eyes. "Stop. I don't want to listen," and she started to cry. Then I started to cry. Clara put her head down, took a deep breath, and pulled us closer to her. She put her arms around us and stopped reading. Then Clara too started to cry.

"Poor Mama," Clara said, "she hasn't had it very easy. I hope Astrid and Margaret are helping her. She doesn't have me or Ruth. The bigger girls need to help....," she stopped to dry her tears. Pulling Eleanor onto her lap, she gave her a big hug. "I love you girls, you know that and I won't let go of you.... you know that.... Are you ready to read on?" She cleared her throat, took another deep breath, and continued.

I miss you girls, but I am so happy that you are there in Norway with Birgit. I know she is good to you. And now Clara has Ole, and they can be your family until we can all get together again. Our new President Roosevelt has a New Deal program to help the economy, and we certainly need some help. I have planted a garden again, but it is so dry and the wind blows so much. They say it is a dust bowl. We needed some money, so Dad deeded the land to the State of North Dakota for $1900. That's about 8,000 kroner. We will be able to live and he can still farm the land.

Please know we love you and want the best for you. I'm sure you are growing into such big girls now. Maybe you can send me a picture?

Love Mama

"Let's write a letter back to Mama," Clara suggested as she went to get paper and pencil. "I think we should tell her that you girls are with me this summer. We can tell her all the things that we are doing together--going on picnics, butchering pigs, tending a garden. That will make her feel better. Why don't you each draw a picture and we'll send them with the letter."

Eleanor drew a stick baby and put red dots all over her face. "Is this how measles look?" she asked Clara. Clara smiled and told her it sure did. I drew a cemetery with a marker that had Christine's name on it. Clara wrote the letter and then we all signed it and she mailed it. The rest of the summer Eleanor pretended to have a funeral for the baby. I'd hear her in our room wrapping a doll in a blanket and setting it on the table. Then she'd sing "Jesus loves me." I distracted her by taking her outside to play. We were both sad.

Too soon summer was over. I was going to be in the fifth grade and Eleanor was going to start school. I was anxious to see my school mates, but I didn't want to leave Clara and Ole.

"You need to get back to school," Clara reminded us. "Ole and I will take you in the car. You can both sit in the rumble seat. We will be back to see you soon. Let's gather your things and be ready to leave tomorrow."

Clara and Ole drove us back to Slemdal. Bibben and Erling were sitting in the garden when we got there. He had his arm around her back, and they looked cozy. I wasn't happy to see him there.

"Welcome home, girls," they said at the same time. "How was your summer?"

"We had a great time together," Clara told them because Eleanor and I just stared at them. "We got some bad news from Mama. The whole family had the measles. Mama had another baby in January who died of the measles and because the winter was so cold, they put her in a box in the garage and hope to have a little funeral in the spring. We don't know about the funeral. She said the Depression is bad and that Ruth lives in another town now.'"

"Oh Clara, that is so sad to hear. I'm so happy we have you girls here with us and that we don't have those worries. Lucky my dad owned the big store in Oslo so we have enough money," she smiled and looked at Erling. "Now for our news. Erling and I were married on July 5. He bought the Knardal farm in Halden and works at the Halden pharmacy, so we will all be moving to the Knardal farm in a couple of weeks. The girls will go to school there."

What? Married? Erling's going to live with us? Moving? A new school?

"Halden is about 230 kilometers from you and Ole. It's on the Swedish border just south of Oslo. It's a beautiful place. The farm has about a thirty-hectare garden with lots of oak trees and fruit. The town has a big fortress that looks out on the Oslofjorden. It's called the Fredrikstad Festning. We can still see each other as often as possible. You and Ole are always welcome to come see us." Bibben spoke quickly I think so we wouldn't have time to complain.

"Congratulations to you both," Clara said. She looked at Ole and nodded so he would say something.

"Yes," Ole said as he nodded his head in agreement. "It's nice to have a partner to share life with. I know Clara and I are happy together. And just think, you have a couple of cute little girls to call your own."

I wasn't so sure about that. Eleanor looked over at me and secretly lifted her eyebrows, rolled her eyes, and frowned. Not much we could do about this. I couldn't take Eleanor home on a ship and a train, and Clara was married and staying in Norway. So we had to do what we were told.

Clara, Ole, Borghild, Eleanor
by Ole's car

Erling took a picture of Clara, Ole, Eleanor and me by Ole's car with the rumble seat. "You girls can send this picture home with a Christmas card. Your family will see Ole's car with the rumble seat, Ole and Clara, and how big you girls have gotten." Bibben smiled at Erling and thanked him for taking the picture.

And then we moved to Halden by the Swedish border.

Chapter Twelve:

Knardal Farm, Halden, Norway

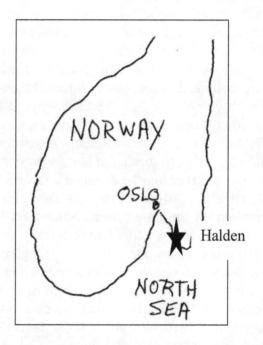

Knardal, an area just south of Halden, is situated on the Idde Fjord which establishes the Norwegian - Swedish border. The Knardal Farm is a family farm in Knardal previously owned by the Stange family. Ragna Stange sold the property in 1932 to Erling Moe Bernsten.

Eleanor and I had to start over again in a new town and at a new school. We wore our new clothes, and we felt like Norwegians. We could speak Norwegian, and I could read and write some. I was nervous about a new school, but I felt like I fit in. Eleanor was six and in the first grade, so she finally had kids her age to play with, and she was doing well in school. She liked to play dolls and school. I'd play with her just to keep her happy. I was ten and in the fifth grade, so I had other things to think about than playing dolls and school. More adult-like things that deal with growing up. My clothes were getting too small. My trousers were too short, my shoes were too small, and I was gaining weight. I wondered if I should quit eating so much, but I was always hungry.

Erling had meetings he attended a few nights each week. He always wore a blue suit-like uniform with an emblem on the brown shirt. Sometimes he wore belt and strap over a tunic. I took a close look at the emblem once when the shirt was hanging in the hallway. It was a red circle with a yellow sun cross in it. It had two yellow swords that pointed upwards in the red cross. I thought it was strange, but I was always glad to see him go to those meetings. Life seemed easier when we didn't have to talk to him.

"What kind of meetings does he go to?" I asked Bibben one night. "He always wears that uniform, but he never says anything about it."

"Oh, he goes to a Rikshird school where they talk about politics and practice things like marching and all. He's belonged to that group for a couple of years.

It's a political organization." I didn't know anything about politics - not at home and not here in Norway, so I just forgot about it.

Eleanor and I made lots of friends, and we liked to play hide and seek at the fortress by the sea. Halden didn't get much snow so we weren't able to toboggan and ski, but the ice on the Loddefjorden gave us a place to skate. We made sails that we could hold when we skated, and sometimes the wind in the sails took us to Sweden! The Norwegian sweater I had gotten for Christmas a couple of years ago was too small, but it fit Eleanor. She wore it when we skated. Everyone thought she looked so Norwegian.

#

"Boya," Bibben called to me. She was sitting at her little desk in the library. "Now that you are almost eleven, I think it would be nice for to you learn to play the piano." I didn't really want to take piano lessons, but I knew I'd never have the chance at home. I thought I should be grateful. "We have a piano teacher right down the street and we can get a piano. Would you like that?"

"Um...Ok," I said reluctantly, but with some confidence. So I took piano lessons. Bibben enrolled both Eleanor and me in dance lessons, too. I wasn't very good at either, but it was fun to try. I wondered if Bibben wanted us busy so she wouldn't have to pay too much attention to us. We were used to having lots of sisters and fun-loving parents. This just wasn't the same. I hoped we could go home soon. It's been more than two years, and Clara had said we'd be going home after two years.

One weekend Erling and Bibben took a trip to Oslo. I told the housekeepers that Eleanor and I would be fine, and that they should take the day off. They did. My friends including some boys from Sweden that we had met at the fortress came over. The boys brought a lot of candy, and we girls dressed up in Bibben's dresses. We pretended we were having a dinner party, and the boys were our guests. We set the table with the good dishes and flowers, and we sat around the table pretending we were eating. After our pretend dinner, we found Uncle Erling's cigarettes and, of course, we smoked. Some of us got sick and threw up. Eleanor cried and said she wanted us to stop. She was only seven, so she wasn't having as much fun as the rest of us.

When Bibben and Erling came home, he discovered his cigarettes were missing. "Come here girls," he shouted up the stairs. "I want to talk to you."

Eleanor and I looked at each other. We were afraid he knew what we had done. "Don't say anything, Eleanor. Let me do the talking. You just agree."

Uncle Erling's face was red, and he sternly asked, "What were you doing when we were gone?"

"Playing house," I said.

"Playing house," Eleanor repeated nodding her head in agreement.

"What else?" and he looked straight at me and waited for me to speak. "What else?" he shouted. "Where was the housekeeper?"

"Some friends came over to play. Um... ah... we tried on some of Bibben's dresses and paraded around," I nodded my head in a yes-we-did-way. "We had a pretend dinner in the dresses. We didn't hurt any of them and we hung them back up."

"Yes, we played house in Bibben's dresses," Eleanor echoed.

"Where was the housekeeper? What about my cigarettes? Did you play house with them too?" his voice got louder and he talked faster. "Who smoked my cigarettes? You? Did your friends smoke too? I saw Swedish candy wrappers in the garbage. Did you have the boys from Sweden here? And where was the housekeeper?"

Eleanor and I looked down. "But we did not do anything wrong. We just told the housekeeper to take the day off." I wasn't sure he would understand.

"If you think you are old enough to tell the housekeeper what to do and be alone here, then perhaps you should be on your own. I guess I'll just marry you off, Boya, to that young, rich bachelor you don't like, and you can be on your way."

I jumped up and down and gritted my teeth. "You can't do that to me. You have no rights on me," I screamed at him. "You stop saying that to me." I grabbed Eleanor's hand, and we stomped upstairs to our room.

"No dinner for either of you tonight," he shouted at us, "and stay in your rooms. I'll tell Bibben about this at dinner." I was happy that I wouldn't have to look at him at dinner.

The next morning everything was fine. No one said anything about our little party or the scolding we got the night before. *A grave ned striksøksen.* It's easier to ignore things just to keep the peace.

Bibben packed open-faced sandwiches, fruit, and lefse, and we all went on boat ride through the Hvaler Islands on Erling's large boat. We boated all day all the way to Stromstad in Sweden. Nothing was said about our party. Eleanor stayed close to me that entire day. No one ever mentioned anything about that day.

#

My eleventh birthday was coming up. It was Mama's birthday too, and I wished we could have a party together like we used to. Bibben said I could invite 3 – 4 friends. I mostly wanted Clara and Ole to come to the party, but they lived too far away. I decided I didn't want a party without Clara.

One evening at dinner, Bibben looked at me and said, "The man who really owns the Halden Farm, Mr. Stange, is the oldest son in the family and this farm really belongs to him. He has the right to buy it back because of allodial rights. That means it's been in his family and he has the right to it because he's the oldest. He will be moving here, so sadly we will be leaving here."

"What? We're moving? What about school?" I asked Bibben. "I thought Erling bought this farm. Eleanor and I need to finish school. Where will we be going? Maybe Eleanor and I should go home."

"Erling did buy it, but Mr. Stange has a long-time legal right to it. So, Erling is required to sell it back. Erling's parents live here in Halden, remember?" I hung my head and bit my lip to keep from crying. "We've had dinner with them a couple of times. They have invited you girls to stay with them until school is out. It's only a few weeks. Erling and I will be going to Hønefoss to find a place for us all to live because he will be working in the pharmacy there." Bibben was quite clear about the arrangements.

"We don't even know Uncle Erling's parents," I said. "Why can't you stay here with us until school is out? Can't we go back to Clara and Ole?" Eleanor started to cry. I couldn't understand all of this. We had just gotten settled and made new friends, and now we were leaving again. "Do our parents know about this?" I asked Bibben. "Does Clara know?"

"I haven't had time to write to them lately, but I will," she replied. "They will be happy for you because things aren't very good at home. The farming isn't going well, the crops are poor, and money is very tight. You have it better here with us. You can continue in piano and dance. And your Norwegian is coming along so well."

I wanted to write home and tell Mama and Dad what was happening to us. I wondered if they know. What could I say? Eleanor and I were kids and couldn't take care of ourselves, but we couldn't get home without help. Maybe Dad could come and get us? We had to do what we were told until we were older. I decided not to write home.

"I think it's best that you stay here and finish the school year," Bibben said. "Erling's parents have a small bedroom that the two of you can share. Oh, and girls, we just got a letter from Clara telling us that she has a new baby boy. He's almost two months old and she is busy with him."

"Do we get to visit them?" Bibben had changed the subject, and I was interested in Clara's baby. "Am I this baby's aunt? Is Eleanor? We are too young to be aunts, aren't we?"

"I guess you would be his aunts," Bibben assured me. "Let's just get you to the end of the school year and then we'll see if we can visit them so you can see the baby. Clara said they named him Per Anton."

What could we do? I wasn't big enough to find a place to live and to take care of Eleanor. We had no choice but to stay with Uncle Erling's parents and finish the school year. So Eleanor and I moved into Erling's parents' house. I was so angry I had a hard time paying attention in school. Uncle Erling's mother walked us to school and at the end of the day walked us home so we couldn't meet our friends at the fortress after school. She was a good cook, but we didn't feel very welcome. Finally the school year was over, and Erling and Bibben came back to Halden for us.

We moved to Hønefoss.

Summer 1935

Chapter Thirteen:
Hønefoss, Norway

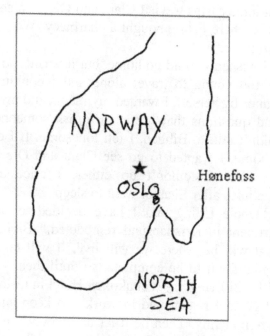

*Hønefoss is a small industrial town in Ringerike
about sixty kilometers north of Oslo.*

Living in Hønefoss didn't last long – just three
months. Just when we were meeting new friends, we

were told that Uncle Erling bought a pharmacy in Kristiansund. We would be moving again.

"Where is Kristiansund? Is it close to Clara?"

"Kristiansund is on the west coast of Norway situated in the islands. It's a coastal town," Bibben explained. "But it is not close to Hov. We will have to plan longer trips to visit Clara and Ole. I'm sorry, but this is where Erling bought a pharmacy. We will need to go there."

I wished I could go home, but it wasn't possible. I was too young to travel alone and I couldn't leave Eleanor by herself. I wanted my mama and my sisters. I had questions that I wanted to ask someone, but I couldn't talk to Bibben. I felt lonesome. If I couldn't go home, I wanted to go see Clara and Ole and the baby. But I couldn't do either. I cried at night sometimes after Eleanor went to sleep.

"Uncle Erling and I have decided to have the apartment in Kristiansund remodeled," Bibben said. "That will be where we will live. It will take a few months for it to be complete, so until then, you girls and I will live at the Vettakollen Hotel in Oslo. Erling will go to Kristiansund to work and keep an eye on the remodeling. Then he'll let us know when we can leave Vettakollen and go to Kristiansund."

The Vettakollen! Yes. I will get to see my old friends and go back to the Holmenkollen School. And Uncle Erling will be away. It sounded okay for now.

And we moved to the Vettakollen Hotel in Oslo.

August 1935

Chapter Fourteen:
Vettakollen Hotel, Oslo

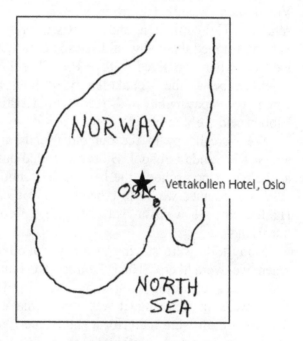

Vettakollen is both a hill and neighborhood in the borough of Vestre Aker in Oslo. The hill lies just west of Holmenkollen and provides a nice view of Oslo and the Oslo fjord. It is in the same general area as Slemdal, an area known to the girls. The Ris Church is in the area. The girls had attended this church when

they were in Slemdal. The church is not that large but quite cozy and built of stone and wooden planks with some nice glass painted windows. It is surrounded by the small cemetery and a few houses.

We were back in our old neighborhood. Vettakollen wasn't far from Slemdal, our private school in Holmenkollen, and our Ris Church Sunday School. I hoped that we would see some of the friends we had when we lived here earlier. We knew we wouldn't be at the Vettakollen very long because when the apartment was ready in Kristiansund, Bibben said we'd move.

We were happy to see our old friends at school and at Ris Sunday School. Bibben enrolled both of us at the Ris dance school, the best dance school in the area. Of course, we hadn't been good at dance in Halden, but we went anyway because we could see our friends.

Many kids were staying at the Vettakollen Hotel when we were there. Their families were attending conferences or doing long-term work in the area. Some were just relaxing. It was easy to make friends because we all were there for a short time. We wrote plays together and performed them in the hotel hallways.

Bibben took sewing lessons while we were in school, and in the evenings, she tried to sew me a coat. She was as bad at sewing as we were at dance. The coat was an ugly brown fabric, the seams were crooked, and it looked homemade. Mama had sewed clothes for us, but she was good at it. Bibben threw up her hands in frustration. *Dritt!* She ended up taking Eleanor and me to the Glass Magazinette to buy us new coats! She didn't want us to wear these nice coats to school, but when she was away, our maid let us wear them!

"Come here, girls," the maid said one day. "Sshhh. Bibben has gone to Krisitiansund for a few days. I think you should wear your new coats to school! We won't say anything to Bibben, but here, put your new coats on and run off to school." The maid understood that I was almost twelve and that kids noticed what everyone wore to school. I wanted to wear the new coat. I was happy when Bibben was gone because I got to wear it. I felt grownup and pretty.

We had a great visit from Tante Mathea when we were at the Vettakollen. She had come to Norway to visit her sister, Berte, and stopped to see her niece, Bibben, and us girls. It was like having company from home. We had fun showing her our new clothes, our schools, and where we tobogganed in the winter. She stayed for a few days then she went to Odnes to see the rest of her family.

Erling returned to Vettakollen to tell us the apartment was ready for us to move in. He didn't say much but packed everything up and loaded it into Bibben's car. He left then for a meeting, and I think he drove to Kristiansund later by himself. We didn't get to see Tante Mathea again. We had to say goodbye to our Vettakollen friends.

We got in Bibben's car to move with her to Kristiansund.

Chapter Fifteen:

Kristiansund N

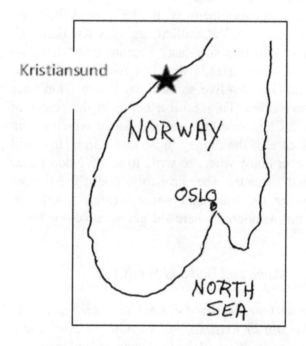

Kristiansund

By the sea on the western coast of Norway Kristiansund N, 550 kilometers northwest of Oslo, spreads across several islands just off the Norwegian Sea. Most people use a ferry system to get around the islands. Most architecture is typically Norwegian with colorful wooden homes and harborside fish

*warehouses. Kristiansund has a rich fishing heritage
and is well known for producing 'clipfish,' a cod that
has been dried and salted.*

We have been in Norway a little more than three years and we had already lived in so many places I couldn't even count them. Well... let's see. Villa Rein, Halden, Hønefoss, Vettakollen, and now Kristiansund. How long will this stay last? Eleanor and I have no chance to make friends that last more than a year. Clara and Ole now live so far away that we don't see them very often. They built a house in the center of Hov, and Clara said Ole was the bursar which meant he took care of the money in Sondre Land. How will Mama ever know where to write to us? We don't hear from her because she probably doesn't have an address for us. I thought about writing a letter to Mama but wondered where I'd get an envelope and a stamp.

Dear Mama and Dad and family,

I'm so lonesome and I want to come home. We moved again to Kristiansund so now we don't know anyone again. We will have a new school and new friends. Kristiansund is by the sea and it can be cold here...

I thought about the letter I'd write and didn't write it. It was sad. I didn't have much good news, and I didn't want to make them feel bad. Maybe after we've been here a while I could write to them.

It was a long, long drive from Oslo to Kristiansund. School had already started when we arrived. I was in the sixth grade. Eleanor was in the second grade and had to wear a uniform. We older students didn't wear uniforms. So I had to dress every day. My pants were too short; my shirts were too tight; my shoes didn't fit; I wanted to talk to Bibben about that and about having some money of my own, but I didn't know how to talk to her. One evening after supper Erling came into the living room wearing that uniform with the sun cross emblem on the sleeve. He was going to one of his meetings again, and Eleanor had gone to her room. I decided to talk to Bibben.

"Bibben. Um... um... I need new clothes for school, and I think I should have some money of my own," I blurted it out. "My clothes are too small. I have no money. How can I learn about money when I don't have any?"

Bibben smiled at me. I could see her eyes moving up and down as she looked at me. "Yes, Boya. I can see that you are growing up. I'm sorry I haven't paid attention to that. I've been too busy with the moves we've been making. I think we'll ask Marie, our new housekeeper, to take you shopping. Your pants are too short, you need some sweaters since we live by the sea which can be chilly. You probably need some new underwear and maybe even a bra. I'll talk with Marie to see what she can do."

"I really think I should get some money each week," I looked straight at her so she couldn't avoid answering me. I wanted some money, and I wanted a purse to put it in. I didn't say anything about a bra.

"Yes, Boya. I will give you some money every week. But I will give you some kroner now while I figure out how much you should get each week. But you will need to tell me how you spend it."

Marie and I went shopping that weekend. Kristiansund didn't have any big stores like Oslo, but I did get some new clothes, new shoes, new underwear and even a bra. I liked shopping with Marie because her daughter was in her late twenties, and Marie remembered how her daughter felt when she was my age. Marie told me that Bibben liked to spend time with Erling since they were newly married. I felt lucky to have Marie.

"Do you think I should have to tell Bibben how I spend my money?" I asked her. "It's not that I will have much, but I just want to have my own and not have to tell her. If she gives me the money, then it's my money. It's not her money anymore. I won't be foolish."

"Well, you can tell her some of how you spend it. That won't hurt you. She may even forget to ask most of the time. Just keep track so you can tell her if she asks."

I liked Marie. She felt like a mother to me. I liked school in Kristiansund and because I could speak Norwegian, I made lots of friends. My school had special activities for kids after school, and that made it easy to make friends. We spent time after school making homemade toboggans for winter. We couldn't toboggan by the Norwegian Sea because it doesn't freeze over. Because there weren't too many cars in Kristiansund, it wasn't too dangerous to toboggan in the streets when they were icy. That was fun!

Eleanor went to a different school, but it also had after-school activities. She didn't make a toboggan, but she played football, did music activities, and watched movies. She made lots of friends, too.

We finally got letters from Mama. They were addressed to me, and Marie always brought them to me because I could read. I didn't need Bibben to read them to us anymore. We got a letter not too long after we got to Kristiansund. Eleanor and I went to our room, and I read the letter to Eleanor.

November 1935

My dear girls,

I'm so sorry I have not written more often, but I think about you every day and send my love. We are in a bad depression here which means the ground is dry, the crops are bad, and money is tight. We are now going into winter and it can be very cold here. I'm so glad you girls are in Norway and can have nice things with Birgit. I'm anxious for you to come back home, but I think you should stay until this depression is over.

Astrid graduated high school and started teaching school right away at Stringer's Country School.

"What's the Stringer School," Eleanor asked.

"Don't you remember that country school that some of the kids went to? We used to see some of those Stringer kids in town on Saturdays when we went to town with Dad."

"I don't remember. I'm only seven, almost eight. So keep reading."

Margaret is still playing basketball and singing with the schoolgirls club. Inez goes to the same school as Margaret but she doesn't play basketball. Rolf is nine, now, and he helps Dad when he can, but mostly he helps me with gardening and butchering. Signe and Ingeborg are still pretty young and play together most of the time.

Van Hook just got a new movie theater. Last week Inez and Margaret saw the movie "It happened one night." The theater has popcorn for sale, too. They had a good time that night.

How are you girls doing? Is school going okay? Do you get to see Clara and Ole? And how about their baby boy? I guess you girls are aunts now. I know that Clara and Ole live a long way from where you are, and I suppose it is not easy to get to see each other. I'm so sorry about that. Maybe you can spend a summer with them sometime.

I will write again soon. Maybe you could send me a picture of you both. I will try to get a picture of us here and send it. Our love to you both.

Love Mama

Eleanor's lower lip began to quiver. "Let's try not to cry, Eleanor," I said. "We can't go back yet. We have no way to do that."

"What about her baby? She hasn't told us anything about a funeral for her baby?"

"I don't know about that, Eleanor." To change the subject, I said, "I've got some kroner. You want to go get a treat?" We walked to a little shop near our apartment and bought a big bar of Melkesjokolade and ate it all before we went back to the apartment.

#

Kristiansund was much smaller than Oslo, so we were able to leave the apartment and play outside or meet our friends. We weren't going to get lost. I liked that because there was a boy in my class. Bjorn. He was cute, nice, and always seemed to be near me. I liked him too, and after school we liked to walk around the Vanndamman Park near the ocean. I offered to walk Bibben's dog, and then I'd meet Bjorn. We'd walk together and talk about school and friends. We'd even walk out to the ocean no matter how rough the weather was. I liked having some of my own money so we could stop for a treat. I had more money than he had, so I'd share. I didn't tell Bibben about this.

"Is that your boyfriend," Eleanor asked me one night. "I see you with him all the time and you were even holding hands yesterday."

"I guess he is, Eleanor. I like to spend time with him because he's nice and he's smart, too. Don't tell Bibben and Erling." I didn't want to say any more about this to Eleanor. She's only eight years old and too interested in it.

Eleanor and I were both in Scouts, and we worked toward badges in cooking and sewing, but we mostly liked reading the Scout magazine about camping. I noticed that every month my Scout magazine had advertisements for Venus napkins to use for mentrasasjon. I secretly read those advertisements. When I was on a summer Scout camp out, I heard the other girls talking about this very thing.

"I knew this was going to happen," one Scout told the girls as we sat around the fire, "when I realized my clothes were too small, I needed a bra, and that I had aches in my lower back. My mother gave me a little booklet about it and bought me those Venus napkins."

Most of the other girls agreed, but some of us just listened. My clothes had gotten too small and Marie had bought me a bra. I guess my lower back has hurt too, but I just thought it was because I was swimming. I decided to talk to Marie about this, not Bibben. I was happy that I had my own money, but I wasn't so sure about going to a store and buying those napkins. I didn't want anyone to see me doing that. I'd have to ask Marie when the camping trip was over.

#

"I think, Boya, that you and I have a lot of things to talk about," Marie said. "Venus napkins is just one conversation. I'll pick up some supplies for you when I go to the market next time. Until then, don't worry about this. It's natural."

I didn't worry about it, but I was curious. When Marie bought the supplies, I tucked the box in my bottom dresser drawer. Lucky it was handy because a couple of months later, I needed those napkins. I told Marie, but I didn't mention it to Bibben. I didn't say anything to Eleanor. She was only seven years old and didn't need to know. Besides, she still liked to play with dolls and her friends. I wasn't interested in playing anymore.

Bibben liked to take us to the new opera house in Kristiansund. Mama and Dad had told us that Bibben would be taking us to the theater and to dance lessons. They said she had lots of money and liked cultural events. So we went to the theater if it wasn't raining or foggy. Bibben didn't like the rain or the fog and wouldn't go anywhere when the weather was not to her liking. The shows at the theater were sometimes okay but sometimes the story was too complicated for kids. Then Bibben and Erling attended and left us in the apartment. Marie stayed with us when they were gone. She always let us have a couple of friends come over.

A ferry boat went back and forth between the islands. It was too cold to ride in the winter, but the rest of the year Eleanor and I and sometimes Bjorn rode from island to island. I was twelve, I could ride without an adult and I could take Eleanor with me. We'd spend an entire day riding the ferry boat and wandering around the other islands. I had some kroner so we could have lunch on the ferry or on a little island.

"I think we should talk about you being careful," Bjorn whispered to me on one of the ferry boat rides.

"What? I don't know what you are talking about, Bjorn. Careful about what?"

"Ssshhh. Speak softly, Boya. This is serious. I'm talking about how strong the German military is getting and how your Uncle Erling wears the NS uniform with the sun cross symbol. Haven't you noticed that?"

"Yes, I have. He goes to some meetings and must wear that uniform. What does the NS stand for? What does this have to do with me?"

"It's a uniform that shows he is a member of the Nasjonal Samling. I read about it in a newspaper. The Rikshird is like the German military and has members between the ages of 18 and 45. Rikshird members have duty a few times each week. Their leader is Vidkun Quisling. I've heard that this Vidkun guy has been visiting with Adolf Hitler in Germany."

"Where did you hear all this?" I whispered. "What does this have to do with me?"

"Ssshh. You are an American citizen, Boya. You told me that. Germans don't like Americans. Germany has already established a few concentration camps for dissenters or foreigners, and some may be in Norway. You could be taken, Boya. This is serious. You need to be alert."

"Bjorn. I don't like this. What can I do about it?"

"Keep your eyes open. Don't give away too much information about yourself. You said you have relatives in Odnes. Your last name is Aadnes. The NS will probably keep an eye on you. Be careful, Boya. Very careful."

Now I had lots of things to think about and worry about. Venus napkins, Uncle Erling and his uniform. NS. And to top it off, Bibben always complained. She didn't like me going on the ferry rides, she didn't like me coming home late from school, she didn't like to take me shopping, she thought the weather in Kristiansund was miserable.

"It's always raining or overcast," she'd complain in the summer. In the winter it was always, "It's too cold and windy and winter is too long. I don't really like it here."

"We are moving to Nes in a couple of weeks," they told us at dinner one night.

"What? Moving again? Why?" Eleanor sat quiet while I complained. "I like it here and I like my friends here. I like the swimming club I'm in. I guess maybe I even like dance. Why do we have to move again?"

"The weather is miserable here, and we need to get further inland. It's better for my health, Boya. Erling just bought the Vøyen Gård in Nes på Romerike. We will live at the farm and he will work at the pharmacy there. The weather will be better there."

"Bibben, where is this? Where are we going?"

"Vøyen Gård is a farm in Romerike. We will be a little northeast of Oslo and a lot closer to Clara and her family. The summer weather is so nice, and it doesn't rain all the time like it does here in Kristiansund. We will be not too far from where we were at Villa Rein. You remember that don't you?"

"Yes, I remember, but that was about three years ago. I have lots of friends here now because we've lived here for three years. The only good thing is that we will be closer to Clara. How much closer? And can we see her more often?"

"Yes, Boya, we will be just a couple of hours from Clara and her family. And, yes, we will be able to see her more often. I have felt bad about being so far from her these past three years, so we will be sure to see Clara."

Why does Bibben have to be the happy one? What about me? What about Eleanor? I wished I was old enough to take Eleanor and go home.

"I think your work at the swimming club teaching kids how to swim and dive is important. You should be able to continue that til the end of the school term," Bibben continued. "Erling and I think you should stay in Kristiansund, Boya, and finish this school term.

Erling, Eleanor, and I will go on to Nes and get settled. I've spoken with Marie, and she has agreed that you can stay with her until school is out. She may move to Nes with us. We'll see."

YES! I get to stay in Kristiansund and live with Marie. I could see Bjorn and my other friends, but poor Eleanor. She cried when she learned of the plans. But what could I do? I couldn't take care of her. I'm fourteen and she's just ten. I'm not old enough to take care of her by myself.

I could tell that Eleanor was sad. She didn't say much and often looked down. "I'll be in Nes before you know it, Eleanor. You'll be closer to Clara and Ole and Per. Just think, maybe you'll get to see that little boy before I will. And Clara had a little girl in January, and you'll get to help her with that baby, too."

Marie helped me pack my things and then we went to her apartment to where I would be staying. We took Eleanor with us so she would know where I would be.

"Let's get you settled, Boya," Marie said. "It will be fun for Eleanor to help you get settled and to see where you will be." She showed us a small bedroom that had been her daughter's bedroom, and the pink ruffled curtains and matching bedspread were just right. "You can arrange your room however you like."

Eleanor helped me for a while before I took her back to Bibben. When we turned to leave, Eleanor's lower lip quivered again and tears ran down her cheeks. She had that pouting look on her face. She didn't say anything just held my hand, looked at me and wrinkled her nose and sighed.

And they moved 500 kilometers away to Nes på Romerike.

#

"Let's spend some time talking about your citizenship," Marie said the next day when we were walking in a park. "We need to speak quietly, Boya. This is serious. You understand?"

"Ahhh, I think Bjorn has mentioned this to me. Is it about Germany and that I am an American citizen?"

"Yes, Boya. You should behave like normal but always be on the lookout. We have young German soldiers that are moving into Norway, and you should not be friendly with them. We know that both Norway and the United States are neutral. But I've thought about this. I suggest you always speak Norwegian, not English." I leaned in closer and listen intently to Marie. "We don't really know what is happening, but Europe is afraid because Germany is so strong. Your Uncle Erling belongs to an organization called the Nasjonal Samling and it favors Germany. I've read that their leader is man named Vidkun Quisling. The Nasjonal Samling has a Rikshird in Odnes and that's where you have family. Have you heard about a Rikshird? It's a training school for the NS."

"Yes. Bjorn talked about that, too. What should I do?"

"I'll be going to Nes with you. Bibben and Erling have hired me to come to Nes and work for them. I can be watchful for you when I am there. I'll be making arrangements for us to move when school is out. You'll be seeing lots of boxes. Don't be alarmed. We'll be okay. Oh, and Boya, a letter came from your mom to Bibben, and since she's gone, the postal clerk gave me the letter. Let me get it for you."

I took the letter to my bedroom and sat down on my bed to read.

April 1938

Dear Borghild and Eleanor,

Uffda how I think about you and miss you. I'm sure you have really grown up in these past few years. We had planned on just two years for you to be in Norway and now I count six years. Borghild you are fourteen, and you and I just celebrated our birthdays! You remember that we share that day. April 20! And Eleanor, you are ten. You are bigger than Borghild was when you girls left for Norway. My it seems like yesterday but at times it seems like it was so long ago. I miss you and I wish we could bring you home, but we've read in the Norwegian newspapers our neighbors get that the Germans have put mines in the waters and it isn't safe to travel by ship. We hear on the radio and read in the newspapers that much of the world is nervous about Germany. The reports say that German soldiers are cruel, and that Germany is planning to take over the world. I want to warn you to be very careful.

I stopped reading to remember what Marie had said to me about being careful. This must be serious, I thought. I was going to talk to Marie and Bjorn about this again soon. I continued reading.

Things here aren't so good either. It's been so very hot and we've had very little rain. The crops the past two years have been almost total failures and we have a lot of grasshoppers. But our friends here think that things are going to improve and that this cannot go on forever. The government has programs to help the farmer, so we do get some money. We had a better crop this year, but the price for the grains was lower, so not so good.

Ruth, Astrid, and Margaret have all moved. Ruth is working in Minneapolis. Astrid and Margaret are both teaching school in different towns. Inez, Rolf, Signe, and Ingeborg are at home with us. Inez is about to graduate high school next month. I'm not sure what she'll do next.

I forgot to tell you about our funeral for Christine. Our preacher was able to come to our house in the spring. Gosh, that was four years ago. Dad carried the box in from the garage and I put a cloth on top of the sewing machine in the dining room. We lined some chairs up facing the sewing machine and Dad carefully set Christine's box on the sewing machine. We had a funeral. We buried her in the Van Hook Cemetery that afternoon. Dad had gotten a spot for her and had dug a hole to put the box in. Her box was put into a steel vault. We all went to the cemetery to bury Christine and then we returned home feeling sad.

Well, this is getting too long. I'm sorry it isn't better news for all, but we have hope. I'll try to write again soon. You try to write home too. I love you both. Say hello to Clara when you see her.

Love Mama

Poor Mama. Life for her hasn't been easy. I'm glad she still has some kids with her, but it's too bad about the farming situation. I wished I could help her, but now I have no idea what will happen to me and to Eleanor. Clara is with Ole, but we must make our own way here, and Eleanor is still so young. I laid my head on my pillow and cried. I thought again about writing to Mama and telling her how sad I am for her.

Dear Mama and Dad and kids,
Hi. I'm still in Kristiansund but we will be moving again soon. Eleanor, Bibben, and Erling already moved to Vøyen Gård. It is a farm in Romerike. That's not far from where we lived before. Anyway, I am staying in Kristiansund with Marie, our housekeeper, until school is out. I'm so sorry for you and the baby and the farming...

I decided not to write that letter. It was too sad; I cried and fell asleep.

#

School was soon to be over and that signaled many goodbyes for me. I spent more time with Bjorn, and we talked a lot about my being careful and what may happen to the two of us. We walked on the Vanndamman most of the time and often stopped to sit on a bench and talk. Bjorn always made sure there weren't others close to hear our conversation. He kissed me several times those days, but we knew that this was the end of our relationship. The day before Marie and I were to leave, I was saying goodbye to the swim team when I heard Bjorn's voice call my name from out in the hall.

"Bjorn! Come in here and say hello to the swimmers," I called to him.

"I can't, Boya. You must come here," and I went to the hall to see him. "I'm afraid for you, Boya. You must be very careful. The news today isn't good. Some say that the Germans want Norway because it can get them to Britain. I heard the name of a man who is supposed to be really cruel and that he may be coming to Norway. His name is Joseph Terboven. Boya, you must keep alert to this. Watch Erling and the others that wear that uniform. I can't protect you now when you leave. Be careful." And with that he kissed my forehead and turned and left. I watched him walk away and knew I would never see him again.

I turned to say goodbye to my swimming friends as tears rolled down my cheeks. We all hugged each other as we said goodbye.

The next day Marie and I left for Nes på Romerike.

July 1938

Chapter Sixteen:

Vøyen Gård - Nes På Romerike, Norway

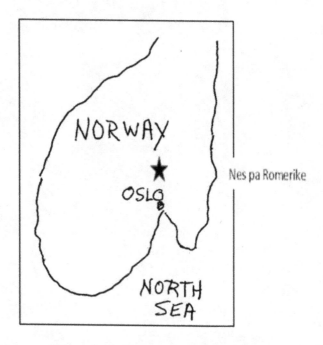

Romerike is a green, lush district located about twenty minutes northeast of Oslo. It is the birthplace of Norwegian Independence and boasts its importance both culturally and historically. Romerike consists of about a dozen communities including Nes and Vormsund. Vøyen Gård is a farm in this district.

My mouth dropped open and my eyes widened when we drove up to a farmhouse. It was a huge house with lots of farm buildings nearby. But we were not close to a town or village.

"Is this Vøyen Gård?" I asked Marie.

"Yes, Boya. This is Vøyen Gård. It is the farm where we will be living. Look up at that middle window on the second floor. I think I see Eleanor looking out."

Eleanor was gone from the window in a flash, and soon the front door flew open and she came running out. She let out a yell and jumped up on me. We both fell backwards onto the yard and laughed and hugged each other.

She had been alone with Erling and Bibben in the country for almost two months. Bibben didn't like for her to go anywhere alone. She was stuck in the house with her toys and books and Bibben and Erling. Now what, I wondered. A new place. A new school. Make new friends. Again and again and again.

"Have you been to the school, Eleanor?" I asked. "Have you seen any kids around here?"

"Yes. One day Bibben and I drove to Arnes. She said that's where we would be going to school, but we didn't see the school."

"How will we get there? Is it far from here?"

"Bibben said that Marie would take us to Arnes to buy bicycles and we would ride them to the school bus. Then we leave our bikes at the bus stop and ride the bus to school."

Marie, Eleanor, and I drove into Arnes the next day to see the school and to buy bicycles. We checked how far we would ride our bikes to the school bus, and we decided it was about five kilometers. That's not such a bad bicycle ride if it's nice outside. But what about when it's cold and winter? What will we do then? The school was locked so we peeked in the windows, but we couldn't see anything. So we went back to the farm. I unpacked my things and arranged my room which was right next to Eleanor's room. Eleanor helped me. She couldn't stop talking about how lonesome she was for me and for Clara and for home. Then we rode our bikes around the farm buildings. This was a bike of my own.

We had a fancy dinner with Bibben and Erling that night. Bibben said it was my welcome home dinner. It was waffles with jam and sour cream, goat cheese, smoked salmon, Jarlsberg cheese, and fresh berries. Bibben suggested at dinner that we visit Clara for a few days because she had called Clara, and Clara invited us.

The next week Bibben had us pack an overnight bag and we drove to Hov to see Clara. Bibben went on to Odnes to see her family. Clara could not let go of us when she saw us.

"It has been too long since I've seen you girls. Look at how you've grown up! Boya --- you are a young lady now! Look how tall you've gotten. And you, Eleanor, you have grown too. How I've missed you both! Come and see my two children. Per is already three years old and Astri is six months old, still a baby. You can hold her if you like. Come here, Per, and meet your aunts!"

"He's so cute," Eleanor said as she sat down on the floor to play with him. I held little Astri and visited with Clara. We had so much to talk about. We wrote a letter to our family in Van Hook telling them that we were together again and that Bibben and Erling had moved to Nes pa Romerike, and that they should send letters for us to Clara because we move so much.

"How was Kristiansund? How was school? I hear you were teaching swimming. How was that? Did you like it there?" She rattled on not giving me a chance to answer. We looked at each other and laughed. "We'll have plenty of time to get reacquainted," she said as Ole came driving up the road.

Ole was tall just like Dad and seemed very Norwegian to me. But then so did Clara. She, too, was tall like Dad, and now her Norwegian was excellent. We spoke some in Norwegian and some in English until Ole interrupted us. He asked us to sit down and listen to what he had to tell us.

"Girls, you are now fourteen and ten years old. You are old enough to know that there are some terrible things happening in our world. You may have heard that Germany is becoming stronger every day and wants to take charge of other countries. Some say their leader, Adolf Hitler wants to take over the world." We listened real close to what he was saying. I remembered this is what Bjorn was saying. "I don't mean to scare you girls, but young German soldiers are everywhere around here, and we aren't certain what they are looking for. The papers say that the German leader, Adolf Hitler, is interested in Norway because of its closeness to Britain. Hitler is interested in Trondheim and Narvik on the Norwegian Sea as well as the Oslofjord and Oslo itself. If he had these two areas, he would control Norway and have easy access to Britain. Remember, you girls are Americans, and my friends have been talking about the need to be cautious. Behave normally. Don't speak English. Act like a Norwegian." We visited quietly the rest of the evening while Eleanor and Per played. Eleanor was acting like his mother.

Hov was like Van Hook. Clara made food like Mama. Homemade bread. Lefse. Boiled beef. Porridge. We stayed up late each night and laughed and ate and played and sang. Ole joined right in and danced with all of us. I thought about Dad and how he'd dance with us girls. He'd pick us up and dance around and sing Norwegian songs and laugh with us. Erling never did that.

When Bibben drove into the yard, we knew it was time to go. Eleanor started to cry.

"Can't I stay and play with Per? I don't want to go back. I like it here."

"We have to go to school, Eleanor. Come on now," I prodded her. "We can come back again, but Clara needs to take care of her family." We all hugged and kissed goodbye, and Ole whispered in my ear, "Be cautious, Boya."

Eleanor and I slept in the car as Bibben drove back to Vøyen Gård. I didn't speak English anymore, and I wore my Norwegian sweater to school the first day. A girl in my class came over to talk to me.

"Aren't you new?" she asked. "You weren't in my class last year. Did you just come here? I'm Kari Bohn and I live at the Greni farm. Where do you live? I think we are in the same class. Aren't you in the Ungdomsskole?"

"Yes, I just moved here. I am in the lower secondary school. Are you?"

"Yes!" she replied. "We can be friends. Where do you live?

"Vøyen Gård."

"I'm at the Greni farm. It's just ten kilometers from Vøyen Gård. I see you have a bike, too. We can bike to each other's farms."

"I'd like that," I told her. I was so happy to have a new friend and was anxious to visit her farm. She knew all the kids in school, so I got to know lots of them and didn't miss my Kristiansund friends quite so much.

A ripple of laughter circled the room when Kari was around, and because I was her friend, my time in school was fun. I loved biking to her house and spending time with her family. They had lots of fun singing, dancing, and telling stories. Kari's little brother, Karl, wasn't in school yet, and he reminded me of my brother Rolf. He was about Karl's age when we left home. I really liked her mom. She was good to me and visited with me. I liked being at school or at Kari's better than I liked being on the farm.

Bibben wasn't involved in our school lives that fall. I didn't really think she would be. We had Marie and a housekeeper who tended to what we needed. One night I overheard Bibben and Erling talking.

"I can't do this, Erling," I heard her say. "I'm too old to have a baby. For God's sake, I'm forty-six years old. I have never wanted children. What will we do? We must figure something out."

My eyes opened wide, I covered my mouth with my hand, and I leaned closer to the door in my room to listen. "Not in Norway. It's illegal here. I checked." She was crying.

"Maybe we should think about going to Denmark or Sweden," Erling offered. "I've heard that all you need is a doctor's note stating that you qualify if the birth is fatal to the mother or there is a chance for birth defects."

I was astonished but I couldn't say anything. I couldn't tell anyone. *Does Marie know? What was going to happen now? How was I going to keep this to myself?*

"I have a doctor's appointment tomorrow," Bibben said. "I'll ask the doctor."

This was all I could think about. I couldn't pay attention in school, and at home I looked at her to see if she looked pregnant or if she was ever sick. I tried to pretend everything was normal, but I was curious and nervous about it. Just knowing and not being allowed to talk about Bibben's condition was difficult.

Two days later, Bibben and Erling left. They didn't tell us they were leaving. They didn't tell us where they were going. They were gone for four days and nights. When they got home, Bibben went to bed for several days. She never had a baby.

#

Kari's mother asked me about my confirmation celebration one day when I was at their house.

"When are you going to have your confirmation celebration, Boya?"

"I don't know. Bibben hasn't said too much about it, but I'd heard that confirmation celebrations are fun and important."

"We are getting ready for Kari's because she turns fifteen soon and that's when you usually have your confirmation. Are you fifteen yet? Most people start planning about a year ahead of the ceremony. It's when you get your bunad, and we celebrate you becoming an adult."

I didn't know if Bibben was planning to have a celebration or not. We did go to church and I knew that confirmation was part of the process, but I hadn't been to any celebration like that so I didn't know much about it. I thought I'd ask Bibben what she thought.

"Ah... Bibben," I found her sitting in the living room with a blanket around her legs and her head in her hands. She looked so sad. I tiptoed over to her. "Bibben, are you awake? I have a question. I'll be fifteen in the spring, and that's when people celebrate

245

confirmation. Do you think we'll have a confirmation celebration?"

"I've thought about that, Boya," she looked down and continued, "but you may have noticed that I haven't been well lately. It hasn't been easy for me to give attention to details. But, yes, you'll be fifteen next April and I think we can plan for a modest celebration next October. I'll talk with Marie so she can help plan it. We can invite Clara, her family, and all your grandparents. I can ask my friend to make your bunad because a bunad has lots of embroidery that takes time to do. I'm not so good at embroidery, but she is. We'll get started soon."

"Thank you, Bibben. Should I be doing anything to be ready?"

"No, Marie and I will take care of it."

"Oh, Bibben, another thing. I've been invited to a party at my friend Kari's house on Saturday. Do you remember her? She's in my class and sometimes we bike together. Her mom said I should come to the party. I could ride my bike there. May I go?"

"You need to ask Marie since she's the one who is really in charge. What will you do if it gets dark? Would you plan to spend the night?"

"I'll ask Kari about that. And I can talk to Marie, too." I left Bibben and knew that Marie would let me go. I skipped all the way into the kitchen to find Marie.

"Kari and her mother said it would be fine for me to spend the night," I explained to Marie. "I'm fourteen and I know how to be careful. I'll just spend the night and then come back the next day. Do you agree, Marie?"

Marie did. Because she had met Kari and Kari's mother, she allowed me to stay overnight. I packed a little bag and rode my bike to Kari's party. Kari had invited ten kids, and we played music, danced, had supper, and played Basse outside. My Basse team didn't win because we couldn't defend our square and the basse hit the ground. One of the boys, Dave, was captain of the team that won. I only met him that day. He was two years older, so he didn't go to my school, but he lived with his parents on their farm in Vormsund only six kilometers from me. We talked about what we liked to do and discovered we both liked to cross-country ski and thought that would be a great sport for us that winter. We agreed to meet again. I didn't tell him I was an American, and I spoke Norwegian all the time. We became good friends that winter and being able to cross-country with him gave me a good chance to get away from the farm and have fun. I felt safe and important and grown up with a boyfriend two years older than I was.

#

More and more German soldiers were entering Norway, and Erling was going to meetings all the time. I noticed several young men and women in Romerike wore the same uniform as Erling especially on the same two days each week he wore it. They all had the NS emblem on their sleeves, and they all walked tall and straight like they were marching. I don't know what they did at their meetings, but I didn't speak to them. When I'd see them on the road, I'd cross to the other side but tried not to be too obvious. I was paying attention to the world around me. I was always afraid, but I didn't dare mention this to Bibben or to Erling. I didn't even tell Marie or Dave.

On Friday, September 3, 1939, all of the talk was about Germany and Poland. Hitler's Nazis had invaded Poland and now war had begun. No one said much at school that day, but everyone appeared nervous. It was as if a dark cloud had come over all of us. We knew Poland wasn't that far from Norway, and now I was certain that the German soldiers and the NS were working together. I kept alert and never spoke English. I was glad that it was Friday so I wouldn't have to go by the German soldiers the next few days.

When school was out that day, I saw a British newspaper, **The Evening Standard**, lying on the bench at the bus stop. It was from September 1, 1939. I didn't want to make it look like I could read English, but I had to read it.

Germans Invade and Bomb Poland—Britain Mobilises.

Germany invaded Poland today. Complete mobilization has been ordered in Britain.

It was true. Now what? Will Norway be next? I have my Confirmation Celebration in a month. *Will Norway be at war? Will we have the celebration?*

Should I ask Marie or Bibben? I decided not to ask but to keep my eyes and my ears open.

Bibben and Marie planned my Confirmation Celebration to take place in October, but since the war was going on, gasoline was being rationed in Norway, and Bibben said that would make it difficult for the Odnes family to come to the celebration. A few of them did purchase train tickets and were able to come. Erling met some of the Odnes family at the Arnes train station just a ten kilometer drive from the farm. It was a small celebration with only twelve guests. Clara and Ole and family were not able to attend due to gas rationing and the difficulty of taking the train with two small children. I don't think Ole wanted to spend time with Erling, but no one said anything about that. I just knew that they weren't at the celebration.

I received lots of gifts, but the typical gift for Confirmation is a bunad. Bibben explained bunads to me as she presented me with mine.

"Each region in Norway has distinctive traditional and formal folk dress. Odnes is in the Oppland County in the Gudbrandsdalen Valley. Our bunads have long, dark blue wool skirts with floral embroidery, a long-sleeved white blouse with tatting on the collar and cuffs. We wear a silver brooch called a solie to close the blouse and use matching cufflinks for the cuffs. We also wear black stockings and black shoes with buckles. Your bunad is just like all the Odnes family members. We all look alike," she said smiling.

"Thank you so much. I will cherish this forever." My new bunad fit perfectly. I felt part of the family when I wore mine. I wished Eleanor had a bunad, but I knew she'd have to wait.

All guests came to the ceremony at the church. The vicar spoke about how confirmation honors a pledge to Christianity as well as formalizes entry into adulthood. I listened closely especially to the part about being an adult, and then we all went back to the farm for the traditional Confirmation Celebration meal. Marie had made several traditional Norwegian dishes. Dad's brother Erik played the accordion and sang, so we all danced. I didn't get a card from home, but they probably didn't know it was my Confirmation Celebration. I felt like I had to be an adult now like the vicar said, and I needed to take care of myself. My parents won't always know what goes on in my life.

All that fall the students in my class talked with each other about the war and Germany and Poland. The talk was about Germany mobilizing in Norway and across the continent, but as young kids we didn't have all the information. We heard a rumor that the Norwegian army was mobilizing. We'd heard something about the British putting mines in the Norwegian Sea to protect Norway, but I didn't dare ask too many questions. We all knew about kids older than we were wearing uniforms, attending meetings, marching, and looking serious. We were glad we were just fifteen, but I was soon to be sixteen and that meant I needed to decide between academic high school and housewifery school. I still had several months to decide but I thought about it often. Either choice meant I'd have to go away to school. How could I leave Eleanor? She was just eleven. I realized she had spent more time in Norway than in America. She was no longer the "little American doll" but looked and acted Norwegian. But she would have to stay with Bibben and Erling if I left. Many nights I'd wake up and think about it and couldn't go back to sleep. Knowing Marie was with us at the farm helped me worry less.

That December the newspapers and radio reported that Vidkun Quisling, the leader of the National Union Party in Norway, had gone to Berlin to meet with Adolf Hitler. Everywhere I went people were talking about German activity on the Danish – Norwegian border. Some said these were just rumors. Some called them unsubstantiated reports. Then the truth became known.

When I awoke to get ready for school in the morning, the living room radio was blaring the news: "The peaceful waters along the shores of Norway are peaceful no longer... Germany has marched into aggression..." I rushed into the living room to listen. It was true... At 5:20 AM, Friday, April 9th, 1940, Germany invaded Norway by air, sea, and land. Germany attacked our seaports and our airfields.

"All Oslo citizens should remain in Oslo" the radio stations blared. "German warships have penetrated Oslofjord. The Blitzkreig has come to Norway." All radio stations from the Associated

Press, German News Agency, NBC shortwave receivers, the BBC were reporting the same thing --- Norway is now under siege by Germany.

I could hear planes flying overhead and occasionally I'd hear a blast or an explosion. But we lived on the farm away from a village, so luckily we had no German soldiers at our house. *Was I supposed to go to school today? Should I wake Eleanor? Will we be staying home?*

Bibben and Marie listened to the radio too, but Erling was gone. I didn't know where he was, and Bibben said nothing about his absence.

"Do you think we should take cover?" Marie asked. "Maybe the air invasion will come closer to us. We should be prepared."

Bibben said nothing but turned the radio to the BBC. It reported that the British and Norwegian armies were mobilizing. "Narvik has been captured by the Germans. Norwegian Foreign Affairs Minister Halvdan Koht has responded with the defiant words *Vi gir oss ikke frivilleg, kampen er allerede I gang.*" Norway was not going to surrender.

Then we heard, "News Bulletin! Denmark's King Christian X is convinced his army could no longer fight off the German invasion. Denmark has surrendered to German forces." The war kept getting closer to us. We all went to a corner in the basement where Erling had another radio. Eleanor sat close to me and held my hand. Bibben switched stations often. It seemed she wanted to find some good news, but all the news was about the invasion.

"What's going on?" Eleanor asked. "Why are we in the basement listening to the radio. What's going on? I'm scared." Bibben and Marie said nothing. Bibben turned up the volume.

"Norway has been invaded by the Germans," I explained to her. "German warships came up the Oslofjord and have captured Oslo. This means war. Listen now... listen to the radio."

Then the radio reported that the entire Norwegian government including King Haakon VII had fled the capital for the mountains in the north. "Let's listen now, Eleanor. He said 'We will not submit voluntarily. But the struggle is already underway.' I missed part of it. Just be quiet and I'll tell you later."

"This is Vidkun Quisling reporting from Oslo. Because England violated Norwegian neutrality by laying minefields in Norwegian territorial waters..."

"What does that mean?"

"Ssshh. Eleanor. I need to listen."

"The German government offered the Norwegian government their peaceful help accompanied by a sincere reassurance..."

"Boya... what is..."

"Eleanor, please be quiet."

"I ,Vidkun Quisling, proclaim the National Union Party in control and as the leader of the National Union Party, I, therefore, am the head of the Norwegian government. Here are the names of the new government officials in my party..."

"It's not good, Eleanor. It's difficult for me to explain, but I don't speak English anymore because I don't want to be identified as an American. We are at war with Germany. I don't know what will be happening with school, but I may have to be moving to another town for school, so you must stay close to Marie if I do. She will help you and explain things to you. Don't be afraid but be careful. Do you understand...?'

We heard a loud knock on the front door, and Bibben tiptoed upstairs to see who it was. I sneaked up the stairs behind her. Bibben peeked out the small window in the door and then opened the door to let some people in. In the entry stood Erling's family with suitcases in their hands. Bibben conversed quietly with them by the door. Then their voices got louder and they interrupted each other.

"So many German soldiers were marching all over Oslo," Mrs. Bernsten said. "People rushing, the pop-pop-pop of guns and sirens. It was terrifying," she put her hands over her ears. "We wanted to get out of Oslo, but the traffic was so heavy."

"Everyone wanted to get out," Mr. Bernsten interrupted. "The highways were clogged and intersections were crowded. The Germans are coming for us. We need to hide."

"Do you have room for us? Can we stay here?"

They had taken a few of their things with them when they left Oslo. They brought their things into the living room and then they all came downstairs. *Where was Erling? Had he contacted them or made connections for their evacuation? I didn't dare ask. I wondered where they would stay.*

Bibben whispered softly with Erling's parents who were waving their arms and crying. I saw them looking around the house, going from room to room, and then suddenly Bibben came back to where Eleanor, Marie, and I were. The Bernstens stood behind her.

"Erling's family will be staying with us for a while, so we'll have to make some changes with our rooms," Bibben said. "Now let's see.... ah, Eleanor should move her things in with Boya. Marie can move into Eleanor's room, and that leaves Marie's area for the Bernstens. That will give them more space." We all just stood there looking at each other.

I began to count to myself... *La oss se. Bibben, Erling, Marie, Eleanor og meg selv lager fem. Erling's familie... seks... syv... høyde... tretten... fjorten... Uffda.*

Now almost fifteen people in the house. The farmhouse was crowded with more people. *How would Marie prepare food for us all? How could she be the housekeeper for all of us?*

"Let's go upstairs so that everyone can get settled in," Bibben said. And with that, everything was rearranged. All day we spent moving things around and listening to the radio. We learned that we should put blackout shades on our windows to prevent light from showing the Germans where to bomb. We were all afraid.

We stayed home from school for several days until we could understand what was happening. Then we learned the bridge at Vormsund was blown to pieces.

My heart ached. Dave lived in Vormsund. Was he okay? Vormsund is six kilometers from Vøyen. Dave is six kilometers from me. The school bus passes through Vormsund. Now what? How will the bus cross the bridge if it's blown apart? How will I get to school? School is about twelve kilometers from the bridge. And Kari? She's about five kilometers from Vormsund. Which part of the bridge did the Germans bomb? Will Kari get to school? My god. What is going on? What are we going to do?

I got on my bike to ride to Dave. When I got to the bridge, I saw rowboats by the shore. I put my bike in one and rowed real fast to the other side of the fjord. German soldiers were standing on the other side. I pretended I knew what I was doing. I couldn't find anyone home at Dave's farm, so I had to bike back to the fjord, past the German soldiers, and row to the other side. I spoke no English. *Keep your eyes forward and smile. Don't look nervous.* German soldiers now on both sides of the fjord. I took my bike out of the boat and peddled as fast as I could to Vøyen. *Only six kilometers, Boya, peddle fast but look normal.*

Bibben met me at the door. "Where have you been? We've been looking all over for you. Not even Marie knew where you were. You must let us know what you are doing and don't leave here unless you tell one of us."

"I'm sorry, Bibben, but I needed to check on the bridge at Vormsund. I heard it had been bombed. It has been. We can't cross the bridge, but someone has

put boats there so we can row across. How will the
school bus cross to get us to Arnes? That is the
question."

"Don't worry about school right now, Bibben. We
have greater concerns."

The days seemed to go by quickly. We all listened
to the radio and tried to make sense of it all. Then on
April 14th the radio broadcast reported that Halden had
been bombed. We were not that far from Halden; we
need to take precautions. The Bernstens were troubled
because they had friends in Halden since they had
once lived there. They tried to call their friends, but it
appeared the phone lines had been cut. I realized I,
too, had friends in Halden. What about the Swedish
boys? Are they ok? It's been just five days since
Norway and Denmark were invaded, and already the
Germans are advancing into Norway.

Bibben sat us all down and told us what she had
heard early that morning.

"German troops are marching in the streets of
Oslo and already are standing guard in front of the
Norwegian Parliament building. The Norwegian army
has already constructed a temporary bridge at
Vormsund, and we could cross now without rowing.
The BBC reported that the British army, navy, and air
force is providing great strength and support to
Norway and that Narvik and the surrounding
countryside have been recaptured."

Things were moving so fast it was difficult to keep
up. I didn't know the names and offices of all the
government officials, but I did hear that King Haakon

VII and his government, refused to give up control
and to recognize Quisling's government. And then the
news: "Today is Monday, April 15, 1940. Prime
Minister Vidkun Quisling has resigned."

Now what? Is King Haaken VII in charge? Who is
in the Parliament building? How could we keep up
with the news? Bibben turned the radio off, shrugged
her shoulders, and went outside. Eleanor and I sat still
wondering what was next. At times I paced back and
forth waiting for some direction. What could possibly
happen to us? I didn't understand; how could I explain
things to Eleanor. Bibben reappeared in the living
room.

"Girls, come here," and Eleanor and I went to her.
"I received a letter today from the Red Cross. It
pertains to you girls. Here is what it says:"

United States Embassy
Oslo, Norway
April 12, 1940
To: Savner Borghild og Eleanor Aadnes

President Franklin D. Roosevelt has directed
the ship the *American Legion to* leave the port of
New York on July 25, 1940, and proceed
to Petsamo, Finland. She is scheduled to arrive in
Petsamo on August 6, 1940. There, she will
embark for the United States on August 16 with
dignitaries as well as Americans in Scandinavian
countries who wish to return to the United States

and who may not be able to return safely any other way.

Our records indicate that Borghild Aadnes and Eleanor Aadnes are American citizens residing at this address. Because of their United States citizenship, Borghild Aadnes and Eleanor Aadnes are allowed to travel to the United States on the *American Legion*.

If Borghild Aadnes and Eleanor Aadnes desire to travel to the United States on this ship, please be advised to report to the US Embassy in Oslo to secure their reservations for passage on that ship. Their papers and reservations will then be secured for passage. They should notify the US Embassy as soon as possible to secure their spot on the ship. The ship will depart Petsamo on August 6, 1940.

If they elect not to secure passage, no further action is required.

"What?... What?" I looked at Bibben with wrinkled brow and wide-open eyes. "What? How does the United State Embassy know where we are? How could they find us? What does this passage mean? Do the Germans have anything to do with this? Are we in trouble?"

"Slow down, Boya," Bibben cautioned. "One thing at a time. I've had to update the US Embassy every year or whenever we move. You girls are United States citizens, and the Embassy always monitors your whereabouts. When we moved to Vøyen Gård, I notified them that you girls were at this address. I have done this every time we moved. You are American citizens, and this notice says that you can secure safe passage back to America so you won't be harmed. Norway is at war."

"I don't even know why we are in Norway," Eleanor said. "I don't remember home. I know I have parents and sisters. I have a brother, too but I don't know them. I've been confused for a long time. And now we are in a war. Does this notice have anything to do with me? What am I supposed to do?"

"Yes, Eleanor, this notice means you and Boya. See, your name is in the letter," Bibben looked at us and pointed to our names. "You girls are free to return to your home and your family. You are also welcome to stay here with us. We will need a few days to decide and to figure out the details. Do not say anything about this to anyone. Not even to Marie. And definitely not to Erling. You understand?"

"Yes," we said at the same time. But how would we get from the ship to our parents? We didn't know. I explained to Eleanor why we were in Norway. I didn't really know why, but I could tell her some things. "Eleanor, Mama and Dad received letter from Bibben and Tante Mathea saying they'd like to have some of Dad's children come to Norway. Farming was bad and there wasn't much money. Mama and Dad decided it would be Clara, you and me. So our neighbor took us to Aunt Thora in Shakopee, Minnesota, and then we took the train to New York and the ship to get here. Do you remember the train ride and the ship ride? You were just four years old.

We've been here for... let's see. 1932 to 1940. That's eight years. Can you remember the train ride and the ship?"

"No, I can't remember. I think I remember Mama and Ruth, and I remember our dolls' names. You said their names were our sisters' names." We all sat silent immersed in our own thoughts. Eleanor put her head in her hands and cried.

The next few days we were silent about our situation. Bibben said nothing. Eleanor said nothing. I said nothing. Erling didn't come home. But all the time I was thinking, thinking, thinking. *What shall I do? Can I leave my friends here? What about Dave? I like him. He reminds me of Dad. What about Clara? Can she go on this ship? But she has Ole and the kids here. What would I do if I went on the ship? What happens in New York? Could I contact Tante Mathea? Could she help me find my way home? I'm an adult now and need to be brave.* I couldn't think of anything else. My mind was in a trap about the war and about the chance to go home. All night I'd toss and turn and wonder.

Eleanor questioned me. "Are you going to go? Who are our parents? How will you find them? Who has money for this? I can't go if you don't go. I'm only twelve and you are only sixteen. Can you take care of me? What if you don't go? I can't go alone. I'm not going." Eleanor too was confused, and I was no help to her.

In the middle of the night of my sixteenth birthday I awoke to a voice talking to me, "Go home, Boya, go home." I sat up in bed and looked around. Nobody. Who spoke? I didn't know, but I decided to go home. The next morning, I woke Eleanor to tell her my decision.

"I am going home on the ship. I am going to go to the Embassy in Oslo and tell them I want to go home on the ship. What about you?"

Boya at sixteen

"What about Bibben? What about Clara? What about Dave? What about Marie? What about Kari? What will you tell them?" Eleanor had all kinds of questions. She had clearly been thinking about this as well.

"I can't tell Dave and Kari, but I must tell Bibben and Marie. They can help me figure this out. I will tell them today. I need to get to Clara somehow. I don't know right now how I can do that, but you must be quiet about this. Do you want to come with me?"

"I'm scared, Boya. I'm scared to go with you. I'm scared to stay here... I can't go with you. Maybe I'll see Clara. I'll have to stay here." Tears ran down her cheeks and onto my shoulder as she clung tightly to me. I cried. At the same time I noticed that she was growing taller. The top of her head reached my shoulders. She was twelve. She needed a sister or a mother. I wouldn't be able to be here for her. I'd have to talk to Marie to help her with growing up.

#

Erling's family spent most of the day pacing back and forth in the library, wringing their hands, bowing their heads in prayer, and whispering. Their faces were always tense. They looked to the dad for hope and advice most of the time, but when they did, he hung his head and didn't have much to say. Marie's room that the Bernstens were now occupying was down the hall from us and at night they sometimes shouted at each other. I couldn't tell what they were saying. We could always hear crying. Their voices got louder and then I'd hear *ssshhh*. Then quiet.

#

I decided I didn't need to wait for Bibben to introduce the topic of the ship to America. I knew what I was going to do. Eleanor and I walked into the living room where Bibben was listening to the BBC. "Bibben," I called to her. She looked up and motioned for us to sit down. We didn't sit. "I've decided I am going to go to the Embassy and make arrangements to take the ship to America." Eleanor didn't wait for a response, but rather just blurted out, "And I've decided that I will stay here."

Bibben stood and hugged us both. "I could tell you girls had been thinking about this. Your pensiveness the past couple of days could be seen in your eyes. I admire your concern to think about yourselves." She held Eleanor out in front of her and kissed her forehead. "We will be fine here, Eleanor, and when the war is over, we can talk about your returning to the United States. But if you want to go home, this is the only time you will have safe travel until the war is over... whenever that may be." Eleanor still wanted to stay.

"Let's talk about how you can get to the Embassy, Boya. I think I have a good idea. You will need to be cautious going into Oslo."

The Vøyen farm manager planned to go to the Vormsund butcher to get some sausage smoked, so Bibben arranged for him to take me with him and drop me at the train station so I could catch the train into Oslo and go to the Embassy. I would inform them that I wished to secure passage out of Petsamo and back to the United States. There I could learn about the process and what would happen in New York. I packed an overnight bag in case I couldn't get back the same day. The next morning when we were to leave, we heard the radio broadcaster announce "Josef Terboven has been made Reichskommissar of Norway with his headquarters in the Parliament buildings. He will reside in the Norwegian Crown Prince's residence in Skaugum."

"Hold deg I kontroll og vær kul, Boya," Bibben said and handed me a stack of kroner. *"Ikke gjør noe dumt."* I told her that I could be in control and I wouldn't do anything foolish.

The farm manager dropped me at the train station on the outskirts of town. I waited for the train to Oslo. I knew it was a ninety-minute train ride, so I hoped that a train would be leaving soon.

An announcement came over the speaker. "No foreigners will be able to leave Oslo. If you are not a Norwegian citizen, you should not get on the train to Oslo." I had to think fast. I couldn't get on the train. I needed to find the farm manager so I could get back to Vøyen. I grabbed my overnight bag and ran back into town. If I hurried, I could catch the farm manager. He had already left the butcher shop. The butcher said he said something about needing lumber. The lumber yard was just up the street, so I rushed and there he was, loading lumber in the back of the carriage. I jumped in with him telling him that I couldn't take the train and needed to go home with him.

When we got back to Vøyen, Erling was there. He did not have his NS uniform on.

"Where have you been?" he asked. "We should always know where you are."

"I rode my bike to the school bus stop to see the new bridge in Vormsund. I need to know how I will get to school." I held my chin up and kept eye contact with him. "I found out that the bus can cross on the new bridge."

He seemed satisfied with that and went upstairs to his family.

Bibben came in and when she saw me her mouth fell open and she gasped. "What? You are here. I thought you were going to Oslo to put your name on the list to go to America. What happened?"

"An announcement came on in the depot saying that no foreigners could leave Oslo. I'm a foreigner if I'm an American. I ran to find the farm manager so I could get a ride home. I guess I won't be going to Oslo, and I won't be going home."

"I applaud you, Boya, for the quick thinking. I have misjudged you. I didn't realize that you have so much control. I'm glad you are safe. Now we need to find a way for you girls to finish school this spring," Bibben said. "There aren't very many weeks left. Staying here and passing by the German soldiers may not be safe. The Vogstads are closer to the school and often take in students. You wouldn't need to ride your bike to the bus stop. I think it would be safer; the Vogstads would be happy to take you in for a few weeks. This is best for you now. Pack your bags. I will call the Vogstads and then have the farm manager take you there."

I knew the Vogstads and was happy to learn that we would be closer to school and especially happy we wouldn't have to pass by German soldiers. Eleanor smiled knowing that she would be able to go with me. I told her that we needed to be tight-lipped and not say much to the farm manager. We were both pleased to get to the Vogstad farm and to learn that Kari was staying there, too. When we saw each other, we jumped up and down, hugged each other, looked at each other in disbelief, and both started to cry.

"What are we going to do?" she asked not expecting an answer. "I'm scared and confused."

I stood tall and put my shoulders back and with confidence I said, "We are going to finish the school term. We are going to pretend nothing is wrong, but we are going to be always alert. I noticed some newspapers in the depot last week that give some information. We must be careful not to be carrying them with us. We could get stopped, but we need to know what they say. Some are in English and some in Norwegian. You check the Norwegian papers and I'll watch the ones in English. We can share what we learn."

The next few weeks Kari, Eleanor, and I walked to school together talking all the while about silly things that were happening in school. We didn't talk about politics nor about Germany. We were careful to look normal and speak softly. When we got back to the Vogstads after school, we would whisper about what we had read and learned. Eleanor always liked to listen.

Kari's and my teacher told us all to be careful but to keep coming to school. She said a resistance movement was forming; it will help Norway fight the Germans. She reminded us that we would be finishing middle school this spring and going on to various forms of high school and those schools were all in different places. Kari and I knew that this spring would be the last time we would be going to school together. She would go on to regular high school and live in a dorm in Oslo. I would be going to housewife school in Sandvika eighty kilometers from Vøyen. We had a sad goodbye when school was over. I rode my bike to Dave's house in Vormsund to say goodbye to him.

"I'm going to be going to school near Sandvika, Dave, but I hope that we can still visit each other. You said you will be at the Romerike folkehøgskole at Jessheim and that's right off the road to Vøyen, so I can stop to see you on my trips home."

"Boya, it is a very long bike ride from Sandvika to Vøyen. Don't ever ride your bike through Oslo but take the road to the north of Oslo so you won't need to ride through the city. Probably fewer German soldiers on that route as well. Jessheim is a little over halfway, so it would be a good rest stop."

"I will do that. The trip may be longer, but it will be safer. Do you think you could come to Sandvika to visit sometimes?"

"I'm sure I will, Boya, but it would be difficult to say when. I'll need to figure out how to stay in touch. See if your school there has a public phone, and if it does, you can give me a call. If not, I think we could send short letters that say what our plans are but nothing else. I don't know if the Germans are reading mail, but we want to be careful."

We took a short walk. Dave was tall and strong just like Dad and Ole. I liked that. We stopped a while by the banks of the fjord and we kissed. I felt strong but safer when he held me. Then I had to leave.

I returned to Vøyen to make arrangements to go to Rosenvilde.

"We are only a few hours from Hov, aren't we?" I asked Bibben. "Could we drive to Hov so we can see Clara before I go to Sandvika? Eleanor and I would both like to see her and her family."

"Yes, we should do that. I should see my family in Odnes, too. I could take you girls to Hov and then go on to Odnes for a couple of days. This house is so cramped with everyone here that it would be good to get away for a couple of days. I'll call Clara and tell her you'll arrive for a couple of days at the end of the week. Erling is here to take care of his family."

Eleanor skipped around and shouted for joy when she heard we would see Clara and Ole and little Per and Astri. The next couple of days Eleanor and I took lots of walks and rode our bikes around the farm just to get out of the house. I didn't mind the Bernstens, but Erling made me nervous. I tried to avoid him whenever I could. We didn't ride off the farm property because we were nervous about the German soldiers on the roads and bridges. Then we put together an overnight bag and were ready to go to Hov.

The ride from Vøyen to Hov was scary. German soldiers were everywhere checking cars and peoples' identification. Bibben must have had some identification card that allowed her to flash her card because the soldiers let us pass without taking time to look closely at her card. They didn't even ask about Eleanor and me. I didn't ask her about that card because I was afraid it may have something to do with the uniform Erling wore. After three hours in the car, we were overjoyed to grab our bags and go to Clara's house.

"Oh girls," Clara started to cry. "I'm so happy to see you and to have you stay with us for a couple of nights. We need to catch up with what's been going on in our lives. How are you?'"

Eleanor and I started talking at the same time. We all laughed and let Eleanor talk first. She told Clara about all the people living with us, about her last days in school, about the letter we got telling us we could go home on a ship. She went on and on not giving us a chance to talk. She got out of her chair and walk around while she talked and sometimes her voice got louder as she punctuated her stories with her hands!

Then it was my turn. I didn't need to talk about the same things, so I told Clara about the last few weeks in school, the Vormsund bridge, my getting ready to go to Sandvika to the Rosenvilde School. I was happy that the school provided room and board so I wouldn't need to have too much money from Bibben. I felt like she owned me when she gave me money.

"Are you going to tell her about your boyfriend, Dave?" Eleanor looked at me out of the corner of her eyes raising her eyebrows at the same time. "Are you, Boya? Are you going to tell her?' As a twelve-year-old she was quite interested in Dave and in my telling Clara.

"Yes, Eleanor, I'm going to tell Clara," I replied. "Clara, I have a boyfriend, Dave. He's a couple of years older than I am, but we like to ride bike and cross-country ski. We have lots to talk about, and he will be at the Romerike folkehogskole at Jessheim. So when I go home to Vøyen, I can stop and see him. It will make a nice rest stop about half the way home. That's about all."

"That's wonderful," Clara replied. "I'm happy for you. You are almost seventeen, and having a boyfriend is not unusual. Does he know you are an American? And what are his thoughts about the Germans?"

"I have not told him I'm an American citizen. He warned me to be careful at Sandvika and when I'm riding my bike home. He doesn't like the idea of the German invasion, and he has talked about getting involved. Maybe he'd join the military or get involved in some resistance movement. He's not sure right now."

"What do you know about the resistance movement?" Clara asked as Ole walked in with Per and Astri. "Did you enjoy your outing?" Clara asked the kids as they jumped onto her lap.

"What's this talk about the resistance? Did I hear that word?" Ole asked. "What do you girls know about it? You must speak softly when we talk about it." He lowered his voice and continued, "I can give you some information, but you must keep it secret. A few underground newspapers are being published. I have a couple of them I can show you. They will keep us informed about the Germans and the resistance. Let me get one. I keep them hidden."

"I'd love to see them," I said. "I want to keep informed on what is happening. I will be alone in Sandvika, and I want to know these things."

Ole returned with a couple of newspapers. "See here. This one reports that Vidkun Quisling resigned on April 15, 1940. He was the head of the National Samling Party here in Norway and a Nazi sympathizer. You can read the article. And, Boya, I think you will be seeing some of these newspapers. We try to share them with others involved in the resistance, but we are very careful to keep them hidden."

I was thrilled but nervous about the newspapers. I had to trust myself and how I handled my knowledge of the resistance. I knew I had to protect my future. This was all I could think about on the ride home.

#

By the end of May, Norway was experiencing many shortages. Shortages of bread, milk, butter, flour, clothes, spirits, and tobacco were felt by most citizens. Not only was gas being rationed, but every member of a household now carried a ration card. Often the card wasn't even usable as the shortages left little to purchase. Many people were planting gardens to keep from starving. Blacked out windows were the norm to prevent bombings from hitting one's home or business. Nazi soldiers had no mercy. They forced their way into people's homes and stole blankets, food, sugar and anything else they wanted. They often terrorized the residents to intimidate them. Early morning sounds of military boots on the streets kept people in their homes frightened for their lives. We were always afraid. Underground newspapers reported that Josef Terboven as the head of the Nazi party in Norway was a brutal man, and now he is the Reichskommissar of Norway and lives in the Norwegian crown prince's residence in Skaugum. Josef Terboven now ordered that all Norwegian news and newspapers be censored.

But during it all, a Norwegian underground was busy. It seemed there was not a unified resistance group but many smaller groups were organizing around the country. Underground newspapers helped the underground to organize and share news. The earliest news showed that on June 7 King Haakon was put on a boat heading to the United Kingdom. Six hundred million kroner was also spirited away in a British troopship and put into a London bank vault.

On June 10, 1940, Norway surrendered to Germany. German leaders ordered the Norwegian military forces to cease resistance and demobilize. Newspapers reported that Germans were certain that the surrender was complete and that resistance had ended. However, the Norwegian underground had already begun to mobilize. *Vi håpet de ikke følte at det var ugler I myra.* We used the Swedish saying about an owl in the bog knowing the Germans didn't understand that we were saying something was not quite right…

#

In late August underground newspapers reported that Crown Princess Martha and her three children were able to escape on the steamer American Legion out of Petsamo, Finland, on August 15. The steamer was heading for New York. 897 people were on board. The cost would be one dollar a day for those on board. *Eleanor and I were supposed to be on that ship. We'd be on our way home if we had been able to get to the Embassy in Oslo. Now Eleanor must depend on Bibben and Erling but mostly Marie. I need to take care of myself.*

Chapter Seventeen:
Sandvika Rosenvilde

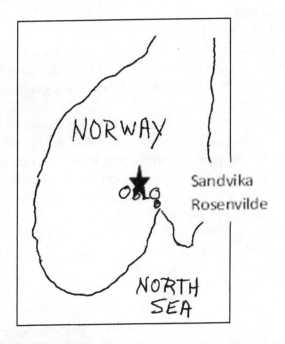

Rosenvilde was a housewife school and infant home located just north of Sandvika, a small railroad junction and shopping center fifteen kilometers west of Oslo. The school served as a high school and orphanage. It enrolled thirty-six students.
It was often referred to simply as Sandvika.

I packed some items and hitched my bike into Bibben's car in August, and she started the drive to Sandvika. I looked back and saw Eleanor waving to me as we drove away. It reminded me of the day we drove away from the farm back home. I could clearly remember seeing my family waving to us as we all cried and the car drove away. That was the last time I saw my Van Hook family, and as I relived that day, tears ran down my cheeks and I muffled a sob into my sweater. Then I straightened up and remembered that I was now an adult. I needed to be strong and take care of myself.

"We are going to stop at the US Embassy in Oslo before we go to Sandvika, Boya. You will need your American passport for identification. You are old enough now to have a passport and the Embassy is the place to get one. It will take us a couple of hours probably, but this needs to be done." I hadn't thought about that, but I realized that she was right. We spent a couple of hours at the Embassy, filling out forms and getting my picture taken.

"Guard this with your life, young lady," the gentleman at the Embassy told me. "Carry it with you at all times. It is your identification now, and you may need to produce it." He handed me my passport. I was proud to finally have my own form of American identification. I held it tightly as we went to Bibben's car to continue the drive to Sandvika. I looked at it several times and felt a type of kinship with my family at home. I tucked it safely into my bag.

"You will need to ride your bike to Vøyen when you have free weekends, Boya," Bibben told me. "Marie is going to need your help now that we have so many living at the farm. You will be studying cooking, baking, laundry, cleaning, handiwork, sewing, and childcare. All good skills you can practice at the farm."

"That means I must ride almost eighty kilometers to Vøyen and eighty kilometers back to Sandvika. And I have only two days on a weekend, so it will be difficult. What about passing German soldiers. How will I do this?"

"You just peddle. They aren't looking for schoolgirls. Be sure to have your identification papers with you in case you get stopped. You will need to prove that you are a student so you should carry student identification. We will watch for you every other weekend. Do your best in school. My best to you now, Boya. Stay safe and we'll see you in a couple of weeks." We unloaded my things. She handed me several hundred kroner and told me to keep it hidden and use as needed. I watched as her car drove away. I was alone.

#

The next months at Sandvika flew by. Once again I had new friends to meet, my future to think about, the war, my sister Eleanor, Dave, and my family back home. I had to protect myself and my identity, so I was suspicious of everyone. I'd wake up in the night and not get back to sleep. In the day I studied cooking, baking, laundry, cleaning, and sewing in addition to taking care of children ranging in age from eight days to two years old who came to the school from hospitals and orphanages. With so much to do, I was busy most of the time. And then there was Dave. He visited me often and was impressed to see what I had been learning. We didn't go out to any activities as it was too dangerous.

"How do you get here, Dave? Is it dangerous? Do the German police stop you?" So much I wanted to know.

"I rode my bike, Boya, so that I could see what your trip would be like. It is a long ride, but I wasn't stopped by any Germans. They were out there, but I kept my eyes and ears open and rode like I was exercising. I think you could do the same. Jessheim is about sixty kilometers. Take the road north of Oslo; don't go into Oslo. I think fewer Germans are on the north road."

"Dave, I need to tell you something that I haven't shared with you," and I took out my passport. "I'm an American, Dave. My sisters and I were sent to Norway to live with Dad's cousin because farming wasn't so good at home and money was tight. I have lots of sisters and one brother in America. Mama and Dad are there with them."

Dave never interrupted me, but when I stopped talking, he took my hand and said, "I've known that, Boya, since I met you. I think everyone in the town knew that. We just never thought it important. I think we should talk about how you should stay safe."

I told him about the letter from the Embassy and my intent to go home on the same ship that the Crown Princess went on. I told him about the announcement in the Vormsund train station and how that announcement kept me in Norway. He nodded his head, let me cry on his shoulder, and he held me tight and told me he'd take care of me. We agreed to see each other often. He could come to my school and I could stop at his school when I peddled home. I felt better.

Every other weekend with my passport in my backpack, I rode my bike the eighty kilometers to Vøyen stopping at Jessheim to see Dave. The ride to and my work at Vøyen were difficult. Vøyen always had guests that needed to be waited upon, and Bibben said it was good to show what I was learning at school even though she didn't always seem pleased with the number of house guests. She was impatient with everything and nodded quickly when asked a question. She was always sighing and was short in conversation. She said that she wished she could live in the city like I did.

It didn't surprise me that come spring, Bibben, Erling, and Eleanor moved to Stange just seventy kilometers north of Vøyen. It was further to Stange than to Vøyen, but it was closer to Clara and Ole, so maybe Eleanor would feel close to family. Erling's family did not move with them but stayed behind at Erling's Vøyen farmhouse. My things at Vøyen went with them to Stange. So, technically, I moved to Stange as well. My things were not particularly important anymore. I was getting along fine with what I had taken with me to Sandvika. I decided I was not going to be riding my bike to Stange. Bibben wouldn't be needing my help since they were there alone. My time with Dave was more important to me, and our relationship was growing stronger. Dave had copies of underground newspapers that he shared with me and told me that sharing those newspapers in secret was an ideal resistance activity for ordinary citizens. Passing an illegal paper to a friend was an individual act of resistance. I could be part of that.

"Terboven is now in charge." Dave showed me articles in the underground paper that told how brutish he was and how he ruled Norway like a dictator. "He has outlawed free speech and public meetings. He has outlawed political parties, and he has tried to force teachers to teach Nasjonal Samling ideology in the schools. The teachers have resisted. Norway hates Terboven."

"I can see why," I said. "Do you think he hates Americans?"

"I can't say, Boya, but he is a horrible, violent man. Norway does not need a leader like Terboven. A protest and public resistance movement is being planned for April 8."

"How involved are you in the resistance, Dave? Are you being careful?"

"Yes, Boya, I'm being careful, but I am a part of the resistance. There will be planned protest April 8th. April 8th will be one year since the German invasion. You can be part of the protest. We are all wearing paperclips on our lapels as a non-violent symbol of resistance, unity, and national pride You can also wear this paperclip on your lapel." And he put the paperclip on my lapel. I wore it with pride.

On Tuesday, April 8, 1941, the protest was held. Dave rode his bike to Sandvika. Traffic across Norway stopped at noon for thirty minutes. Nobody went into the stores or used a car, tram, or telephone. Lots of Norwegians wore a paperclip on their lapels. Dave wore a paperclip. I wore a paper clip. I was part of the resistance to Germany. We were united in protest and resistance.

The resistance movement became more organized each month. The central organization called MILORG for **mil**itary **org**anization had oversight on activities and missions for those in the resistance. I had a sense that both Ole and Dave were members, but neither said so.

That summer Dave and I joined in the moving of horses into the mountains for the summer. We bicycled to the Vinstra train station north of Lillehammer to meet the farmer whose excursion we had joined. We rode his horses sixty kilometers through the lush, spring valley to the mountain farm where the horses stayed. We stayed at the mountain farm for several days enjoying nature and the wilderness. It was on that holiday that I decided to leave Rosenvilde and move to Oslo to hopefully study at the Vettakollen hotel to be closer to Dave. I learned that earlier that summer my Grandpa Sterud had passed away, and I missed his funeral. Sadly, mother never saw her father after she left Norway.

When we returned to Oslo, I stopped at the Vettakollen school office to inquire about admission and learned that it was accepting three new students. I could be one of them. Dave went with me to Sandvika to collect my things and tell them I would not be back. One of my Sandvika friends handed me a new underground newspaper. It reported that Terboven had ordered the submission of all radio receivers and newspapers. If Norwegian citizens did not comply, Terboven promised to deliver a harsh punishment. The underground found a way to smuggle shortwave radios from Sweden and England.

We moved my things to the Vettakollen Hotel, and Dave began a new adventure. He had taken an apprenticeship on a farm south of Oslo and was able to obtain one of the smuggled radios from Sweden and keep it hidden. He was able to stay in contact with the news as German terror escalated.

Fall 1941

Chapter Eighteen:

Vettakollen Hotel, Oslo

Ah, the Vettakollen! I was back in the neighborhoods where we had lived when we first got to Norway. Slemdal, Holmenkollen, and Vettakollen were all familiar to me. But now rather than being in elementary school, I was finishing my high school studies at the Vettakollen Hotel. I was a guest at this hotel years ago, and now I was part of the student staff. It was exciting to be staying and studying at the hotel. Several German soldiers and NS people who had duty to patrol the nearby area also lived at the hotel. I maintained a low profile while at the same time I read and shared the underground newspapers and wore a paperclip. I didn't flash the paperclip, but I did have one on my lapel. I noticed that several of the other students wore paperclips as well. We had a secret bond of resistance and winked at each other in recognition of that bond. Perhaps the Germans would think it is part of our hotel uniform!

Mrs. Vidkun Quisling also lived at the hotel with her dog. We students never saw her husband, but quite often she asked one of us to carry her dog up and down the stairs because it was too fat to get up the stairs by itself. We laughed at her behind her back. She kept to herself most of the time but often ate in the restaurant. We'd serve her meals, clean her room, and provide any service she requested. She rarely visited with any German soldiers that were staying at the hotel. We served those Germans as well, but we didn't speak to them.

Travel in Oslo at this time was difficult due to the war and the presence of so many German soldiers who obeyed Nazi orders and often terrorized citizens. A couple of my fellow students told me about being out late one night and being stopped. *"Haende Hoch! Still Stehen!"* We had all learned that that meant hands up and stand still. We had laughed about what to do if the Germans gave that command and then *"Pssierschein!"* Pssierschein meant to hand them our identification card. How could we do that if our hands were up? We thought those commands were foolish when said together, but those students said it wasn't funny at all the night they were stopped. We believed then that Norwegians could never trust that they wouldn't be mistreated, brutally beaten, and imprisoned. We all had to be very careful in our travels, and I felt this intensely since I was a young, vulnerable American woman. I was an easy target.

#

On December 7, 1941, Japan attacked Pearl Harbor. I was glued to the news and listened closely to the BBC broadcast of United States President Franklin D. Roosevelt's speech to the Joint Session of Congress. "Yesterday, December 7, 1941, a date which will live in infamy, the United States of

America was suddenly and deliberately attacked by naval and air forces of the Empire of Japan... I ask the Congress to declare....a state of war..."

Now what? What about my family at home? Will they be safe? Will America come to the aid of Norway? Will I see Dave again? How will Eleanor understand this? I should have taken Eleanor and gone home on the ship out of Finland. No matter. I cannot turn the clock back; I must go forward. My thoughts rambled. No coherent sense in them; they just came at me from all directions. I must make some sense of this. *Do I dare call Dave? He needed to be near a phone to take a call. How could I get to him? I'm an American and now America too is at war with the Nazis. Am I safe?* I was certain if the German soldiers entered my room they would look for underground newspapers under my mattress and in my closet. I hid them instead inside the folds of my dirty clothes figuring the soldiers would not check there. I reread them often just to reassure myself that what I believed was right. I wrote a quick note to Dave and dropped it in the mail hoping he would get it.

A couple of days later, I was called to the hotel office and there stood Dave. He had bicycled to my school to check on me and to talk about what was happening. Outside the hotel and far from any entrance we walked, and in whispers, we decided that we should meet in secret from then on. He was in the resistance, and I was an American. We couldn't let each other get hurt because of our allegiances. We crafted an itinerary of where and when to meet. We both tucked our itineraries inside the soles of our shoes and said our goodbyes until we could meet again.

German schools had indoctrinated some of the youth in Nazi ideology for the past decade. These indoctrinated young men were my age, and now they were soldiers. They were instructed to follow the three "Criminal Orders" issued by the High Command. The underground papers reported that these three orders explicitly rejected the laws of war and encouraged soldiers to commit atrocities. Soldiers received the "Guidelines for the Behavior of the Troops" which instructed that "this war demands ruthless and aggressive action against Bolshevik agitators, snipers, saboteurs, and Jews, and tireless elimination of any active or passive resistance."

The soldiers harmed and arrested anyone who looked or acted suspicious. I was afraid all the time, but I kept abreast of information through the newspapers and what others were saying. I stayed clear of Mrs. Quisling and her dog but joined in the regular Christmas holiday festivities at the school. The school kept its Christmas celebration so some of the students stayed on to celebrate with and care for the children. I didn't want to go home to Stange and to Bibben and Erling, so I volunteered to stay at the school.

#

Dave sneaked into the school over the holidays so we could see each other. We agreed to meet in late February. We both bicycled to our secret location, hugged each other a long while, and then on February 29, 1942, we became engaged. I don't know how they learned about our engagement, but Bibben and Erling came to the Vettakollen about a week later. They were not happy! "You are too young." "A war is going on." "How will you live?" *Where do Bibben and Erling get their information?* Dave and I didn't think we were too young. We had fallen in love, and we were happy to have each other. Because Bibben and Erling were unhappy about this engagement and because I didn't want to spend any more time with them than necessary, I spent most of my spare time with Dave's family on the Eggum farm near Vormsund. The distance from the Eggum farm to Hov was about a three-hour drive, so we could see Clara and Ole who now had three children: Per, Astrid and Anne. Anne was born at the end of April, and I had not had a chance to see her and hold her. I was anxious to visit. Dave and I had lots of fun with the kids and enjoyed our time with Clara and Ole. Clara and Ole were both happy for Dave and me, and they invited us to stay with them any time.

Ole and Dave got along well. "I want you to know, Ole, that I have both a short-wave radio and a regular radio, but I keep both hidden. Because of these radios and my access to the underground newspapers, I can tell you about what goes on in the country. I share this information with Boya, and I am very protective of where and how we meet. I love her and will protect her."

"I can tell that you love each other, and I see you are a man of character. I'm happy to have you with Boya and in the family. Now I want you to come with me." Ole took Dave downstairs into his potato bin. They were downstairs for several minutes and spoke quietly. I wanted to know what they were talking about. I asked Clara what she knew.

"Lots of things happen around here, Boya, that I don't ask questions about. I know that Ole is involved in the resistance, but I can't know all about that business. I think you should not question Dave too much about it either. It's dangerous."

#

Later that spring while at the Vettakollen, one of the school leaders took me to the Berg School for an appendectomy. The Germans had taken occupation of the nearby Aker Hospital, so the Berg School had become the local hospital with classrooms serving as hospital rooms with ten patients to a room. Somehow Erling found out I was a patient there and came to visit me. *How did he find this out?* I feigned pain and fatigue so I wouldn't need to spend too much time with him. I was determined to limit contact with him.

I'd lie awake at night in my hospital bed and wonder how all this happened. I'd review in my mind what my life had been like the past ten years and what it was like now. Sent away from my home. Not able to return not only because Clara got married, but also because I couldn't get to the *American Legion* ship leaving from Petsamo. Moving all the time. Being in the middle of a war. Having a strict stepmother and a stepfather who, I knew, was a follower of NS. A brother-in-law and a fiancé who were in the resistance. And Eleanor, dear Eleanor, whom I hadn't seen for some time. I didn't know anything about my family in America. Did they know what was happening to us? It was too much. Riding my bike was no longer fun. My muscles tensed up and my sweaty palms gripped the handlebars when I had to pass by German soldiers. I feared being stopped and interrogated. They would see my American identification. I didn't know if I was safe. I hesitated making the trips to Dave, and I had decided months before that I would not visit Stange.

Fall 1942

Chapter Nineteen:
Grini Prison Camp, Bærum, Norway

*Grini, originally a women's prison located just
outside Oslo, was established as a German
concentration camp on 14 June 1941. The largest
concentration camp in Norway, Grini served as a
transit camp for the continuation of prisoners to
camps in Germany and Poland. Prisoners worked in
manufacturing, agriculture, and other manual
labor. Almost 20,000 men and women experienced
imprisonment under German conditions at Grini.*

I was enjoying a beautiful early fall morning in
my room at the Vettakollen Hotel with a few hours to
myself before I had to report to work with the
children. Light, cool breezes floated in through the
open window moving the curtains back and forth. The
musty smell of fall and the crunching of dried leaves
underfoot occupied my attention as I watched the
children play outside. Then the sounds quickly
changed. I heard rhythmic stomping of boots in the
short hallway outside my room. My heart skipped
several beats as my eyes surveyed my room to be sure
no underground newspapers were visible. I had been
careful to keep those papers and anything American
hidden. The sounds of boots stopped in front of my

door. Bang! Bang! Trying to remain calm, I peeked out the door. Eight German soldiers pushed open the door and charged into my room. The one in front shouted, *"Sie arden verhaftet."* I was being arrested.

"Why? I'm a student here. I – I – I work with the children. They need me here."

"Gather a few things including your American passport. You are coming with us."

I did as I was told and put a pair of pants, underwear, a sweater, my hairbrush, my US passport, what was left of the kroner Bibben had given me, a package of Venus napkins, and my toothbrush and toothpaste into a bag. One soldier held tightly onto my arm as they marched me down the hallway to the stairwell, down the stairs, and out the front door to a German war truck. I was pushed up and into the backend of the truck. Four German soldiers jumped in behind me. I was held at gunpoint. We drove about ten kilometers to Møllergata 19. I knew this was the Oslo police house. I had heard that it had been taken by the Germans to be used as headquarters for the Nazi security police. The Gestapo!

When I got inside, I saw maybe twenty young girls. I didn't recognize any of them. We all looked closely at each other but were afraid to speak. What was going to happen to us? Then all but one of the soldiers left the room. The soldier guarding us looked to be about the same age as most of us. He said nothing but stood at attention and looked sternly in our direction. At one point he left the room. Some of the girls whimpered.

One of the girls came close to me and whispered in my ear.

"This is the German Gestapo. I don't know why we are here." The door creaked and began to open. She moved quickly away as the young guard reentered the room with another official. I held onto my bag of clothes. We were all silent avoiding eye contact with the soldiers. *What were they going to do to us? Would we be safe in numbers?*

"I have the Americans here. What have they done?" the guard asked the official. "I was told to bring them here."

"They have done nothing, but the Americans have interned some Germans in America. We will intern these Americans just the same. Get them in the back of the trucks outside."

We were herded into the backs of the trucks parked outside the police house and driven northwest out of Oslo to a place in Bærum. Squished and afraid of what might become of us, we rode in silence at gunpoint until we reached the main gate. I recognized this place as Grini women's prison, but it appeared to have more buildings than I remembered. An electric fence stretched around a large area containing several buildings. Then I recalled reading in an underground newspaper about how the women's prison camp outside of Oslo had been taken by the Germans and repurposed for a concentration camp.

#

"Get your things," one guard shouted, and the soldiers began to push us out of the truck. We stumbled over each other as we were marched to the main building. "Get over by the wall there. Wait for instructions. Don't talk and don't move."

Several other detainees were standing in a row with their hands in the air and their noses touching the wall. I recognized the Star of David on their shirts and I knew they were Jews.

What will happen to me now? Will Dave know where I am? Will I be here long? Will they move us to another site? Settle down. Don't let them know you are afraid.

The rhythmic tick-tock of the clock on the wall broke the silence while it measured three hours as we stood at attention and waited for instructions. We weren't the ones with our hands in the air and our noses on the wall. In some strange way, I felt lucky. We were guarded by several young German soldiers who walked back and forth and talked amongst themselves. It must have been their commanding officer who finally came in and spoke to the main guard. When he left, the main guard stepped forward and surveyed the room counting how many girls were detained there.

"When I point to you, step forward and hand me your passport and your valuables," the guard pointed to the girls that were with me in the back of the truck. "Thirty of you will follow this guard to the third floor. I'll point to you and count to thirty. The rest wait," and he started pointing at us individually. "*Eins...*

zwei... drei... vier... fünf... zwanzig..." and at twenty-three he pointed to me. I quickly handed him my passport and valuables and got in line. *"Achtundzwanzig.... neunundzwanzig... dreißig. Halt!"* And the thirty of us were marched up three flights of stairs to a long narrow room, like a hallway, that had bunk beds three beds high, one toilet, and two wash bowls. We stood in fear after the guard shouted, "If you ever look out those windows, you will be shot." And he pointed at the highest windows in the room. I vowed never to look out those windows.

"Put your things under your bunk. Top bunks under the bottom bunk. Your eating utensils are on your bed. Take them with you to mealtime," and the guard clicked his heels, swiftly turned and left the room. We each found one cup, one plate, one spoon, and one fork on our bunk. He returned in a few minutes and marched us to a different barracks where six female prisoners were sewing dresses and drawstring pants. These were to be our uniforms. We were each issued two dresses, two pair of pants, and a pair of shoes. We were then marched back to our barracks. "Put one dress, pants, and your shoes on and put your street clothes in your bag under your bunk. I'll be back in ten minutes."

We did as we were told. Some of the girls cried; one started reciting the Bible aloud. "Blessed are the peacemakers for they shall be called the children of God." "Do not fear little flock." She recited one verse after another.

"Be quiet," one of the girls said in a loud whisper. "The guard will come back and who knows what will happen to us. You must be silent."

As the skies darkened so did our room. We had not eaten since we were first pushed into the truck. We were starving. Soon a guard appeared and shouted, "Bring your eating utensils. We are going to the cafeteria" Our first supper was four very thin slices of sour bread, the kind made from unripened grain from Poland. It had been mixed with paper and acid to hold it together. We were given a small piece of margarine and a tablespoon of plum jam as thin as water.

The guard picked up a margarine and a tablespoon of jam. He shouted at us. "Use half tonight and bring the other half back at breakfast." We were so hungry we ate it all. Our barracks were silent all night. At breakfast we got four pieces of the sour bread again and a cup of water from a faucet. We had no margarine or jam. That was all. We were still starving.

We were marched back to our room in silence. One of the older girls whose bunk was close to mine whispered to me, "Who are you? Why are you here? Does anyone know you are here?"

"I'm Borghild. I don't know why I'm here. Maybe because I'm American. I don't think anyone in my family knows I'm here. Who are you?"

"I'm Anna. I'm American, too. No one knows I'm here. The Gestapo took me without any notice. How will our families know where we are? We need a plan." She was silent. "Sshh, I think I hear someone coming." We were silent for a couple of minutes. She continued, "I thought maybe we could write our family's names and addresses on paper and then give that paper to each other? If you get out, you can contact my family about me? I will do the same for you."

"Good idea," I whispered back. "We could use toilet paper. I have a pen. Do you?"

"No. Can I borrow yours when you are done?"

"Yes."

The sound of heavy boots in the hall signaled that someone was coming. The guard returned and marched us outside to a long table holding pans, a bucket of water, and potato peelers. We were to peel potatoes all day. This was our duty assignment. The day dragged on and on. Standing in place for hours was difficult, and I could see others twisting their backs and shifting their feet to get some relief. Dinner was the same meal we had had the day before.

That evening, I stayed on my bed in silence, and in the dark on the toilet paper, I wrote names and contact information. I listed Dave, Clara, and Ole, but I did not list Bibben. I had moved out of Bibben and Erling's house last year. I didn't think they needed to know where I was. Eleanor, my poor younger sister living with Bibben had no idea what had happened to me. I hid the paper in my underwear hoping to finish it later. I couldn't put it under the mattress as I thought the guard may look there. I handed my pen to Anna.

The next morning we were marched again to the cafeteria. Two slices of bread, no butter, tea, no sugar.

Then we were marched to our duty station. It was colder outside than yesterday, and we had no sweater nor jacket. The water holding the potatoes was cold and our hands turned red with cold. Other prisoners were harvesting potatoes, carrots, cabbage, and onion. A guard caught one of them eating a carrot and marched over to him.

"You... you are stealing food. You have carrot in your mouth." He grabbed him by the arm and threw him to the ground. "Spit it out! You must pay for stealing, so now you will run back and forth on this field ten times. Back and forth. You understand me? Run. Then come back to me." The prisoner ran back and forth. The guard counted: *eins... zwei... drei...* The prisoner looked weary and he was only on his third pass. He had seven more to go. *Vier... fünf... sechs*. And on this pass the prisoner fell to the ground. No water was offered. I started to cry. The guard shouted *"aufstehen"* and pushed him up into a standing position. The prisoner stumbled to his feet gasping for breath. I watched out of the corner of my eyes. No water was offered. *Sieben... neun... zehn.* And his ten times were accomplished. Exhausted, the prisoner fell at the feet of the guard. No water was offered. "Pushups now," the guard shouted, "you will not steal food." And the prisoner tried to do a pushup. Using a heavy stick, the guard whipped the prisoner over and over. The prisoner fell to the ground unable to get up. The guard whipped him a couple more times and then left him on the ground. No food. No water.

I was terrified. I was mad. What was I going to do? I was not going to steal food. All of us had watched what had just happened, and no one said anything. We didn't dare help the prisoner. The one girl who always recited the Bible in our barracks looked at the prisoner on the ground and said, "Blessed are those who are persecuted for theirs is the kingdom of God." I wondered where God was in this. I thought about what the vicar said at my confirmation about being an adult. I thought about myself as an adult. I'm eighteen, and I need to be in charge of my life. I must keep my head about me. I said nothing to anyone when we were in the open field a couple of times a day. I just tried to breathe fresh air and keep my eyes down. I didn't know how I could escape.

Every day we marched to our work duty station where we peeled potatoes to be put into the camp soup. Out of the corner of our eyes we watched brutal attacks while we peeled potatoes. The cries of pain, the sounds of whipping, the shouting in German. We tried to keep our moods light and to cover the horrific sounds around us. We quietly sang Norwegian folk songs and told each other about ourselves. Most of us were young American girls that had done no wrong. What were they going to do with us?

We were never given lunch but were given twenty minutes at noon to play games. All we had was a ball and a bat. Some of us played. I played just for the exercise so I could stay strong. Some of the older prisoners who weren't on the potato peeling line sat and rested. Weary. Starving. Tired. Scared. The guards looked the other way.

After work duty we were forced to march around the camp singing Nazi songs. The goal was to *nazify* us. We tried to sing as we marched, but we didn't know the songs, so we pretended to sing. Some who weren't singing were beaten. Some were made to crawl on their bellies in the dirt. This went on for about an hour before we were marched to our barracks and given a few minutes to gather our eating utensils and march to supper. Some nights we had cooked dry fish with grey sauce. We also had potatoes with the peels left on. I decided our peeled potatoes were for the soldiers and officers. We were so hungry we ate the peels. We called it "bodysweat." Many of the older prisoners got sick. Coughing, vomiting, and crying. There was nothing we could do to help them. The guard marched us back to our barracks.

The girls on the top bunks decided to look out the top windows -- the very windows we were told not to look out. These girls could see where all the prisoners lined up in the morning and at night and then made to march in step. They quietly told the rest of us what was happening. Every day prisoners were punished in that yard. Some prisoners were whipped while they did pushups. This after a long day of work and almost no food.

"Stop looking," one of the girls said. "You will get shot, and maybe so will we. You must stop."

"I can see some prisoners lined up," one of the girls whispered. "Here comes a police wagon. They are loading those prisoners into that wagon. Where are they going?" But no one knew. The next morning we heard one of the guards shout at the prisoners. "Do as you are told, or you too will be sent to Trandum."

Trandum. Trandum. We knew Trandum was the end of the line for prisoners. Prisoners were shot at Trandum.

One of the girls began to quietly say the 23rd Psalm. "The Lord is my Shepherd...yea though you walk through the valley of the shadow of death, fear no evil." I tried to believe it. I tried to not fear the evil around me, but it wasn't easy. Then she began to quietly sing "Nearer My God to Thee." Others joined quietly in the song.

One day we were taken to the first floor to be checked by a doctor. My finger itched so much that I thought I had gotten scabies. Lucky for me it was just normal eczema that probably got worse when peeling the potatoes. It itched and itched, but nothing could be done to make it better. I just had to endure the itching and the weeping of the sores. Edith stood beside me and quietly asked if I had brought any Venus products. I shared what I had with her when we got back to our barracks. Now what was I to do when I needed them?

For dinner one night all we got was a tablespoon of sugar with our soup of potatoes and rutabagas cut up with their peelings left on. I was happy to eat the peelings for more nourishment. Sometimes a few peas had been added or maybe some beans. Another time we got a half piece of thin sausage. We called it

"Storm Soup." It was held in a large wooden pail with a ladle for scooping. Once I saw the bottom of the pail. It had sand and dirt in it. Often many of the girls were sick in the night.

A couple of times we were taken to a large room for showers. A guard handed each of us a small towel but no soap. We showered in our uniforms as a way to wash them and our underwear. We used the radiator or the hot water pipes to dry our clothes. First, we tried to cover ourselves, but soon we just walked around naked. People were losing weight and looking thinner each day.

It seemed like months had passed, but it had just been ten days when a guard entered our barracks, came over to me, and told me to pack whatever I had and join him in the hallway. I was afraid. I didn't know what he was going to do with me, but I got my few things together. I was careful when I put the toilet paper from Anna in my shoe. I didn't dare say anything to her, but I looked at her with hope and fear. I met the guard in the hallway and looked straight at him in defiance. He handed me my passport but not my kroner.

"You are free to go."

Free to go? Go where? Go home? I looked squarely at him with raised eyebrows and questioning eyes.

"Yes. You are free to go. Go down the path here and out the front gate. Hurry now." He pointed to the path that went past the barbed wire fence and out to the road.

I was shocked, but I looked straight ahead putting one foot in front of the other. Don't look back, I told myself. Keep moving ahead. I got to the end of the path, looked up, and there stood Erling in his NS uniform.

"Boya," he shouted, "here, come over here." I didn't want to see him. I didn't want anything to do with him. I quickly looked around to decide what I should do. He came closer to me and said, "You are free. I have been all the way to Terboven to get you free. Terboven gave permission for your release. Now come with me."

I was so angry. I was angry at him. I was angry at the Gestapo. I was angry at everything. Grini had so many older people who were still in the camp. They were weak and hungry. They were being beaten if they didn't obey. They didn't have much fight left in them. They didn't know their destiny and they were trapped. I heard crying all the time at night. These older people needed help. Why should I, young and healthy, be the one released. It was wrong. I turned away from Erling and walked away. I didn't look back at him. He knew.

He knew I didn't like him. He knew I had been suspicious of him for a long time and wasn't going to go with him. I quickly assessed what I should do. Hurry, Boya, and get away from Grini. You need food and water. You have about ten kilometers to get back to Vettakollen. That's a long way.

Then I heard Erling behind me. "Boya, stop. STOP! You need to stop and listen to me." I started to run. Erling pulled his car out in front of me, jumped out, and made me stop. "Get in the car, Boya, you cannot run from Grini in your uniform or the soldiers will think you ran away. They will capture you, torture you, and send you away. Now, get in my car. I'll take you to the Vettakollen." He knew more about what I needed to do than I knew.

I realized he was right. I needed to get out of that uniform, and I couldn't just undress on the street. I got into his car. We rode in silence. *What was I going to say to him? Should it be thank you? How could I thank this Nazi sympathizer who was like a stepfather? Yet he had just gotten me out of Grini.* He stopped in front of the Vettakollen Hotel and reached his arm across me so I couldn't get out of his car.

"Now listen to me, Boya. You have your passport and I'm giving you the letter from Josef Terboven that freed you from Grini. You must carry this letter in your passport. If you are ever stopped by a German soldier, you must show this letter. You will not be taken prisoner if you share this letter. Here, take it now and tuck it in your passport. It will keep you free."

I wasn't sure what to do. Should I take the letter? Should I be carrying a letter from the Nazi leader in Norway? I looked at Erling. He nodded a *yes* to me. His nod meant "take the letter." I took the letter, put it in my passport, and looked right at him. "How did you know where I was? And how did you know I was in the hospital? I want to know. "

Erling looked sternly at me and in a quiet voice said, "Mrs. Quisling at the Vettakollen has kept an eye on you for me. I was nervous for you because of all the German soldiers living in the hotel. She told me you had been taken to the hospital, and she told me you had been taken from the Vettakollen by some German guards." I put my head in my hands in disbelief. I stared at him with my eyes wide open. If Mrs. Quisling had been informing him of my whereabouts, then he knew everything I had been doing. I gasped and shook my head. He knew about my sneaking away with Dave. I felt violated. Perhaps that's how he and Bibben knew I was engaged.

He continued to talk. "I went to the Møllergata 19 to see if you had been taken there. Their records showed you were transferred to Grini. I hurried there, but they wouldn't let me see you. I went through every channel, but eventually I went to Terboven to get permission for your release. It's in the letter I'm giving you. Be careful, Boya, be very careful."

I didn't know if I should thank him, if I should hug him, or if I should just get out of his car. I reached over to shake his hand, and he handed me a few hundred kroner. "Take care of yourself now." I grabbed my bag of clothes and got out of his car still wearing my uniform. I watched him drive away.

As I walked into the Vettakollen Hotel lobby headed for my room, I noticed Mrs. Quisling sitting by the corner window in a big chair with her dog at her feet. She looked up at me and then looked out the window. She knew then that I was not a prisoner. I hurried to my room before anyone could see me. I didn't want to have to explain to my student friends where I had been, and I sure didn't want to be stopped by the German soldiers who lived at the hotel.

When I got to my room, I took my uniform off, threw it in the trash, put on my own clothes, and looked at Anna's paper in my shoe to see whom she wanted me to contact. The address was Arnes. She was from Arnes, the very town where I had gone to school a couple of years before. I didn't know her there, and we hadn't shared that when we wrote on the toilet paper. I hoped I could get to Arnes in the next few days to tell her family where she was. But first I needed to eat. I was starving. I had some old bars in my room that I gobbled down, but I was still hungry. I knew I needed to leave the Vettakollen. I could not be there with the Germans and Nazis occupying the same hotel. I would go to Dave's parents in Vormsund. I had money for the train, but I also had a bicycle I needed to keep. I decided to leave much of my stuff behind and ride my bicycle sixty kilometers. I hoped I could get a good night's sleep before my long ride. I crawled into bed, closed my eyes, and just as I was nodding off, I heard footsteps in the hall. Too close! The steps stopped at my door. I hid under my covers and prayed that it wasn't the German soldiers coming after me again. No heavy boot noises. I listened more closely. I heard a light knock on my door and then footsteps going back down the hall. I tiptoed to the door and peeked out just as Mrs. Quisling was turning the corner at the end of the hall. I looked down and discovered a bag. Did I dare take it? It must have been left for me. I quickly took it into my room and cautiously opened it. Food. Mrs. Quisling had left me some food — fruit, bread, Norwegian goodies, and a note. "Be careful." Huh. She and Erling were my protectors. I ate some of the food but decided to save some for breakfast. I thought I would be safe in the hotel that night. I slept well, and I decided to leave quietly early the next morning.

Sunrise and a check on the placement of my passport containing the letter from Terboven, a warm sweater, the leftover food, my kroner, and a quick look around my Vettakollen surroundings and I was ready to climb on my bike. Wait. If I were to be stopped and searched, Anna's information in my shoes would be discovered. I put on two pairs of underwear and tucked her note between them. I quickly moved through the hotel lobby glancing around to see if Mrs. Quisling was anywhere in sight. I wanted to give her quick nod of thanks, but she was not around. I put my backpack on, got on my bike, and rode away. My whole body felt the movement of the bicycle. I reviewed the last couple of weeks. I had come through a horrendous experience that so many others who have been taken will not survive. I had the two people that I disliked the most that were my rescuers. Angels had been watching over me. Here I was engaged to a member of the resistance, sister-in-law to a resistance member telegraphing messages to the Special Operations Executive (SOE), carrying what I called a freedom note from the head of the

Nazi party in Norway, fed by Vidkun Quisling's wife. How would my family in Van Hook ever put their heads around my life? I wanted a letter from home, and I hoped when I would finally get to Clara that she would have heard from Mama.

Just peddle, Boya. Just peddle and enjoy the scenery and the crisp fall air. You will not have "storm soup" for dinner tonight. You have a light lunch with you as well as kroner to buy yourself something for lunch. Then I realized that I did not have a ration card. I wasn't really a member of a household. In a sense, I was homeless. I knew each family member was given one ration book. I didn't need one as the Vettakollen took care of room and board. I was now on my own. I rode my bike past women working their gardens to provide food for the family. They were stooped over to harvest even the last little bit of whatever they could of potatoes, turnips, carrots. I recalled the prisoner who had stolen a carrot and was brutally beaten by the guard. I'll bet that prisoner is still there and starving. Once again, I was angry.

I had been pedaling for over four hours and was half-way to Dave's parents. I hadn't been stopped by one German soldier yet, and I hadn't seen many of them on this ride. But I was hungry and thirsty, and I needed the toilet. I rode into the small village of Lillestrom. The long queues at the market and no ration card made me think I should just keep going. No chance for food here. I stopped in the little park next to the market and got off my bike. A young girl in the park came over to me to chat. She looked closely at my shirt.

"I see you have a paperclip on your lapel," she said. "I have one, too. Do you live around here? I like your bicycle. Where are you going?"

She was intent to visit, and since it had been some time since I had had a regular conversation, I engaged her for a time with my story. "I don't live around here. I just left my school at the Vettakollen Hotel. I'm riding my bicycle to a farm near Vormsund. I am moving there. I just have what's in my backpack. I'm hungry and thirsty because it's been a long ride. But I'm about half-way to my destination."

"I have some fruit I'd share with you if you'd like. I also have half a bread loaf I'd give you."

"I have a little food in my backpack, but I'd certainly share with you." We sat in the grass and shared a picnic. It was good, and I was thankful to have someone to share it with. I was certain we just looked like two schoolgirls in the park. I gave her two ten kroner coins. She was thrilled. And then I thanked her and told her to take care of herself. I got on my bicycle and pedaled down the road. I reached the Eggum farmyard shortly after dusk, took off my backpack, and knocked on the door.

"What?" Dave's mother was astonished. "What? Boya, is this you? Come in, my dear," and she took my backpack, gave me a hug, and led me into her kitchen. "Sit down. Let me get you something warm to drink and something to eat. You look tired and weary. Did you ride your bike all the way from Vettakollen?"

"Yes, I did. I have quite a story to tell you, but I'm so happy to be in your kitchen! And yes, I am hungry and thirsty. I'll gladly eat what you offer!" Through the kitchen window, I saw Dave's dad striding briskly up the yard to the house. Dave and his dad both had broad shoulders that signaled confidence. Dave was tall like his dad, strong, sure of himself, yet soft-spoken. The kitchen door opened. Dad hung his fall coat on the hook by the door and walked up to the table. He smacked the palm of his hand on his forehead and ran over to me, picked me out of my chair, and danced me around the room.

"What have we here? It looks like a friend of Dave's!" he winked and smiled, put me down, and then he took a drink for himself. "I'm happy to see you, but what brings you here?"

I didn't know where to start with my story, but it poured out. I told about the Vettakollen, my schooling and the children, and Mrs. Quisling and her dog. And then I told how the eight soldiers arrived at my door and took me away. My emotions finally gave way, and the tears flowed. Mom and Dad Eggum were horrified. Their mouths dropped open and they gave heavy sighs of concern. At times I was interrupted to make clarification or to just give them a time to catch their breath. Then I showed them the Terboven letter. They were speechless.

"Terboven? Terboven signed this note to free you. How can we understand this? He is a Nazi, we are in war with the Nazis, Dave is in the resistance, and here you have been freed by Terboven, the head of the Nazis in Norway!" Dave's dad leaned back on his chair, clenched his hands above his head, and shouted "*herregud.*" He slumped forward and rested his chin in his hands. "*Så ironisk, men her er du!*"

"Yes, ironic," I agreed, "and here I am. Would you like to see the letter again?" I handed it to them. They huddled over it, read it, and reread it.

"Mein Gott, ich Himmel. Mein Gott, ich Himmel. This is unbelievable." Dave's dad shook his head. "I believe you must keep this close to you. It's your freedom." He handed me the letter, and I tucked it back in my backpack.

"You, my dear, you are family, and you will live with us," Mom said. "We always have room for more. Dave is still at his apprenticeship, but we will try to call him and let him know you are here. I know he would come home. Let me see now. We have my brother Håvard, Dave's brothers Kristian and Bjorn, and Aunt Lille. Oh yes, and we have two young boys from Oslo living with us. You know many farms are taking in city kids who don't have enough food. They will spend the winter with us. And we have the maid, the welder, and the farm workers who help with the farming. And sometimes we take in others who need shelter or food. Sometimes we have had up to sixteen around our table. But all are welcome here! We will find a room for you, too."

"How do you do it? How do you feed everybody? Does everyone here have a ration card? I've read that all meat, oats, and eggs need to be given to the German soldiers. Is this true?"

"Everyone here does not have a ration card because some are here without the Germans knowing. And, yes, it's true that the Germans take our food. They register and count everything and take what they want. We had a garden this summer and Dad has hidden potatoes, carrots, and onions in a hole underground so we have something for winter. We are careful with how we cook and how much we eat. But first, let's get you settled. Dad and I will find a spot. But first, let's try to call Dave."

The call went through. Some of the telephone lines in the area had been cut, but the call went through. "Boya? Where are you?"

"I'm at your parents' house. I can't tell you the story on the phone, but I will tell you when you get here. I'm no longer at the Vettakollen. Do you think you could come home?"

"Yes. Are you safe? I'll be home in a couple of days. Boya, be safe. I love you."

"I love you, too, Dave, and I want you home with me." I started to cry. "Hurry now and you be safe."

I was home, and I wanted to make this my home and not the farm in Stange with Bibben and Erling. I'd have to think about Eleanor and her future, but I knew I couldn't live with Bibben and Erling anymore even if Eleanor was still there with them. I needed to get to Arnes and then to Clara and her family in Hov.

I wanted to get to Arnes to visit with Anna's family. Arnes was just five kilometers from the

Eggum farm, and I knew I could ride my bike. And I had the Terboven letter for protection. I hoped Anna's family wouldn't ask why I was released. I visited with Dave's parents about this concern, and we decided I should not tell Anna's family why I was released.

"I don't know if they should know about Erling, about his involvement with the NS, about how he went to Terboven. I think I should say that I don't know why I was released. The most important news for them is where their daughter is right now."

Dave's parents agreed that I should say I didn't know why I was released, but they thought I should carry the letter with me in case I was stopped by German soldiers.

I rode my bike to Arnes a couple of days later, met Anna's family and told them about her and the conditions at Grini. They shook their heads and cried. They knew that she and her friend Edith had been taken, but they didn't know where they ended up. I could confirm that a few days ago they were at Grini. I took the Terboven letter, but Anna's family didn't ask why I was released. I left feeling bad that I was free while they had to deal with Anna's situation. I rode my bicycle back to the farm knowing that I had accomplished my mission and the letter would keep me safe. As I neared the farmyard, I spotted a tall, strong, broad-shouldered man standing by the house. Dave! I knew it was Dave! I pedaled faster calling his name, jumped off my bike and into his arms. I really was home now!

#

Early winter Dave decided to join the Norwegian Civil Service. We decided to go to Hov to see Clara and Ole and the kids before he had to report for duty. We realized that trying to get to Stange on this trip would be difficult as it included a much longer drive. We didn't want to ask Bibben and Erling to drive Eleanor to Hov. I wanted to tell Clara about my time in Grini and about my Terboven letter, so I didn't want to have Bibben and Erling there. So we made plans without a chance to see Eleanor.

It was exciting to see Clara and her family! Being at Vormsund with Dave and his family and then spending time with Clara and her family made me feel like I had two homes. I was at peace and felt comfortable even though a war was going on. Dave and I and Clara and Ole sat up late that first evening as I told them about my being arrested, taken to the Møllergata 19 and on to Grini, my time at Grini, and my release. I told them about Erling and the Terboven letter. They agreed that I should keep the letter but carry it with me only when necessary.

Then Clara announced that she had received a few letters from home and that Mama had apologized for not writing to all of us, but she thought we were all in a different place and didn't have addresses for Eleanor and me. She was right. I was in Kristiansund, Eleanor was in Stange, and Clara was in Hov. Then I was at Sandvika and then at the Vettakollen. How could Mama keep track of us. Clara said Mama and Dad were concerned about us when she'd learned that Norway had been invaded and that the Germans had taken over. She was sad that she had sent us to Norway, sad about the Depression and her inability to bring us home or to come and visit, and sad about our current lives in Norway. She had written that she was "helpless." Clara had written to Mama and Dad and told them about what was going on and where we all were. Then she handed me the most current letter.

October 1942

Dear Girls,

I hope this letter gets to all of you. Clara, maybe you can save it and share it with Borghild and Eleanor. It seems I'm always apologizing about not writing more often, and for that I am sorry. I love you all --- and Clara your whole family too. I wish I could meet Ole and my Norwegian grandchildren. Maybe some day we can all get together and tell each other about our lives. Maybe even hug each other and cry a little bit!!

I may have told you that Astrid moved and got a job as a riveter in the shipyards in Portland, Oregon. It's a good job. So many men enlisted when the US entered the war last December that women began to fill their jobs at home. Working as a riveter was one job, and now Astrid is a riveter. Margaret quit teaching and moved to Minot to marry Byron. Byron works on the railroad and won't be going into the military. They got married in June. Inez met a fellow, Ray, who became her steady boyfriend. She came home and told us she was pregnant. Dad wouldn't let her stay at home, so she and I took the train to Coeur d' Alene because Ray was there. Inez stayed there with him, and I went on to Portland to Astrid. I left Dad at home with Rolf, Signe, and Ingeborg.

It was good to be with Astrid. I got a job cleaning apartments during the day when Astrid was at work. This gave me a little money so I could help with expenses and save a bit. The Nesheims, remember them in Van Hook, well they had moved to Seattle, so after a couple of months, I left Portland and went to Seattle. I am in Seattle right now staying with the Nesheims. I love it here. It reminds me so of Norway. Mountains, the ocean, light breezes, some snow. It makes me lonesome for home. I think I may have to go home to Dad and tell him we should leave the prairie and move to Seattle. I guess I'll have to see what he says. President Roosevelt's New Deal was good for America during the Depression. It put people back to work and restored faith in the American system and gave us a sense of hope. I just don't know how long we should keep struggling as farmers. The weather is so unpredictable that it's not easy to make a living.

Anyway, I'll be headed back to Van Hook soon. Inez and Ray got married in Minot in September. Ray is in the military and had to leave, so Inez is staying with Margaret and Byron. I think she will have that baby soon.

I love you girls, miss you, and will write when I get home. Stay safe in the war.

Love, Mama

Sitting beside Clara was like sitting beside Mama. Clara was tall like Dad, but she had a voice like Mama and her arm felt cozy like Mama's. "Let's do the math, Clara," I said. "How old was Mama when you were born?"

"Let's see. Mama was born in 1894 and I was born in 1914. Mama was twenty. And if we left Van Hook in 1932, then Mama was 38. I was eighteen when we left Van Hook and you were eight. Eleanor was four."

My lips quivered; tears welling up in my eyes ran down my cheeks. I am eighteen and the same age Clara was when we were sent away. I have spent more than half of my life in Norway. And now I am engaged to be married to a Norwegian. Maybe I am a Norwegian? But I have an American passport. I guess I will be a Norwegian citizen when I marry Dave. Can I be a citizen of both countries? These were things I'd have to learn about. For now, I felt safe. I put my feet up on the coffee table, took hold of Dave's hand, and smiled at Clara. She smiled back, got up, and left Dave and me for some time to be alone.

Winter 1942

Chapter Twenty:
Vormsund, Norway

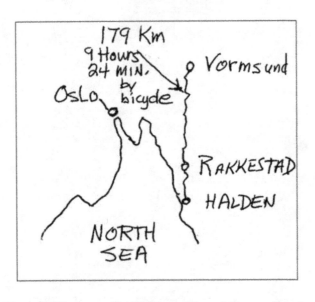

*Vormsund, a small village in Nes på Romerike, is
located fifty-four kilometers northeast of Oslo.
The Eggum farm is one of the farms in the Vormsund
area and is five kilometers from Arnes.*

The days seemed to fly by that winter. Dave's
orders took him to Halden about one hundred fifty
kilometers south of the farm. That's just far enough to
keep him from living at the farm, yet close enough

that I could get to see him. I wanted to keep busy, but I also wanted to be part of the family. I immersed myself into farm life helping with chores. Something was always going on. We cooked, cleaned, or wove fabric. We didn't have running water in the house, so we hauled water for drinking, cooking, or bathing. We either boiled water to wash some clothes or we took the clothes to the Åa laundry by horse and carriage.

A basic feeling of insecurity was always in the air. We kept our eyes open to see if any German soldiers were in the area. Some area farms had been invaded by the Germans; some of the neighbors were beaten and had their food and household supplies taken. We were lucky to still be unharmed; however, just like the others we had black-out curtains to make it difficult for German planes to orient themselves and find targets for bombs. Farm areas weren't necessarily bomb targets, but Vormsund isn't too far from the Swedish border. Bombings kept Norwegian citizens from trying to escape to Sweden. We were on standby ready to take shelter in case an air-raid siren blared.

Not everyone in the household knew Dave was part of the resistance movement. We kept it quiet that he had a smuggled radio and illegal newspapers hidden in the house. If the soldiers were to discover that, the farm would be a likely target. Regardless, his dad, mom, brothers, and I sneaked into the cellar to listen to the radio broadcasts. We shared whatever illegal papers we could get our hands on. We never spoke of these things in public.

Barb Solberg

We were all worried about the potential trouble at the heavy water factory in Rjuken, a small town about two and a half hours west of Oslo. Heavy water is used to produce nuclear power and weapons. It had been big news in the late thirties, that Norsk Hydro had built the first commercial heavy water plant and that Norsk Hydro shipped heavy water to scientists in Europe for physics, chemistry, and biomedical research. Germany was certainly interested in capturing that plant and making heavy water for use in a nuclear war. We all worried.

Christmas came and went. We had a small celebration, with a Christmas tree Dave's dad had cut in the forest. We didn't share gifts because going shopping was dangerous, and we didn't have the traditional meal because of all the rationing and the need to conserve food. Dave's mom had put up jam during the summer as a special treat for Christmas. The jam was sour because there was a lack of sugar, but it gave important vitamins we wouldn't be getting otherwise. We all shared the jam and layered it on our lefse!

Dave was able to come home on occasion, and we especially enjoyed the spring weather when we could go outside for walks in the countryside. I felt so secure when he was home. He watched out for me and shared some of what he did in his civil service duty. He rarely mentioned his participation in the resistance movement, but I knew that he was still involved. Then he'd have to report back to his camp. I always hated to see him go, but I knew that his service would be over come fall, so I kept looking ahead to that time.

I missed Dave but being with his family was a comfort. His mother was easy to talk to, but some things I had to keep in my heart. I worried about various issues, but I was especially worried when I missed my period. Now what? Am I working too hard hauling laundry? Am I being too cautious about eating right so there is food for others? Am I starving and it's affecting my health? Days went by. Nothing. I had to decide what to do. I knew I was pregnant. Dave was in Halden. I needed to get there to tell him before I said anything to anyone else and before I started to show. What should I say to his parents? I decided to discuss a visit to him with his parents, but I couldn't tell them about the pregnancy. I had to talk to Dave first.

We all agreed that the best transportation for me to Halden was my bicycle. But first I had to apply to the authorities to get a license to go to Halden. The authorities advised me to take the inner road through Trogstad, Mysen, to avoid the Germans. They also told me that I needed to go to the Halden police to get special permission to go to Idd Church where I had arranged to meet Dave. Dave's dad and I checked the maps and discovered the trip was about 140 kilometers. That meant about eight hours of pedaling, but I would have to stop to use the toilet and to eat. I knew I could do that trip. The late May weather was stable; trees had leaves, warm breezes filled the air, and the sun spent long hours warming the earth. If I left early in the morning, I could make the trip in one day. Hopefully, I wouldn't be stopped by any German authorities. I packed a large backpack with food and clothes. I hid the Terboven letter deep inside the backpack just in case.

"Be careful," Dave's mom and dad said. "We want you back!"

"I will be careful," I assured them. "I have so much to look forward to." And I got on my bicycle and pedaled down the road. I felt free in the middle of a war not just because I was out in nature and on my bike, but mostly because I had a secret weapon for safety --- the letter. I had plenty of time to think about that letter, about Erling, about Mrs. Quisling, about my safety. How could I thank them? Should I thank them? Was I a traitor because I had that letter? I tried to put these thoughts out of my mind. I didn't need to think about that now. Now I needed to think about being pregnant, telling Dave, discussing the future. What would Dave say? Would I go home to North Dakota or was Norway my home now? The miles quickly rolled behind me and by noon I was more than halfway to Halden, and the back roads I was on had no German soldiers. I was safe so far, and I was going to make it to Halden in one day. I knew the Halden police station would be open all night. I needed them to give me permission to go to the Idd Church to meet Dave and to contact Dave to meet me there. It was early evening when I arrived at the police station; they looked at the large backpack I was lugging and asked to see inside it. They wondered if I was escaping to

Sweden. I told them my story, and they gave me permission to go to the church. They also contacted Dave to tell him I was in Halden and on my way to the Idd Church.

I was exhausted but also exhilarated to see Dave. We fell into each other's arms and tears of joy ran down my cheeks. I was happy to be safe, happy to be with Dave, happy I hadn't been stopped by the German authorities, happy to share the news that we were going to have a baby, and happy that we could make some arrangements together. We agreed that we should get married as soon as possible. I would tell his parents, and he would arrange permission to get married. I left the next day to head back to the farm with one stop in Rakkestad to see a relative of Dave's mom. Two days later I pedaled into the farmyard.

Lots of conversation ensued about my trip, and when that ended, I told them why I went to Halden. "I am excited to tell you that Dave and I are getting married. You are going to be grandparents. You see, I am going to have a baby. Dave is getting permission to come home for a wedding, and we'd like you to help us with the arrangements."

Their eyes opened wide, and smiles spread across their faces. "Well, I'm not old enough to be a grandfather," Dave's dad said, "but I'm sure I'll work into that role!" He laughed and came over to give me a hug. Mom stood up, dusted her hands off on her apron, and said, "Well, my dear daughter-in-law, we better get busy making arrangements. How soon do you think we can get this together?"

"Because I'm an American citizen and considered a foreigner in Norway, the soreskriver in Sørumstand needs to provide the proper papers for me to get married. We would have the soreskriver marry us legally, and then we would go the priest's office in Arnes for a Christian blessing. We can make these arrangements as soon as we hear when Dave can get a leave."

"This sounds like a good plan," Mom said. "Let's have a nice wedding dinner after the marriage. We have some family here, and I'm sure you'd like to invite your sister and her family. What about Eleanor? What about Bibben and Erling?" We decided to invite them all.

The wedding was set for July 10, 1943. Dave's brother and his wife were our attendants. I was happy to be able to fit into my bunad, so we both wore our bunads. Dave's mother brought out her Norwegian bridal crown, a treasured family heirloom. It was made of silver and attached to a long veil. I was proud to wear it.

The rain poured down that day, but still there was joy in the air. Clara and Ole came to celebrate; Bibben, Erling and Eleanor did not come. We had a celebration dinner at the farm – much laughter and dancing. Dave's mom and I had made two traditional Norwegian wedding cakes: a Bløtkake which is a sponge cake filled with cream and topped with icing and fruit and the popular Kransekake, or a tower cake.

Now I had three families: Clara's family and Dave's family in Norway and our family in Van Hook. Dave's mom had both flags on the dinner table – the Norwegian flag and the American flag. This was the happiest day for me. I couldn't wait to write home and tell Mama and Dad and the family about Dave and our wedding. The bad news was that Vemork had been captured by the Germans. Germany now had heavy water.

Two days after the wedding, Dave had to report to a new station for the remainder of his civil service duty. He had to report to Tynset about three hundred kilometers north of Vormsund. I went with him to Arnes where he caught the train. It was a familiar trip to Arnes for me because that is where I'd catch the school bus when I was younger and living at Voyen. When we got to the train station, Dave was told to ride in the cow wagons because the Germans occupied the passenger wagons. I hoped he would be safe and write often. He wouldn't be back to the farm until he was discharged in the fall. It was going to be a long couple of months for me. I cried as I waved goodbye to the train and turned and headed back to the farm. Memories of waving to my family in Van Hook washed over me. I couldn't help but cry and wonder if I would ever get back to America again.

Clara and Ole had waited at the farm hoping that I would go home with them for a few days. I was happy to do so and quickly packed my bags. I wanted to talk with Clara about pregnancy and childbirth. Our sister relationship was changing!

When we got to Hov and their house, several newspapers and a letter from Mama were waiting. We were both anxious to read the letter from home; Clara quickly opened the letter.

July 1943

Dear Girls,

I hope this letter finds you all well. I also hope that if you aren't together, that Clara will save the letter and share it when she sees you. Perhaps you, Clara, could write and let me know where Borghild and Eleanor are so that I can write to them too.

I left Seattle and went home to Van Hook. I got home on April 1. It was good to be back and see Dad and Rolf, Signe, and Ingeborg. They seemed to do just fine when I was gone. I told Dad that I wanted to move to Seattle because it is just like Norway. He agreed to sell the land and move the family to Seattle. I'm not sure when all this will happen, but I hope soon. I think Rolf may decide to stay in Van Hook. He's already seventeen and has friends here. He could finish the school year here. But Signe is just thirteen and Ingeborg is just eleven, so they should come with us. I'll let you know when we make that decision.

Prices have picked up here the last few years. I think the war effort is part of the reason. That could mean that farming would be better, but we have worked so hard and suffered so through the Depression. I think it's time to move on. We aren't getting any younger, and hard work is not easy. Dad is now fifty-three and shows signs of hard work. I too have worked hard. We could find jobs in Seattle, and several of our friends from Van Hook have sold and moved to Seattle. I think you girls would like it there. Perhaps we can all get together there in the next few years.

Greet Birgit for me and thank her for caring for you these past years. I'll write again when we make some decisions.

Love Mama

"Can you believe this? Seattle? I'm not sure where that is. Let's look on the map and see where that is." Clara went to her dresser and brought out a map of the United States. "Seattle is on the other side of the country. Look here, Boya. It's by the Pacific Ocean. That's a long way from Van Hook!"

"I'm happy for Mama," I said. "If she's found a place she likes that reminds her of her home in Norway and they can find work there, then I think it's a good idea."

"Maybe they'll be able to make enough money to come to Norway and see us," Clara said. "I'll bet that trip would cost a lot of money. And they still have the two little girls to raise."

"Poor Mama. She's been raising kids since she left Norway. Have you ever counted how many there are?"

Clara laughed out loud. "Oh yes, Boya. When I had our second – Astri - , I did count how many Mama had. Eleven of us except Christine died. Do you remember that? And now I have three kids. Uffda for Mama. "

"Yes, I remember the baby dying. Mama wrote to us about that. Eleanor pretended to have a baby and had funerals most of one year. She played Mama most of the time. But I hardly remember Mama. Sometimes I feel like I don't have a mother. I've been away for eleven years now." Tears rolled down my cheeks. "Do you think I'll ever see her again? Or Dad? I don't even know the two little girls. And now I barely see Eleanor. All our other sisters have moved all over. I think only Rolf is still in Van Hook. What a life we've had!"

It was so good to be with Clara and Ole. Ole worked as the municipal treasurer in Hov and quietly continued his work with the resistance movement. Both Ole and Dave were secretive about their involvement and their work, so if the Germans came to our house, the rest of us would not have anything to share. It wasn't strange for one or both to be called out in the night for some kind of mission. As the war progressed the resistance movement became stronger. Ole spent lots of time in his potato bin sending messages. We worried about them, but we trusted them and were proud to have them fighting for Norway.

Clara and Ole read the Hov-to-Odnes area newspaper so that she could keep up with whatever was happening. I asked Clara "Do you ever read about that fellow from Odnes that was in your class?" I don't know what made me remember him, but he was curious to me.

"Interesting that you ask," Clara said. "I saw an obituary in the paper for a Johanne Walle, and it said her only surviving relative was a son, Helge, who lives in Odnes. She died on June 10. The obituary didn't say if she was ever married, but it did say that she worked most of her life at the Odnes Hotel."

"Ah…do you think she may have known Dad? He worked at that hotel, didn't he?"

"Yes, I recall him saying that he worked there. I wish I had known this. I would have talked to her when I was there. I guess that's not possible now! Maybe we'll run into her son sometime."

"I don't think he'd know Dad, do you? I think Dad left Norway when he was about twenty. Isn't that guy about your age?'

"I think so. At least close in age. Maybe we'll run into him sometime when we go to Odnes. We'll need to remember this."

We busied ourselves with her kids and cooking, gardening, visiting. Clara had some fabric and she helped me sew a few maternity clothes. She parted with some of hers, but she thought she may keep a few just in case she got pregnant again. The time went by too quickly, and soon I had to return to Vormsund.

Dave was discharged from his service in the fall of 1943, and I was so happy to have him back home. My months of pregnancy were passing quickly, and although Dave's parents were outstanding and I enjoyed their company, having Dave home made me feel more secure. Dave's mom gave me old sheets to sew baby clothes for our soon-to-be little one. This kept me busy. Dave was at home most of the time, but he was secretly away as well. He couldn't tell me where he was going, but sometimes in the late evening, he left the house. It was on those nights that I had difficulty sleeping and worried so about his safety. I assumed that he participated in resistance missions.

Christmas came and went just like the other war years. We were able to celebrate the holiday with a scaled down celebration - - not all the foods, not all the gifts, not all the family celebrations. We did have a Christmas tree that Dave cut down, and with the traditional candle lights on it, it felt festive. We learned that King Haakon was expected to deliver a Christmas message over the BBC, and we were anxious to listen to that broadcast. We shared the stories we had heard about his escape to London, how the crown jewels were not taken from Norway but were hidden somewhere, and how King Haakon VII continued to love and care for our country while he was in exile with his son Crown Prince Olav. We gathered around the radio as Dave tuned in the BBC.

When we heard King Haakon's voice, we all held hands while some cried.

Dear Countrymen: It is long since I last spoke to you and now that Christmas is here again, I would like to take the opportunity of sending you all a greeting.

First of all I want to thank you for the fight you have waged ceaselessly for Norway's cause, and for your faith in the justice of this cause which filled you with strength to continue resistance in spite of all the kinds of tyranny to which our enemies resorted.

My heart bleeds when I think of all those who have lost their dear ones as a result of war, and when I think of the anxiety suffered by those who have members of their families or relations in prisons at home or abroad.

All of us working over here for our country are filled with admiration for your unflinching resistance. The sacrifices you are constantly offering on the altar of our mother country are a great encouragement to us and spur us on to continue the work.

Conditions at home have deteriorated year by year but your unquenchable resistance has shown our enemies there is one aim for which we will never cease fighting – our freedom and independence...

The progress of the war makes us entitled to believe that we are now approaching the end, even if we must still be prepared for losses and great sacrifices. But we who are aware of the enormous resources of our allies do not for one minute doubt that in the end our cause will triumph...

I am not able in a Christmas greeting to include all those who are in my thoughts, but of all those away from home we will in the first instance remember our seamen who perhaps more than any others feel the loss of Christmas at home and who courageously and loyally brave all dangers and bring glory to Norway's name, who by sailing all the seas show the whole world that Norway's flag still flies freely.

Wishing you a Merry Christmas and a Good New Year I conclude with the traditional words, "God save our Motherland!"

Dad went to the cupboard and took out a big jar of homemade liquor. He poured each of us a short glass of the heimkok; we clinked our glasses with a toast to our King and Norway's future. Mom led us in singing the Norwegian National Anthem followed *by O Holy Night.* Our conversations revolved around two topics: the possibility of the war coming to an end and the reality of the upcoming birth of our baby. We were all anxious to have a new little one to give our attention to. The wait ended on January 21, 1944, when our little girl, Ragnhild Eggum, was born.

I wanted to share all this with my own mama. I wanted to tell her I'm a mother and she is a grandmother. I wanted to tell her how cute my little girl is. I wanted to share this experience with her, but I've heard that sometimes now, due to the war, the mail takes six months to be delivered. I don't know where my mama lives now since her last letter said she wanted Dad to move to Seattle. Where are they?

#

The last couple of war years in Norway were a real struggle. Oslo was headquarters for the German armored division, so our trips to Oslo were only for emergencies. Norway had been a neutral country in WWI and had hoped to stay neutral in this war. But as Germany swept north, Denmark and Norway were attacked and now Germany controlled both Denmark and Norway. Huge military tanks roam the roads to intimidate us and fill us with fear. Always questions like *Will the German patrol allow passage through the identification stations? Will I be stopped and tortured by the police?* In addition to the tanks in Oslo, German infantry divisions can be found throughout Norway and their strength is overwhelming. The sounds of German army boots marching through cities and villages instills terror and panic in all of us. Often the soldiers enter homes and simply take whatever they want including food and blankets. Residents hand over their limited amount of food and are happy if they aren't terrorized, beaten, or shot. Consequently, people are anxious and starving, and the nation's health is suffering. I've read in the underground papers that after Germany occupied Norway, the daily caloric intake of the average Norwegian went from 2,500 calories down to only 1,500 a day. And now four years into the war, the average Norwegian can find only enough food for 1,237 calories a day.

#

The underground newspapers reported on activity at the Vemork hydroelectric plant. Germany controls the plant, and the British Special Operations Executive's mission (SOE) to destroy the plant to keep the Germans from engaging in nuclear warfare has had some failures. Operation Grouse dropped four men into the area to provide intelligence on October 18, 1942. Just one month later, two British gliders carrying thirty-four commandos who were to destroy the plant crashed; all survivors were shot. Another attempt, Gunnerside, on February 28, 1943, dropped six new agents to join the four dropped in 1942; they were successful in destroying important equipment. The next attempt by Allied aircraft dropped more than 400 bombs on the facility on November 16, 1943, causing partial damage. The Germans continued to control heavy water. So much of the talk around the dinner table is about heavy water and what could happen. No one feels the end of the war is imminent.

The Norwegian civil resistance has had some great triumphs, but the country seems exhausted. Farmers store and hide as much garden produce as they can to help survive the winters. Many farming families have taken in young, starving children from Oslo. These same farmers serve in the resistance movement. Many have built mountain cabins used for resistance training, storing of munitions, and housing for resistance soldiers. Many operate illegal short-wave radios sending to and receiving messages from the SOE in Britain. Many leave covertly in the night for secret missions. Nothing seems safe. Everyone is hungry. Blackout shades are pulled down in the evenings so German planes can't identify places to bomb. It is a dark time.

The general Norwegian public did not know what was going on with the heavy water plant, but word was that after the last attack, the Germans made plans to move the heavy water to Germany. Heavy water would be put on a ferry boat that crosses Lake Tinnsjø, the deepest lake in Europe, and moved on to Germany. On February 20, 1944, the world cheered the news that the ferry boat carrying heavy water from the Vemork factory across Lake Tinnsjø and on to Germany was sunk and the heavy water drowned. The battle for heavy water on Norwegian soil ended. I read that the Norwegian Resistance Movement was instrumental in this success, and I was excited to read this to Dave. He looked at me, grinned, and nodded "yes." I wondered if he or Ole had been part of that operation.

Then word came that the Allies were preparing for final and decisive attacks against the Germans. On June 6, 1944, the Allied forces invaded northern France through beach landings in Normandy. The Norwegian resistance, now more organized than ever, was on constant alert and readiness. The tide was beginning to turn. It was becoming clearer that Germany was losing the war. How long would it take?

We wanted to celebrate. I wanted to see Clara and her family. I wanted to share my little girl with my sister. But we were not free to move about as we wished. It was still too dangerous to take a chance especially with a small child. We stayed home. I missed the birth of Clara's fourth child on June 29 --- Maia.

#

On December 26, 1944, and against the rules forbidding gatherings without government permission, we had friends over and decided to arrange for sleigh rides on New Year's Eve. We called friends, family, and neighbors from all over Norway to invite them to a great party. We planned to use thirteen horses with toboggans, to keep warm in sheep skins, and to carry torches. Everyone was to bring some food, some type of replacement for coffee since coffee was rationed, and moonshine since liquor was forbidden.

Our farm boys accompanied me to Oslo to pick up Arne Lie, a twenty-three-year-old actor, and an opera dancer/singer and her mother. From our neighboring area came four fiddlers and their ladies, all relatives of Dave's dad. We met at the Eggum farm and divided ourselves into the different toboggans hooked up to horses. A friend, Johan Mustad from Voyen, brought his own riding horse, carried a torch, and covered himself with a large Norwegian flag. This was all quite illegal.

The weather that night was bitterly cold, but the moonlight sparkled on the snow and in the trees. An accordionist pushing and pulling the bellows while fingering the buttons and keys rode in the lead toboggan while an opera singer's strong mezzo soprano voice coming from the middle of the parade lead the singing. The music was invigorating. Norwegian folk songs, Christmas carols, national anthems. All our voices carried cheer through the valley. Mom and Dad Eggum welcomed everyone back into the warm farmhouse complete with a tasty smorgasbord. We danced all night! We agreed to have a similar party next New Year's Eve!

We ushered in 1945 with great success, and at the same time we were anxious about the continued attacks the Allies were planning. The BBC announced SOE airdrops at 7:00 pm and 11:00 pm in coded messages like "the dog is on the roof" or "lions are ferocious." Dave knew what each message meant. An airdrop consisted of several parachutes containing arms, radio equipment, and supplies dropped for the secret army units staged in Norway. Local resistance members moved to the drop area, secured the supplies, and stored them in outhouses, barns, and various hiding places in the area. Years after the war we learned that Ole, Clara's husband, had been part of the February 23, 1945, pickup from a drop in Sondre Land. A Canadian pilot from Saskatoon, Canada, - Harry Wilkie - dropped 2.5 ton of materials near Hov to be used during the liberation days in 1945.

During this winter and despite the war, Dave built a house that included a basement and second and third floors. Dave and I and Ragnhild moved in! We had running water but no water heater. I heated water in a large boiler to do laundry. Diapers and baby clothes were boiled by themselves, then I'd change the water and boil the white clothes, then the colored clothes, and lastly the work clothes! In the spring, summer, and fall, I could hang the clothes outside, but in the cold of winter, I'd hang them around the house. It took more than one day to do the laundry. All this while the war continued and little Ragnhild learned to crawl and walk and talk! She was such a joy and a relief from war worries.

On May 1, 1945, mid-morning, Dave hollered for me to come quickly to our hidden radio. I grabbed Ragnhild and down the stairs we ran.

The BBC broadcast a newsflash:

"This is London calling. Here is a newsflash. The German radio has just announced that Hitler is dead. I repeat that. The German radio has just announced that Hitler is dead."

We gathered around the radio to listen to the news. Almost as quickly as it started, the war ended! The BBC news flashes came like a falling row of dominoes; one event set off a chain of similar events. Hitler committed suicide on April 30; he shot himself in the head. Soon after, on May 7, Germany unconditionally surrendered to the Allied forces in Europe. When Josef Terboven heard the announcement of Germany's surrender, he detonated a 50 kg of dynamite in a bunker hideout on the Skaugum compound and blew himself up. The war officially ended on May 8th, and on May 11, Norwegian loyalists arrested Vidkun Quisling and his aides for treason. Quisling surrendered and was imprisoned at Mollergata 19. By May 11, the resistance forces had taken back control of Akershus Fortress in Oslo and had raised the Norwegian flag! On June 7 King Haakon VII returned to Norway. The streets in Oslo and around the Royal Palace heralded a party atmosphere. The occupation was over, and constitutional life could function normally for the first time in five years. The long process of reconstruction could begin.

Trials for those accused of committing war crimes began. Erling Moe Bernsten's pharmacy license was suspended on June 19th for his involvement with the NS. Around 50,000 other Norwegians who had been members of the Nasjonal Samling, were found guilty of treason; twenty-five were executed.

In August, the trial for Quisling began. "I have in all my thoughts and deeds been led by a love for the Norwegian people," he said during the trial. He was sentenced to death for crimes of high treason. His appeals were rejected. During the early hours of October 24th, Quisling, dressed in a white sweater and gray knickerbockers, was brought to the grounds of the Akershus Fortress. A doctor pinned a white target over Quisling's heart. Quisling was blindfolded and bound to a temporary wooden wall. The firing squad took its place; Quisling was the target.

#

Dave and I were ecstatic. The war was over, his work with the resistance was over, and I was pregnant again. We were happy that our second child would not be born in a war-torn country. "I suggest we make a trip to Hov to see Clara and Ole and their kids," Dave said. "I'll go to Stange and get Eleanor so we can all be together."

I so wanted to see my sisters and thoughts of this trip filled my heart. We made plans to go. I called Eleanor, who, by now, was seventeen years old. I had missed so much of her life and wanted to catch up. She was thrilled to know that Dave would drive to Stange to get her. Erling had gone to Kristiansund, and Eleanor was alone with Bibben. We decided it best not to take Bibben to Hov with us.

The reunion was glorious. Hugging. Talking. Laughing. Bouncing our children --- all 5 of them – four of Clara's and one of mine – on our knees. We talked about how they reminded us of our brother and sisters at home. Cute little towheads with rosy cheeks and happy smiles. We didn't know our sisters and our brother as adults, so our remembrance was when they were kids. Our kids quickly warmed up to Tante Eleanor. Clara managed quite a smorgasbord, and Ole had saved a few bottles of moonshine just for the occasion! We were a family – an American family but now also a Norwegian family. Clara set the US and the Norwegian flags on the table. We sang both national anthems.

PART THREE:
ONE FAMILY – TWO FLAGS

April 1942

Chapter Twenty-One:
Van Hook, North Dakota

Asta leaned across the kitchen table in the Van Hook farmhouse and took hold of Martin's hands. Looking straight into his eyes, she said, "Martin, it's time to leave here." She paused. "It's time to leave Van Hook for a better life." Martin looked down for a few seconds and then looked at his wife's aging hands and tired face and took a long deep breath then exhaled. Asta waited before she added, "We have tried to make a go of it here, Martin, but it's no use. We are no further ahead now than when we got here thirty years ago."

Martin paused and then cautiously said, "Well, yes and no, Asta. It hasn't been easy, but we have survived and raised several children who are doing well. We still have three at home here to raise. We have fully paid our debt to Peter. But you are right. It hasn't been easy. But we do have friends and memories here."

"Remember what you told me years ago, Martin, when you told me about your son in Norway? You said, 'sometimes you need to leave things behind.' Well, Martin, it is time to leave Van Hook behind. I've been to Seattle and it is lovely --- so much like Norway. Come with me, Martin, move to Seattle. We have Van Hook friends who packed up and left here and are now part of a large Norwegian community in Seattle, and there we will find our old friends and meet new friends. Lots of work there, too, Martin. Work in the defense industry. Work where you get a check without worries about rain and wind. Come with me, Martin. Let's move to Seattle."

Martin hung his head and sighed a long-suffering, spiritless sigh. He buried his face in his hands, scratched his head, slowly reached down and squeezed Asta's hands and then he broke the silence. "Yes," he shook his head, "yes, Asta, you are right. We have both worked hard. You are a wonderful partner in all this. I don't think we failed. So many things got in the way. The weather, the Depression, the war. We do deserve the chance to finish our lives with a regular income – a check each month. And you, Asta, deserve to live where you'd like."

"Oh Martin," Asta smiled, got up from the table and put her arms around him. "I don't think we have failed. But I do think Seattle is just like home --- the fjords, mountains, and forests back home. Oh Martin, it's beautiful and there are lots of jobs in defense, in fishing and in construction. An area in Seattle called Ballard has many Scandinavians. Let's do this, Martin. Let's sell the farm and take the kids to a new land. I'm going, Martin. I don't have any more patience for this prairie. I want us to go to Seattle. Won't you come along?"

Martin's deep breath and contemplative look gave Asta pause. She waited for him to respond. Then finally, "You have probably heard the rumors just as I have, Asta. Rumors suggesting a dam might be built somewhere around here and the powers that be will flood this area. I've seen surveyors all around here. Nothing in writing, but we could possibly lose this land anyway."

"I've heard those rumors, Martin. I've thought about them, but I've mostly thought about taking a chance on a new life. Give something pleasant to the kids we still have at home."

Martin and Asta reviewed their family. Asta said it all out loud, "Clara, Borghild, and Eleanor have probably made Norway their home. Clara married a Norwegian and they have a family. Borghild and Eleanor virtually grew up as Norwegians. Borghild was eight and Eleanor was only four when they left here, and that was ten years ago. Now Norwegian teenagers. How tragic that they are experiencing German occupation. Ruth is married. Astrid works in Portland but plans to move to Seattle. Margaret and Inez made lives of their own. Just Rolf, Signe, and Ingeborg at home, and Rolf is almost sixteen."

"Let's think more about this, Asta. Let's think about how our friends did this. Perhaps we can come up with a plan. A move may take some time since we'd need to deal with the kids, the house and farmland, and the move. One step at a time, I guess."

"I think the kids here are old enough to be part of this conversation, Martin, don't you?"

"Ja, Asta, I think so."

Conversations about moving to Seattle occupied much of their family time. Martin and Asta emphasized how they made decisions. They talked about how they decided to leave Norway for the United States and what a journey that had been. They recalled how they decided to send the three girls to Norway and what a journey that has been. Both journeys were meant to create a better life. Now they faced a new journey, a new horizon, and hope for a better life.

The girls, Signe and Ingeborg, were hesitant, but after several discussions about the benefits of moving to Seattle, they warmed up to the idea saying it might be exciting to live in a city. Just thinking they'd have some money and life by water and mountains made it attractive. Enough of the wind and the prairie. Enough of dry years running on hope that the next year would be better. Rolf would stay in Van Hook, tend the farm, and go to school. He turned seventeen in May and at age eighteen he'd need to register with Selective Service and would probably join the army.

Asta's mind was consumed by two issues: the upcoming move and the need to contact her daughters in Norway. No letters had been received from them for several months, and Asta was not certain if they were okay. She wasn't even sure about Borghild and Eleanor's living situations although she was quite certain that Clara and Ole had put roots down in Hov. Determined to make contact, she reached out to the American Red Cross regarding the sending of a civilian message. It was possible, but the delivery of the message would take a back seat to any military message to POWs and their families. These messages were restricted to twenty-five words and had to be about family news only. All messages were sent to the International Red Cross headquarters in Geneva from there they were sent on to their respective destinations. She decided to send the telegram.

Asta provided the message: "Hello girls --- Just to let you know we are not forgetting you and hope all is well. Ruth, Marg and Inez all married. All well. Mother." And sent the message to Clara in Hoviland on October 29, 1942.

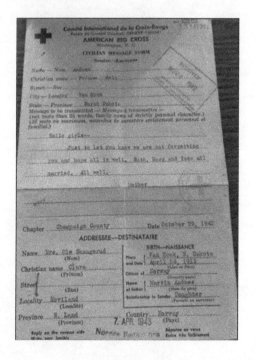

In August 1943, Martin closed his savings account, took the cash, loaded the car, and pointed it westward. Asta packed sandwiches, crackers, cookies, and cheese into a traveling icebox.

Rolf waved goodbye to his family as they drove out of the farmyard. Martin, Asta, Signe and Ingeborg waved back and headed west, once again leaving some things behind.

August 1943-1947

Chapter Twenty-Two:
Seattle, Washington

Montana's miserable August heat made the four-day trip to Seattle seem long. Stopping at a roadside creek in Idaho gave relief to the girls as they threw off their clothes and jumped in. Laughter, cool breezes, and a picnic provided just the psychological lift the four needed. Dried off and refreshed, they climbed back into the car and drove into what looked more like Norway at each turn. Asta grinned and talked and talked and talked about Seattle, about fjords, and about mountains. "We're heading for home," she giggled.

"Seattle is just like home. Just think, we'll see some of our old friends soon. Maybe we can find a house in Ballard!"

Halvor and Orma Nesheim, old Van Hook friends now living in Ballard, were excited to greet them, invited them to stay, and set out a hearty, Norwegian feast of smoked fish, cheese, lefse, pickled herring, fattigmand, and rommegrot. Halvor shared valuable information about the area, jobs and places to live.

Within a couple of weeks, Martin bought a three-bedroom house for $1600 on a contract for deed with a down payment of $1100 and the remainder of $500 plus interest to be paid later. He found work in the

shipyards supplementing family income with freelance jobs. Asta swept the Boeing wind tunnel, Signe, pitched in at home cooking and cleaning. Ingeborg, just eleven, was happy when everyone got home in the evening. Martin and Asta felt quite settled by the middle of October. They were close to comfortable in "little Norway."

Martin in front of the Nickerson house

\#

Soon they realized that the war had an impact on probably every community in the United States. Applications for ration cards for various commodities including gasoline, butter, sugar, meat, dairy, coffee, dried fruits needed to include an address for the applicant. Ration cards would be sent by mail on July 21, 1943. Martin and Asta were between addresses during the application period so initially they did not have ration cards, hence no commodities. They had some money, but they couldn't purchase the goods available only through ration cards. Asta had never wasted food, so her prudence in the kitchen and with leftovers allowed her to provide meals until their ration cards arrived.

"Martin! Just think. We have done it again. We left Van Hook for a better life, and it's okay that we sacrifice now for the sake of the war. We are not starving, and we made the move. I'm so happy, Martin, in spite of it all. We know how to work hard, and here we are in 'little Norway' living and working side by side with our friends. I knew I couldn't stay on the prairie any longer. I love you, Martin, and thank you for joining me here." A wide grin flashed over Martin face. "We each get a check every two weeks, Martin. We have no worries about money now. We aren't rich, but we are rich in soul and spirit."

Martin took her hands in his as a tear rolled down his cheek. "You made a good decision for us, Asta. You made a good decision. *Å være midt i smørøyet. (We are in a good place.)* Now if we could just hear from our girls in Norway. I've heard that the mail isn't reliable during the war, and Germany is in control of Norway. Pray God that they are safe."

Asta found paper and pencil and sat down at her kitchen table. Deep in thought, she wrote a list of her children in chronological order including where they lived. She looked up, smiled, and thought of the last two girls who were still with her and Martin. They should know the names and particulars of their siblings. She recalled that Signe was just three when the girls left for Norway, and Ingeborg was not yet born. This list should be helpful to them as well.

Clara – now 29 – married to Ole – lives in
Norway —3 children – Per, Astrid, Anne
Ruth – now 28 – married to Ray – lives in
Minneapolis –
Astrid – now 25 – lives in Seattle
Margaret – now 23 – married to Byron – lives
in North Dakota
Inez – now 21 – married to Ray --- lives with
Margaret and Byron – 1 child – LesLee
Borghild – now 19 – lives in Norway
Rolf – now 17 – lives in Van Hook
Eleanor – now 15 – lives in Norway
Signe – now 14
Ingeborg – now 9

She taped the list to the cupboard so Signe and
Ingeborg can get to know their sisters. Tears rolled
down her cheeks as she realized she had children who
didn't know each other, and she had grandchildren she
had not yet held. How could she ever make up for this
lost time? Could she and Martin ever afford to bring
their Norwegian girls home? Could she and Martin
afford to visit Norway? Would she ever again see her
parents or her brothers and sisters? Perhaps they had
passed away and she hadn't heard the news. She was
happy to be in Seattle, her new Norway with fjords
and mountains, but she had missed so much. And she
missed her family – her kids in Norway.

"Why don't you write to them once a month and
ask them to return a note," Martin said. "They don't
know our new address here in Seattle and they should.

Let's make another chart so we can check off when the monthly letter is sent and then record when we get one back."

Asta liked the idea. She had just a few cards to write: Ruth, Rolf, Margaret and Inez, and Clara. Clara would share it with the other two girls. And Signe and Ingeborg were with them.

October 29, 1943

Dear kids,

> *We have moved to Seattle. Rolf is in Van Hook. Astrid is not far from us. We have a 3-bedroom house, and you are all welcome to come to see us. Dad and I have jobs – dad in the shipyard and I'm at Boeing. Here's our address... 332 W. Nickerson. Seattle, WA. Please write back and send pictures if you can. Here's a picture of me and the girls.*

Love Mor

Soon letters arrived from Ruth, Margaret & Inez, and Rolf. Things seemed quite well with those four. Months passed, however, with no word from Norway. Asta continued to write to Clara hoping to hear how the girls were doing. She thought perhaps her worrying caused her to feel sick most of the time. She noticed she had wounds that healed slowly, she felt fatigue, she was losing weight but was hungry all the time. She asked a friend for the name of a doctor. Her appointment revealed that she had diabetes. This meant a diet change, a life routine of blood sugar testing with the daily "dip and read" urine tests, and subsequent insulin shots. The doctor advised her to carry her insulin and testing supplies with her to work in case she wouldn't get home. He also advised that she keep a month's supply of insulin since during war time shipping was often interrupted. The best foods for a diabetic, he said, were meat, fish, eggs, cheese but stay away from starch. The very foods she was advised to eat were on the rationing list, difficult to get, and expensive. Blood sugar levels took on a new meaning for her. Now her worries included not only her kids in Norway but also her health.

Eighteen months passed with no word from Norway. One day Martin brought home two **Nordisk Tindende** newspapers one of the guys at the shipyard shared with him. Just looking at articles written in Norwegian gave Asta comfort. She quickly noticed the second page headlines: **Norway's Postal Service Impacted by WWII**. Her mouth dropped open in surprise as she read that twenty-four Norwegian postal ships were sunk along the Norwegian coast and forty-nine officials were killed in the line of duty.

"Martin," she shouted. "Come here. Did you read this?" she showed him the article. "Do you suppose our girls either aren't getting my letters or their letters aren't getting here? Or maybe both?"

"This could be an answer to your worries, my dear. I don't think the girls would not write home. I have both read and heard that since the United States got involved, Germany has retreated in many places. I don't know about the Pacific Front, but I do know that bombing raids on German cities are increasing and that British and American troops have crossed the Rhine. Just hang on, Asta, I think this war is ending and we will hear from our girls."

They looked at each other, tears rolling down their cheeks, yet excited at the thought of hearing from their girls in Norway. Martin, a big man, picked Asta off her chair and danced her around the kitchen. Signe and Ingeborg came running down the stairs when they heard their mother's shouts of joy!

"What is this?" Signe asked. "Have you two gone nuts? Did we hear from our sisters?"

"Not yet," Martin told her. "But just you wait. We will real soon." And he danced Signe around the kitchen and then went for Ingeborg. Tears. Laughter. Hugging. Excitement.

"To think that we might be a family sometime. Wouldn't that feel good?" Asta's twinkling eyes and broad closed smile brought everyone to tears. They hadn't had this much joy in years. This was a great day!

Asta's dream of having some of her family around was coming true when Ruth called to say that since her husband was away with the Army, she and her one-year-old daughter would love to take the train to Seattle in April. Could they really come and stay for a while?

Asta's dreams were coming true. She would have some of her children with her and with them came grandchildren. Ruth's husband was serving in the US Army but so was Asta's only son, Rolf, who was stationed nearby at Fort Lewis, Washington. Could Rolf's wife stay with Martin and Asta? Oh, and by the way, Rolf's wife is expecting! Asta would hold some of her grandchildren.

January 1946 - October 1947

Chapter Twenty-Three:

Norway

The New Year's celebration last year had been so fun that the family hoped to repeat it this year. It brought everyone back together. Even though food was still scarce and employment opportunities were tough, enough had occurred to make the celebration important. The war was over, the Germans were gone, friends could gather without fear, and very slowly food was appearing on the store shelves. Time to celebrate the new year and Norway's liberation.

As many family and friends as possible gathered early on New Year's Day at the Eggum farm in Vormsund to share hugs, food, mulled wine, singing, dancing, and sleigh riding. Strong, calm horses with thick winter coats pulled the sleighs steadily through the snow-laden forest with bells jingling on their harnesses and torchlights guiding their way. Breaking the charm and wonder of the beautiful snow scene, rousing choruses of *Ja, Vi Elsker* and *Norge i rødt, hvitt og blått* filled the air expressing love of their homeland. Norwegian flags waved in the air and on the sleighs! Freedom.

Clara and Ole and their five kids joined from Hov. Boya, pregnant with their second child, and Dave and their daughter joined the celebration. Eleanor came from Stange. The eleven together with Dave's parents and their neighbors created quite a gathering. There was laughter, there was singing and dancing, there was eating. The party in the midnight sun went on for hours and rang in 1946. Sharing the celebration with Eleanor added an extra element of joy, and Boya was happy to learn that Eleanor planned to stay with them for a few weeks. Certainly she would be around when Boya gave birth.

In the late evening hours, Eleanor announced to her sisters that she was making plans to go to America to meet her family. "I am homesick," she said, "and I don't even really know them. I was so young when I was sent to Norway, and I want to go back. I'm going to look into the possibility for me to do so." The other two girls hugged her and encouraged her go home to see her parents and the sisters closest to her.

Boya celebrated with the best of them until she had to call it a night. Her second child was due any day and Boya needed rest. Dave took her and one-year old Raghnild home shortly after midnight. Two weeks later their second daughter was born. Happy to be together with her family, Eleanor stepped into the role the older girls remembered belonged to their sister Ruth, and Boya shared stories of how Ruth had cared for the young ones and helped around the house.

Clara wanted to see her sisters and the new baby. Ole agreed to drive Clara and the kids to Boya and Dave's house. Tucked in Clara's purse was a letter from home and with the letter was a picture of their mother and their two little sisters, Signe and Ingeborg.

Seattle, Wash, Jan 4th, 1946

Dearest Clara & familie, Borghild & familie,

Guess you are wondering why you don't hear from us, and I'm really ashamed about how careless it seems. I left all the letter writing to Ruth and Signe, but now Ruth has left and Signe is so busy and almost never home, so guess I'll have to get a letter written myself. It was so good to receive your and Borghild's letter on Xmas Eve – felt you were not so far away from us. Rolf was home too – he was lucky he was stationed at Fort Lewis, Washington, for six months. He had to join the army in November and first went to Fort Snelling, Minneapolis, before he came out here. He is also so homesick and was lucky because now he can come home almost every Sunday. His wife and little son, born 16 Dec, are coming out in a couple of weeks and will stay with us as long as Rolf is out here. Guess they look forward to that – they are just kids, but maybe it is just as good they get married and settle down. She is Norwegian – related to the Reisches in Van Hook – a kind and nice girl and a lot of fun.

...

8 Jan

Just home from work and found M. Westby's family picture in the mailbox- all of them good looking and nice to get. We are – all of us living in this house – gone during the day. I leave at 7 in the morning, Martin 7:30, Signe and Ingeborg leave for school right after. I'm the first one to get home, 4 o'clock, then Ingeborg and Martin. I have coffee ready for them when they get here. Signe goes to work right after school and doesn't come home before 7:30. So now you see our timetable, washing clothes, ironing and clean the house when we can. I have been working at a restaurant since we moved here 2 years ago.

Signe has also had a job after school the whole time. Martin has worked in the shipyard, so time goes so fast. Ingeborg went to see Inez in Montana last summer and Signe and I left in August and we all spent almost a month in Van Hook. The girls were so homesick for their friends and the farm, but after coming back to Seattle they seem to like it better here. We still have the farm, but when Rolf joined the army, Eugene Thomas started to rent it. Do you remember him, Clara – he's married to the youngest of the Reisch's girls – believe they were in Ruth's class. Don't think we will move back to ND. Martin likes living in Seattle and the weather too. Now it has been raining for the last three months though. Ruth came out in April last year and stayed with us that summer until Ray got out of the army. Now they live in Minneapolis where his family is staying.

This is almost like old days --- writing and receiving letters to you and from you. Over the last years we have been wondering and wishing you were back here. As for me, I think USA is the best country I can think of. Living in ND for 30 years was just difficult. We would still be there if I had not decided to go West. Three years ago Inez and I traveled out here – she was going to Idaho to see her sick husband and I joined here. I was allowed to be gone for two weeks, but I kept on to Portland, Oregon, and worked there for three months before going home. From then on I was finished with the farm and all the bad years.

Since then the farmers around Van Hook have had good crops and become well-to-do. A big dam is also being built – it will take ten years and give a lot of people work. Missouri River from Garrison to Stanley and 1000 farmhouses will be under water. Our farm will be flooded but Wales' farm will not be so the railroad will go there. They are starting this spring. There will be a lot of jobs here for the next 2 – 3 years- and if you can come over I'm sure there will be plenty of work. Nobody knows what is going to happened in the future. Right now we have strikes going on like the telephone, telegraph, but our streetcars start on Friday so guess most of us will have a vacation. But if only this inflation will stop, things will be back to normal again.

About the package, Clara, I hope you can get or make some warm clothes for the kids. Would like to know what you got, sent shoes for Ole first – did he get them and did they fit? How about the children's shoes? Did you have to pay duty on them. You see I had to wait til shoe rations was over here before I could get them. Any cotton or wool underwear or wool stockings can't be had, only you are pregnant. Tried to get some yards for Borghild but gave up. Did you get the yarn I sent? I have sent 14 packages, one with spices to Eleanor, the rest of them to you and Borghild from all of us here because we couldn't send more than 1 package a piece every two weeks. Still have some other things I'm going to send – if you can't use it, give it to somebody else. Did you get the overcoat – thought maybe if it didn't fit Ole, maybe Borghild's husband could use it. Let me know what you got, Clara. There are so many rumors about packages begin stolen and the duty so high. Hope you got the shoes anyway.

We sure hope you can make it here – Ole might have to take any job he can get until he learns the language. He can also go to night school and learn whatever he wants to. And Borghild – tried to get a few things for her, but the stores are open just one hour after I am through working so that doesn't give me much time to look around. You should have seen the stores the last 2 – 3 years – hardly any material of any kind – no cotton of course – and what we get now is so bad and costs 50 -65 cents. You can hardly get stockings – have to stand in line for a whole block – so you see it took all to make USA win the war.

All the factories made materials needed for the war. But we won and that was the main thing. I

*worked at Boeings for a few weeks building
airplanes. So many people working there – it was
an interesting time.*

*And the pictures we got- so nice to see you
and all the kids – so pretty and Boya's family too
– how we love you all. You are all so nice looking
– should like to have a picture of Eleanor too. Is
she as tall as Borghild & you? It would be so
much fun if you could come over. I'm ashamed to
send this scribble but better next time. Do write to
us once-in-a-while. It is so much fun to get a letter
from you.*

Love mor

So much news and so much joy knowing what
their family was doing, learning that they had moved
to Seattle, their sisters had married, parents were
working. All seemed well, but they had not received
any packages from home like Asta had mentioned.
Asta had said, however, that they had received the
Christmas letter and picture from Clara. It was time
for the girls to consider together a trip home.

"I am certain that I am going," Eleanor shared. "I
have some schooling to finish this spring, and I'll
need to save some money, but I'm going to do this. I
am going to write to Tante Mathea in New York to
see if she could meet me there. I suppose I'd take the
train to Seattle. *Å få blod på tannen*, girls, I am
inspired. I am going to write to Mama and Dad and
tell them I am coming home!"

"I think you should do this, Eleanor," Clara said. "Ole and I have been talking about going sometime soon, too. We will need to figure this out, but we are going to take all five children with us the way it stands right now. This would be a big trip, and we would need to have long term visas and stay for a few years. We'll see."

Excited and motivated, Eleanor spent the next several months finishing school and making arrangements. She mulled over what to pack. Should she pack winter clothes or was Seattle warm? Was it rainy? Should she take her bunad? In the final packing, her bunad was nicely layered at the bottom of her trunk below her Norwegian sweater. She neatly packed several pictures of her sisters and their families, places she had lived in Norway, pictures of Bibben and Erling, a Norwegian flag, and pictures of her schools and school friends. She would have plenty to share about her life in Norway.

The United States Embassy issued her passport on August 22, 1946, and she boarded the Norwegian American *Stavangerfjord* in Oslo on October 19. Tante Mathea would meet her October 29 in New York. With no memory of her short life in Van Hook, Eleanor was going straight to Seattle!

Ten days on the ocean gave her plenty of time to think, review her life, remember what she could of her American family, decide what to wear when she got off the train to meet her parents. What would her sisters think of her? Would she be able to pursue her nurse's training in America? How long would she stay? Would she go back to Norway? Which side of the Atlantic would make her most homesick for the other side? These were questions she could talk about with Tante Mathea because Mathea clearly had two sides of the ocean as well. Eleanor jotted these thoughts in her notebook.

Tante Mathea met Eleanor at the pier, generously shared her time and thoughts, and graciously showed her around New York City before taking her to Grand Central Terminal to continue her trip to Seattle. Tante Mathea handed Eleanor a small purse with an undisclosed amount of money, kissed her goodbye, and sent her to her family. Several days with the Great Northern Railway rumbling on the tracks gave her time to digest what she and Tante Mathea had discussed. Two countries --- one on each side of the Atlantic. Loyalty to both sides. Family on both sides. "Not an easy decision," Tante Mathea had told her. "Let time and experience help you decide, Eleanor. Don't worry about it now."

Eleanor exited the train in Seattle wearing her bunad thinking it would help her parents find her. Martin and Asta needed no bunad. They knew their daughter and raced to her, hugging her, kissing her, holding her out in front of them to take a good look at her, and speaking Norwegian with her. Martin loaded her trunk in his car and away they went to her new home in Ballard to meet her two little sisters.

November 10, 1946

Dear Sisters in Norway,

I am in Seattle with Mama, Dad, Signe and Inkie! They call Ingeborg "Inkie," and Astrid "Ozzie," and Inez "Inie." So I told them that we now have a Boya. Our sisters here are beautiful, and I am so happy that we studied English in school because they don't speak much Norwegian. We are having a great time getting to know each other and we giggle all the time. We are sharing the upstairs of Mama and Dad's two-story house. Inkie is fourteen and Signe is seventeen so I am the oldest. They both tried on my bunad and it almost fits them. They both go to school each day, so I am at home. Rolf and his wife, Rogene, are here with us. They have a little boy, Ronnie, and she is expecting again this winter. They also live upstairs since there are two bedrooms. The only problem is that we have one bathroom in the whole house on the first floor. But I wait until everyone who needs to go somewhere leaves. Then I get ready.

I'm talking about continuing my nursing training here while I am here. I don't know how that will work, but I'm going to check into it. I can't just sit around. Signe helps me think about how to get into nursing school here since she is almost done with high school and is thinking about what's next for her.

Seattle is like Norway with mountains and rivers. The weather is nice, but Inkie said it rains a lot at this time of the year. The area we live in is Scandinavian so Dad brought home some sweet treats the other day. Just like home! The train ride was long but pretty in many places. I'm lonesome for you two and your kids. I hope you are making plans to come to America. I think we should get everyone together here so we can all take a good look at each other!! They all liked the pictures I brought with me and Mama put them on the kitchen cupboards for everyone to see.

Love, Eleanor

Eleanor addressed the envelope, got a stamp from her mom, and put the letter in the mail. She wondered every day if her letter was in Norway yet, but she knew it had to make the reverse trip she had just made so that would mean about three weeks. She continued to think about nursing school.

#

Clara called Boya to share the news in Eleanor's letter and to report that she and Ole were planning for themselves and their entire family to travel to the United States and to stay for an extended period of time. Clara needed a US passport and Ole needed a Norwegian passport but the kids traveled under their parents' passports. Clara's passport arrived first on January 22, 1947, and Ole's followed on February 11,

1947. Ole's brother agreed to move into the Hov house and care for their mother. That way they could keep the house because they planned to return in a few years. They applied for a five-year visa, and on March 7, 1947, Clara and Ole and their five children ages 11, 9, 4, 2, and a baby, hoped to board the Norwegian American ship the *Stavangerfjord* in Oslo and sail off to America. However, sea ice had made Oslo port inaccessible for ships; the Norwegian American Line instead rented a train to take over four hundred United States travelers from Oslo to the port in Bergen.

"I thought we were going on a ship," eleven-year-old Per asked his dad.

"Yes son, we are, but the port here in Oslo is iced in and the ship cannot enter. So, we will take the train to Bergen to get on the ship. Look at all these people that will be on the train with us. I've heard over 400 will ride the train to get to the ship."

"I see, Dad, and listen to them all singing *Ja, Vi Elsker*. See, they have their hats in their hands. Some are crying, Dad, and waving the flag. Maybe they are sad."

"Could be, Son. Some may be moving to America and their families wonder if they'll ever see them again. This is why we are going to America – so your mom can see her family and they can get to know us and we can know them. Your mother will have to tell you the story on our trip. You ask her about it some quiet day on the ship."

The train steamed out of the Oslo station as the platform filled with people waving, crying, and shouting farewell disappeared around the bend. The ship departed the Bergen port on March 7, 1947, arriving in New York Harbor on March 17. Clara and her family regrouped in a hotel for a couple of nights to prepare for their train trip to Seattle and her parents.

#

Asta and Martin immediately connected with their Norwegian grandchildren who were fluent in Norwegian. Grandpa Martin joked with Per and Astrid, took them to the pier and out for Norske sweets in Ballard's corner Scandinavian shop. Asta held onto the little ones, rocking, singing, and bouncing them on her knee like they were riding a horse.

Rida, rida ranka
Hästen heter Blanka
Liten riddare so rar
ånnu inge sporrar har
Nar du dem har vunnit
Barndoms ro forsvunnit.

It was good to be home with her mom and dad, but Clara had business to tend to with her dad. She invited him to sit with her on the porch steps after dinner one night.

"Ole, you watch the children. I'm going to talk to Dad about Helge."

Martin and Clara stepped outside. Clara looked her dad straight in the eyes. "Dad, do you know about your son in Odnes?"

"Ah... yes.... I know some about him," Martin stammered.

"Does Mama know about him?"

"Ah...yes… I told her after you girls went to Norway. I didn't mean to keep it from her, but I thought you might meet him. Did you?"

"Ja, Dad, I did. He was in my class when I studied in Odnes that first year. Do you want to know about him?" Clara looked right at her dad and paused for an answer.

"Ja, that would be ok."

"He's a fine man, Dad, quiet, never married, rode his bike all over town. He's lived in Odnes or Fluberg most of his adult life. His mother died in June 1943. We saw her death notice in the paper. Ole and others knew about him. I talked to him before I knew who he really was, but he knew about the three of us girls. Don't you think he should be part of our family? Don't you think he should be here with us? He looks just like you and Rolf, Dad. Tall, good looking, well built, strong."

"This is good to hear, Clara. I made a mistake, and I couldn't make it better. I'm so sorry for them. I met your mother, and I knew that she was the one for me. I'm so sorry."

"It's okay, Dad. I was pregnant when I got married. Boya was pregnant when she got married. These things happen, but I think you should tell the rest of the family and we should include him. Will you do this while we are all here?"

"Ja. Let me talk with Mama first so she knows I will tell."

Clara planned to hold her dad to his word. She didn't ask him anymore about it, but she would be paying attention.

#

Boya and Dave and their two children were left in Norway, but not for long. Martin had inherited some money in Norway and shared it with Boya so she could come home for a visit. Dave's parents were not overly excited to let them take their two small children with them to America, so they convinced Boya and Dave to leave the two kids behind. Raghnild, almost four, and Anne, almost two, were left with Dave's parents while their parents went to America. When Dave and Boya left the farm to board the Stavangerfjord in Oslo, there was laughing, there was hugging, and there was crying. The ship pulled out of port on October 8, 1947 and arrived in New York harbor on October 18. The train took them to Minneapolis to sister Ruth's for an eight-day visit before they continued on to Minot to visit Margaret and Inez. Margaret and Byron drove them to Van Hook so Borghild could show Dave where she was born and where she had gone to elementary school. They continued to Seattle.

November 1947

Chapter Twenty-Four:

322 West Nickerson

Ballard, Seattle, Washington

The house on West Nickerson in the Ballard district was aflutter with activity. Martin was pleased that he had purchased a two-story house since Clara & Ole and their five children were now camped in the living room leaving the upstairs to Martin, Asta, Signe, Ingeborg, and Eleanor. It was a messy, cluttered, fun-filled house that felt quite empty after Ruth and her two girls went home to Minneapolis. Then Rolf took his wife and two boys home to Van Hook. When those seven left, the Nickerson house had extra space. The only caveat was one bathroom, and when all but three of them went to work or school each morning, the bathroom was busy if not crowded. And it was hectic and messy, but love filled the air as they prepared a party for the arrival of Borghild and Dave.

"Clara, why don't you, Eleanor, Signe and Inkie plan a party. You could be getting it ready while Dad and I go to the train station to pick up Boya and Dave," Asta said. "We are so anxious to hug them and welcome them home. How about a big plate of fruit and sweets – things they haven't seen for a long time because of the war. Let's straighten up this part of the living room, Clara. It's where we will have Borghild and Dave live. It will be crowded, but we will be together again."

The girls agreed to rearrange the living room and put a party together. The neighborhood store had everything they needed for food, and the girls had fun getting it all ready.

"Martin, just think. In a few short hours, we will have Clara, Borghild, and Eleanor all back with us! It has been seventeen years, Martin, seventeen years, and they have grown into women – women with Norwegian voices and customs. Husbands and children of their own. In a way, it's like bringing Norway back to us." Asta cried. Martin cried. They held each other for a long time.

"Yes, Asta. We will have them back with us but for who knows how long. We have Astrid and Signe and Ingeborg, and we have had Ruth and Rolf. All we need now is to have Margaret and Inez with us. Then we will be complete. We need a family reunion right here on Nickerson! We can do it, Asta. We can make room."

While Martin and Asta drove to the train station to fetch their daughter and her husband, the girls prepared the house. Hoping to recognize their little eight-year-old Borghild, now twenty-three, a wife, and a mother, Asta and Martin waved as the train rolled in. Will Borghild recognize them? The pictures Eleanor and Clara shared should help! Asta thought about the picture with the X's she had sent to Norway.

She paused a bit until she noticed a young, pretty blonde woman with a tall handsome young man by her side climbing down the steps.

"Dave, *Se der vifter de med et norsk flagg. Det må være dem.*" Martin's waving a Norwegian flag was the giveaway! Borghild raced to her mother's arms and sobbed. "I'm home, Mama, I'm home."

#

The three Norwegian girls were elated to see each other, but Eleanor was particularly happy to introduce Boya to Signe and Inkie! Her two closest sisters – now reunited as the youngest trio of the family. There was hugging. There was crying. There was laughing. There was sharing. Norway had come home to America! It was time to get the rest of the family together in Seattle.

"Let's call Ruth, Margaret, Inie, and Rolf and tell them to get on the train and get themselves out here!" Astrid (Ozzie) was taking charge. "We have plenty of room and good lord, we all grew up sharing beds anyway. We can do it again. I'll call them but when should they come?"

"How about around Thanksgiving?" Asta suggested. "Clara's kids will be home from school, Dad and I will have a couple of days off work, and we will have a couple of weeks now to prepare."

The four remaining kids agreed that they would take the train to Seattle for the holiday. Ruth trained to Minot where Margaret and Inie joined her. Rolf joined at the depot in Stanley, and the four of them headed west on the new Empire Builder laughing, crying, and reminiscing. They were going to be a family for the first time.

"We haven't all been together, ever," Margaret reminded the other three. "Inkie was born after the girls left for Norway. It won't be the entire family since Christine died as a baby," she murmured sadly. "I wonder how Mama and Dad feel about this gathering? We'll have to be very helpful since they are getting older. Let's see, Dad is 57 and Mama must be 54. Ozzie wrote to say that Mama's health isn't good, so we need to be helpful!"

Martin picked his kids up at the King Street Station in the late afternoon. "My god," Margaret said, "You look just like Dad, Rolf. And look how tall you both are! Ruth and I are both tall but what happened to Inie??" They all laughed.

"Someone needs to be the same size as Mama," Martin laughed. The ride to the Nickerson house was alive with laughter, joking, and anticipation. As they neared the house, two flags flying in the front yard announced one family with two flags. They were all home! Noisy laughter, hugging, crying, sharing stories, eating together, drinking together, having family fun that had been missed for so many years. Short Asta fell in love with her two tall Norwegian boys: Ole and Dave. They melded right into the family fold. One night Martin had all his kids line up in order of height. Clara, Astrid, Rolf, Ruth, Margaret, Borghild... on down to the shortest.

"Seems each baby we had, Asta, got shorter!" Martin teased. "Now let's line up according to age." The lineup barely changed. "How many of you girls have a bunad?" Asta, Clara, Boya, and Eleanor. The other girls tried on their sisters' bunads and danced around to *Ja, Vi Elsker* with the Norwegians taking the lead. Dave grabbed a Norwegian flag off the table and lead a parade around the living room. Everyone danced and sang. Every night was like this. So much fun.

The ten Aadnes siblings in Seattle 1947
Back row: Inez (Inie), Eleanor, Borghild (Boya),
Margaret, Astrid (Ozzie), Ruth, Clara
Front row: Ingeborg (Inkie), Rolf, Signe

One night at dinner, Clara looked at her dad with a questioning eye. Was he going to share the information about Helge? Martin saw the look and nodded yes to his oldest.

"Ok everyone, I have something to say. And I want you to know that your mother knows this story, so don't worry. Here it is," he paused, took a deep breath, and spoke. "You have a half-brother in Norway."

"I knew it," Boya blurted out. "I knew it. It's Helge in Odnes, isn't it."

"Yes, Borghild," Martin said. "That is who it is. A little of the story without much detail. His mother worked in the Odnes Hotel."

"I knew it," Boya said, "We read her story when she died, didn't we Clara?"

"Yes, Boya, we did."

"Did you know this and not tell Eleanor and me?"

"Yes, I did. Ole and I decided it was Dad's story to tell, so I waited until we all got together and he was ready to share the news."

"Go on, Dad, tell us about him," Eleanor said.

"I think you may know more about him than I do, but I can tell you that I had met and fallen in love with your mother. We decided to marry and come to America. I didn't tell her about the baby until you girls had gone to Norway. I wasn't hiding it; I felt bad about it. But I couldn't fix it. I'm sorry, but I loved your mother and wanted to be with her. I had to leave him behind."

Asta listened quietly. She knew the story, but she let Martin tell it, and let the Norwegian girls, especially Clara, tell about Helge. When it quieted down, Asta said, "I think he should be included in the family. He's a brother, you know. We have come a long way and many years have passed. He should meet his siblings and hopefully his dad. I welcome him."

All the girls and Rolf were curious about Helge. Clara had a picture of him, and she had some stories she could tell. Boya had always watched him from a distance, but now she knew who he was and that he was a brother. Eleanor was just learning about this news for the first time, just like the other kids. They all agreed that they would include Helge when they got together again. A family picture was taken so a special copy would be sent to Norway with Boya and Dave when they returned.

The days flew by and soon it was time for Ruth, Margaret, Inie, and Rolf to board the train to head east to their respective families. Their carefully packed bags contained pictures of siblings, special gifts from Norway, notes they had written each other, and a small flag of each country to put on their tables. Their early breakfast was quiet at times and at times full of chatter. There was laughing. There was hugging. There was crying. Clara, Borghild, and Eleanor stood beside their mother along with Ozzie, Signe, and Inkie while Martin loaded bags into the car. Ruth, Margaret, Inie, and Rolf climbed in with their dad. Asta cried as the car drove away. They all waved. Soon the car disappeared into the traffic heading to the train station leaving their mother and Clara, Borghild, Eleanor, Inez, Signe, and Inkie behind.

Chapter Twenty-Five:

Seattle, Washington

The house on Nickerson quieted down after the family gathering. Boya and Dave and Eleanor had gone back to Norway. Ozzie had married and was teaching math in Seattle. Signe and Inkie had both graduated from high school; Signe was married. Clara and Ole and their now seven children had moved into the house next door. Asta and Martin and Inkie were alone.

Asta noticed her urine was often pink and foamy, and her hands, feet, face and abdomen seemed to swell. She called the Seattle doctor she had been seeing since 1947. He thought she might have uremia and referred her to a nephrologist for tests. The test results indicated chronic nephritis, a serious, life-threatening disease that can evolve from diabetes. This condition coupled with uremia put Asta in the hospital for treatment and observation. Attempts to control blood sugar and insulin response were not effective.

Asta passed away at 2:20 AM on April 1, 1951, in King County Hospital at the age of 56 years. She had twenty-one grandchildren. Two daughters and two of the grandchildren were living in Norway. Funeral services were held at the Wiggen & Sons Mortuary in

Ballard with burial in the Pacific Lutheran Cemetery in Seattle.

Asta saw her entire family together only once.

The End

Epilogue

Martin Pederson Aadnes died July 19, 1960, in the King County Hospital of injuries suffered in a fall on Nickerson Street near his home. Funeral services were held at the Wiggen & Sons Mortuary in Ballard with burial in Pacific Lutheran Cemetery in Seattle next to his wife.

Clara and Ole Skaugrud maintained homes in both Seattle and Hov traveling back and forth every few years. They brought five children with them from Norway with two more born in the United States. Ole was buried in Hov; Clara died in Seattle on May 27, 1982. Clara's ashes were carried to Hov and buried with Ole in the Hov Church Cemetery.

Ruth and Ray Schaust lived in Minneapolis their entire lives. They raised three children. Ruth died in a nursing home in Minneapolis on February 18, 1992. She is buried by her husband in the Fort Snelling Cemetery in Minnesota.

Astrid (Ozzie) became a famous golfer in the Pacific Northwest, helped write the Seattle Public Schools math curriculum, and died in a nursing home on March 26, 1988.

Margaret and Byron Varberg lived in North Dakota. They raised four children. Margaret died on March 9, 2006, with funeral services at First Lutheran Church in Minot, ND, and burial by her husband in Rosehill Cemetery, Minot.

Inez (Inie) lived in Walla Walla, Washington. She and Ray had three children. Inez died on March 21, 1989, and is buried in Evergreen Washelli Memorial Park, Seattle, Washington.

Borghild and Dave Eggum worked in Seattle to gather enough money to return to Norway. They met Eleanor in Chicago in July 1948, and the three returned to Norway on July 19, 1948. Boya and Dave took over the Eggum farm and raised five children all of whom remained in Norway. Borghild passed away on April 21, 2001 and is buried in Norway.

Rolf and Rogene lived in North Dakota and raised six children. Rolf died September 3, 1982, in the Veterans Hospital in Fargo, North Dakota. He and his wife are buried in the Van Hook Cemetery beside baby sister Christine.

Eleanor finished nursing school in Seattle and returned to Norway with Boya and Dave in July 1948. She married Ole Eggum in 1952, and in 1954 they purchased Store Odnes. They had one daughter. Ole died in 1966 but Eleanor remained at Store Odnes, changed her name back to Aadnes. Their daughter remains at Store Odnes and has restored the Odnes Hotel. Eleanor passed away in 2010 and is buried in Norway.

Signe was the last of the siblings to pass away. She was a steady companion for her several of her sisters during their final years. She died in Seattle on April 26, 2013. She had one son.

Ingeborg Aadnes Vitro passed away June 6, 2007, at home in Cupertino, CA, after a courageous eight year battle with two types of cancer. She had three sons. She directed her ashes to be scattered in Puget Sound.

Christine Aadnes. Died at two weeks of age a victim of the measles epidemic in January 1934. She is buried in the Van Hook Cemetery.

Helge Walle lived in the Odnes area his entire life. He never married. He was a carpenter who liked to play in the Odnes Musikkorps, take a drink, and ride his bike. In 1972 he borrowed money to come to America to meet his siblings. He died on February 13, 1994 and is buried with his mother in Fluberg.

Bibben and Erling Moe Bernsten remained in Norway, settling in Rena. Erling regained his pharmaceutical license in early 1950s. Boya and her family reunited with them during the Norwegian Holiday Pentecost in 1946. Erling passed away in 1969 and Bibben in 1980.

By 1982 two of the Aadnes children had passed away: Clara and Rolf. Margaret and Signe decided to hold a family gathering at the homestead in Van Hook, North Dakota. In 1987, a family reunion was held. Family members submitted family pictures and information for a family booklet. A few local family members picked chokecherries from the trees Martin had planted years before and made chokecherry wine for toasting Martin and Asta at the banquet. Seven siblings and many extended family members including those from Norway came to meet each other. Gathering round the hole where the original homestead had been located, the Norwegians, wearing their bunads, placed a Norwegian flag in the spot where their mothers had been raised. They sang the Norwegian national anthem. The Americans placed an American flag next to the Norwegian flag and sang the national anthem. Tears around!!!

The family decided they should gather every five years. In 1992 they gathered in Odnes, Norway, at the family site. In 1997, they gathered at Ocean Shores, WA. In 2002 it was back to Norway to the Odnes family home. In 2007, the family gathered in Mandan, North Dakota, on the Missouri River. In 2011 it was back to Odnes, Norway. In 2016 over 150 gathered at Laguna Beach, CA. They will gather again in 2022 in Odnes, Norway.

Martin and Asta would be amazed to see how five generations later their family still gathers.

Aadnes children including Helge circa 1980
Front row: Eleanor, Signe, Astrid, Margaret, Inez
Back row: Ingeborg, Borghild, Helge,
Rolf, Clara, Ruth

Ole Skaugrud was indeed one of the Norwegian Resistance team who on February 23, 1945, executed the pickup from a drop in Sondre Land. A Canadian pilot from Saskatoon, Canada, - Harry Wilkie - dropped 2.5 ton of materials near Hov to be used during the liberation days in 1945.

This photo (courtesy of Robert Skaugrud) was taken at their forty year reunion. Ole is on the right.

Acknowledgments

Family stories and histories surface at unexpected times, in unexpected ways, and in no particular order. When those stories spark curiosity about family puzzle pieces, then those whose curiosity has been sparked are fascinated and may relentlessly pursue the rest of the story. This is what happened to me.

I was initially intrigued about my grandparents' story in 1975 when I visited Norway to meet my mother's sisters, Borghild and Eleanor. They took me to the home of my grandmother's youngest sister, Else, who showed me the old, yellowed photograph of the kids --- the photograph with the x's over the heads of the three sisters sent to Norway in 1932 – the one on the cover of this book. I was told how those X's would help their Norwegian family recognize the girls when they arrived at the Oslo pier. I wanted that photograph but didn't feel it appropriate to ask for it, but I never forgot about it. We traveled on to Store Odnes to the home of my grandfather's family then owned by Eleanor. Puzzle pieces were appearing and begging me to search deeper into this family puzzle. All these years later, I am touched by what I learned on that trip, and without those sparks, I may not have pursued the story any further. To Else, my great aunt, I owe my gratitude. She never met her sister, Asta, but she saved that picture for over forty years. I was fortunate to have been able to see it and hear the story.

In the 1950s Eleanor and her husband purchased Store Odnes, and over the years have preserved the family history there and have shared it with so many of us. Without that purchase, we probably would have lost that historic connection. And today, Eleanor's daughter, Astri, owns Store Odnes and has preserved the family history there and also shared it. My gratitude to this mother – daughter team who have kept the foundation for the family.

Many family members wondered about the lives of the girls when they were in Norway. How would we ever know their stories. Then, in 2015, my sister and I went to Norway to visit our cousins. We were all sitting around a coffee table in the Odnes house having Aquavit when Borghild's daughter, Birgit, brought out a notebook and began to share its contents. When her mother learned that she had terminal cancer, she wrote her story! The story of her life in Norway! Birgit began to translate. I took copious notes until Birgit said her daughter would probably translate it for me! What a treasure that puzzle piece has been. It provided the bones for Part 2 of **What We Leave Behind**. Thank you to Borghild, Birgit, and Karen for this piece of the puzzle.

And to my mother Margaret, the fourth child, I am indebted for her love and for her sharing of the story that is the Prologue to this novel. She told how she would hear her parents at night discussing which girls to send and how her chest would hurt as she cried and hoped they wouldn't send her. And even though she left home at sixteen, she kept a treasure trove of family documents that provided pieces to the puzzle.

And to all the sisters in the family who crossed the Atlantic many times to visit each other what gratitude the rest of us have for them. They held the family together. I recall how much fun these sisters had with each other --- the laughter, the cards, the toasts, the silliness – so much captured in pictures my mother had kept. Mom said their dad always had fun with the kids, and that characteristic carried through into future generations. Even today when we all gather for our five year reunions, there is laughter, toasts, silliness, singing, and a genuine love for each other. Our gratitude to the sisters for holding on to each other in spite of all odds.

Long before this story had taken the form of a novel, I was accepted into the Little Mo' Writers Incubator sponsored by Humanities North Dakota. I was somewhat nervous to share my writing with the group, but they provided just the support I needed. The instructors, Deb Marquart and Tayo Basquiat, offered helpful comments including the encouragement of "You've done the research now digest it and write the narrative." And that set me free. Thank you. To the other seven participants, I thank you for reading my "stuff" and offering your feedback and encouragement.

All puzzle pieces don't come from family members. How can we adequately thank those who archive history? I am indebted to the State Historical Society of North Dakota for all the gathering and curating of the state's history. Included in that archival endeavor is the Mountrail County Historical Society who gathered homesteader stories, town histories, and township maps and published them. These organizations made it possible for me to get to know my grandparents' neighbors years after they had passed. Van Hook quickly became more of a community of friends than just a place on the map. To the county courthouses, specifically the Mountrail County Court House that helped me find my grandfather's homestead documents. What a source of details those documents are! Documents that provide information on how the homestead was proved up --- buildings, crops, neighbors' testaments regarding the homesteader's character. I learned how hard my grandparents worked just by reading what the neighbors testified to. This recorded history gave life to my family's story. And to those people across the world who have digitized documents available on the Internet so one can research without all the travel that was necessary in the past. Thank you!

To Robert Skaugrud, a member of the Aadnes family Facebook group, who posted the information about the Skaugrud brothers and their participation in the Norwegian Resistance Movement in WWII. I am thankful for that piece of family involvement in WWII. He provided the reunion picture of the group who stopped Hitler from getting the heavy water. Thank you for saving and sharing that piece.

Once the story had been written, a number of readers provided suggestions, editing comments, and overall insight. A thank you to Kathy Dixon, Donna Erwin, and Sarah Vogel for offering suggestions in such a kind way. I appreciate the time you took and the talents you shared helped make this novel a reality. And thanks to my grandson, Daniel, who suggested that a map of Norway be part of each chapter when the girls were moved around. I liked that suggestion and incorporated it.

Thank you to BookLocker for facilitating ease! To Angela the co-owner, to Todd the book cover designer, and to Brian for the book trailer, thank you all and the others in your group whose skills have helped make this story available.

To my daughter, Jessica, a thank you for sharing your marketing skills for the trailer and cover. I sure did need that help!

To my son, Jon, thanks for being you and listening to me talk about this story time after time. Thanks for carrying on this heritage.

And to Jonah Lantto of the Good Talk Network in Minot, North Dakota – Thank you for listening to and taping the story, and for listening a second time to fix the rough spots, and for listening to the final edited version! You are probably now a "full-fledged" member of this family. Just a downright than you for your reaction to the story. I have enjoyed story hour in your studio.

A special thanks to my sister, Bev Rohde, who not only read several of the revisions, but also answered her phone the many times I called for encouragement. "You've come this far. You can't quit now." If she had quit answering her phone, this story would still be in folders in my file cabinet waiting for someone down the road to take up the charge! Thank you, Bev, thank you for being the wind beneath my wings!!

How does one thank a spouse who has been beside me during the years of gathering, sorting, storing, wondering, writing, crying? Reading and rereading one manuscript after another. Encouraging me to tell the story. Drawing the maps for the book. Simply, thank you. Thank you, Rich.

And to all those people in the world who save things and wonder what might become of all that "stuff." I say, go forward with pride. Leave some breadcrumbs behind to spark interest in the family story. Someone will probably thank you in abstentia!

To Martin and Asta whom I never knew: I hope my vision of your life is fair and appropriate. Thank you for your courage and persistence under such difficult times. You can be proud of what you have left behind!! To your children who hung on to each other over all the years --- thank you.

Resources

1953. *Norges apotek og deres innehavere. N.p., n.p, 1953.* 605-606.

Aaraas, Olav. 1994. *We Won the Land: An Exhibition on the History of Norway.* Lillehammer: De norske Bokklubbene A/S.

n.d. *Access Geneaology: A Free Genealogy Website.* Copyright © 2021 Access Genealogy | Home of Free Genealogy. Accessed November 10, 2021. https://accessgenealogy.com/wp-content/uploads/2013/08/North-Dakota.jpg.

Carlson, Don. n.d. "Geneastory." *John H. Kasa.* Accessed September 12, 2020. http://geneastory.com/genealogy.

Christopher Tietze, M.D., F.A.P.H.A. 1967. November. Accessed December 9, 2020. https://ajph.aphapublications.org/doi/pdf/10.2105/AJPH.57.11.1923.

Editors, History.com. 2009. *Adolf Hitler commits suicide in his underground bunker.* November 24. Accessed February 24, 2021. https://www.histoy.com/this-day-in-history/adolf-hitler-commits-suicide.

Eggum, Borghild Aadnes. 1991. "Personal Story." Translated by Kara Gurholt Merrell.

n.d. "Everyday Life." *Archiverket.* Accessed December 9, 2020. https://www.arkivverket.no/utforsk-arkivene/andre-verdenskrig/hverdagslivet.

Fraser. 1924. "Federal Reserve Bulletin." *Discover Economic History.* October. Accessed September 21, 2020. http://fraser.stlouisfed.org/files/doc/publications/FRB/pages/1920-1924/27545_1920-1924.pdf.

Ganzel, Bill. n.d. *Farming in the 1940s: Food for War.* Accessed February 23, 2021. https://livinghistoryfarm.org/farminginthe40s/money_02.html.

Goldberg, Jasper. 2011. "Norwegian Teachers Prevent Nazi Takeover of Education, 1942." *Global Nonviolent Action Database.* May 31. https://nvdatabase.swarthmore.edu/content/norwegian-teachers-prevent-nazi-takeover-education-1942.

n.d. *Idd of Enningdalen Historielag.* Accessed March 5, 2014. idd.no.

n.d. "Jessie Birdsbill." *Family Search.* Accessed June 22, 2021. https://ancestors.familysearch.org/en/278T-N4D/jessie-birds-bill-1898-1949.

n.d. *Josef Terboven (1898-1945).* American-Israeli Cooperative Enterprise. Accessed November 11,

2020. https://www.jewishvirtuallibrary.org/josef-terboven.

Juhl, Kourtney. 2019. "Norwegian Civil Resistance of the Nazi Occupation: 1940-1945." *The Cross Section.* November 11. Accessed December 13, 2020. https://crosssection.gns.wisc.edu/2019/11/11/norwegian-civil-resistance-of-the-nazi-occupation-1940-1945/.

Samuelsen, Anders, ed. n.d. "Knardal." *Idd Og Enningdalen Historielag.* Accessed May 5, 2014. http://www.idd.no/.

Lee, Alma. n.d. ""My Prisoner of War Days"." *Telling the Truth.* Accessed October 19, 2020. https://www.tellingthetruth.info/history_pioneering/norwayB.php.

Lund, Raghnild. 2002. "University of Southeast Norway." *A Hundred Years of English Teaching: A View of Some Textbooks.* February. Accessed April 17, 2021. http://www-bib.hive.no/tekster/hveskrift/notat/2002-02/not02-2002-lund.pdf.

McLaughlin, Michael. 2003. "The Slaying of a Quisling." *The Barnes Review.* September/October. Accessed September 20, 2019. https://barnesreview.org/the-slaying-of-a-viking-the-epic-of-vidkun-quisling/.

Mellgren, Doug. 1995. "To The End, 'Traitor' Quisling Proclaimed his Innocence." *AP News.* October 24. Accessed September 21, 2020. https://apnews.com/article/17bd03969f72d42f8d7f e475a38a2186.

ND State Historical Society. 2021. "Lesson 4; Topic 5; Section 1." *North Dakota Studies Grade 8.* Accessed July 26, 2021. https://www.ndstudies.gov/gr8/content/unit-iv-modern-north-dakota-1921-present/lesson-4-alliances-and-conflicts/topic-5-modern-government/section-1-introduction.

Nissen, Hanrik S., ed. 1983. *Scandinavia during the Second World War.* Translated by Thomas Munch-Petersen. Minneapolis, Minnesota: The University of Minnesota Press.

2018. *Norway in World War II.* March 30. Accessed July 13, 2020. https://www.lifeinnorway.net/norway-world-war-two/.

n.d. "Norwegian Collaborationish Forces During WWII." *Feldgrau: German Armed Forces Research 1918 -1945.* Accessed June 3, 2014. https://www.feldgrau.com/ww2-norwegian-axis-forces/.

1910. "Sixty-First Congress Session II Chapter 264." United States Congress. 455 - 459. Accessed June

17, 2021. https://www.loc.gov/law/help/statutes-at-large/61st-congress/session-2/c61s2ch264.pdf.

Solberg, Barb. 1977. *Martin and Astat (Sterud) Aadnes.*

2018. "Suicide Josef Antonius Heinrich Terboven, the Reichskommissar for Norway." *World War II Graves.* October 13. Accessed November 20, 2020. https://ww2gravestone.com.

The Minot Daily News. 1948. "Martin Aadnes Family Has Reunion; Three Daughters Home From Norway." June 7: 6.

The Minot Daily News. 1945. "V-E Day Proclaimed; European War Ends." May 8.

2019. "The Norwegian Bunad." *Life in Norway.* February 25. Accessed January 5, 2021. https://www.lifeinnorway.net/bunad/.

Thomas, Robert B. 1918. "The Old Farmer's Almanack: 1919." Boston: The Old Farmer's Almanac, Incorproated.

Trueman, C N. 2015. *The Red Cross and World War Two.* May 25. Accessed March 18, 2021. historylearningsite.co.uk.

Van Hook Journal. 1914. September 24.

n.d. *WWII Escape described in MInister Florence Harriman's book "Mission to the North".*

Accessed December 21, 2020.
https://no.usembassy.gov/mission-to-the-north/.

Questions for Discussion

1. It seems that all the intentions of the characters in this true story are honest, but hurdles were thrown in front of them and changed the course of their lives. What are some examples of those honest intentions? What were the hurdles that changed those intentions? Have you had honest intentions that have been changed by unforeseen hurdles? How?
2. With which character did you identify and why?
3. This is the story of strong women. Identify those women and discuss their strengths. Where did that strength come from? Did they ever falter?
4. List all the "things" that got left behind. Which characters had to leave those identified things behind? What have you/your family had to leave behind?
5. Could you send three of your children away? Under what circumstances? Discuss the emotional upheaval that causes for all parties.
6. Did you learn anything new about Nazi occupation of Norway during WWII? What? How about immigration? Ellis Island?
7. Can you identify any circumstances in your family history that prod you to learn more about your heritage? Will you follow up on that? How?
8. What will you leave behind?

About The Author

Barb Solberg, a native North Dakotan, earned both BS ED and MA degrees in English/communication from the University of North Dakota. She spent most of her professional career teaching speaking and writing. She has published in a number of magazines and newspapers. In 1995 she became a pioneer in the field of online learning working as an instructional designer, faculty developer, and international consultant. In 1996 with Harcourt College Publishers she authored a student guidebook to help students navigate the World Wide Web and online learning platforms. Retired now, she and her husband have two adult children and five grandchildren and live in North Dakota.